NOW I'LL TELL YOU
EVERYTHING

BOOKS BY PHYLLIS REYNOLDS NAYLOR

Shiloh Books
Shiloh
Shiloh Season
Saving Shiloh

The Alice Books
Starting with Alice
Alice in Blunderland
Lovingly Alice
The Agony of Alice
Alice in Rapture, Sort Of
Reluctantly Alice
All But Alice
Alice in April
Alice In-Between
Alice the Brave
Alice in Lace
Outrageously Alice
Achingly Alice
Alice on the Outside
The Grooming of Alice
Alice Alone
Simply Alice
Patiently Alice
Including Alice
Alice on Her Way
Alice in the Know
Dangerously Alice
Almost Alice
Intensely Alice
Alice in Charge
Incredibly Alice
Alice on Board
Now I'll Tell You Everything

Alice Collections
I Like Him, He Likes Her
*It's Not Like I Planned It
    This Way*
Please Don't Be True
*You and Me and the Space
    In Between*

The Bernie Magruder Books
*Bernie Magruder and the Case
    of the Big Stink*
*Bernie Magruder and the
    Disappearing Bodies*
*Bernie Magruder and the
    Haunted Hotel*
*Bernie Magruder and the
    Drive-thru Funeral Parlor*
*Bernie Magruder and the Bus
    Station Blowup*
*Bernie Magruder and the
    Pirate's Treasure*
*Bernie Magruder and the
    Parachute Peril*
*Bernie Magruder and the Bats
    in the Belfry*

The Cat Pack Books
The Grand Escape
The Healing of Texas Jake
Carlotta's Kittens
Polo's Mother

The York Trilogy
Shadows on the Wall
Faces in the Water
Footprints at the Window

NOW I'LL TELL YOU EVERYTHING

Phyllis Reynolds Naylor

 Atheneum Books for Young Readers

NEW YORK LONDON TORONTO SYDNEY NEW DELHI

With special thanks to Corie Hinton,
a Peace Corps volunteer (2008–2010)

*   *   *

ATHENEUM BOOKS FOR YOUNG READERS
An imprint of Simon & Schuster Children's Publishing Division
1230 Avenue of the Americas, New York, New York 10020

For information about special discounts for bulk purchases, please contact Simon & Schuster Special Sales at 1-866-506-1949 or business@simonandschuster.com.
The Simon & Schuster Speakers Bureau can bring authors to your live event. For more information or to book an event, contact the Simon & Schuster Speakers Bureau at 1-866-248-3049 or visit our website at www.simonspeakers.com.
Also available in an Atheneum Books for Young Readers hardcover edition
The text for this book is set in Berkeley Oldstyle Book.
Manufactured in the United States of America
First Atheneum Books for Young Readers paperback edition September 2014
2 4 6 8 10 9 7 5 3 1
The Library of Congress has cataloged the hardcover edition as follows:
Naylor, Phyllis Reynolds.
Now I'll tell you everything / Phyllis Reynolds Naylor. — 1st ed.
p. cm.
Summary: As Alice McKinley begins a new phase as a student at the University of Maryland, College Park, she experiences many changes, both expected and surprising, that lead her into a future her seventh-grade self could only have imagined.
ISBN 978-1-4424-4590-1 (hc.)
ISBN 978-1-4424-4591-8 (pbk.)
ISBN 978-1-4424-6161-1 (eBook)
[1. Coming of age—Fiction. 2. Universities and colleges—Fiction.
3. University of Maryland at College Park—Fiction. 4. Friendship—Fiction.
5. Family life—Maryland—Fiction. 6. Maryland—Fiction.] I. Title.
PZ7.N24Alw 2013
[Fic]—dc23   2012040626

To all the Alices,
whatever their names,
who helped me write these books

CONTENTS

1
THE U OF M

The day I left for college, Lester borrowed a pickup for all my stuff.

"Anything that can't fit in the back can't go, Al," he said.

"I've got to take my beanbag chair. That's a *must*," I declared, jumping down off the back end and wiping my hands on my cutoffs.

"*Take* it! *Take* it!" Dad said. "Just promise you'll leave it there."

We joke that while some kids suck their thumbs all through childhood and others hang on to a blanket, I've kept my old beanbag chair as a sort of mother substitute, a lap to cuddle in when things get tough. Mom died when I was in kindergarten, and I've had that beanbag chair almost as long. I'm even too big for it now, but I could always use it as a hassock, I figured.

All morning Elizabeth, Pamela, and I had been carrying things out to the truck. Gwen's brothers had helped her move the day before, and Liz would leave for Bennington the next day. I was taking some stuff to my dorm at the U of Maryland and was lucky Liz and Pam were still around to see me off. We were standing out on the driveway in our shorts and T-shirts, studying the mountain of junk in the pickup, trying to think of anything I might have forgotten.

"Ironing board?" said Elizabeth. She's the gorgeous one, with creamy skin, thick dark eyelashes, and long, almost black hair.

"*Nobody* uses an ironing board at college, Liz!" said Pamela. "You just fold up a towel on the floor and iron on that, if you iron at all."

A gnat blew directly in front of Pam's eyes, and she tried to smash it between her hands. Sweat dripped off her face and onto the front of her purple tee. We were all perspiring like crazy.

"Toaster?" said Elizabeth. "What will you do if you crave a grilled cheese sandwich at midnight and everything's closed?"

"Are you kidding?" Pamela exclaimed. "All you need is your iron. You put cheese between two slices of bread, wrap it in foil, and press down on it with a hot iron." She lifted her blond hair off the nape of her neck, as though even talking about ironing made her miserable.

"Your ingenuity is amazing," I said. "Next you'll tell us an iron can broil a steak and bake a potato. Can it help me with my homework? Hand me that box, Liz, and let's see if we can't squeeze it in beside my suitcase."

I've known Elizabeth Price and Pamela Jones forever, it seems. Well, since sixth grade, anyway. Pamela, a natural blonde, slim and talented, is going to a theater arts school in New York and is letting her short hair grow out so she can play more parts. Elizabeth's been admitted to Bennington in Vermont, and I'm going to Lester's alma mater, which is only about a half hour from our house. Like, I'm the adventurous one. Gwen's going there too—premed.

I think Dad believes I've grown up so close to him and Lester that I'm afraid to get too far away. So he insisted I live on campus, which is fine with me. It's about time he and Sylvia had the house to themselves. They've only been married three years.

"Oh, God!" I said. "Sheets and towels! I didn't pack any at all!"

Pamela looked at the stuff we still had to squeeze in. "We made a mistake. We should have stuffed clothes in your mini-fridge and wastebasket before we put them on the truck. There's all that empty space inside." We collapsed on the front steps and took a break.

"I can't believe I have to go through this all by myself tomor-row," Elizabeth said.

"What about *me*? My dorm room's half the size of yours, and I'll have to keep most of my stuff under my bed. I'm still not through sorting." Pamela groaned. She was already looking like an actress. She had plucked her eyebrows into thin crescents over her eyes and wore black mascara and eyeliner. *A lot.*

We gazed wearily out over the yard and across the street,

where Elizabeth's big white house sat handsomely on its manicured lot.

"I remember when you first moved here from Takoma Park," Elizabeth said. "Mom and I were sitting out on the porch watching you guys carry things in."

"And you were wearing matching skirts," I told her.

"*Skirts!*" She turned and looked at me. "We *were*? You *remember*?"

"You looked so perfect to me, and I was so envious. The perfect mother and daughter, sitting there reading a magazine together. . . ."

"Don't remind me," Elizabeth said quickly. *Perfect* is like poison in her vocabulary now, she's trying so hard not to be.

"We've been through a lot together," said Pamela, and sighed. Then she asked, "If you could look into the future and see what was happening at some particular age, which age would you pick?"

"Thirty. I'd pick thirty," said Elizabeth. "I figure that whatever I'm doing then will more or less dictate how the rest of my life is going to turn out."

"I'd choose a year from now, to see if I was going back to New York," said Pamela. "If you don't have talent, they don't encourage you to return." Both Pamela and Elizabeth looked at me.

"I'm not sure I'd want to know," I told them.

"Why *not*?"

"Because I'd probably pick age sixty or something, to see if I'd still be alive. And what if I wasn't?"

"Don't be morbid," said Pamela, and then, looking for a brighter note, "What's the latest from Patrick?"

"He's finished work on that book for his professor and is starting his year of study abroad. Loves Barcelona. Says he'd love to live there someday," I told them. The way I said it made it sound as though Patrick was just any guy, not the boyfriend I'd had almost continuously since sixth grade.

"I don't know how you stand it, Alice," Liz said, putting into words what, I'll admit, I'd wondered about myself.

"I don't know either, but—as Patrick says—the sooner it's over, the sooner he'll be back in the States." It was oppressively humid, and I thrust my lower lip out and blew, trying to fan my face. But it didn't help.

The front door opened behind us, and my brother came back out. Les got his MA from Maryland last December and just found out he'd been hired as the assistant director of a conference center in the mountains of West Virginia, where corporations hold retreats and sales conferences and couples come to get in touch with their inner selves. He starts September first. Dad always wondered what Les would do with a philosophy degree.

"I *told* you I was going to sit on a mountaintop so people could come to me and ask the meaning of life," he joked.

Now he was standing beside us in shorts and sandals, staring at the pickup truck, which seemed to list to one side.

"Say, Al, you really travel light!" he said. "Sure you don't want to take the piano, too?" His dark brown hair matched his eyes, which always, *always* seemed to be hiding a smile.

Elizabeth and Pamela gave him their immediate attention. Lester's single at the moment, and they've had crushes on him since they were eleven. *All* of my friends love Lester.

"Aren't you just the teeniest bit sad to see your sister off?" Elizabeth asked, in a voice she reserves only for Les.

"Been wanting to boot her out since the day she was born," Lester said. "Hey, I'm getting rid of all three of you, come to think of it. At last!"

"When are you going to get married, Les?" Pamela asked. "Or are you going to stay a bachelor all your life?"

"Oh . . . maybe twenty, thirty years from now I'll think about it," he said. And then, "Sylvia's got lunch ready, Al. And then we'd better get going."

I sniffed under one arm. "Oh, gross. I've got to have a shower first."

"How about you, Liz? Pamela? Want some lunch?" Lester said.

"Can't. I'm getting a manicure in twenty minutes," said Pamela. "Liz is coming with me, and we need to clean up."

"Well, let's get a move on," Lester said, and went back inside.

Elizabeth, who was sitting between Pamela and me, put one arm around each of us. "Do you remember what we promised once? That we'd always get together like this, no matter how old we got, and share our secrets?"

Pamela was grinning. "You mean, tell each other when we lost our virginity." One of the hundred silly things we'd said. Pamela had already lost hers, so the rest was up to Liz and me.

Elizabeth gave our shoulders an exasperated shake. "You know what I mean. I just hope we're always like this. They say you make your closest friends in college, but I don't see how anyone could be closer than we are."

"There's always texting," Pamela said.

"It's not the same," said Elizabeth.

"So if we can't actually get together, we'll make it a conference call," I suggested, knowing I'd better get inside.

We jokingly sealed it by placing our hands on top of each other's, the way kids do in grade school.

"Till Thanksgiving, then," I said.

"Or Christmas," said Pamela.

"Or even spring break," I added.

"Sisters forever," said Elizabeth. And because she was so serious and solemn about it, we laughed.

Sylvia had lunch ready when I went inside—chicken salad with pineapple and almonds, my favorite. Dad gave me a bear hug before we even sat down. He had the look of a bear too, sort of pudgy and cuddly, his head slightly balding on top.

"Well, honey, it may be a while before you're here at the table again," he said.

"Probably all of one week," said Lester. "Wait till she tastes the food at the U. She'll be home every weekend, I'll bet."

"College food is mostly carbohydrates, as I remember," said Sylvia. "Potatoes, pasta, beans, bread . . ." She was all in coral today—light sweater, pants, loafers. As always, my stepmom looked stunning. "Come home whenever you want a good pot roast."

"When will we see *you* again, Les?" Dad asked.

"Oh, I'll be back from time to time," Lester said. "But I'd think you two would enjoy some privacy for yourselves."

Dad put one hand on Sylvia's shoulder. "We manage," he said.

I had to put my sheets and towels on my seat in the pickup and sit on them. It was the only space left, and my head almost touched the ceiling. I already had a box of books under my feet.

"I'll bet Dad and Sylvia are secretly glad to see me go," I told Les as we backed down the drive and watched them waving to us from the porch. "Do you realize they've hardly been alone since they married?"

"Yep. He's never had the chance to chase her around the table naked," Les said.

I gave him my most sardonic look. "Yeah? Is that what married people do?"

"How do I know? I've never been married."

"Do you remember when you were dating Marilyn Rawley, and for your birthday she said she'd cook your favorite meal in the costume of your choice?" We both started to smile.

"And I chose surf and turf, with Marilyn dressed in high leather boots and a leopard-skin bikini," Les said, and we laughed.

"Did *you* ever chase *her* around the table naked?" I asked.

"Hey! She had on a bikini, didn't she?"

As more and more of my neighborhood disappeared behind us, I wasn't sure if I was feeling nervousness or excitement. I guess I'd call it nervous excitement. But just when I thought I was being cool about heading for college, I heard myself say, "Sylvia says Dad's afraid I'll become 'sexually active' at Maryland."

"Good old Dad," said Les. "Well . . ." He paused. "You know what to do, don't you?"

"What's this? A facts-of-life-before-I-go-off-to-college talk?" I said.

"Hey, you brought it up."

"If I have any urgent questions, I'll call you," I joked. Then, "Everyone makes sex sound so dangerous."

"It's dangerous, all right. It's dynamite!" said Lester, and grinned. It's hard to have a serious conversation with my brother, but I had myself to blame.

"The voice of experience," I commented.

"Not nearly enough," he sighed.

The first week at Maryland, it was hard to take it all in. Like a whole city, with everyone around my own age, and a smörgåsbord of activities to choose from. I wanted a bite of everything. The bulletin boards were crammed with invitations from sororities and fraternities, notices about movies and lectures, announcements of student trips abroad—all inviting me to join something, protect something, attend something, discuss or support or audition. There were even fliers taped up in the restrooms:

ACTORS NEEDED FOR CROWD SCENE IN '50S FILM! HIV TEST-
ING IN PRIVATE! OKTOBERFEST IN GERMANY! REBUILD HOUSES IN
HAITI! HOW WILL YOU VOTE ON IMMIGRATION? JOIN THE DEBATE
ON GLOBAL WARMING!

I wanted to try them all! Of course, as I discovered when I
asked about it, you had to have a passport and enough money
for airfare to attend Oktoberfest in Germany or even to build
houses in Haiti. But you could pile in a car of students driving
to a protest somewhere, and there was no one to stop you. Your
parents wouldn't even know you'd been gone. If you wanted
to skip three days of school to be part of a crowd scene in a
local movie, your professors didn't take roll. You might miss
an important handout and really screw up an assignment by
missing classes, but that was up to you. The freedom was both
heady and terrifying.

Every time I passed Testudo, the huge bronze turtle in front
of McKeldin Library, I made a habit of rubbing its nose, just for
fun. The book we received at orientation said it was supposed
to bring good luck on tests, but then an upperclassman saw me
do it, and she said you rubbed it if you didn't want to graduate
a virgin. And someone else told me she'd heard that if a virgin
ever graduated from Maryland, the thousand-pound sculpture
would fly. Which is why it's still there, I guess.

I made up my mind I'd do at least one new thing a week: a
foreign-language film, a debate on same-sex marriage, a talk by
our congressperson, helping students register to vote. I thought
I was busy in high school working on *The Edge*, but it couldn't

compare with this. It seemed as though someone had turned a dial and my whole life had sped up a notch.

As for my dorm room, however, the only way to describe it was "semi-hideous." The cinder block walls had a fresh coat of yellow paint, but it still looked as stark as a women's prison. The mattresses sagged a little, and the sea-green drapes were missing some hooks. That's why people bring so much stuff from home, I realized. You have to cover every square inch of space with your own things to make it seem remotely livable, and Amber and I did a pretty good job of making it livable, though the stuff we added was mostly mine.

I brought the rug and a green comforter for my bed; a lamp, bulletin board, and mini-fridge, and a funny poster—a take-off on the famous painting *American Gothic* with dogs' heads taking the place of the farmer and his wife. Amber contributed some throw pillows, a second lamp, and enough pictures of her boyfriend to cover one wall. These were good for a start. We figured we'd be adding other stuff as the year went on.

Before I'd met Amber Russell, I'd already seen her tattoos in Facebook photos—the dove on her ankle, the angel on her thigh, and the butterfly on her midsection—and they were cool. But once we shared the same room, I discovered pretty quickly what I didn't like about her: She seemed to migrate all over the place.

By day two her cosmetics and lotions had crowded mine on the bathroom shelf, her books were strewn everywhere, and her clothes pushed mine into a corner of the closet, where they cowered, begging me to rescue them. When she kicked off her shoes (which she invariably wore without socks, so they smelled), they always seemed to land over by my bed, and I was forever stumbling over them. She was like an oil slick that kept taking over more and more of the surface space, and there was no way to contain her.

She wasn't all that careful about personal hygiene, either. She'd drop used tampons in the wastebasket without even wrapping them up; she let sweat-soaked T-shirts hang in the closet for days on end without washing them, till I hated to even open the door to our room. And she showered only when she felt like it.

But the maddening thing was, her boyfriend was always hanging around, usually as sloppy as she was.

Tolerance, I told myself. Different people have different priorities, that's all. Hygiene wasn't high on Amber's list.

Gwen and I got together whenever we could. There was a large house off campus—a gift to the university—where premed students could live at half the usual rate, so Gwen, understandably, chose to stay there, which was a bit of a bummer for me—we would have been such good roommates.

"So how goes it?" she asked one Friday a few weeks into school, when we'd managed to meet for dinner at a Burmese restaurant in town.

"I love my classes," I told her, "but—God! Amber's a slob! She *smells*! Our room stinks. I can't stand going in there at night."

"Huh! Mine's the exact opposite. She even wipes off the toilet seat after she uses it!" Gwen said.

"Amber doesn't even use toilet paper when she pees!" I complained. "You ask how I know that? She pees with the door open."

Gwen burst into laughter. "You only have to put up with her for a year. Next fall you can choose someone different. Of course, you could get someone worse."

"Impossible," I said. Through the window, I watched a guy in a corduroy jacket cross the parking lot and come inside. He paid for an order at the cash register and took it out to a girl in a waiting Toyota. I concentrated on Gwen again. She'd recently had her eyebrows shaped, two beautiful black curves extending out toward her temples, against her mocha brown skin.

"Your mistake was not saying something right away," she told me. "You've let it go this long; she probably figures you're okay with it. You've got to talk to her."

I sighed. "You know I hate confrontation."

"Then you've got to decide which you hate more: talking to her about it or slob city."

"What are you going to specialize in, Doctor? Psychiatry?" I asked.

Gwen ate another bite of her lemongrass beef and pointed to the last piece of my roti pancake. When I shoved it in her direction, she ate that, too, still thoughtful. "I don't know. Pediatrics, I think. Or maybe Ob/Gyn. Remember what they told us when we were hospital volunteers? That there's only one happy ward in a hospital, and that's the maternity ward? What do you hear from Patrick?"

"I'm trying to follow your train of thought here," I said, and we laughed. "He's having a blast. He e-mailed me about all the different people in his classes—a guy who's climbed Mount Kilimanjaro twice; a girl who's joining the Peace Corps; a guy who pays his way through college by fishing; an artist; a priest . . . *He* gets to meet all these fascinating people, and I get Amber."

"So plan to visit him over spring break or something."

"Don't think I haven't considered it," I told her. "I've even priced airline tickets. But that's months and months away. I'll probably seem pretty boring compared to all his friends there."

"He's coming back to you, remember," Gwen said.

"That's one thing to be happy about," I agreed.

When I got up the next morning, there was a wet towel on the bathroom floor, along with Amber's underwear, and a washcloth in the sink. A bottle of shampoo lay on its side on the shelf, and a thin puddle of slippery goo oozed across the shelf, surrounding my makeup. *Arrrghhhh! Enough!*

I whirled around and marched back into our room. Amber had thrown off her covers and was engaged in a giant stretch. Her T-shirt was bunched up around her waist, and the butterfly tattoo on her midsection seemed to spread its wings as she moved.

"Amber, your stuff's taking over that whole shelf in the bathroom," I said. "I'd really appreciate it if you'd clean it up."

She opened her eyes and squinted at me. "Just push it to one side. I won't care."

"Well, *I* care. And it's also annoying to keep stumbling over your shoes and things."

"O-*kay!*" she said, yawning. "Don't have a spaz."

There! I told myself. *That wasn't so hard.* It *was* possible to assert myself without a shouting match.

When I got home from classes that day, the towel was back on the rack and Amber's underwear was gone, but the shampoo bottle was still on its side, and pink liquid was now dripping off the edge of the shelf. I capped it, cleaned up the mess, and wiped off my cosmetics.

Things were a little better after that. For a week, anyway. Then I noticed she was using my deodorant stick.

"Hey, Amber, that's mine," I said.

"Oh. Do you care?"

"Well . . . sure! I mean, it'll be used up twice as fast, and I'm paying for it."

"I'll buy the next stick," she said.

I think it was that night that I woke up around two or three to a rattling sound, and my first thought was that Amber had locked herself out and was trying to wake me up. I lifted my head and listened.

It was a steady, rhythmical, squeaking sound, and then I realized that Amber had her boyfriend in bed. I didn't know if I was more angry, surprised, or embarrassed.

"Oh, you're so good . . . you're so good," Jerry's voice kept murmuring.

Little breathy moans from Amber. Her bed frame rattled louder as it knocked against the wall.

I didn't turn on the light, but I got up and went to the bathroom, slamming the door behind me. I heard the guy swear.

After I'd flushed the toilet, I went back to bed. I could hear the two of them whispering in the darkness, so I put my pillow over one ear and went back to sleep.

In the morning Jerry was gone, but he'd left his socks behind. Amber came out of the bathroom, brushing her teeth. She had on a wrinkled sleep-shirt with SURF CITY written on the front. She wasn't smiling.

"Thanks for nothing, Alice. You could at least have waited," she said.

I was sitting on the edge of the bed and stared at her. "Excuse me?"

"Jerry was pretty pissed off at you. You were banging around at the critical moment, and he lost it."

I knew exactly what Jerry had lost, but I said, "If he's looking for his socks, they're under your bed."

"You know what I mean," Amber said. "Let's have a little consideration."

I couldn't believe it. "Are you serious? I'm wakened at three in the morning by you and Jerry, and I'm the inconsiderate one?"

She simply went back in the bathroom, and this time she closed the door.

I called home.

"I can't stand it, Dad!" I said. "I shouldn't have to put up with this!"

"Then don't. Talk to your resident adviser and see what the rules are. Are men allowed in women's rooms?"

"Huh?" I said. "This is the twenty-first century, Dad! Of course they are! But we're supposed to show consideration. Amber claims I didn't show her any when I interrupted *them*."

"Well, honey, I'm here if you need help with life-or-death decisions, but I think this falls in the solve-it-yourself category," Dad said.

One thing about Amber, she didn't hold a grudge. She went right on as though nothing had happened. I hid my shampoo and deodorant, and she even asked if I had any. I lied and said no, and she washed her hair with hand soap.

I was facing a huge assignment due on Monday and knew I had to work on it all weekend. On Saturday afternoon, though, Amber decided to do her laundry—the first time I'd actually seen her do any at all. Jerry came by, and they started stripping down her side of the room—sheets, towels, shirts—stuffing everything in a pillowcase to take to the washing machines in the basement. I headed for the library with a stack of books.

I worked right through dinner, stopping only long enough to get a tuna wrap and a bag of chips, but by nine that night, I'd had it. My eyes could scarcely focus and my head throbbed. I knew I had a full day of writing ahead of me on Sunday and wanted only to go to bed and sleep.

When I got back to our room, Amber was sitting at her desk, painting her toenails, one foot propped on our wastebasket. We talked a little about exams and grade points, and then I undressed in the bathroom, pulled on my pajamas, and got into bed.

My pillow had a dirty-hair smell that wasn't mine, and I could almost bet that Amber had borrowed my pillow. I was too tired to start an argument, though, so I turned it over and stretched out.

My foot touched something between the sheets, however, and suddenly I sat up, threw off the covers, and saw a rolled-up condom at the foot of my bed, along with Amber's underwear.

I leaped out of bed.

"Look!" I shouted, pointing.

Amber turned. "Oh! Sorry!" she said. She stuck another wad of cotton between her toes and padded over to retrieve the condom.

"This is *my bed*!" I yelled. "What were you *thinking*?"

"Well, *my* sheets were in the wash, and Jerry doesn't like to do it on a bare mattress," she said. She shrugged. "You were gone, so . . ."

"It's *my bed*!" I screamed again.

I think I went a little insane. I pulled off my sheets and flung them on the floor. Then I grabbed Amber's underwear and tossed it out the window. I picked up her shoes, which were on my side of the room, and threw them against the wall. I scooped up everything of Amber's that had migrated over to my section and dumped them on her bed.

Amber left and didn't come back that night, or the next or the next. Gwen heard she'd moved into Jerry's room. I wondered what *his* roommate thought of that! Every so often, she'd come back to get some more clothes or drop something off, but we didn't talk much. And that was fine with me.

2
SURPRISES

With Amber gone, Gwen started coming to my dorm more often, and then we simply used Amber's bed as a couch. It was a good place to hang out, and I found I was making friends more easily than I'd expected. Sometimes someone would ask if a visiting friend could crash there for a weekend, so it became a guest bed when needed, and I liked meeting friends of friends.

I'd always heard that high school students were more independent thinkers than middle school kids and that there was even less of a herd mentality in college. That's one of the things I hoped would happen when I got to Maryland—that I'd be released forever from worrying about whether I had the "right look" or wore the right brand-name jeans, or if I was hanging out at the most popular places.

But it wasn't quite that simple, because sometimes I felt there was a competition to see who had the most individualistic look, and the professors were no exception.

Fun, though. There was the professor who dressed like he belonged in a law office, and one who looked as though he slept in his clothes. And then there was my Sociology 101 teacher, who walked into the lecture hall on the first day of classes in knee-high boots and a leather skirt.

As the weeks went on, though, and she appeared in an ultrafeminine dress with a ruffled collar one day and a denim skirt the next, we began to realize that she was making a statement about society's attitude toward women based on superficial appearances. Valerie Robbins and I tried to guess how her outfit punctuated her point at the end of each lecture. Male and female equality? Woman as dominatrix? Sex in the workplace?

"I think she's trying to establish a position of authority," Valerie had said that first day. "All she needs is a whip."

Valerie was a tall, thin girl who fascinated me because she ate twice as much as any other girl I knew but complained that she couldn't gain an ounce. I'd pay almost anything for her metabolism. She was also the kind of friend who didn't just welcome you with open arms, she *enveloped* you in whatever project excited her at the moment, and Valerie was always into projects.

"You've got to help me," she said the third week of October. She'd been going with this guy Colin for a year and a half— they'd met in high school—and he was a sophomore here at

Maryland. His birthday was coming up on Monday, and he had bragged that no one, ever, had been able to surprise him—he was that good at detecting signs and signals. Valerie wanted to prove him wrong.

She brought two friends—Abby and Claire—to my dorm room around noon on Sunday and told us her plan. The four of us were going to her uncle's house in Adelphi that afternoon to bake cupcakes, Colin's favorite. That night she and another couple were taking him to dinner to celebrate because it was the weekend. But at three o'clock in the morning on Monday, the four of us would sneak into his dorm, stand outside his room, and belt out "Happy Birthday." When he admitted defeat, he'd get the cupcakes. What did she have to lose but a good night's sleep? And the rest of the cupcakes would be ours.

Val had the car, Abby had the two cake mixes, and after a trip to the local Giant for the rest of the ingredients, we drove to her uncle's, where we promised to leave some cupcakes in return for the use of the kitchen.

We divided each cake mix in half. To half the chocolate, we added coffee instead of water; to half the vanilla, we added maraschino cherry juice.

Abby was a little powerhouse—small for nineteen, but hardly fragile. The oven mitts gave her the look of a boxer, and she was definitely the director of this operation.

"Fill each cup just two-thirds full," she instructed. "You don't want the batter to spread out over the top as it bakes."

"I hope Colin's worth all the trouble," said Claire, a tea towel tucked into the waistband of her jeans. Her widely spaced eyes surveyed the cupcake pans still waiting to be filled.

"No trouble for me. I love baking," Abby said. "Someday I'm going to enter a bake-off and win ten thousand dollars. All I need is a recipe no one has ever thought of yet."

"If I won ten thousand dollars, I'd start a rare-book collection," Val said.

"I'd use it to open a consignment shop," said Claire. And we all agreed that would be perfect for her. Claire's wardrobe was indefinable, because she could throw together the most unlikely combinations and look great. She wore her long brown hair pulled straight back, away from her face, so that all the attention was directed to her body and the flow of her clothes.

Everyone looked at me.

"If I had ten thousand dollars, I'd fly to Barcelona to see my boyfriend five times," I said, and told them about Patrick.

Sitting around that kitchen table, watching the cupcakes rise through the glass window in the oven, I was feeling pretty good about college so far. Eight weeks into the semester and I'd already made some friends, got rid of a roommate, and knew my way around the whole campus. Not as hard as I'd imagined, and if I didn't feel really close yet to these girls, I was feeling comfortable.

Valerie, Claire, and Abby spent the night in my dorm room. Valerie came back from her dinner with Colin around eleven, and we decided it was easier to all bed down in one room than set an alarm in four different rooms on campus. Valerie and I slept on the floor in sleeping bags, and I let Claire and Abby have the beds.

When the alarm went off at three, it felt like we'd only been asleep for fifteen minutes. Ugh. How could we possibly pull on our clothes and sleepwalk all the way over to Colin's dorm? But somehow we all managed to get our teeth brushed so we wouldn't asphyxiate Colin when we surprised him, and ten minutes later we were wider awake than I'd imagined, sneaking across campus under an October moon. When we saw a security car making a turn, we ducked behind a hedge and it rolled slowly by. We felt like prisoners on the verge of escape, waiting out the beam of a searchlight.

Finally there we were at the side door. It was a known fact that our key cards opened the side doors of at least two of the buildings on campus, and one of those buildings was Colin's dorm.

We went up a flight of stairs, our feet making light echoing thuds on the metal steps, and opened the fire door. We were all so used to noise in the halls—at all hours of the day or night—that the absolute quiet was a bit unnerving. But down the hall we went to room number 231 and found the door . . . ajar.

We stared uncertainly at each other. There was no way Colin could have found out what we were up to, because the four of us had been together all day Sunday and none of us had called anyone. Whichever of Colin's roomies had come in last simply hadn't bothered to close the door behind him, we decided, so we stepped inside.

No lights were on in the small living area. On either side, there was a door to a two-man bedroom. Valerie pointed to Colin's door.

"Ready?" she whispered, and we faced in that direction. "One . . . two . . ."

A large figure suddenly loomed in the doorway beside us, blocking the light from the hall, and we screamed—all four of us together.

"What the hell?" A shadowy hand swiped at the wall for the light switch, and there was Colin in his boxers, his rumpled hair hanging in front of his eyes, just returning from a trip to the bathroom.

There were rustlings in both bedrooms, voices in the hall, and somebody appeared brandishing a lacrosse stick.

"Wait!" Valerie yelled.

"Val?" Colin said, staring at her, then at us.

"He's surprised," I said.

"Happy birthday!" Val and Abby and Claire cried in unison.

"I don't believe this!" Colin said, finally beginning to smile, and I thrust the box of cupcakes in his hands.

"We broke your record, admit it," said Val.

"Hey! People are sleeping here! Trying to, anyway," said one of the roomies.

"We're going," Val told him. "Happy birthday." She kissed Colin's bemused face and pointed toward the cupcakes. "Share."

* * *

I was almost as excited about Thanksgiving this year as I was for Christmas. I hadn't seen Pamela or Elizabeth since September, and most of my other friends would be home too.

Liz texted regularly, but we had to go on Facebook to find out anything about Pamela. She called once, though. She said the theater arts college works you to death, and I said, what else is new? We agreed to get together the Friday after Thanksgiving.

Usually I can get someone to drive me to the Metro in College Park, and then I get off at Silver Spring, where Dad or Sylvia picks me up. But I had a lot of things to carry this time, including laundry, so Dad drove over to College Park and waited for me outside my dorm. We'd talked about getting me a used car, but the Metro was so handy, and student parking so iffy, that I'd decided to wait.

I threw my stuff in the backseat and slid in up front, leaning over to give Dad a kiss. I love the way his face lights up when he sees me.

"Four whole days!" I said. "And I got most of my assignments done, so I can just hang out. Is Les home yet?"

Dad edged the car into traffic on Route 1. "Coming in this evening. And a friend of his is driving in from West Virginia tomorrow."

"Male or female?" I asked.

"A young lady, actually."

The older my dad gets, the more he sounds as if he were born in the 1800s. Any female under forty is always a "young lady."

"Have you met her?" I asked.

"No. Les just said it's someone he wants us to meet. Her name is Stacy."

I looked at Dad. "Where's she going to sleep?"

He broke into laughter. "Now, where have I heard *that* before? You haven't changed a bit."

I laughed too. I used to ask that about Sylvia all the time when she and Dad went anywhere overnight before they were married, but this time I was simply protecting my room. "I just want to know if I'm supposed to give up my bed or if she'll be shacking up with Les."

Dad grimaced. He hates that term. "I haven't the faintest idea, and I'm not about to ask. Lester will have to work that out himself," he said.

I was impatient with the way traffic was creeping along, so I turned on the radio but kept it low. "How are things at the Melody Inn?" I asked.

"It's been a busy fall, and business is picking up, I'm glad to say."

I asked about various employees and music instructors, and then the big green exit sign for Silver Spring loomed up ahead, and once we were off the beltway, it wasn't long before we were home. Dad pulled into the drive, and we each carried some bags inside.

Sylvia hugged me and gave me a peck on the cheek.

"I smell something baking already," I told her. "The whole house smells wonderful."

"I'm so glad both you and Les could come for Thanksgiving," she said, and accented the last word with an extra squeeze before she let me go. I figured that, much as she and Dad liked having the house to themselves, they also enjoyed sharing it again, especially around the holidays.

I loved being back in my room. A whole double bed to myself, recently painted walls, old treasures. . . . Sylvia had faithfully watered my huge rubber plant, which now reached the top of the windows. I lay down on my bed and smiled happily up at the ceiling. So many dramas and traumas had passed through this room. The night Sylvia slept with me, for example, before she and Dad married, when a blizzard kept her here at Christmas; the time I hid Pamela here when she ran away from home; the way I cried after Patrick and I broke up back in ninth grade. . . . Right now it was great remembering all of that, because—happy or sad—each experience was a part of this room.

My cell phone started ringing almost immediately. Everyone was checking on everyone else to see who would be around this weekend. We had the decency not to plan to get together till after Thanksgiving—to spend Wednesday night and Thursday with our families—but we all looked forward to the next day.

Jill and Justin were settling into life as new parents to a baby boy, but almost everyone else except Patrick—and Mark, of course—would be back. There was particular sadness in that, because if it weren't for the accident that took Mark, we'd all be meeting at his place. But everyone promised to show up here on Friday.

"I've really missed Nathan," Elizabeth told me when I returned her call. "He's so *cute*, Alice! He calls me 'Mommy Two.' Would you believe he's five years old already?"

While I had been home several times since September, Liz—way up in Vermont at Bennington—hadn't been home until now.

"I can't wait to see him," I told her. "I can't wait to see everyone!"

When I heard Lester come in, I rushed downstairs and almost knocked him over as I threw my arms around his neck.

"Hey! What do they feed you on campus? Stimulants?" he said, grinning.

I gave him a big sloppy kiss on the cheek and hugged him again. Then I let out a shriek. "You're growing a beard!"

"You noticed."

"You're all prickly!"

"Women love it," Les teased. He turned to Sylvia and hugged her next, then Dad. "It's sure good to be back," he said.

"And Alice isn't even going to see her friends till Friday," Sylvia told him. "Such restraint!" She had held dinner till Les got here, so we sat down almost immediately to eat.

Our dinner that evening must have lasted two hours. We just sat around and talked over coffee and Sylvia's lemon sponge cake—helping ourselves to second and third slices.

"So what's our coed doing these days?" Les asked me. "How's the roommate?"

"You don't want to know," I said, but I told him anyway.

"Could have been worse," he said. "Amber and Jerry could have been having sex in your bed with you in it. Now you've got the best of all possible worlds—a private bedroom for half the price."

"Tell me about you and Stacy," I said, and then was embarrassed that my thoughts had gone from beds to Les and Stacy.

"What about her? You'll get to meet her tomorrow. Her family's in Arlington, but she's going to have dinner here and then drive home tomorrow night."

I could swear I saw relief pass over Dad's face. Sylvia's, too.

I loved being home that night. I felt so special, somehow. Both Les and I coming back to the old homestead—both of us in new locations, with new lives.

"You miss me?" I asked him at one point.

"Not a bit," he answered, but his smile said it all.

I don't know what I expected when Stacy Houghton arrived— a model, maybe. The real Stacy was only an inch or so taller than me. She wasn't what you'd call beautiful, but she was definitely attractive, with short, semi-curly hair and a small button nose between the lenses of her stylish glasses. Her lips were delicately shaped, like twin peaks. I just hoped I wouldn't goof up and call her Tracy, a woman Les proposed to once.

"Hello, Alice. Hello, everyone. Sylvia . . . Ben . . . ," she said, looking us over.

"Welcome!" said Dad, smiling and taking her coat. "We're so glad to have you!"

She was wearing a white sweater, with tiny pearl earrings, and if she used makeup at all, it wasn't noticeable. She and Les exchanged a quick kiss, and I saw his hand linger on her waist. And then we were all moving to the kitchen for a glass of cider and to help Sylvia with the finishing touches, so by the time we were ready to eat, we didn't feel like such strangers with Stacy.

Dinner was everything you'd want it to be on Thanksgiving. Dad carved the turkey, and we all carried food to the dining room table in a happy parade.

I studied Les and Stacy throughout dinner. She was in her last year at the university in Morgantown, she told us, working on a degree in phys ed, but had a job on weekends as a swim instructor at the Basswood Lodge and Convention Center, where Les worked.

"And she's a state swimming champion," Les said proudly, then added, with a grin, "She hasn't entered any swimsuit contests, but she could win some."

Stacy just laughed. "Not my line," she said.

A bundle of energy, that's what she was—the quick way she moved, responded. The more I watched her and Les, in fact, the more they seemed exact opposites of each other. Where Lester was laid-back, Stacy was intense. Where Les was careless—his napkin, his knife, and his fork strewn every which way over his plate—Stacy was precise. And yet, when I saw their eyes meet, the warmth of those glances told me they liked each other very, very much.

It's funny the way you grow up with one idea about a person and don't really start noticing other things till you're older. I'd always thought of Lester as sort of a playboy, but sometimes when I'd hear him discuss world problems with Dad, I'd think, *I didn't know he cared anything about that!* So I guess it wasn't too surprising that Lester was in love with a woman who was intelligent and energetic, yet different from any other woman he'd ever dated.

And Dad . . . I turned my attention to him next. When you're a kid, you believe your parents' main occupation in life should be taking care of you, as though they should be thinking about your feelings twenty-four hours a day. And then you grow up and realize that your dad has needs and interests that have nothing to do with you at all.

The other thing I was feeling as we sat around over dessert, laughing at my roommate stories (a lot funnier now that they were in the past), was that it was the first time I felt like an adult with my family. I was more than just the kid sister now. And I liked that feeling. Liked it a lot.

I got a call from Patrick later and ran upstairs to take it in my room.

"I was hoping you'd pick up," he said.

"Where *are* you?" I asked, curling up on my bed, the phone tucked under my ear.

"Well, at the moment I'm sitting on a bench near the

entrance of the Plaza de Cataluña in the early evening, wishing you were here."

"There in Barcelona?"

"Yeah. And I'm looking up at a statue of a guy on a . . . Wait a minute, correction: a *woman* on a horse—a naked woman on a horse—holding a small sailing ship above her head."

"I don't get it. Why is she on a horse?"

"I don't get it either, but a bunch of us are exploring the city, and the others have gone in search of a restroom. You home?"

"Yes. And it's so great. The whole gang's getting together tomorrow. I really miss you, Patrick. Seven more months till you're home again."

"Where are you going to meet tomorrow? It would have been at the Stedmeisters' . . ."

"I know. That's on everyone's mind. So I've invited everybody here. Les is home too, and he has a new girlfriend."

"That's a surprise?"

I laughed. "*She* is. And they're obviously crazy about each other."

"Uh-oh," Patrick said. "I see the gang moving off . . . they didn't know I was over here. Gotta hustle."

"Happy Thanksgiving, Patrick," I said, "even though you're not celebrating it." I didn't want to carry on about how much I longed for him, because it was depressing, for one thing, and because, technically, we weren't in an exclusive relationship. We usually kept our remarks to the I-miss-you variety. This time, though, I said, "I love you."

He could still make me laugh, even four thousand miles away.

"I'm sending you a kiss by proxy," he said.

I was smiling already. "And how does that work?"

"Well, there's a mail truck parked at the corner . . . and I'm walking over"—I could tell he was moving because his words were fading in and out—"and I'm putting my arms around the back of the truck, which is a little hard to do because I'm still trying to talk into the cell phone . . ."

"I'm not as wide as a truck, Patrick."

"I know, but partway will have to do. And now I'm pressing my lips against the door, a long, slow kiss . . ."

"Mmmmm," I said, pretending to moan with pleasure.

". . . and a pedestrian is looking at me like I'm loco and is probably going to call the *policia* right this minute," Patrick finished. *"Adios, querido!"*

The local language of Barcelona, Patrick had told me, was Catalan, not Spanish, and I was bummed because I'd wanted to practice my high school Spanish with him. But the tourists all came with their Spanish dictionaries, Patrick said, and the locals humored them, so he occasionally threw in a Spanish phrase when he called.

I was glad that his last words to me were funny and affectionate, the way I wanted him to remember me. Then I looked up *querido* in my Spanish dictionary and was pleased that it meant "sweetheart."

***

Liz, Pam, Gwen, and I agreed to spend the night at Elizabeth's after our other friends had left. It was fun seeing everyone again. Tim, Pamela's ex, had that movie-star unshaven look, while Keeno—now at the Naval Academy in Annapolis—had just the opposite: a buzz cut. Karen was home from Penn State; Lori and Leslie were still together, we heard, but had decided to move west and were headed to Washington State. Penny and her folks had moved to Delaware, and no one knew where Brian was at the moment. We'd just lost touch.

All we did was talk. It sounded like a zoo, everyone trading YouTube favorites and gossip. To tell the truth, it was a relief when everybody else had gone and just us girls headed over to Liz's house, closing her bedroom door behind us.

"Whew!" she said, hugging us all over again. "Oh, man, I have *missed* you guys!" Texting, we all agreed, could never compete with this.

She looked great too. Pamela was the scrawny one now, but she didn't deprive herself of any of the snacks Mrs. Price had made for us. We sprawled across the beds in Elizabeth's room just like we used to, the twin beds with their same ruffled white bedspreads, and talked about our lives—classes, subjects, grades, professors, fun. . . .

Gwen told us about going to a sign-language poetry festival I'd seen advertised on campus but hadn't attended, where deaf students expressed themselves visually, and for the millionth time I thought, *This is another cool thing we didn't see back in high school.*

Liz was into contact improv and demonstrated with Pamela

on the rug. She put on a CD of Debussy's *Afternoon of a Faun*, and as each of them began moving her limbs in slow, rhythmic motion to the music, they gradually touched, curved together, rolled, separated. . . .

"What's it supposed to be? Modern dance? Wrestling? Orgiastic? *What?*" asked Gwen.

"Just bodily expression," Liz explained after their brief demonstration. Pamela had already been introduced to it earlier in the fall at her school, but it was new and wonderful to Elizabeth.

"I could sure use some dancing," I said. "I've gained six pounds."

"Awwk, tell me about it! The Attack of the Freshman Fifteen! I've gained seven," said Gwen, who still had eleven years of school ahead of her.

"So what do premed students do for fun, Gwen?" Pamela asked.

Gwen stretched out full on the bed and propped more pillows behind her.

"Well," she said, "the first day I walked into our residence house, some of the freshmen had gathered there in the living room. There was a huge box of LEGOs on a coffee table, and while we were talking, one of the older students put one in her mouth and started chewing. There was a loud crunch, but it didn't seem to faze her. I was like, *Whoa!* And then I realized they were edible LEGOs."

We laughed. And she said, "It's like we're always starving! And get this—every year, they tell me, one of the upperclassmen is selected to be our scout, and he has to keep track of every reception being held on campus—a promotion, a secretary's birthday, parents of incoming freshmen, retirement party, whatever. And then he assigns one of us to sign up as a server if possible, or simply be a drop-in, and to come back with pockets loaded. And birthdays . . . We've got a cupboard full of cake mixes, and whenever someone's hungry, we think of a birthday to celebrate if we're not having one ourselves. A couple weeks ago we had a birthday celebration for Trotsky—"

"Trotsky?" asked Pamela.

"Yeah. Born on November 7, 1879. We had a red cake, and someone made a pin-the-axe-on-the-Trotsky game out of cardboard. The month before that, we even had a celebration for Donald Duck."

"Oh, man. I'm in the wrong dorm!" I said. "Maybe I'll change my major to podiatry. That's feet, isn't it? I think I could handle feet."

"You ought to visit me next Halloween," Pamela chimed in. She was sitting cross-legged now on the other bed, a long turquoise scarf wrapped twice around her neck, a royal-blue streak in her blond hair that now almost reached her shoulders. "Practically the entire school joins the Halloween parade in the Village."

"How did you dress?" Liz asked.

"The pope," said Pamela.

"The pope?" I cried. *"You?"*

"And I was escorted by two nuns, both guys," she said. We

screamed with laughter. "You should have seen us. One of my friends was a grasshopper. We drew our characters' names from a hat, and had to judge each other on how well we did. We were doing great until about one o'clock, when we ended the night in a bar and the pope was wasted so the nuns had to drag him outside." She reached for another Dorito. "I'm crazy about one of my instructors, though. Wish we could date faculty." She looked at Gwen and me. "How are the guys at Maryland?"

Gwen shrugged. "Like guys everywhere, I guess. Some nice, some jerks. Bigger selection to choose from, though." She turned to Liz. "What's it like up there at the North Pole?"

"Sleepy," Elizabeth told her. "Definitely sleepy. Except on weekends. Then everybody's out to hook up with someone."

"Yeah, tell me about it," said Pamela. "Have any of you met someone special?"

"No. Still seeing Austin occasionally. But he'll be a senior at Howard next year, and I don't know where he'll take a job after that," Gwen said. She looked at me. Guess I was next.

"It's hard to compare guys with Patrick, but there's one guy, Dave—Dave Larson. We hang out sometimes."

"Yeah?" said Pamela, waiting.

"Just the 'nice friend' category," I said. "Come on, tell us about the guys in New York. There's got to be someone other than your professor."

"Well, there's Jake. He wants to do repertory theater. Weird and passionate. Passionately weird or weirdly passionate, I'm not sure which."

We just looked at her and grinned.

"Passionate with you?" Elizabeth asked.

"Yeah. We've slept together a couple of times," Pamela said, and took another sip of her seltzer water.

For Pamela, sex was probably just part of her life now, I thought, but I didn't feel quite as adult as I had before. Sometimes it seemed as though the whole world was divided into girls who had done *it* and girls who hadn't. As though Pamela and Gwen were on one side of a wall and Liz and I were on the other, just looking over.

Liz must have been feeling the same way, because she said, "At Bennington that's all some girls talk about."

Pamela just shrugged. "No big deal. Stuff happens. That's it."

But I *wanted* it to be a big deal. I wanted it to be with someone I loved, anyway, someone who was more than weirdly passionate.

"Yeah," Gwen said, "when you're still a virgin, you obsess over it. It's huge. But once it's happened, there are so many other things to think about."

What I was thinking as our talk drifted to "other things" was my conversation with Patrick the day before, trying to remember every remark, each reply. . . . I remembered saying, "Seven months till you're home again," but I couldn't remember what he'd said next.

"I love you," I'd told him.

And he said he was sending me a kiss by proxy.

We'd laughed.

3

CHANGES

It came on slowly.

I didn't get phone calls from Patrick anymore, I got text messages and e-mails. Occasionally photos of landmarks and stuff—rarely of him. He'd tell me how busy he was, what he was studying, where he was going on his next expedition, how much he loved Spain. *He's moving there for good,* I thought. Should I give him the dates of spring break and ask if he'd like me to come? Or don't ask? Just say I'd be there, that if he had classes I'd be glad to tag along?

Then the tone changed ever so slightly:

Much as I love Spain, I'm feeling more and more unsettled. Like I'm still on some kind of academic track that's going to take me straight out of the University of Chicago and into a suit and tie.

I replied in a joking tone: *I don't know—I think you'd look pretty good in a suit and tie.*

But he didn't joke back. A week later I got:

The students here are so different . . . they've seen so much, done so much. . . . Sometimes I feel I'd just like to take a couple years off and really do something different. With my hands, I mean. Where I can see I've done something constructive—made something, built something, planted something, I don't know.

Am I making any sense?

And I answered:

It sounds a little like burnout to me. You've been going 90 miles an hour all your life, Patrick. No wonder you'd like a break. . . .

The perfect time for me to suggest a visit, so I did:

Speaking of which, spring break begins here on March 20, and I can buy my own ticket. I'd love to see Barcelona with you. Should I come?

There. No beating around the bush. I was free, I was flush,
I could come.

It was another week before he answered:

*Great idea, but our projects are due around then, and I'll
have to give mine my whole attention. Also, as I told you, I've
been feeling pretty unsettled. Not depressed, just like I want
to try something different. I'm even thinking about joining
the Peace Corps.*

*I talked to a professor here, and he thinks there may be
a way I can get at least a little credit for the Peace Corps
toward my degree when I go back to Chicago. But the beauty
of the PC is you don't know where they'll send you, and that
sort of appeals. . . .*

I couldn't swallow for a minute after I read it. My throat was
dry, like all the moisture in my body had been sucked out with a
giant vacuum. It was what he didn't tell me that felt like ice in my
gut. He wasn't coming home. And then it got worse: Patrick had
mentioned a girl in his class who wanted to join the Peace Corps.

I squeezed as much as I could into spring break, and I had the
funds to do it—from having saved part of my weekly allowance
all through grade and high school, and the monetary gifts from
relatives, to investing the money I'd earned working part-time
at the Melody Inn and, for the last summer, on the cruise ship. I
could afford to cut loose now and then, I decided.

I spent the first three days in New York with Pamela, meeting her new friends and going to shows; an evening in Georgetown with Valerie, Abby, and Claire, then an overnight back in Silver Spring; a visit to Valerie's family in Frederick; a wild last-minute trip to Philly to meet Abby's cousin on leave from the navy, just because she thought we'd hit it off (but we hardly had a decent conversation the whole evening); a Saturday helping out at the Melody Inn; and finally, the last rainy Sunday at home, help-ing Sylvia go through boxes of stuff in our attic that had been there for years—things that had been moved twice: once from Chicago to Takoma Park, then to our home in Silver Spring.

There were things that my mom must have received as gifts that she didn't want—a silver-plated butter server, a decorative bread box. I found old Christmas decorations, framed prints that had hung in the hallway back in Chicago, an ancient potty chair. . . .

"Everything that's going to Goodwill, I'll put on my left," Sylvia said, the sleeves of her blue shirt rolled up to the elbow. "If there's anything in this batch that you really want to keep, Alice, just say so."

I was perched on top of our "keepsake trunk," because everything in there was a keeper. My little brown monkey that wore diapers, Lester's childhood drawings, a tracing of Mom's hand with my little hand traced inside of it. . . . I used to come up here on rainy days—just like this one—and go through them.

I surveyed the assortment of stuff in front of us. "Well, that potty chair can go," I said. "Les and Stacy may need it long before I will."

"Hmm. Hadn't thought about that," she said, reconsidering it. She brushed one hand over the pink and blue bunnies painted on the lid. "But aren't we being a little premature?"

"I don't know. I just have the feeling Stacy's 'the one,' don't you?" I said.

"Lester's had a lot of girlfriends."

"True. And he almost married one. But . . ."

Sylvia slid the potty chair to the right. "What the heck. If I don't have grandchildren, I'll put it out in the yard and plant flowers in it."

We laughed. "I'd still put my money on Stacy," I said. "She's got enough energy for both of them. Les told me they went on a scuba diving trip last month. Maybe they'll move in together."

"We'd be the last to know," said Sylvia, reaching for another box and sliding it toward me to open.

"Tablecloths," I said, lifting the flaps and holding one up.

"They're all yours if you want them," said Sylvia.

"I don't even have a table," I told her. "Out."

When Sylvia pulled over the next box, she read the label and handed it to me. "Your mom's," she said.

I knew exactly what it was. It had been in our attic forever but I'd never opened it—a large flat box, the kind a winter coat might come in, all the edges sealed in blue tape.

"Her wedding dress," I said, one hand caressing the lid. "Aunt Sally told me once that Mom found it in a secondhand shop and fell in love with it." I'd seen it in my parents' wedding photo, but I hadn't actually touched it. Sylvia waited, probably hoping I'd open the box, and I was tempted. But I couldn't bear it if the moths had got it or it was discolored. That disappointment could wait for another day.

"Definitely a keeper," I said, putting it in the pile to the right, and Sylvia only nodded.

One of the things I liked most about college was that we spent more time talking with guys than we had in high school. And when Gwen spent the night with me on weekends, we talked a lot about our futures, what we wanted out of life, not just Elizabeth's or Pamela's latest news.

"I keep thinking, okay, so I'll have invested eleven or twelve years of my life earning the 'MD' beside my name, but when do I get to have fun? Am I sacrificing too much?" Gwen said once.

"Sometimes, when things get really crazy, I think about taking a year off," I confided. "But then I wonder if I'd ever come back."

With our new guy friends, we talked about an even larger variety of topics. When the high school gang used to sit around the Stedmeisters' pool, for example, when did we ever talk about the Supreme Court's ruling on health care or about gun laws or immigration? When did we ever all go to a Woody Allen film festival or a political debate? Or go on a crazy two-o'clock-in-the-morning search for vending machines on campus, looking for loose quarters so that one of the guys, who only washes his clothes on found quarters, could do his laundry? College definitely had its benefits.

Those of us who stayed on campus over the weekend often plotted against those who had gone away. Like the guy who always spoke in clichés, his favorite being the one about not being able "to see the forest for the trees." So when he was away one weekend, we went into the woods and gathered all the fallen branches and limbs we could carry, dragged them into his dorm late one night, and filled his room, floor to ceiling. Ah, the beauty of a no-curfew life!

Someone knocked on my door one evening about seven as I was madly typing the last paragraph of an essay I'd scribbled out earlier. Claire and Valerie were holding a bag of potato chips hostage until I finished, but *they* were eating most of them.

"Come in!" Valerie yelled, her nose buried in a physiology book.

It was my friend Dave; he wanted to eat off campus that night and was looking for company. A square-faced blond, only slightly taller than me, he had cobalt-blue eyes, large hands, and had been on the university wrestling team the year before but gave it up to raise his grade point average. Jag, a new friend who'd transferred from a university in Bombay a year ago, was with him.

"Anyone interested in *food*?" Dave said, looking at me, then at Claire and Valerie. "We're heading for Ledo's."

Val held up the bag of chips. "Dinner," she said. "No, seriously, I already ate. Want some?"

"Hey! You're giving away *my* dinner!" I yelped.

"I want real food," said Dave.

"Doesn't have to be pizza," said Jag. "We could go somewhere else."

"Pizza's fine; I'll go," I said. "I'm starved. Claire?"

"Nope. Val and I are going to a movie at the student union. Enjoy!"

I went in the bathroom and put on some lip gloss, combed my hair, and then the three of us went out.

It was a gorgeous spring night, and there were couples all over campus. I walked between the guys, and we jokingly jostled each other for room on the sidewalk. Both of them were business majors, and Dave was a sophomore. Last semester he'd taken sociology as an elective, and that's where we'd met.

"Cold?" Dave asked. "Want my jacket?"

"No," I told him. "I'm okay."

The air was heavy with a damp sweetness that mingled with the smell of wet concrete and earth. The smell of spring. The night breeze was like a caress through my hair—the kind of breeze, the kind of night that could make you feel in love even if you weren't.

We decided against driving to Ledo's and went to a neighborhood café where they had the best Monte Cristo sandwiches, a favorite of mine.

"So . . . ," Dave said when he'd finished his sandwich. He's a fast eater, and I'm usually only halfway through by the time he's done. He sat tweaking a plastic straw in his hands. "Any idea what you're going to do this summer?"

"Something different, but I don't know what," I told him. "What are you guys going to do?"

"My uncle's a painter. I'm going to work for him. Slave wages, but it's better than nothing," Jag said.

"I usually work for my dad in his music store, but I'd like to do outside work. Your uncle doesn't need another helper, does he?" I asked.

"Unfortunately not."

"Sign up with a temp agency," Dave suggested. "That's what I do."

"How does that work?"

"You tell them what you can do—type, file, cook, paint, whatever—and if a company needs a temporary employee, the agency will send you there for a week or however long they need someone."

Jag saw some friends at another table so he excused himself, and Dave ordered a piece of pie.

"Somehow I thought you'd be traveling this summer," he said, studiously carving out a forkful of apple and crust.

"No . . ."

Without looking at me directly, he asked, "What about that Patrick guy?"

I didn't answer for a moment. "What about him?" I said finally.

His blue eyes studied mine. "Well, is he out of the picture? Just wondering."

"I still hear from him," I said. "I got a postcard last week."

"Hey! A postcard! He's got class!" Dave grinned, but he let it drop.

"I don't know," I said honestly. "I was hoping he'd be back in the States this summer, but now he's talking about joining the Peace Corps."

"Hmmm. That's a two-year commitment, isn't it?"

"Yeah," I said, offering nothing more.

Dave studied me thoughtfully for a moment or two. "Why don't you come to the mountains sometime for a weekend? My folks would be glad to have you."

"What mountains?"

"Blue Ridge, western Maryland. We could do whatever you like—hike, swim . . ."

"Well, maybe," I said, and was embarrassed to discover that my first thought was where I would sleep. "Do you have room?"

"A bedroom all to yourself." He gave me a playful grin. "Of course, if you'd like to share mine . . ."

I laughed, and Dave was all business again. "You said you wanted to be outdoors more. That's about all there is where we live—mountains, valleys . . ."

"Sounds nice. I'll keep it in mind," I said.

I had to admit I was attracted to this guy. Patrick was pretty sophisticated, but every once in a while he used to do something childish, like speak with a British accent for a day. Dave didn't act like that. He was a bit more casual, more quiet, but he could always make me laugh. Just little things, like, he'd make funny little stick people out of straws when he was waiting for me to finish lunch—have them talk to each other, describing the inside of my mouth, maybe. Or I'd just catch him watching me, smiling, ever ready to get a napkin for me, open a door, share his coat—a mixture of humor and consideration. Maybe Dave had outgrown kid stuff by now. But then, maybe Patrick had too. It had been almost a year since I'd seen him.

We walked all around campus that evening and just talked. Walked, talked, sat on a stone bench under a budding cherry tree as petals rained down on us, and talked some more. When we finally got up to go back to my dorm, we passed under an arch of branches that gave off a sweet scent—linden trees—and Dave leaned over and kissed me. I wouldn't call it passionate, but it was more than just friendly. And I realized that I might be having some of the same kinds of feelings for him that I'd had for Patrick. Was this possible?

Lester and Stacy got engaged in May. Even after predicting to Sylvia that Stacy was the one, I was still in shock.

"I can't *believe* it!" I cried when he told us. He'd made a quick trip home to celebrate my nineteenth birthday, and at my request we had all my favorite dishes for dinner. When else could you have tortellini with vodka sauce and chicken Alfredo both at the same meal?

"Why?" he asked.

"You've only known her since Thanksgiving!"

"*You've* only known her since Thanksgiving. I've known her a little longer than that." Lester stared quizzically down at the two dishes of pasta before him, then shrugged and took a spoonful of each. Sylvia tried to hide a smile as she passed him a huge spinach and strawberry salad to go with it, my one healthful suggestion for the meal.

"I just didn't think . . . I thought you'd be old and gray by the time you settled down," I said.

Les tipped his head in my direction and pointed to his hair. "A couple there already."

"Well, *I* think it's exciting, Les, and I really like Stacy," Sylvia said.

"So do I, and I'm happy for you," said Dad. "When's the wedding?"

"We haven't set a date yet. She's still debating whether or not to go for her master's, because the job prospects might be a lot better if she had one. I think she needs to make up her mind about that first." He turned to me. "Would you please stop staring at me bug-eyed and eat?"

I obliged. "Well, I'm happy for you too, Les," I said. "*Really.* So that makes three of us."

"Good. So what do you want for your birthday? I didn't have time to get you anything. But I will."

"I want to bring some friends to the wedding," I said, giving him a wide, determined smile.

He grinned. "I think that can be arranged," he said.

I took Dave's advice and signed up with a temp agency for the summer. On the days when I didn't get called in, I helped out at Dad's music store, but by the end of July, I was sick of temp work. Probably half the time I didn't get called at all, and when they did send me out on a job, it was hideously boring—file clerk, receptionist, stock girl, shampoo girl.

I really wanted to be outdoors. Where were the dog-walking jobs, playground supervisors, car washers? Taken, taken, taken, they told me, if there were any at all.

And then on a Monday night, I got a call. A construction company on an emergency road repair needed a flag person for one day—their flagman was sick. Only one day, low pay, did I want it?

The following morning I was up at four and putting on my raggedy jeans for ventilation, a thin cotton shirt over a tank top, and a blue bandana around my head. I slathered myself with sunscreen, made a sandwich, filled a thermos, grabbed my sunglasses, and was off. I drove Dad's car to a two-lane road north of Gaithersburg, slowing down when I saw a few cars parked on the shoulder near a bulldozer.

It may have been a two-lane road, but it was a busy one, and it curved and disappeared behind a line of trees. I parked and got out, studying the five men drinking water from a cooler on the back of a pickup. I was supposed to check in with someone named Ed, so I went up to a guy holding a clipboard. "Are you Ed?" I asked. "I'm the flag girl today."

The men stopped talking and looked around. "No," said the man, peering at me over the rim of his safety goggles. He nodded toward the guy in a faded baseball cap, so I went up to him.

"Ed?"

"No, that would be the man over there in the checked shirt," he answered.

The men exchanged smiles, and I looked about suspiciously, but I was a good sport, so I turned to the man in the checked shirt, and he said, "If you're looking for Ed, he's—"

"No," I said, "I'm looking for the boss."

"In that case, it's me," said a guy with a tattoo on his bare shoulder.

"Nah, that's me," said the guy with the clipboard.

By now, though, they were all laughing, and I laughed with them.

"Sorry, we're just having a little fun with you," the clipboard guy said. "I'm Ed Crawley, and these SOBs are your partners for the day."

"I'm Alice," I said, and the other men called out their names, grinning broadly.

The men were repairing a sewer line that led to the houses farther out. The left lane of the curving road had already been blocked off.

Ed explained my job, which could hardly be more simple: I was to stand at one end of the long stretch of construction with a sign on a pole that said SLOW on one side and STOP on the other. Shorty, the guy with the tattooed arm, was at the other end of the broken pavement with his own sign. When Shorty turned his sign to SLOW for oncoming traffic on his side of the road, I turned mine to STOP, and vice versa. Shorty called the shots. If my attention wandered and I didn't respond, he'd give a loud whistle and I'd go into action.

The only thing I could say for the job was that it got me outdoors. There was more physical action for me at a filing cabinet than there was out here on a country road.

As the morning heated up, I edged more and more to the right to keep in the shade, until finally there was no shade at all. The trickles of perspiration running down my legs and back were maddening.

I'd been standing there for five hours when I realized I had to pee.

A Porta-John sat somewhat precariously back near the pickup truck, and I couldn't help but wonder if it would tilt if I went inside, but I had no choice. I couldn't just put down my sign and walk off, however. I tried to get the attention of one of the men, but a jackhammer was going, and no one could hear me. I must not have been able to get Shorty's attention, because he kept waving his line of cars on through. The next and the next and the next . . .

When someone saw me at last and took my place, I ran for the Porta-John. I barely made it. I pulled the door closed behind me and tried not to look down the hole, managing to hold my breath most of the time until I escaped back into fresh air. I even thought about going without water so I wouldn't have to use the john again, but that wasn't a good idea.

At twelve we opened the lane back up temporarily and sat down under a single tree beyond the truck. When I unwrapped the sandwich I'd thrown together that morning, though, it was disgusting. The bologna was warm, the cheese had melted, and the whole thing drooped. I was holding it between two fingers when Ed noticed.

"Don't eat that," he said. "Here." He handed me half a beef sandwich, the meat a quarter inch thick between the bread slices, all of it still chilled from the cold pack in his bucket.

"I can't eat yours," I protested.

"Yes, you can. I've got another to go with it, and a piece of cake."

"Now what's she up to? Takin' our lunch?" called the guy in the bandana, who had been working down in the trench. "Here, skinny gal, have some chips." And he passed the bag over.

I smiled and took a handful. Nobody had referred to me as skinny since second grade, and I was grateful for the candy bar someone gave me too.

But lunch hour is never a full hour on a construction gang. A half hour, at most, and then we were back on the job. SLOW . . . STOP . . . SLOW . . . STOP . . . My arms were hot to the touch from the sun. Even taking off the cotton shirt barely made a difference.

By three o'clock I had to pee again—I'd downed two cups of water from the big cooler on the back of the pickup and could have drunk more. The Porta-John had been in the sun all afternoon, and just lifting the metal latch burned my fingers.

I considered leaving the door open for a moment, but it faced the men and the road, so I didn't. Sweat rolled down my face.

The stench from the toilet was overwhelming, and the toilet paper was gone.

Trying not to retch, I got it over with as soon as possible, pulled up my jeans, and wished for the fifteenth time that I'd worn shorts, then fumbled for the door latch.

It wouldn't turn.

No! I gave it a hard jiggle. Nothing. I was stuck! I was sweltering! I was being cremated alive!

I bore down with all my strength, but I couldn't even see the latch through all my sweat. The guys must have been playing a trick on me—just waiting till I got inside. This wasn't funny! I'd die!

In a panic I banged on the walls of the Porta-John, and finally I heard a man's voice say, "Alice? Turn the handle."

"I *am*!"

"The other way," he instructed, and suddenly the door flew open, and I almost fell out, gasping for air. I'd been in such a hurry to leave that I'd been turning the latch the wrong way.

"You all right?" asked the burly man in the bandana.

I smiled sheepishly. "I am now," I said, and wiped my arm across my forehead.

"Easy does it," he said. "Only thirty more minutes to go."

At three thirty we put the safety cones and the tools in the truck and finished off the water.

"Thanks for helping out," Ed told me. "I see they've got you down for the bulldozer tomorrow. Come a little early and Lou will show you how to drive it."

My mouth fell open.

"I thought she was going to run the jackhammer," said Shorty, and then I knew they were joking again. I thanked them for putting up with me and couldn't wait to get back in Dad's car and turn on the air-conditioning.

Note to self: On construction jobs bring water, bring ice, bring toilet paper.

4

PLANNING AHEAD

I sat hugging my knees, my forehead pressed against them, feeling vaguely sick to my stomach. The letter was crumpled between my chest and the anthropology book on my lap, and a gust of October wind rustled the crisp leaves that had blown up the steps of McKeldin Library, where I'd been for the last ten minutes.

Was I relieved that Patrick had written me first? Would I have written him? It wasn't a phone call. Wasn't an e-mail. It was one and a half pages long, handwritten, one of the few letters I'd received from him in my life.

How long had I known him? Seven, eight years? Ever since sixth grade. We'd broken up once but had gotten back together, and when he went to college, a year ahead of me, it was understood we could go out with other people. But the understanding was a sort of veneer over the feeling that he and I were really special to each other. Now I wondered if I was the only one who had felt that way.

I turned my head sideways and stared up at the bare branches that were dancing in the wind.

I've been putting this letter off because I wasn't sure how I felt, and I'm writing to say that I'm still not sure. . . .

How had I known what the rest of the lines would say before I'd even read them? But the deeper question was one I was afraid to ask myself: Was I possibly feeling the same way?

Patrick found that he was around women he liked very much, and wanted the freedom to get even closer. Maybe it was a mistake for us to get serious about each other, he wrote, especially because he'd been accepted into the Peace Corps.

What was the big deal? We'd already agreed we could see other people, so what was he telling me—that he was cutting me out of his life? That I was no longer special? The Peace Corps was no surprise. Once he had mentioned it, I knew he would follow through. That was Patrick. The rest? Trying to fence Patrick in was like trying to harness the sea. And yes, if he wasn't sure about me, he *should* be going out with other women.

But damn it, Patrick! I stood up and the anthropology text and notebook in my lap tumbled to the step below. I kicked them the rest of the way down, ignoring the guy in the hoodie who was passing below and gave me a wary glance.

This was the second time Patrick dumped me. And he was

being so damned civil about it. Didn't he have any feelings? What about the way we'd been together on that bench at Botany Pond? What about the way we'd held and touched each other in the limo coming back from the Bay Bridge? The way we'd kissed?

The binder had fallen open and papers were blowing around. I discovered I was crying as I went down the steps to pick them up. Had Patrick cried at all when he wrote the letter? How long had he thought about it? Hesitated, even? Wondered how I'd take it?

My papers collected and the books in my arms again, I began walking down the sidewalk, not caring where I went. The thing was, I found that I kind of liked a number of the guys here at Maryland. As the girls had pointed out, the selection was bigger in college. More diverse. I hadn't met anyone I liked *more* than Patrick, but I'd met several whom I felt I could maybe like as much, Dave in particular.

Was I overreacting to hide the possibility that the letter might have been going the other way?

Tears again.

There's so much ahead for each of us, Patrick wrote. *I just didn't want to keep anything from you and wanted to make sure you weren't expecting more from me. You're the last person on earth I'd ever want to hurt, Alice. . . .*

But I *was* hurting! How could he think I wouldn't? We had a history together. We'd watched each other grow up. How could he ever feel that close to anyone else? How could I? And yet . . .

Dave was incredibly thoughtful, Jag was crazy smart, Travis

had a wicked sense of humor, and what about the other guys I hung out with when a bunch of us got together on weekends? Who knew how I'd feel about them when I got to know them better?

But I wasn't looking around for someone else; why was Patrick?

A couple was coming toward me and I made no room on the sidewalk. I wasn't even thinking about them until I noticed them parting to make way for me.

Patrick was right, of course, about expecting too much of each other. I knew that. I'd always known that. But how should I answer? Telling him that there were other guys I was attracted to sounded like trying to get even. Telling him I was about to write the same kind of letter wasn't entirely true and read like revenge. Telling him I was crushed and bleeding was both true and a lie.

I realized I was heading away from my dorm, so I turned and started back. This time I allowed myself—forced myself—to face what I was really feeling. Was it possible that just as I clung more to home than other girls seemed to, I used Patrick as my buffer against the world? My shield against having to explore more on my own, get to know other guys, allow myself to love and lose? Did every girl who lost a mother when she was small carry that around forever? When was I going to approach life minus a security blanket, trusting that whatever happened, I'd be strong enough to handle? I came to a bench, so I sat down and unfolded the letter again:

Would it be easier if we didn't call or text each other for a while, just to see how it goes? It might be a good time to try it because I've been assigned to Madagascar and have been told that my village is two hours by bicycle from the nearest town. No electricity, no cell phone coverage. I've started a blog and will be posting notes whenever I'm in the capital, but I don't know how often that will be. I just want you to have the same chance that I do to explore and meet new people, and I hope you believe me when I say that you still, and will always, mean a great deal to me.
Patrick

Why couldn't I just live with that? Why not let that last line sustain me and throw myself into new friendships, a new relationship maybe, and see what would happen?

And finally, back in my dorm when I'd sat at my computer motionless for twenty minutes or so, my feelings going back and forth like a pendulum, I put my fingers on the keys:

Dear Patrick, I wrote. *Understood. Really. Always, Alice.*

Abby was my roommate my sophomore year. After the "outbreak of Amber," as I called it, Abby was a refreshing change. She respected my space, kept her own reasonably neat, and I certainly never found her underwear in my bed.

Now that the second bed belonged to Abby, the whole gang hung out here sometimes, with as many guys as we could comfortably squeeze in. Besides Dave and Travis and Jag, there was Cole, the basketball player, and James, who was inheriting his family's farm, and Pete and Andrew and other guys I went out with occasionally for a sandwich or to a club, and that's how the big shave-off took place in our room.

I'm not sure how "No Shave November" got started. I think it was originally a charity event to raise money for men's health awareness or something. But guys all over campus had been growing competitive mustaches or beards—whatever—and then, on the first of December, we had a big shave-off. At some schools, I'd heard, women take part and don't shave their legs for a month, and sometimes, for the big shave-off, they removed hair from . . . uh . . . other parts of the body as well.

We were content to watch the guys try to outdo each other, and in they came with handlebar mustaches, goatees, shoulder-length hair, dreadlocks, and we girls supposedly had the pleasure of shaving them or watching them shave each other.

"I hope somebody's going to vacuum this up," Abby said as we watched Cole's reddish locks fall, hit or miss, into the barber's apron that we fashioned from a sheet. Colin had the arms of a vinyl raincoat tied around his neck, and soon his hair was sliding down the front and, some of it, anyway, into a trash basket.

"Isn't there some way to recycle hair?" Val said, waiting with a mustache trimmer. "Fill mesh bags with it to surround an oil spill or something?"

We shrieked as Travis posed for a picture with only half

of his handlebar mustache shaved off, and we made him pose for another with Dave, who had run a razor up both arms from wrist to elbow.

But James won first place when he stripped off his shirt and presented his hairy back to the girls.

"Wow!" I said, running my hand over the silky mat of black hair. "I had a cat once that felt like this."

James pretended to purr. "Live it up. I'm all yours."

I contemplated that vast expanse of shiny blackness. It was like a virgin forest, and I felt like an axman about to destroy it forever.

"Uh-oh," said Claire, "she's got that look in her eye."

I put down the scissors I'd been holding and borrowed the narrow mustache trimmer instead. Then, bracing my left hand on James's shoulder to steady myself, I turned the gadget on and carefully shaved out the letters A-L-I-C-E, to much laughter.

When we got a hand mirror and showed James his back, he spun me around and sat me on his lap. Then everyone got their cell phones and took pictures of us. Valerie sent one to my laptop, and hers was the best. There I sat, straddling James, who was looking over his shoulder and grinning, his face pressed up against mine, with A-L-I-C-E etched on his back in crooked but definitely readable letters.

I e-mailed the shot to Liz and Pamela and Gwen and also to Lester. For a brief moment I fantasized about forwarding the photo to Patrick, but then I wisely closed my laptop.

* * *

Abby and I were in Valerie and Claire's dorm room one rainy night, having just shared a gigantic white pizza, delivered right to us. The driver had looked so wet and miserable, we asked if he wanted a slice. Instead, he gratefully accepted the extra tip we gave him before he took off. We hung a DO NOT DISTURB sign on the door to discourage anyone else from dropping by and raiding our dinner. You can't believe the power of pizza. One whiff, and there's a mob knocking. Claire had gone to a game, so when we were done, we'd put our leftover slices in their little fridge for her.

"Ah," Valerie said, sprawling out on her bed.

"Ah," I echoed, lying beside her, head to foot. Abby lay on the other bed, lazily hitting a balloon up in the air and watching it drift down again for another swat. Occasionally the balloon would come over our way, and I'd maybe give it a kick with one foot. There was something about our contentment that reminded me of the way Pamela and Liz and I, and sometimes Gwen, used to hang out in Elizabeth's bedroom with the twin eyelet bedspreads, the matching curtains, everything that made that bedroom so "Elizabeth."

For just a moment I felt a sudden rush of homesickness sweep over me, and then it was gone, but in those few brief seconds I realized how much those friends were like sisters to me, and I wondered if Abby and Valerie could ever mean as much to me as they did. Wondered whether you have to have a history with someone to feel the same closeness.

We'd been to each other's homes once or twice over holi-days, and I'd met their families—Claire's in Baltimore, Valerie's in Frederick, and Abby's clear over on the Eastern Shore. But it wasn't the same as driving over to Gwen's, or walking to Pamela's, or looking across the street to see if Liz's light was on. Still, there was something about living together all these months the way we were that had a sisterly feeling, and I was glad the three of us had stayed in that night instead of going to the movies in the rain. It was another tragic Italian classic and, masterpiece or not, I wasn't in a Fellini mood.

"What made you decide to major in history?" I asked Valerie, barely raising my head as I bounced the balloon with my knee. This time when it drifted toward the closet, no one went after it.

"I don't know. Sort of like following a continued story, I guess."

"You plan to teach it?"

"God, no. What I'd *really* like is to work in a museum. Acqui-sitions or something. I'm totally addicted to *Antiques Roadshow*. Why did you choose counseling?"

"I haven't exactly made it official," I said. "I just like listen-ing to people."

"Eavesdropping, she means," Abby joked.

"Well, that, too," I laughed. "I mean, do you ever wonder why someone would become an exterminator?"

"Oh, please!" said Valerie. "Just the thought!"

"Or a proctologist," said Abby. "I mean, of all the parts of the human body, someone chooses—"

"Uh, we just ate," said Valerie. "What about you, Abby? You decide on a major yet?"

"No," Abby told us, and turned over on her side, propping her head on one hand. "I'll probably go through four whole years and still not know. 'Getting away from high school,' that was my major."

"You and me both," said Val. "I used to think, 'If these are the best years of my life, shoot me now!' It wasn't so bad after I met Colin, though. We hung out together a lot, and the MSG—"

"Monosodium glutamate?"

"'Most Snotty Girls'—then they left me alone."

"Why did they pick on you?" I asked.

"There had to be a reason? One of them told me I was too tall and wore the wrong clothes for my height. They wanted to do a makeover on me—even cut my hair—and I declined."

"Because . . . ?"

"Would you trust someone brandishing a pair of scissors who would just as soon chop off your legs? So they posted a photo of a tall, skinny, naked girl—a behind shot—on YouTube and put my name under it. One of their parents eventually put a stop to it, but walking out of that school with my diploma was the best thing that had happened to me up to that point, and that's pathetic."

"Sounds awful!" said Abby. "I never had to deal with anything like that. Mostly, I just wanted to get out in the *real* world and *do* something. Except I didn't, and still don't, know what that something is."

We lay still, thinking that over.

"Maybe that's what college is all about," I said finally. "Helping us discover who we are."

"A short, dumpy girl sick of studying, but she's hopeful," said Abby.

"A tall, skinny girl with heart," said Val.

I laughed. "An in-between girl who's thinking Claire doesn't like white pizza nearly as much as I do, and I can even enjoy mine cold."

"Okay," said Abby. "Let's eat the rest and destroy the box."

I met Jared, a music major who was apparently an amazing saxophone player, in line at the cafeteria, making small talk. For some reason, I mentioned the Melody Inn and that led to his telling me that he plays in a band for weddings and stuff. We had lunch together a few times, went to a jazz concert, and in April he invited me to a friend's afternoon wedding just so I could hear him play. It was quiet at the U because there were no big finals scheduled, and a lot of kids had gone off campus for the weekend.

It seemed like a good idea at the time, since he assured me that the reception was a buffet—they didn't have to set an extra place for me—and he was doing a special number on the sax.

He and the clarinet player—a guy named Blake—were picking me up for the reception, which was being held in Langley Park. I put on a navy-blue sheath that I save for special occasions and my sling-back heels, and as I stood in front of the mirror putting on my makeup, I suddenly realized that I had a pretty good figure—not perfect, by any means, but there was a nice curve to my breasts, a slim waist, hips maybe a little more narrow than they ought to be, but . . . well, I looked great, actually.

"Hey, *babe*!" I said to myself in the mirror. Then I went outside to wait for the guys.

Jared did play well. He had long fingers and a narrow face and shoulders. His hair was short and dark and curly, and he was handsome in a nervous sort of way.

I sat at a table with some friends of the groom, and I could tell that several of the women had their eyes on Jared and commented on his playing. They'd crowd around him after a set, or they'd gather around him at the bar, and I'd stand off to one side counting the number of girls who hit on him. But after a while I started counting the number of drinks he'd had.

I was glad Blake was driving after the gig was over, because he'd had only a beer or two.

"This was a lot of fun," I said to both of them when we reached my dorm. "It was great hearing you play, Jared. Thanks for inviting me."

I was surprised when he got out of the car too, because he lived off campus with some grad students.

"I'll walk," he told Blake. "The air will do me good. Jush keep my sax at your place, will you?"

"Jush?" I said, laughing. "Jared, are you drunk?"

"I'm fine!" he said, a bit too loudly.

"C'mon, I'll drive you," Blake called, leaning toward the passenger window.

"I'll *walk*!" Jared said. "Air will do m'good."

"O-kaay," Blake said, and drove off.

I hadn't really planned to spend the evening with Jared. I'd wanted to catch up with Pamela and Liz, answer their last texts and e-mails. But I remembered the orange juice and cheese in my little fridge, and I figured the least I could do was offer him some juice. Maybe I'd change into jeans and we could walk around campus a little—sober him up. It *was* a gorgeous spring evening.

"I've got to meet some friends later," I lied as he followed me up the steps, stumbling a bit, and down the hall to my room. "But maybe we could take a walk? Let me get out of these shoes."

He slipped one arm around my waist as I put the key in the door, and no sooner were we inside than he pulled me close and gave me a long French kiss, thrusting his tongue in and out of my mouth and moving his pelvis against me with each thrust.

I pushed away from him. "Jared," I said, still trying to be polite, "cool it. How about some orange juice?"

He gave me a surprised, hurt look. "What's the matter, baby? You're *hot* in that dress!" He gave me a pouty, chiding look and reached out for me again more gently, this time kissing me more tenderly, and I decided to chalk up the clumsy pass to alcohol. I wanted to get outside but needed to ditch the dress.

"Why don't I put on jeans and sneakers and we can walk?" I suggested again. "It's beautiful out."

In answer, Jared stretched out on my bed and closed his

eyes. "Ahhh," he said. "Whatever y'shay. I'll jush lie here fo'a minute. Tell me when ya ready."

I took my jeans and sweatshirt into the bathroom and closed the door. It occurred to me that he might well be asleep by the time I got changed, in which case I'd walk over to the library and let him sleep, hoping he wouldn't throw up on the rug or something. At least he was on my bed, not Abby's.

I slipped out of my dress and was just bending down to step into my jeans when the door opened and Jared stood there, naked from the waist down, fully erect.

"Oh, baby," he said, and pulled me toward him, thrusting between my thighs.

"Stop it!" I cried, pushing at him, but he yanked me closer so that I couldn't wriggle free, then forced me around and started walking me backward toward the bed. His hand wormed its way under the waistband of my panties.

"Jared!" I yelled. "Cut it out! You're drunk."

But the bed hit me behind my knees, my legs buckled, and I fell back with Jared on top of me. He was trying to get my underwear off.

"No!" I screamed at the top of my voice. "Don't!"

He put one hand over my mouth. "Shhhh," he kept saying. "Hey, baby, I'm good! I'm easy!"

"No!" I cried, and bit his hand.

I scratched at his face and managed to push him up just enough that I could bring a knee to his groin, and he tumbled off the bed in a howl of pain.

I leaped over him and ran out into the hall in my underwear, screaming.

Two senior girls coming down from the third floor stared at me, then rushed over.

I was leaning against the wall, my heart pounding, and one of the girls grabbed my arm.

"Are you okay?" she asked.

I jerked my head toward my room, then shakily followed them inside.

Jared lay on the rug in a fetal position, holding his groin. He swore at me when I appeared.

"Did he . . . ?" one of the girls asked, looking at me.

I could hardly talk, my breathing was coming so fast. "Tried to," I said, looking about for something to put on. I didn't want to step over Jared to get to the closet.

I explained what had happened as Jared got to his feet, picked up his trousers, and hobbled into the bathroom.

"Campus police," the other girl said to me, holding up her cell phone and thumbing the number.

"We're staying with you while you report it," her friend said. "You *are* going to report it?"

For one brief moment I thought of the fun afternoon, the way he'd played at the wedding. He was drunk, after all, but . . .

I breathed through my mouth to slow myself down.

"Absolutely," I said, nice guy or not. Drunk or not.

Jared came out of the bathroom.

"The campus police want to talk to you when they get here," the girl with the cell phone told him.

"You've got to be kidding!" Jared said, and turned toward me. "That's the thanks I get for a great afternoon?"

"I thought a simple thank-you would be enough," I said icily.

"Get the hell out of my way!" he said, pushing through the two girls in the doorway and disappeared down the hall.

"It's okay. You know who he is, right?" one girl asked. I nodded. "Better get dressed," she said.

They stayed with me when two officers showed up and I told what had happened. The girls confirmed some of the details, and the men took down Jared's name and where he lived.

"Are you injured? Do you need to see a doctor?" one of the officers asked.

"No, I was lucky," I said.

"And you were smart," the second man said. "You did the right thing to report this. Many girls don't, and it happens to someone else."

Dave heard about it the next day—the ruckus, but not the details—and we walked over to the bookstore together. Halfway through telling him, when I got to the part where Jared was on top of me, one hand over my mouth, I was startled to hear myself sob.

Dave stopped walking and gathered me in his arms. "I wish I'd been there," he said, stroking my hair. "He wouldn't have got very far."

That night I dreamed of Dave.

* * *

I learned that Jared had been put on probation. Partly because I was a little afraid of him retaliating in some way, I began hanging out a lot more with Dave. I made sure that I was always around people on campus, that I always walked with someone at night. I heard that Jared was transferring to George Washington in the fall, but I found I really liked being with Dave.

I guess it was about this time that I started feeling more serious about him. He wasn't just my friend anymore; he was my protector. And it was a small step from seeing Dave as the muscular guy who would keep me safe to imagining him as my lover.

I began thinking about him at night after I'd gone to bed. Dreamed about him sometimes. Dreamed that we were getting ready to make love . . . all the touching and kissing leading up to it, but—as in all my dreams, good or bad—I woke up at the critical moment. *Darn!*

Our kisses became more passionate and his caresses made me crazy. The problem was that there was only one month of school left now, and finals were coming fast. I'd always said that when I had intercourse for the first time, I wanted it to be in a private place, with someone I really liked, with all the time in the world, and plenty of opportunities to see each other again. I wished it were back in January, starting a new semester, because Abby went home sometimes for the weekend and I could have had our room to myself. Myself and Dave. Now I was lucky to have time enough to go back home and pick up a few summer clothes.

"So, what's happening with you these days?" Gwen asked, driving us back to the old neighborhood one Sunday in May.

"I wish I knew," I said. "I just feel unsettled." Where had I heard that word before? "I honestly think I was more certain of my life when I started college than I am two years into it. Now, *that's* scary. I was wondering . . . Do you ever think of giving up medicine—switching to something else?"

"Only a couple times a day, and I've hardly even started yet," she said as she exited the beltway.

We had visited both our families, shamelessly doing our laundry at my place, and picking up some of Gwen's summer skirts at hers. We'd taken time to cut her beloved Granny's toenails, and—at my place—do the dishes for Sylvia.

"Could I send some cherry pie back with you?" Sylvia had asked.

"Do sharks have teeth?" Gwen had replied, and Dad chuckled as he packed some up for us.

Now heading back to the U, we lowered the windows and drank in an occasional whiff of lilacs.

Gwen looked over at me. "Why? You thinking of switching fields?"

"Sometimes I feel like changing bodies," I told her. "Dave's applied to work on a construction job in Pennsylvania this summer. If he gets it, he'll be gone most of the time. I've got applications in to seven different places, and I don't really want to work at any of them. I don't want to go back to temp work, and even Dad doesn't want me to work at the Melody Inn. Maybe I need a whole new me. Go get a brain transplant or something."

Okay, to be perfectly honest, I was probably comparing my life to Patrick's again, and that was a hopeless cause. Also—I couldn't help myself—a couple of days ago I'd checked out his Peace Corps blog:

I thought I picked up languages pretty fast, but these villagers really laugh at my Malagasy, and I like to make them happy. Their language is so unlike any others I know, but I've already learned that they randomly add a "y" at the end of English words to make it Malagasy. "Bank," for example, is "banky." The volunteer I'm replacing and I biked the 24 kilometers to the village on a beautiful road that sometimes runs along the beach. Stayed at his house that night and the next, which will soon be my house—two little rooms, one public that everybody feels free to walk into, day or night, and the other room just for me. Wood frame, tin roof, and some kind of grass siding.

People here are more in-your-face and loud. Come right up to me and tell me I'm too tall, like there's something I'm supposed to do about it. But overall they're warm and welcoming, and I think I've inherited a grandmother. The Peace Corps doesn't want us to start any big projects right away

*because all of them depend on volunteers. I'm just supposed to
go around making friends and improving my language skills.*

I should have stopped reading then, because the next paragraph read:

*The only other volunteer I know from our training group is
Jessica—from my year abroad in Barcelona—but she's in
another village, so I'm pretty much on my own.*

What's she like? I wondered. Do they bike to each other's
villages? What is *he* like now—all these new adventures so far
from home?

But it wasn't just Patrick. Liz was staying in Vermont for the
summer because she got a job in a bookstore there, and Pamela
had applied for a summer theater program in London. Worst of
all, Dave would be working up near Harrisburg.

"And I've got another internship this summer, so you're
feeling left out. Is that it?" Gwen asked.

"Exactly," I said. "Big waaaah."

We were relating all this to Claire and Abby that evening as the
four of us came back from an impromptu volleyball game. As we
climbed the steps to our dorm, Abby said, "I'm going to Oregon
for the summer to work for my aunt in her catering business.
She needs someone to do the baking. Why don't you come too,
Alice?"

"As what? Chief taster?"

"You said you like to bake."

"I said I like to make my dad pineapple upside-down cake for his birthday, courtesy of Duncan and Dole," I told her.

"That's all you've ever baked?"

"Chocolate chip cookies. A devil's food cake once. Blueberry muffins."

"Do you like it?"

"Of course!"

"Then come! We'll stay with my aunt. There's room."

I stopped walking and stared at her. "Are you serious? Where in Oregon?"

"Eugene. Of course I'm serious! She lets me keep half the profits. We bake twice as much, that's twice the profits."

Two weeks later we were flying United to Portland, Portland to Eugene, and then we were sitting in the back of Aunt Jayne's minivan chattering away while her springer spaniel in the passenger seat rested his paws on the open window and lolled his tongue at the passing cars.

5

THE OREGON EPISODE

Eugene, Oregon, is a lot like Maryland in that it's hilly in places and there are loads of trees. What's different is that in Maryland, most of the houses are brick. Here, they're frame and you don't see all the subdivisions where whole blocks of houses are built by the same developer—door to left, door to right, door to left . . . all down the street.

A yellow two-story will overshadow a rambler. Picket fence around one, unmowed grass at another. Abby's aunt Jayne lived on a dead-end street at the top of a hill, with a steep driveway and a vegetable garden in the front yard.

"Here we are!" she said as she brought the van to a stop at the top of the drive and yanked the emergency brake. "Shangri-la Jayne." And Spirit, the dog, took that as his cue to leap about the front seat as though demons possessed him. When Jayne went around and opened the door for him, he promptly leaped out and peed a steady stream around an azalea bush, then faced the car again, tail wagging like a windshield wiper, as Abby and I crawled out and reached for our bags.

There were two old beat-up bikes in the garage, both fitted with large wire baskets front and back. Jayne explained that sometimes—to save gas—she did her marketing or deliveries by bike if the orders were small enough but that the bikes were ours for the summer. And then we were sitting in Jayne's kitchen, a canary chirping at us from an antique-looking birdcage in the next room. Jayne treated us to peach-mango tea and her walnut bars, and I wiggled my bare toes in pleasure.

"What do you think?" Abby asked as we unpacked later, standing between a single bed with its faded patchwork quilt and a metal army cot. There was a blind on one window but not the other, tie-dyed curtains at both; a seashell lamp on the bedside table; and a dream catcher, some Mardi Gras masks, and a few scattered watercolors on the walls.

"I think it will be a blast!" I told her, because Jayne herself looked like an expatriate from a sixties commune. She had an angular face devoid of makeup, deep-set gray eyes beneath her graying bangs, and a girlish smile, as though life still were capable of surprising her. She wore a kerchief around her head, tied in back beneath her hair, and a baggy cotton jumper over a tee. It was going to be two months with a housemother whose smile alone gave you the sense that she was up for whatever mischief you might think of next.

We helped unwrap dinner—little parcels of food from a farmer's market—and after dinner Abby and I rode the bikes all around the university neighborhood on miles and miles of bike trails along both sides of the Willamette River, with a bike bridge to cross over now and then.

"I love it here!" I called to Abby, feeling a remarkably cool breeze after such a warm day. "The weather's perfect!"

"You wouldn't think so if you were here the rest of the year," she called back over her shoulder. "This is the sunny season. The rest of the year, it's like England."

I could do with a little England, I thought. I could live with these one-of-a-kind houses, with the bikes and the breeze.

"When were you here last?" I asked, watching Abby's bare legs make slow revolutions on the pedals.

"I come every summer for a short while. Last time I came for the whole deal, I was twelve."

"Was Jayne ever married?"

"Yeah. They divorced when I was small. I hardly remember him. Now she says she's too busy to fall in love."

That evening we sat around the wood-burning stove in the living room, and I marveled that it could get cold enough to light a fire. Jayne poured each of us a cup of wine in Japanese teacups and told us about the koi pond she was planning to dig in her backyard if she could figure a way to keep the raccoons out.

She chattered on about the plants she would need and the fish she would buy, and when my head began to dip and jerk, and the teacup felt weightless in my hand, I snapped to and saw Jayne smiling at me.

"Okay, girls, off to bed. Quilts in the chest beneath the window. Who gets the cot?"

There were no definite hours working for Jayne. On Mondays and Tuesdays she made casseroles of one kind or another, packaged and labeled each one, and delivered them to steady customers on Wednesdays. Thursdays and Fridays, she cooked for the Saturday Market downtown.

Abby and I did some of the grocery runs for her and helped with the peeling and dicing and cleanup. Jayne loved doing the seasoning, the experimenting and sautéing, but she was glad to turn over much of the baking to us. When Saturday came, we rose indecently early, packed our treasures into assorted boxes and plastic milk carriers, and hauled them all to the back of the minivan.

When we reached the Park Blocks, we set up our folding tables. Farmers were already unpacking crates of lettuce and radishes, mushrooms, beets, and early peas, and it wasn't yet seven in the morning. When the sun comes out in Eugene, though, it's like a sacred moment, people see so little of it the rest of the year. In Maryland, I spend most of summer trying to hide from it.

The Saturday Market was a feast of color. More tie-dyed

clothing than anyone sees in a normal lifetime. Watercolor paintings, tablecloths, and quilts. Shelves of pottery, wood bowls, and birdhouses, as well as the kind of kitschy lawn ornaments that you always hope your neighbor won't buy.

If your eye isn't drawn to the food stalls, your nose will take you there. Abby and I had each downed a banana muffin on the ride in, but as customers arrived, we could smell the empanadas and sausage rolls that were already becoming someone's breakfast.

We artfully arranged the cookies and brownies we had baked, along with Jayne's custard pies, and smiled at everyone who even looked our way. She was right—the food sells out every time before noon, which gave Abby and me a chance later to wander through the aisles and check out the competition. Not that it mattered, because only the most crumbly or lopsided items were left on the tables, and those were hastily disposed of by a markdown after twelve o'clock.

"Are these what I think they are?" I asked Abby as we stopped at one of the tables.

"Yep," said Abby, checking them out. "Pipes for smoking weed." The seller, a long-haired guy wearing a beaded necklace and a leather vest over a bare chest, beckoned to us, but we smiled and moved over to inspect the recorders and guitars across the way.

The Saturday Market had elements of a carnival, for not only were there panhandlers ready to greet you, but some of the customers themselves were a major attraction. In the time we worked the table, from early morning to afternoon, we saw the Tattooed Man, the Girl with the Thousand Piercings, the Fat Lady, the Thin Lady, and the Multi-dyed Hair Man, and we had lots of fun naming them, the infinite variety of the human race.

I wanted to check the stalls one last time to see what I might like to look for the next time—jewelry for Sylvia, maybe. There was a silversmith, as I remembered, and we made our way down an outside row—past the leather belts and bags, past a young man sitting on the ground, head in his arms. We couldn't see his face, but he wore a navy-blue knit cap that covered most of his head, with a few blondish curls hanging out. A hand-lettered sign on cardboard beside him read PLEASE HELP.

We studied him as we drew closer.

"Do you think he's sick?" I asked Abby.

"Stoned, probably."

An open cigar box sat in front of him, but only three dollar bills lay inside. "Should we stop?" I wondered.

She shook her head. "Whatever he wants, we haven't got, and we need to get back to help Jayne."

I reluctantly started to follow when the man raised his head and stared right at me. His eyes didn't have the look of someone who was stoned, but his face had a yellowish cast and the skin under his eyes was dark.

"Hi," I said. "You okay?"

He almost smiled. "Not really. But I need to get home bad." His voice was scarcely audible.

Abby turned around and came back where I was standing.

"Where's home?" she asked. We'd both bent down a little to hear him.

"Seattle," the guy replied.

I wondered if he had AIDS. I looked at his hands, dangling listlessly from his knees, but he didn't have any telltale blotches. His knees could have been bony beneath the worn jeans; I couldn't quite tell.

"So what do you need?" Abby asked.

"Eight dollars more." It seemed an effort for him to get the words out.

I wondered how much I could ask. "Does anyone know you're coming?"

That faint smile again. "They'll know when I get there, but I . . . really got to get home."

I think we all agreed on that. I slipped my bag off my shoulder and found a five. Abby added another.

"That's too much," the man said quickly, and reached toward the bills in the cigar box.

"Keep it," Abby said.

"And good luck," I added.

He thanked us and slowly got to his feet. "Do you know the way to the bus depot?"

"I think it's back that way," Abby said, pointing. "You'd better ask. We're from out of town too. What's your name?"

"Christopher," he said, and then he gave us an almost full smile. At least his teeth looked good. He took good care of those. "Thanks a lot."

"Our good deed for the day," Abby said as we headed back to Jayne. "That was my last five. We'd better make a good profit on those pecan bars."

I was both surprised yet half expecting it when I got a phone call from Sylvia telling me that Les and Stacy were getting married at Thanksgiving. They'd set a date.

"Wow!" I kept saying. "Can you plan a wedding in five months?"

"Well, they have. They've taken care of all the arrangements, and Les sounds as sure and happy as he's ever been. We just wanted to let you know in case you were making other plans for Thanksgiving."

"I'd cancel anything to be at Lester's wedding. Tell him that. This is terrific," I told her, and ran to tell Abby and Jayne the happy news.

One June night, I was half wakened by a noise somewhere in the room. I felt a breeze from the window and perhaps a curtain blowing about. But then I heard just the lightest step, and my eyes opened wide in the darkness.

I could make out Abby's figure in bed, so knew she wasn't walking around. Jayne—tiptoeing in to get something? A second later I sensed that someone was in the room, and was afraid to turn my head. The footstep again, and instantly I thought of Jared, following me here and wanting revenge. And just as I moved to turn over, he was on top of me.

I screamed with every muscle in my throat, and then he licked my face. *Spirit!*

Abby tumbled out of bed, trying to reach the floor lamp and knocking it over. Noises in the hall, and there was Jayne in the doorway, one hand on the light switch.

Spirit was curled up beside me, and I lay with one hand on my chest, afraid my heart was bursting through.

"What in the world?" said Jayne, her hair half covering her face.

"Spirit," I said. "He jumped up on me, and I thought . . . I thought . . ."

"Post-traumatic stress, Jayne," Abby explained. "She thought it was a guy."

"Well, he *is* a guy," I said, patting Spirit's head. "A rather hairy one. I'm sorry, everybody."

"You guys must have left your door ajar. He'll do it every time. Come on, Spirit," Jayne said. "Pick on someone your own size."

After they were gone, Abby asked, "You still think about him?"

"No more than I have to," I said. "Let's get some sleep."

Dave and I were e-mailing more. We didn't do much of that on campus, and now that I was clear across the country, it felt strangely intimate to see our thoughts on a screen.

He'd gotten that construction job in Pennsylvania for July— would be finished by August.

I want you back, he wrote, and those four words said a lot.

That night before I left, the way he'd held me . . . "Makes

me wild waiting for you," he said. "Think how much I'd enjoy a night to remember all summer long."

But we didn't have all night. I'd still had packing to do. And I clung to my wish to have all the time in the world when we did it for the first time.

Now, lying there on a cot in Oregon, I began to wish I hadn't been so particular. I'd heard that first times weren't so great for the woman, but I would have enjoyed the rest of it, wouldn't I? And Dave would be over the moon. Or not. He was a man I really liked and respected. Loved, even.

Now we had to wait till I got back.

I'll be at the airport, he promised. And there was time for us both before school began.

Spent the last two weeks of June at the Olive Garden working—late shift. Someone's on vacation. I was next on the wait list. They tell me that story is true, by the way— about their salad.

"What story is that?" Abby asked when I read his e-mail aloud.

"That a girl came for an interview once, concerned that because there are topless restaurants where the waitresses are naked from the waist up, Olive Garden's 'bottomless' salads meant . . ."

"O'm'god," Abby said, and both she and Jayne broke into laughter.

Jayne had just washed her hair. She'd treated it with conditioner and was now sitting at the window, letting the sun dry it naturally, threading her fingers through it every once in a while. "So who's this Dave guy, anyway? Someone special?" she asked.

"A good friend," I said. "Part of the crowd we hang out with."

Abby gave me her famous half smile. "More than a good friend. I've seen the way he looks at you."

"He looks at *all* the women. He's a *guy!*" I said, and went on clipping recipes from the stack of newspapers Jayne had been collecting for several years. "He's really fun to be around— makes funny remarks about how I look—my eyes, my hair. The 'haystack' he calls it, the way static electricity affects it."

"Remember when he gave you that comb shaped like a pitchfork?" Abby said, laughing. "He just loves everything about you. Lights up like a Christmas tree when you walk in the room."

It was all true, and what I didn't read aloud were the last few lines of Dave's e-mail: *When I kissed you before you left, I didn't want to let go. . . . Right now all I want is you in my arms again. Three months is too long, Alice.*

And I replied, *Sometimes all I can think about, Dave, is you.*

Truthfully, I checked Patrick's blog now and then to see if he was having second thoughts about the Peace Corps. He wasn't:

Learning to adapt to a lot of things, like the rats as big as kittens that scratch their way into my house at night, having their babies and fighting in my walls. Lots of reggae music here, and that I can take.

Had my first trip into a primary rain forest—huge, gorgeous trees. Saw a lemur—they look like moving teddy bears. One did me the honor of peeing on my head.

I'm really fond of the elderly woman who's like a grand-mother to me. Last night she told me about the "hungry season" in Madagascar, when rice is so expensive. Life is hard in these villages. I'm here as an environmentalist, and the two projects I'd like to start are a garden and a com-post pile, and making some kind of a solar oven/food-drying system like they taught us during training. But I still need to be more fluent in their language. The one phrase I've been good at, when villagers talk to me, is "Mora mora azafady!" meaning, "Slower, please."

I wished I could be that definite about something. At the same time I was yearning for Dave, I found I was liking Oregon a lot—liking the freedom from the clock. I could understand Abby's satisfaction in making a *product* she could see and feel and *eat*. The idea of being self-employed began to look a whole lot better to me than going back to school for two more years. I mean, this was basic survival by the work of your hands. Maybe I could persuade Dave to move out here! Or maybe I should change my major from education/counseling to business! Then

Dad would know that I was serious, that I could run a business by myself.

What I especially enjoyed was creating my own recipes. I'd done it only twice so far, but customers complimented Jayne on them the following week. Especially my chocolate date cake with the cream cheese frosting. I was working on coconut-orange bars with an almond crust, and Jayne said I was a natural in the baking department.

"Do you ever think about doing this as a career?" I asked Abby one Sunday as we were getting ready to go out for the evening.

"What? Working for Jayne?"

"Starting a business like she has. Catering or something."

"Not really. I wouldn't want the pressure."

"Pressure? What pressure?" I said, thrusting a comb in my hair. I reached for my dangly jade and silver earrings. "Except for Saturdays, she doesn't ever set her alarm."

"That's the Jayne you see in the summer—when business is best at the Saturday Market," Abby said. "You should see her around income tax time. I spent spring vacation here once, and she's got all sorts of stuff to worry about. She even had court costs once, when somebody sued her in small-claims court for food poisoning. She was scared she'd lose her house."

"So what happened?"

"The woman who sued told the judge she'd had diarrhea for a whole weekend after eating Jayne's seafood lasagna. And she said she'd seen inside Jayne's kitchen when she'd come to pick it up, and it hadn't looked too clean. She was suing her for seven thousand dollars."

"And . . . ?"

"Jayne had proof she'd passed inspection and said none of her other customers had been sick. And when the woman said she'd settle for a year's worth of meals instead of the seven thousand, the judge threw the lawsuit out."

We were still chuckling over that when we set out for a little dive that Abby had found the last time she was here. Moroccan-style kebabs and great espresso.

The restaurant was buzzing when we got there and seemed to be a seat-yourself kind of place. We stood just inside the door reading the menu posted on the wall, debating the merits of lamb stew over beef kebabs, when suddenly Abby poked my arm. "Alice, doesn't that guy look familiar?" she asked.

"Which guy?"

"The one with the curly hair. The table in the center there, with the girl in the red shirt."

I studied him a bit more intently, and sure enough, it had to be him. We were positive when the girl threw back her head in laughter and said, "Oh, Chris!"

As far as we could tell, he had recovered completely from his jaundice (or theater paint) and was in no hurry to get to Seattle.

"C'mon," I said. As we headed to the table next to them, which had just been vacated, I slipped my bag off my shoulder and hung it on the back of one of the empty chairs.

"Well, Christopher, hi!" I said brightly. "Imagine seeing you here!" The girl was still smiling as she looked up at us waiting for an introduction, but Chris's face had undergone a rapid-fire transition from pleasure to surprise to dismay and, finally, to phony friendliness. If his eyebrows could type, they would have written, *Okay, I'm busted, but help me out here and I'll be eternally grateful.*

"Hel-lo!" he said. "Sit down! Sit down! Have a beer on me!"

I could tell by Abby's grin that she decided to play along, so I did too, just for the heck of it, and we pulled over chairs from the next table. If we worked this right, we might even get a whole meal out of it.

"Alice and Abby," I said to the girl, to Christopher's obvious relief. "We're just visiting Abby's aunt for the summer—helping out with her catering business."

"I'm Gretchen," said the blond girl. "Isn't this place great? I'm crazy about the hummus."

"Mmm, we'll try it," said Abby. "What else would you recommend, Chris, seeing as how it's on you?"

I struggled to keep from laughing, but I knew we had him. We could just tell that this was a girl he wanted to impress.

"Uh . . . everything on the menu is great," he said.

"Where did you guys meet up?" Gretchen asked.

Christopher immediately interrupted. "Actually, I'm flush tonight, so order whatever you want."

"Thanks!" I said. And then to Gretchen, "Oh, we just run into each other now and then. We sell at the Saturday Market, so we see dozens of people."

We talked about Oregon in general as we ate our dinner and were having a rather nice conversation when Chris told Gretchen that he was involved in fund-raising for a nonprofit organization. We began to wonder if the organization might possibly be him. We also noticed that he didn't leave us alone with Gretchen for even a moment. When he wanted another pitcher of beer, he signaled someone to bring it to us.

But we wanted to make sure he didn't pull a scam on Gretchen—somehow leaving her paying the bill.

So before we left, after thanking Chris for the dinner, I said, "Hey, weren't you driving up to Seattle for a few days, Chris? How did that go?"

"Nah, something came up at the last minute and I had to put that off," he said. And then, reaching for the bill, he added, "Nice to see you again. Gretchen and I are going to a movie. Be well."

"You too," Abby told him.

Muggy is muggy no matter where it is, I decided around the first of August, when I was baking, a sweatband around my forehead to keep sweat from dripping on the miniature quiches I was taking from the oven. Jayne said she couldn't afford air-conditioning, and since it always got cool at night, that was something to look forward to. Which didn't make any sense to me, unless she did all her baking at night.

"Do you ever wish you were on someone else's payroll?" I asked her when we escaped to the porch between batches.

"Only when I think about getting sick," she said, holding

her iced-tea glass against her cheek to cool herself. "Would be nice to have health insurance. And of course there will be no cruises on the Nile or trips to Florence in my lifetime, and I don't suppose I'll ever be able to redo my kitchen . . . but I'm happy with what I've got, so why tie myself to a time clock?"

"But do you miss being around coworkers?"

"Never really had any, so what's to miss? I'll admit I love the Saturday Market just so I can hang out with other cooks. And I've got my now-and-then boyfriend. But . . . I've always been sort of a loner, and it suits me. What can I say?"

We took a couple days off to go to the ocean, and I loved it. The Oregon coast is so different from Delaware and Maryland. Few motels to be seen, no fences into the ocean anywhere. You don't see many bathers, the water's so cold. At some places there are seals, not swimmers, and huge boulders rise out of the water like humpbacked giants warning people away. Little inlets hold minute ocean treasures if you're quick enough to catch them before they swim off. Once we'd had a taste of the coast, we had to brace ourselves to go back to Jayne's hot kitchen.

Abby was a great roommate because, like me, she enjoyed her "alone time" each day, just to sit and read or wander by herself into town. Usually we strolled in together, but occasionally I explored on my own, and on one of those days, I discovered a Planned Parenthood clinic a few blocks away.

It's something I'd been thinking about a lot. Along with thinking about Dave. I hadn't considered seeing a doctor about birth control before because Patrick wasn't in the picture. I hadn't been "saving myself" for him exactly, it was just that, until recently, when I'd thought about sex with anyone, it was Patrick I was thinking about. But now . . . there was Dave.

I opened the door and stepped inside.

The nurse practitioner was a woman of about fifty—around Jayne's age, I guess—welcoming and friendly, but also very matter-of-fact. MRS. EDWARDS, her nameplate read.

"I think I'd like some kind of protection in addition to condoms," I said. "I just don't like the idea of depending entirely on the guy."

"Good thinking," she said. "Do you want me to go over some of the choices with you before your exam?"

I swallowed. "Exam? Today?"

"Yes," Mrs. Edwards said, pausing. "Are you having your period?"

"No," I said. "I just thought . . . Well, it's okay. Yes, I'd like to hear about the choices first." Anything to delay it. I mean, a little conversation first would be good, along with a tranquilizer maybe, and a dark room so I wouldn't have to look at her looking at me.

So she told me about the rhythm method, the least reliable, and who's going to carry a thermometer along on a date, anyway? Condoms, of course, and she jokingly reminded me that they come in all colors and flavors. There was a weird thing they called a "female condom," like a plastic bag I could stick in my vagina with the edges sticking out. *Not!* I told her. A diaphragm, flat and round, that I could insert over the cervix; an

IUD, or intrauterine device; spermicidal jelly; birth control pills; a patch or injections . . .

How did sex get to be so complicated? I wondered. You don't see guys going to Planned Parenthood before they become "sexually active," as the doctors call it. Every woman you see making love in the movies is obviously on the pill or the patch or something, because you never see *her* fumbling around in her bag at the critical moment for the little compact with the diaphragm in it or the tube of spermicidal cream.

"I think I'd like to start on birth control pills," I told Mrs. Edwards.

"We can do that, but you'll need to get refills from your own doctor. The pill is ninety-nine percent effective, but you shouldn't rely on it alone for at least a week after you first start."

"No problem there," I said.

"Good. Now, I'm going to step out and you need to take off everything from your waist down, and we'll have a look. We want to protect the health of your partner, too." Meaning that they don't want him catching anything from me.

So there I was, five minutes later, lying on the exam table with a sheet over my midsection, my feet in the stirrups, sliding my bottom down to the end of the table, staring at the funny cartoon taped on the ceiling above me of a woman in a hospital gown with a look of terror on her face standing straight-legged right up in the stirrups and the doctor saying, *"Please, Mrs. Jones, try to relax."*

My fingers clutched the edges of the table, and I closed my

eyes, like if I couldn't see Mrs. Edwards, she couldn't see me.

"Okay. I'll be gentle," she said reassuringly.

I'd rather it was a man telling me that, actually—that he'd be gentle. I'd rather have been in a man's arms. . . .

"Just part of being a woman," Sylvia had once said of the necessary pelvic exams we go through in our lives.

It only took a minute or two, and then, just as gently, Mrs. Edwards withdrew the speculum and covered my knees and bottom with the sheet once again.

"Everything looks good," she said. "You'll want to use plenty of lubrication the first time. And if you decide not to go on the pill, I'd suggest you use both a condom and a full plunger of spermicidal cream. We'll give you a pamphlet about the pill, and of course you'll need to talk with your regular gynecologist soon after you get home."

I sure could understand why impulsive couples just *did* it without all this mess. But forever worrying about an unplanned pregnancy was definitely not on my "want" list. I left with a little packet of pills, another of condoms, some pamphlets on birth control and safe sex, and a small sack with a tube of spermicidal cream and a plastic plunger.

"Have a good day?" Abby asked me when I got back—Abby, the girl who's already had at least two intimate relationships. She was lying on the cot reading a bodice ripper showing a woman on the cover with her dress hiked up to her thighs and a bare-chested man with anything but safe sex on his mind.

"Yeah, I did."

She studied the little package I dropped in my dresser drawer. "Shopping? Buy something cute?"

"Planned Parenthood."

"Ah!" said Abby. "It's about time."

Jayne said we outdid ourselves with our milk chocolate cupcakes on market day. Each had peppermint frosting and a cream filling that oozed out of every bite. They sold out first thing. Abby and I sat behind the baked goods table, watching the panorama before us—the endless variety of people—while Jayne presided over the packaged casseroles: the Swedish meatballs, the spinach quiche, chicken and dumplings . . . all the things we'd sampled during the week.

Our attention was drawn to a young couple sauntering by. The girl was probably a sophomore in high school, the guy somewhat older. He was wearing a tank top over his muscular frame, showing off the tattoos on his arms and back. She was also in a tank top, braless, a long sarong-type skirt, and an embroidered headband low on her forehead.

They stopped to look at the handmade jewelry in the booth across from ours, and there was something about the girl that was so artificial, so awkward, it was almost embarrassing to watch. While the guy inspected the metal belt buckles, the girl seemed to find it impossible to let him be. She toyed with the hair at the nape of his neck, and when he brushed her hand away, she extended one hip and gyrated slowly against him. The more time he gave the two girls behind the display table, the more insistent the girl became, until finally she wrapped her arms around his neck and began running her lips along his cheek, drawing the furtive looks of passersby.

"I can't stand it," Abby said.

"She must be terribly insecure," I mused.

Abby turned and stared at me. "Are you kidding? She probably thinks she's God's gift to men."

"If she is, then I feel sorry for her, because she's not enjoying herself one bit," I said, watching the way the guy ignored her. Finally the couple moved on, the girl still draped around his body, publicly coaxing a kiss from him.

"You always excuse people, did you know that? Even when they're awful?" Abby said. "Don't you simply dislike some people? Other than Jared, I mean."

I was genuinely surprised. I remembered how I had both envied and loathed Pamela in sixth grade; Penny, when she came between Patrick and me; and I never did care much for Dad's assistant manager, Janice Sherman; or Mr. Hensley in seventh, with his horrible breath.

"Not true," I said. "I can think of plenty of people I've disliked."

"But, I mean . . . people like that girl, who put on a big show. I just wanted to go over and tell her how obnoxious she really was."

"She *knows* that, Abby! And she's miserable. Couldn't you tell? If she felt good about herself, do you think she'd have to try so hard for her boyfriend's attention? She was totally desperate."

"Hmmm. Maybe you're right. I'll try to think of her as a comedy act," said Abby.

By noon the banana date bread had sold out, and the only items left were a few casseroles of baked ziti.

Abby and Jayne wanted to look at some gauzy skirts at the other end of the market, so I kept watch over the table and took orders from people who wanted a particular item the following week.

And there they were again, the no-bra girl and her tattooed guy, back at the jewelry booth across from me. The two young women behind the counter were pretty and jewel-bedecked themselves, obviously eager to sell. They bantered and parried with the guy in the tank top, who had just slipped a heavy cross around his neck. It rested against his hairy chest wrong side up, and one of the saleswomen reached across the table and adjusted it for him. This gave him an excuse to grab her hand flirtatiously and ask about the ring she was wearing.

I couldn't tell if the girl with him looked more annoyed or pleading. She slipped one hand through her boyfriend's arm and gave it a gentle tug.

Stop, stop! I wanted to call. *Laugh it off and stroll on.* Instead, she tugged more aggressively, and this time he pushed her hand away, then turned his attention to the second young woman, fondling the copper necklace that nestled between her breasts. I saw his girlfriend's cheeks flush, and for a moment I thought she was going to intervene. She recovered, however, and fanned herself with a brochure from her green bag, lifting her long hair up off the nape of her neck. She even playfully fanned her boy-friend. But then, when she still got no response—no recogni-tion at all, in fact—she reached for the hem of her tank top and pulled it up over her head. Then she shook her hair out and faced her boyfriend, naked from the waist up.

My mouth dropped in astonishment, and this time the boy-friend noticed.

And he laughed.

Then the two women selling the jewelry laughed.

There was something so pathetic and sad in the girl's com-plete vulnerability and the guy's callousness that it brought tears to my eyes. She stood there helplessly, doused with embarrass-ment, and reminded me of Pamela, back when we were high school sophomores on our trip to New York, the way she had humiliated herself with Hugh. Of myself, the way my heart broke when Patrick and I broke up in ninth grade.

And right then I realized I needed a job where I was working with people. Baking was fun and creative, but I think I'd really miss counseling; I'd miss helping kids through some unbearable times.

When the girl finally walked away, holding her tank top against her chest this time, the guy made no move to follow. He whistled for her once, as you would call a dog. She stopped, turned around and looked at him, but when he laughed and whistled again for her to come back, she kept going, and I silently cheered her on.

* * *

Dad called to find out if he should meet me at the airport.

"You know," I said, "I've been toying with the idea of not going back to school. Of maybe staying out here and trying my hand at the catering business full-time."

"Alice . . . ," Dad began.

"It's really fun," I said. "And I'm more creative in the kitchen than I thought. Jayne needs a baker, and the nights here in Eugene are great!"

"Alice," Dad said. *"Come home!"*

I laughed. "Gotcha," I said. "But catering has its moments."

"Don't do this to me," Dad said, laughing now. "I'm too old."

"No, you're not, you're just right," I told him. "But to answer your question, you don't need to come to the airport. Dave's picking me up, and I'm going to his folks' place for a few days before school starts. I'll be home Tuesday."

"Okay, sweetheart. See you whenever," Dad said.

On our last day in Oregon, Jayne took us tubing on the Willamette River. It was almost enough to make me change my mind yet again and stay there.

We each had a giant inner tube, and we floated along, our arms and legs draped over the sides of the tube, the rubber— warmed by the sun—blissfully comforting, a counterpoint to the cold water lapping at us from below as our bottoms bounced along with the current.

Every so often, another tuber would drift into view and

we'd wave. I tipped my head back and offered my throat to the sun, wiggling my toes in delight.

"I'm going to miss you girls," Jayne said at one point as our tubes lazily bumped together, and we floated as a clump for a few minutes.

"Women," Abby corrected. "Once we reach the age of twenty, we're women."

"News to me," said Jayne. "I still feel like a sixteen-year-old, as long as I don't look in the mirror."

"Stay that way, Aunt Jayne," Abby said. "Forever sixteen, that's you."

We watched another group of tubers round a bend out in the middle, where the current was stronger. One of them had a cooler on his lap and was tossing cans of Budweiser to the others.

We waved. They waved. And suddenly I said, "Abby, do you see who I see?"

And there he was, Christopher, who recognized us and lifted his can of Bud in salute. The second thing we discovered is that they were all naked. We suspected it when we saw the bare breasts of the women, and we were sure of it when someone in their group upended one of the tubers and we saw his white bottom do a flip-flop in the water.

"Forever sixteen," Jayne mused, smiling blissfully up at the sky.

6
THE FIRST TIME

What I *didn't* tell Dad about going to Dave's house was that his folks wouldn't be there—they were in Boston for the week. And, not too surprisingly, Dad didn't ask. Perhaps he just assumed, the way I'd said it, that they would be. Or perhaps he was showing respect for my privacy, now that I was twenty.

I wonder sometimes if he misses those crazy mealtime discussions we used to have that mortified Les, but who else was I to ask questions of if not Dad and Lester? Other girls had their mothers, while I had Aunt Sally, and Sally's answers were about as helpful to a nine-year-old as a bra with a D cup.

The plane banked and turned in its approach to Reagan National, and I looked down on the familiar monuments—on the Potomac River, the Capitol—and thought how different it was from Eugene. Not better, just different. But it was home. When you live in the Washington area, everything sort of runs together—Maryland, Virginia, DC—and what happens in one place makes news in all three.

"Are you nervous?" Abby asked, hands folded over her bag.

I turned away from the window and settled back in my seat. "Nervous?"

"You haven't stayed in the same position for more than five seconds. Wouldn't have something to do with Dave, would it?"

Was she kidding? It had everything to do with Dave. And yes, I was nervous. And excited. And a little bit scared.

"Just excited to be home," I said.

"Me too." Valerie was picking her up, and they were going out to a new club that had opened in College Park over the summer. "Hope you and Dave have a good time." She looked at me knowingly. "A *really* good time."

"We'll try," I said, and that sounded so naive and pathetic, it made us both laugh.

He met me at the baggage counter and pulled me into a hug, followed by a kiss about as long.

I backed away finally and smiled up at him. "Hi," I said, and he grinned some more.

"Sure glad you're back," he told me. He looked a little heavier than he'd been when I'd left, a little fuller around the jaw, but mostly his shoulders seemed broader. Whatever; it looked good on him. Especially in his bright red Terrapins T-shirt.

Wanted to make sure I knew I was back in U of M territory, I guess.

He picked up my luggage, a bag in each hand, as though they were mere five-pounders, and we made our way out the double doors.

"Hope you're hungry tonight, because I'm cooking," he said. "How does grilled steak, garlic mashed potatoes, and asparagus sound?"

"Garlic?" I said in dismay, then felt my face flush.

He smiled without looking at me. "Or not," he said, and we headed over to the parking lot.

We were strangely quiet as we drove. Dave looked over at me occasionally and asked general questions about Oregon. We were like high school freshmen on our first date, I thought. So weird to go from good friends to . . . something more. Maybe we should wait. . . .

I began to feel slightly panicky, and Dave must have sensed it because he reached over and caressed my arm, and his smile reassured me.

The traffic began to thin out at last after we exited the beltway, and the farther we went, the more rolling the land became until we could see the misty rims of the Blue Ridge Mountains far off. I was looking at the mountains and thinking about the matching blue bra and bikini bottoms I'd bought in Eugene.

Sex must be so simple for guys. I'd been to Planned Parenthood, got the pill, bought the K-Y lubricant, the panties . . .

Dave had probably just walked in a drugstore and bought a package of Trojans off the shelf. Done.

At his house Dave carried the cooler he had brought into the house, and we put all the food in the fridge.

"It's beautiful here," I said, looking out the sliding doors beyond the kitchen. "Not a house in sight from back here."

"There are some great trails, but we'd need to go while it's still light enough to see," Dave said. "Are you up for a short hike before dinner?"

"Love to!" I said. "I'm wild to stretch my legs."

Dave had put my bags in the guest bedroom, so I traded my sandals for sneakers and we set off, following one of the trails up into the foothills for a couple of miles, enjoying the rich earthy scent of the woods.

Looking at Dave's broad back as he went ahead over the rough places, stopping to hold back branches to let me pass, part of me wanted to grab his arm and say *Now!*, and part of me wanted to go until we were both too tired to even try. I could say I got blisters. Splinters. Blisters and splinters. An allergy to pine trees. A plain old panic attack . . .

At the top of a bluff, however, we stood looking out over the valley, the dusk outlining everything in sharp detail—the trees, the shrubs, the stretch of meadow in white and yellow and lavender—and this time when we kissed, our bodies pressed together, I felt I was ready and followed him back to the house.

* * *

There was a wait, however.

I was in his arms again, my lips pressed against his chest. He smiled down at me and cocked his head toward the kitchen. "This?" he said, then nodded toward the bedroom. "Or that?"

"Dave . . . it's . . . my first time," I said.

He stood absolutely still for a moment, then gently pushed my hair from my cheek. "Really?"

"Really."

"Well then . . . I suggest we eat dinner first."

That made me laugh, and I leaned back away from him. "What? We need extra carbs or something?"

I loved the way his mouth sort of dipped at the corners when he smiled at me. "We need extra time, that's all. And we've got all night."

I don't remember a whole lot about dinner. I remember peeling the potatoes and cutting them up to boil while Dave grilled the steaks. I remember Dave lighting two candles in the dining room and feeding him a stalk of asparagus, which we had undercooked.

Mostly, I remember trying to get myself ready in the guest bathroom while he cleaned up the kitchen. I'd been good about taking my birth control pills, so didn't have to worry about that. I showered from the hike and checked myself over in front of the mirror. My teeth! I had to brush my teeth. What about my navel? Any lint in there? And, horror of horrors, my pee smelled of asparagus!

I cut the price tag off the blue bra and put it on, but before

I put on the bikini, I took out the tube of K-Y jelly and read the directions on the box: *Squeeze tube to obtain desired amount of lubricant. May be applied directly onto condoms. Reapply as needed.*

What was the desired amount? When did I apply it to condoms? How did I know when to reapply? Who wrote this stuff?

There was a light tap on the door. "Need anything?" Dave asked.

"Do we have condoms?" I answered, a little embarrassed to admit I had some.

"Yeah . . . I'm okay with that."

"I'll be out in a minute," I said.

I took the tube out of the box, flipped open the snap cap, and squeezed. A large squirt of clear jelly shot across the bathroom and hit the wall.

Look how much I wasted! I thought, and wondered if I should try to use part of the glob sliding down toward the baseboard. No, that would be gross. So I cleaned it up and tried again. This time I got a tablespoon or so and applied it the best I could. Then I pulled on my underwear, checked my teeth once more, and went into the bedroom, feeling strangely wet and gooey between my legs.

Dave was sitting up on one arm, the sheet pulled up to his waist. He smiled at me and held the sheet open for me to slide under. "Wow!" he said. "I always liked you in blue."

I quickly got in beside him without looking under the sheet. What is the girl supposed to say to the guy when she sees him naked for the first time? Is "wow" appropriate? If she doesn't say anything, is it an insult?

The air-conditioning was on and the room was cool, making it natural that I snuggled up against him. And somehow, reverting to good-friend status, I heard myself saying, "This is all sort of awkward for me."

But Dave didn't seem to mind. He kissed my forehead and said, "You'll get used to it." And then he kissed me for real, and I felt myself getting excited. I touched him and felt the condom. Dave caressed my breasts and let his fingers explore me, and after a while I heard him breathing more quickly and he edged up over me. "I'll be gentle," he whispered.

"That's what the doctor said," I told him, and then hated myself. Why couldn't I think of sexy things to say?

Dave chuckled. "Oh, I love the way you said that," he teased.

What? We were joking around? My first time having sexual intercourse and I'd made the guy laugh?

"Oh, Dave," I said. "I'm really so awful at this."

"We haven't even started yet," he said. And then he lay back on his side and smiled at me. "I can wait," he said. "I think."

I didn't say anything the next time we tried, and neither did Dave. We were too intent on making it happen, but it hurt!

Somehow I thought in the back of my mind that pain was mostly an old wives' tale. Maybe a little pain. But I found myself pushing him back a little. He eased up some.

"I'm sorry," he said, but he pushed again.

Maybe we had the wrong angle, I thought. Maybe the

position wasn't right. How did movie stars get by with just a tiny wince, followed by mind-numbing ecstasy?

And then, suddenly, he was in. I felt myself give down there and could feel him inside of me. The strain on his face and the way his head tipped back told me that he was coming. And then he collapsed on his elbows, his head tucked down by my shoulder against the pillow, and I nuzzled his cheek.

I think we both slept for a while, though at some point I went in the bathroom and cleaned myself up. I'd bled some, so I worried about the guest sheets, which we'd launder before we left. We should have put a towel beneath us.

Then I stopped and looked at my face in the mirror.

"Well," I said to my reflection, "you don't look a bit different."

Sometime in the night Dave would have made love again if I'd wanted, but I was too sore. He offered to put his hand on me as Patrick had done, but I didn't want any touching for a while.

"Just hold me," I whispered, kissing him, so he did.

We mostly lazed around the next day. We danced and kissed and walked down to a stream and back. Dave drove to town later and brought back some gyro sandwiches and a Greek salad for our dinner.

The evening had cooled down enough that we could have a fire in the fireplace, and I helped Dave bring in wood and arrange it on the grate. Then we sat on the couch together, each with our separate laptops.

At one point Dave nudged me to look at his screen, and I leaned over. He had accessed his Facebook page and changed his status from "Single" to "In a relationship." He was looking at me intently. "Okay?" he asked.

"Okay," I said, and changed mine.

Gwen and Pamela and Liz and I got together one last time before we went back to school. Liz had been dating a number of guys up in Vermont, none of them particularly special, she said, so she focused more on the fun stuff to do there and told us how— after the first big snow last year—she and some of her friends had borrowed trays from the dining hall and gone sledding on a nearby hill.

Pamela had taken a course in modeling and another in advertising. Her big project last semester had been to film three short commercials, featuring herself in each one.

We gathered around the computer screen in my bedroom and played her DVD.

In the first sketch she was dressed in a leopard-skin body-suit and was draped seductively, catlike, over the hood of a car. We laughed and cheered. It was so obviously sexist, so obviously Pamela, but she was good at it, I'll admit. The next, surprisingly, was a commercial showing Pamela as a young mother with a five-year-old daughter, dressed in matching jogging suits and running along a neighborhood street together, their blond hair backlit by the sun, both of them the picture of health. This was supposedly an ad for a new protein breakfast bar, and Pamela looked just as natural in that as she had in the first one.

The third commercial showed Pamela in a black formfitting dress, standing in an elevator, looking gorgeous. A business executive gets on, gives her the eye, and makes a comment, which she ignores. He follows it up with a suggestive remark, which she also ignores. Then her cell phone rings, and when she answers, it's clear that she's an executive in the same company he is, even higher up the corporate ladder, and you can see him electronically dwindling down to the size of a mouse in one corner.

"Pamela, those are good!" Liz said, speaking for all of us.

"So . . . so . . . Pamela!" Gwen said. "What's your field now? Are you still in theater?"

"Oh . . . I don't know," Pamela said. "I'm going out with a guy in advertising, and he's opening some doors for me, so I'm sort of leaning in that direction. It would certainly pay better than theater. But, work aside, how are things going with you guys?"

"Alice has been going out with a guy named Dave," said Gwen. "In fact, she spent last weekend at his place."

"His parents' place," I corrected as everyone focused on me. "But no, they weren't there."

"Aha!" Pamela said.

"He's nice," I told them, turning my chair away from the computer and meeting the gaze of all three friends sitting expectantly on the edge of my bed. "And yes," I added, "We. Were. Intimate."

"Well, well," said Pamela. "You *have* been busy this summer."

I couldn't read Elizabeth's face. Surprise, I guess. "Wow! So I'm the last one," she said finally.

"Don't do anything rash," Gwen said dryly. "It's not a contest."

But Liz was still staring at me. "Do you hear from Patrick at all?" she asked. "I mean, are you going to tell him about Dave?"

"What do you suggest? A telegram?" said Pamela, and Elizabeth's face flushed.

I was glad we weren't back in ninth grade, because I would have been expected to give out details. But I knew how it felt to be considered the naive one, so I added, "We haven't been in contact for months, Liz. All I know is what I read on his Peace Corps blog." I turned back to the computer and typed in Patrick's blog address.

What I didn't tell them was that somehow I found it easier to deal with my feelings about Patrick by keeping up with his work in Madagascar, not treating his blog as if it were something dangerous I couldn't bear to read. This helped me see him as another interesting friend in my life, one of many. When it came on the screen, I read it aloud:

"RICE TRAINING! It went so well. Even though the road is washed out at this point and no vehicles are going in or out, we managed to bring in a Malagasy man from Diego to do the training. I found two men who could read and write and were really interested in learning with me, and Jessica brought two women from her village. It was three days of

going into the rice field in the mornings, with lectures at the school in the afternoons. The guy was GOOD, and it was great to see people from my village frantically taking notes and asking questions. Basically, this is just a very regimented way of transplanting rice so that the yields are two times, four times, even up to ten times the amount of rice they would get from traditional methods.

I'm still extremely happy to be here. Jessica feels the same way. Yeah, I have my moments, but this is where I need to be right now.

"It's *so* Patrick, isn't it?" Pamela said. "He can make friends anywhere. I'll bet you could plunk him down anyplace on earth and he'd pick up the language."

"I wonder what he'll do after the Peace Corps," said Liz.

"He'll find something," said Gwen.

No one mentioned Jessica.

My own interests were closer to home as I started my junior year. I'd managed to snag one of the newer dorms, and this time Abby and Claire were rooming together, and Valerie and I were just across the hall. The four of us were in and out of both rooms so often, it was hard to tell who lived where.

I wanted to spend more time with Dave, but I was particular about where we made love. The only time I was willing to use our dorm rooms was when our roommates were away for the weekend. I'll admit that planning one of these nights together was pretty exciting, but as far as the library stacks or the dorm lounges, those weren't for me. Dave claimed he could do it anywhere, and I believed him.

"Just think how exciting it would be to try it in the shower," he said one night, nuzzling my neck. We were lying on my bed together, fully clothed, because Valerie would be coming in later.

"The one on the bottom would drown," I said, pulling out one of the eyebrow hairs that grew in a different direction over his eye.

"No, we'd be standing. You against the wall," he teased.

"I'm having a hard time imagining the choreography."

"We could manage," he said, and we kissed again.

I was feeling more comfortable with Dave—about my body, about his, about sex in general, even though I was still pretty new at it. I was really careful to take my pill regularly, and Dave never objected to condoms. I wondered what it would be like to be actually married and not have to bother with pills and condoms unless you wanted to. To have a place you could be together every night without worrying about someone walking in.

One of the things I discovered was that the more freedom you have—no curfew about getting in at night, no restrictions on whom you could have in your room—the more decisions you have to make for yourself. Whom you sleep with, where, what kind of birth control to use, how to respect your roommate's privacy . . . all grown-up stuff, and no parent to make the decision for you.

I was ready.

1
SCOO

The big event on my mind was Les and Stacy's wedding coming up in November. True to his word, Les allotted four of the invitations to me. I wondered if I was going to be in the wedding party, but I found out there would be only one attendant, the maid of honor—Stacy's best friend—and a best man, so naturally, I understood. With both Les and Stacy living in West Virginia, we were just happy that the wedding was to be here in Maryland. Even better, Stacy sent me a little note asking if I would be in charge of the guest book. She said that she and Les would like me to buy whatever dress I would like to wear—something I really loved—and to send the bill to them. *You'll be the first beautiful thing people see when they enter the church,* she wrote. Wow!

Meanwhile, there was school, and I lucked out on some of the most popular classes, especially Human Sexuality, for which the two hundred seats usually filled up within the first three days of registration. I also loved Fundamentals of Design, one of my electives, and even the classes for my major were becoming more interesting, more specific: the Autistic Adolescent and the Social Basis of Behavior. Now that I'd flirted with the idea of changing fields and turned it down, I felt recharged, more certain I wanted a job working directly with people. Maybe that's why a note on the bulletin board at the student union interested me. Both Valerie and I stopped to read it: *Need to be needed? Your school needs you. Hear us out over pizza and calzones.* And it gave a time and place, a conference room in the administration building.

It's a fact that almost any offer of free food on a college campus will attract at least a small crowd, but perhaps the suggestion of work involved kept this one to about thirteen people. Val and I knew only one, James Whitney, whom we'd shaved last November. Platters of pizza slices and calzones were on the conference table, along with a coffeemaker and a note that told us to help ourselves. The organizer herself, one of the assistant deans, was late, and three of the guys devoured a calzone each and edged out the door before anyone could pin them down.

After seven minutes had passed and the organizer still hadn't shown, a tall guy in a Terps sweatshirt, coffee in hand, looked about the room and said jokingly, "I suppose you're all wondering why I called you here today," and we laughed.

So did the assistant dean, who came in just at that moment,

professional-looking and cheerful in her black slacks and gold sweater, her dark hair swept away from her face.

"Sorry. A meeting ran over, and I finally just had to bolt, but it looks like you were in good hands here with . . ."

"Marcus Kelly," the tall guy said.

". . . with Marcus. Have a seat, everybody. Introduce yourselves and have some more food. There's another pizza in the warming oven." She poured a cup of coffee for herself as we told each other our names, and then she sat down. "I'll be brief and give you the basics. We can get into specifics later. The university is starting a new initiative, and we need your input. We're concerned about our image and want to improve relations with the residents of our College Park community, not just by what we don't do—hopefully, no more overturning cars after a football game or leaving beer cans on neighborhood lawns after parties—but by establishing interactions with residents in a constructive way. Students and residents as neighbors, not strangers. This is just a brainstorming session, so I'd like to hear any ideas you might have, no matter how far-out."

Someone suggested a volunteer cleanup brigade after games, but the dean said that was still just a breaking-even kind of thing. She was looking for plusses—making a difference by adding something that wasn't there before.

"Maybe transporting elderly or handicapped people around?" red-haired Samantha said.

We vetoed that. "The only free time students have is on

weekends; the elderly don't have doctor appointments then, and most of us don't have cars," someone said.

"Plus, liability if anyone got hurt," Marcus added.

Another ten minutes of debate, another few slices of pizza. If there's anything college students hate more than warm beer, it's boring meetings that go nowhere.

Devon, the guy next to me, said, "If we're looking at service projects, they need to be something that the Kiwanis Clubs and churches wouldn't already be providing."

"Car wash?" I offered.

"Or a free raking job when the leaves fall," suggested another girl.

Then we started to come alive.

"Yes! Something that's outdoors, where we can meet the whole neighborhood—anyone who stops by," said James.

"I like it," said the dean. "If expenses are minimal, the university will spring for it. And of course we can provide the buckets, the rags, the rakes . . ."

"The pizza?" asked Marcus. "We've got to have bait."

"And the pizza," said the dean, and checked her watch. "I've got to pick up a kid at soccer. You guys are great. Could you work out the details and leave them with my secretary?"

I thought about the Saturday Market in Eugene, people selling what they did best—baked bread or woven baskets.

"Why don't we start a . . . a sort of registry?" I suggested. "Get students to sign up for whatever they do best."

And guess who got appointed registrar?

Marcus agreed to be chairperson.

"We going to have a name for this?" James asked, eyeing, then reaching for the last calzone.

"That would help," said Valerie. "What are we, exactly?"

"Obviously an outreach program of some kind," said a guy at the end of the table. "Community Outreach Organization? COO?"

"Hmm. How about SCOO—Student/Community Outreach Organization?" said Samantha. "And if we could put a 'P' on the end . . ."

Everyone likes big ideas, but nobody likes details.

"Naw, naw, naw!" Marcus groaned. "Just SCOO. So-Come-On-Out. That's what we're trying to say, isn't it?"

So *SCOO* it was, and for a start, we settled on a car wash the second Saturday of October, a leaf-raking in November. Then, to get the publicity going and to persuade our friends to join in, we came up with a motto: "Do it for your community. Do it for your school. Do it for yourself."

"See you at the car wash," Valerie told the others as we stood and stretched.

"Beer party after?" asked Devon.

"Sure, why not?" said Marcus.

"We can probably talk Claire and Abby into taking part," I said to Valerie as we walked back across campus, "and I'll work on Dave." I liked the idea of extending ourselves beyond the campus in even a small way, being part of the adult world we'd be entering all too soon.

But Claire met us in the hallway when we got up to the second floor and couldn't wait to tell us news of her own.

* * *

"Come on in," she said, motioning toward one of the two beds, where Abby was sitting, legs pulled up with the soles of her bare feet touching. Abby put aside the magazine she'd been reading and patted the spread.

"Show's about to begin," she said as we sat down beside her. "I have no idea what it is, but Claire's been waiting for you guys to get back."

Claire's face was beautifully made up, the blush applied just so on her cheekbones, the eyeliner perfectly smudged on the lids, eyelashes long and luxuriously coated with mascara, eyebrows delicately arched and extended, dwindling to fine lines of brown out toward her temples.

"Wow, Claire, you look great!" Valerie said. "What's the occasion?"

"I just want to share something wonderful, and I can hardly wait to tell you about it," Claire said. She reached down and pulled out a shiny magenta case from under her bed. *Magic Myst,* it read in silver script across the top. She ran one hand over the letters, then said, "This may well pay my way through college," and she opened the case.

Like a jewelry box, two flat shelves slid out sideways. The bottom of the case, the shelves, and the inside of the lid were filled with cosmetics of every kind.

"My God! It's the Avon Lady!" Abby joked.

"No, better than Avon," Claire said. "There are specific colors for every skin type and hair color, and all of these are scientifically formulated for the skin cells of women aged eighteen to twenty-two. Anyone can use them, of course, but they were created especially for college women."

"The skin cells know if you're in college or not?" Valerie quipped, still thunderstruck by the extensive display propped on the other bed.

"You know what I mean, Val," Claire said. "I've been using these for the past two weeks, and I can tell the difference. I could never go back to Revlon or Clinique, believe me."

"So . . . are you selling this stuff or what?" I asked.

"That's the best part," Claire said. "I don't just sell the product. Every customer gets a free skin cell analysis but, better yet, I sell executive assistantships. Here's how it works. . . ."

I began to get an uneasy feeling.

Claire was ready for her demonstration, and she unfolded a chart that she propped against the lid of the Magic Myst case. She pointed to a little silhouette of a woman near the top. "I make money two ways: by selling cosmetics and by selling executive assistantships. I get fifteen percent of the price of the cosmetics, but I get thirty percent for each assistantship."

Next she pointed to three little silhouettes below the figure at the top. "And I get a percentage of the sales of each of the assistants. When these girls sell either products or assistant-ships, I get a percentage of those sales, too."

Now she was pointing to a row of nine little women below the three. "Technically, there could come a point where I wouldn't have to sell any more cosmetics at all because I'd be making a lot from the percentages of all the girls below me, and they'd be getting a percentage of all the women below them. I am *so* psyched!"

"Gosh, Claire, are you sure about all this?" Abby asked.

"Sandra explained—"

"Sandra?"

"My friend at GW referred me to her. She said she'd heard about this fabulous way to make money, and the cosmetics are terrific, too."

I'll admit she looked great.

"Sandra took me out to dinner four times, and no Big Macs either. She knows some great restaurants in Silver Spring, and we talked all evening. She even picked me up in her BMW. No hard sell or anything, except she won't be in the area again for six months or so. . . ."

"What did you have to do to get this?" Valerie wanted to know. We were still sitting on the edge of Abby's bed. Nobody had settled back against the pillows.

Claire lovingly released the hinges on the flat shelves and closed the case. "Well, that was the hard part, because you have to buy the case and you have to buy your own cosmetics. But, like Sandra pointed out, all I have to sell are two executive assistantships and I will have paid for my case, and from then on, I start making money every time the women I recruit make a sale."

"How much does a case cost?" I asked.

Claire winced a little. "Well, it comes with an executive assistantship. Just three hundred dollars, but—"

"Three hundred dollars!" we cried, all together. "Claire, where did you get the money?"

"It's okay, it's okay," Claire said. "I went off the meal plan and used that money."

"You what? That's over two thousand dollars," I said.

"Well, I bought a friend's car too—a down payment, I mean—because I expect to be making a lot of sales off campus and . . ." She saw the shock on our faces. "Believe me, I've thought all this through."

I was still trying to run the calculations through my own head. For the last few years, relatives had given me mostly checks and cash for presents, knowing how desperate I was to have some savings when I'd finished college, and the thought of risking a big chunk of that on makeup . . .

"Well, wow!" said Valerie. "What can we say? Good luck and all that."

"Thanks. I didn't even try to give you the full demonstration, but I'll give you the price list of all the cosmetics, and I'll even give you the package deal. Moisturizer, makeup base . . ."

"How much is a package?" I asked.

"Blush, lip gloss, mascara . . ."

"How much?" Val insisted.

"Forty-nine ninety-five," said Claire.

"Oof," said Valerie. "It'll be a while."

Claire glanced up at the crazy clock above Abby's bed on which all the numbers were in Chinese. "Gotta go. I'm meeting up with a senior over in South Campus Commons. Sandra said she sold an assistantship to her last week, and the two of us are the only ones on the whole campus selling Magic Myst. So it's sort of a partnership. See you guys later."

When she had gone, we sat for a few seconds, pondering what she'd just told us.

"You think she's lost her mind?" asked Valerie.

"No, but she may have lost three hundred dollars," said Abby.

"Not to mention her food allowance for the semester."

"Well, maybe she'll surprise us all and get rich," I said. "Meanwhile, Valerie and I went to an interesting meeting this afternoon, Abby, and we've got a proposition to make."

"Not you, too!" Abby said. "I don't want to hear it."

I'm not sure if it was the gorgeous October day, or the sugges-tion of a beer party later, or the appeal of the leaflets Samantha distributed around campus ("People Who Need People"), or the little quips tacked up on bulletin boards: *If your dad's car was here, would you wash it?* and *A neighborhood in need of love. . . .* I'm not even sure what drew the committee members to SCOO—probably different for each student. Devon was plan-ning to attend divinity school after he graduated, and Marcus had relatives in the neighborhood. But maybe, as the pamphlets said, we were just people who needed people or who liked being needed ourselves. Whatever the reason, the car wash was a hit.

The university supplied the hoses and sponges and a fresh box of Krispy Kreme doughnuts each time the last one ran out.

We had students who knew nothing at all about SCOO drawn to the scene just by the scent of the doughnuts, and then they found themselves washing the hubcaps of a Buick. We assigned Dave to stand out on the circular drive to direct traffic.

"You sure there's no charge here?" a puzzled woman asked as she watched James and Valerie attack the mud on her Jeep.

"It's just a thank-you to the community—a chance to meet our neighbors," James assured her. "You a native Washingtonian?"

"No, we moved here from Idaho when my husband got transferred. Where are you from?"

"Frederick."

"Where Barbara Fritchie stuck her old gray head . . . ?"

"Yep. That's the place. House is still there."

A beefy man in sweatpants and a tee was talking to some of the guys about the Terps quarterback this season as we scrubbed the roof of his Honda.

Pickup trucks, sports cars—we even had one or two smart cars and a Mini Cooper.

It was one of those times I wished we could bottle all the smiles and good feelings we got that day. I think we hit an emotional chord with the *If your dad's car was here . . .* line. It reminded us of autumn days back on our own driveways— washing the car, mowing the grass, being part of the family— and getting a little of that here. If we couldn't do it for our own family, we could do it for someone else's. Maybe some of those people had children or grandchildren at colleges halfway across the country, and for this one afternoon we were stand-ins.

"Three Krispy Kremes . . . only three left," a large guy from the wrestling team was calling, holding the box high above his head as he walked around gathering up trash. "Going once, going twice . . ."

By four o'clock the trash was gone, the hoses, sponges, and squeegees carted off, and the assistant dean, who had arrived for the last hour with two kids in tow, couldn't have been happier. Neither could we.

"Got a good neighborhood vibe going. Great job, everybody," Marcus said.

We headed back to our dorms to clean up, then meet up again at Chipotle, and after that, on to RJ Bentley's Filling Station, a favorite local hangout.

Dave rubbed my shoulders as we sat at the bar, his big hands kneading the muscles between my shoulder blades. It felt delicious.

"Thanks for helping out today," I told him, above the music and chatter. "We had a good turnout."

"Get many takers for November?"

"Not yet. I'm trying to get people to sign up for anything at all—whatever turns them on. How about you?"

"I don't know. I'm a fair poker player."

"Anything else?"

"Paddling a canoe?"

"Uh . . . keep going."

"Shampoo a dog?"

"You're getting there," I told him.

8

BACHELOR NO MORE

I loved the periwinkle-blue dress I'd bought for Lester's wedding. Gwen helped me find it, agreeing that I'd be the "first beautiful thing" people laid eyes on when they walked into the church on Cedar Lane. It had a jewel neckline and elbow-length sleeves, with two layers of fabric beneath the hem, each a slightly different shade of periwinkle.

I'd accepted the fact that Stacy would have only a maid of honor at her wedding, and that I wasn't it, but no one was giving her a shower either, I found out. What happened was that all of Lester's friends there in West Virginia planned a so-called bachelor party, but something the girls could enjoy too—simply an evening out for everyone, with the guys paying the bill. Then the girls planned a party, guys included, and the women picked up the tab. Instead of a shower, Stacy and Les were going to throw a housewarming party after they moved in together, and friends could look around and bring them whatever they didn't have. I guess there are as many ways to get married and celebrate as there are happy couples, and once I realized that, the rest came easy.

Stacy liked our church in its wooded setting, and that made up for a lot. Dad and Sylvia were elated.

So was I, but I had my own plans. If Les thought he and Stacy could get married without any high jinks from me, he was mistaken. The first person I called after I'd found out they'd set the date was Pamela.

"We've got to do *something*!" I'd told her.

"Trust me," she said, so I did.

Now that Pamela had an associate's degree from her theater arts school, she was working for an advertising firm. But she still had a lot of contacts at the school. So she recorded the musical accompaniment to a popular Gershwin song and changed some of the words for us. A day before the wedding, she arrived with a CD.

We had celebrated Thanksgiving at a country inn near Stacy's parents' place in Virginia. The rehearsal dinner was scheduled for Friday night and the wedding for Saturday evening. Gwen and Pamela and Liz and I spent most of Friday practicing our performance. Both Gwen and Pamela had professional-sounding voices, and Liz did all right too. My job was simply to offer the toast in my beautiful new dress, so Les wouldn't suspect a thing, and then announce our surprise.

"He'll be impressed," I said at the end of our last practice session.

"He'll be in shock," Pamela said. "I'll see to that."

I was at home Saturday morning helping Les pack. Both of us had spent the night in our old bedrooms, and now he was shifting stuff around in his suitcase, ready for the honeymoon. I ironed a couple things for him and kept finding a lump in my throat more often than I liked. Even though he didn't live there anymore, and Sylvia had turned his room into a guest room, his closet shelves still held a lot of his stuff. Just seeing the old college sweatshirt hanging askew on a hanger and the top hat he'd worn one New Year's Eve as a joke made me wish for a moment I could stop time—or at least dial it back a little.

I sat on the edge of his old bed, folding the things he'd just brought up from the dryer, handing him the ones he wanted to take. I thought about how he would now have a wife with him whenever he came back to visit and wondered if we would ever have the private talks we used to have, just him and me.

"Les," I said, "how did you know that Stacy was the one for you?"

He put another shirt in his suitcase. "Bells rang, my pupils dilated, my palms perspired."

"Really. I want to know."

"Well, you know what they say: What's important isn't whom you marry but when."

"That's ridiculous."

"Think about it. If you marry when you're young and immature, chances are you'll just choose someone who's cute and makes you laugh. But when you wait till the grand old age of twenty-*eight*"— he cleared his throat—"you're more sure of what you want."

"But how did you know it was Stacy?"

"There wasn't a green light flashing, that's for sure," he said. "Mostly, I felt I'd met a person I wanted to spend the rest of my life with. That I didn't need to look any further."

"But how can you be sure?" I persisted.

"You can't. There's not just one person in the world who's your type. There's a whole group with the same likes and dislikes. But you want to spend your whole life looking for all of them? You just feel that everything's right. You're at peace with yourself." He looked over at me. "Why? Would we be talking about you, by chance? Are you in love?"

"I don't know."

"Dave? I think I met him once."

I nodded. "I really like him a lot. There are times I think I love him."

"And Patrick?"

Had I ever, in so many words, told Les that Patrick had dumped me?

"I haven't seen him in so long, Les."

"He doesn't write? Call?"

"Neither of us writes or calls anymore. I think it's better this way. We're both seeing other people. And he's in Madagascar, remember."

"True. Just take it slow and easy, Al. Enjoy being with Dave and see what happens."

"I am," I said, and grinned.

Les paused a moment, a quizzical raise of an eyebrow. Then he continued his packing. "As I said," he repeated, this time with a smile, "take—it—slow."

Saturday morning it rained, but then the weather changed, and by evening the November sky was clear once more. I had been invited to the home of one of Stacy's friend's parents', where she and the maid of honor were getting ready. Actually, I think I'd been asked primarily to keep my eye on the flower girl, the four-year-old daughter of the maid of honor, whose husband would be chauffeuring people from their hotels to the church.

Natalie was a little brunette charmer, still wearing her pajamas from her nap until it was time to put on her dress. The child was in constant motion, and trying to keep the rollers in her hair was nearly impossible. But what just about drove us all crazy was her endless chatter.

I followed her around from room to room as she checked everything out, and there seemed to be not one picture or plant or knickknack that she didn't want to touch or smell or sometimes even lick if it looked especially shiny.

"When is Momma going to come out?" she kept asking, and I knew now why the bedroom door stayed closed.

"She's helping Stacy with her makeup and her hair, and when she's done, they'll both come out," I explained.

"I'm going to have curls," Natalie said. "I'm going to have curls here and here and here." She pointed to her forehead and temples. "And when I walk, I have to take tiny steps, like this"—she demonstrated—"and even if somebody waves at me, I can't wave back, because the petals will fall off the flowers if I do, and even if you run a vacuum sweeper, it won't pick them up, because you know why? They might be wet. And once I went outside and there were petals on our driveway and I slipped and fell down and there were flowers stuck to the bottom of my shoes. . . ."

I'd left my heels at the door and had been following Natalie around barefoot—trying to read a story to her between the chatter and playing a game of old maid and listening to her plink out "Happy Birthday" with one finger on the piano. I was as relieved as she was when at last she was called into the bathroom by another of Stacy's friends to be cleaned up and ultimately delivered to the church.

"'Bye, Alice!" she called as she traipsed up the stairs. "I'll see you at the wedding! And remember not to wave."

I slipped into my beautiful periwinkle, tea-length dress, then collapsed on the sofa and rested my feet on the coffee table. I think I actually fell asleep for a moment or two before I heard a rustle from overhead and opened my eyes to see Stacy coming slowly down the stairs in a silk dress all soft and shimmery, like a candle flame.

"Oh, Stacy!" I said, going over and helping her down the last few steps as her maid of honor lifted the material off her feet.

Stacy showed me that underneath, the entire dress was lined with a pale shell of pink fabric that made it seem to glow. It had a full skirt and a sleeveless top with a plain neckline to show off her grandmother's string of pearls.

"It's perfect," I told her, admiring the short silk organza veil with a pearl-studded tiara against her short brown hair. "Lester will love it."

"It was only the second dress I tried on," she confided, "and I knew this was the one."

I got to ride in the limo with her to the church, and I went in first to make sure that Les wasn't around when she came inside.

Once Stacy was safely in the bridal room, I took my place at the podium in the vestibule. I loved standing there by the guest book, meeting all of Stacy's and Lester's friends, and greeting the many people who knew Dad from the store or Sylvia from school. Uncle Milt and Aunt Sally had not been able to come, due to my uncle's health, but their daughter, Carol, my beautiful cousin, came with her husband. She and Larry were living in Pennsylvania now and had driven down for the day.

"Carol!" I cried, throwing my arms around her.

"Gosh, Alice, you look great!" she said. She didn't look so bad herself. She had a short, breezy haircut and wore an olive-colored dress showing just the right amount of cleavage. "Did you ever think we'd see this day?"

"Nope. And neither did Les," I said, laughing.

It was time for the families to be seated, so Carol and Larry went in next, then Stacy's mom, in her lacy mauve dress.

Dad and Sylvia looked almost like a bridal couple themselves as they went down the aisle to their pew, Dad handsome in his tux and Sylvia looking exceptionally lovely in a pale blue dress with a corsage of white roses and lily of the valley.

When I got the nod that the ceremony was about to begin, I left the guest book and was seated next to Dad and Sylvia. I passed Liz and Gwen and Pamela on my way down the aisle, and we exchanged smiles. All three had come in black as we had planned, with various little jackets and colored scarves.

I slid in beside Dad, and he gave my arm a squeeze.

Candles were lit in every window, and bouquets of pink chrysanthemum, rose-colored gladiolus, and white orchids lined the altar.

The music changed now to the processional, and a door on the right-hand side opened. Out came the minister, followed by Lester, looking absolutely terrifically handsome in a midnight-blue tuxedo, a rosebud in his lapel, his face serene and happy and confident, just the way a bridegroom's should be. He had chosen one of his roommates from their house in Takoma Park to be his best man. Paul Sorenson, tall and bespectacled, was smiling almost as broadly as Lester. They stood sideways to the altar, looking expectantly up the aisle, as the maid of honor, in a rose tea-length dress, came down.

I'd thought I'd heard Natalie's chatter out in the vestibule a moment before, but now the music drowned it out. I was glad to be seated on the aisle so I could see everything, and as I swiveled around in the pew, I could tell by the smiles on the faces across from me that the flower girl was on her way.

I leaned forward a little, and there she came, in her ankle-length dress, her dark hair gently curled and lapping her shoulders, face intent, her feet in her white Mary Janes, taking slow, cautious steps along the carpet. At this rate, I thought, she'd still be in the aisle when the bride came in. Something, however, seemed amiss, and as I looked at her more closely, I realized she had something in her mouth, and she was trying hard to contain it. On first glance, it appeared her tongue was going from left to right, but as she came closer, more hesitant still, the lump was too large and too round to be her tongue. A thin blue liquid was just forming in one corner of her lips, and her eyes found mine and widened in panic.

As she came close to me in the aisle, I leaned forward and put my hand under her chin, palm up, and obediently, gratefully, she spit out a huge, once-blue gumball. It must have been someone's insane idea to keep her from talking during the ceremony, but now she soldiered on, step by step, and I caught Lester's grateful eye just long enough to know that I had played a major part in the ceremony after all. I had a sticky hand for the rest of the service, of course, but Dad loaned me his handkerchief and all was well.

Neither Les nor his bride could contain their wide smiles as Stacy came down the aisle. As they drew closer to each other and her dad released her arm at the altar, Les's expression alone seemed to enfold her in his arms. I found myself swallowing, and swallowing again. Her gown was just as beautiful from the back, for there was a huge bow at the waist with ties all the way down to the hem.

The vows were simple and personal, and one of the things the minister said to Stacy was, "Throughout your married life, remember that inside every man is a little boy." And to Lester he said, "Inside every woman is a little girl." You never know what they're going to say at a wedding.

Dad was holding my hand and also Sylvia's. I glanced over at him once and saw his eyes glistening, and I swallowed some more so I wouldn't cry. I can only guess what he was feeling, but I think he was wishing that Mom could be here to watch her boy get married.

"One down, one to go, Dad," I whispered jokingly after the last "I do" to help him pull himself together.

It was after Les and Stacy had been pronounced man and wife, and a half second before Les released Stacy from their long kiss, that a deep sigh came from the groupies, and everyone broke into laughter and applause. I don't think it bothered Les in the least, because his happy smile as they came up the aisle extended all the way to Liz and Pamela and Gwen.

The reception was held in a Bethesda hotel, and we all stood around with our glasses of champagne while the DJ announced the entrance of the parents, then the happy couple. They danced to "You're My Everything," and Les looked at Stacy as though she were the only one in the room. Then he danced with Sylvia while Stacy danced with her father, and I was surprised when, at the next number, Les danced with me.

"Wow!" I said, looking up at my brother, a married man. "Can this be happening?"

Les grinned down at me. "Better check out Dad. He still standing?"

I laughed. "Everything's going great, Les. The ceremony was beautiful."

"Next time it'll probably be you," he said.

After we were ushered into the adjoining room for our dinner, the band took a break, and we had canned music for a while as Les and Stacy made the rounds, greeting guests and meeting old friends. But after the salad course, when Les and Stacy were back at the head table, the DJ announced the toasts, and Paul Sorenson was first. To me, he always seemed the most serious of Lester's two roommates, but once he'd become the owner of a sailboat he called "Fancy Pants," I never saw him in quite the same way.

George Palamas, the other roommate, was there with his wife, and he laughed and applauded loudly when Paul told what it was like living with Lester—the man who never met a sport he didn't love, a beer he wouldn't taste, or a chance to discuss philosophy with anyone who could stand to get in marathon sessions with him.

Then it was the DJ again. "Let's hear it for Stacy's brother, Kenny Houghton, who will give the next toast. Kenny Houghton, everybody!"

People clapped as a short man I recognized as one of the ushers got up and made a warm tribute to his sister, then to Stacy and Les as a pair.

Dad was next. He jokingly told of his surprise that Les was settling down, "but after I met Stacy, I wasn't surprised at all," he said. "It seemed as natural as the return of spring, and I couldn't be happier on this day to welcome Stacy into our family."

"And now," the DJ intoned, "we will hear from Lester McKinley's delightful sister. Put your hands together, everybody, for Alice McKinley!"

Maybe it was the champagne, but I felt just as beautiful as the lovely Stacy, in my periwinkle dress and my four-inch stilettos. I took the wireless mike and stood facing both the head table and the other diners. "I just want everyone to know how much this day means to me," I said. "I'm getting rid of a brother and gaining a sister-in-law, *finally*." Everyone laughed. I turned directly to Les. "Seriously, Lester, this is really a marvelous day, and at last there's another girl in the family. You've seen me through the terrible twos, the awkward eights, the freaky fourteens . . ." Les was nodding emphatically, to more laughter from the crowd. ". . . And now you have someone else to listen to your philosophizing." Stacy smiled as though she understood exactly what I was talking about.

"But I want you to know," I said, "that the departure of Silver Spring's most eligible bachelor has left a lot of grieving women behind." I saw the smile on Lester's face suddenly freeze. "And it's only right that three of them are here today to receive public acknowledgment of their sorrow. Our apologies to Gershwin."

At that, Pamela, Liz, and Gwen rose from their chairs, the colorful scarves and jackets now removed, and with small black veils covering their hair, they soberly made their way to the microphone as laughter cascaded from table to table and Lester's mouth dropped in astonishment. The strains of "The Man I Love" filled the room, and with Pamela in the middle holding the mike, Gwen and Liz leaning in on either side, they enunciated each word perfectly as they sang:

"One day he came along,
The man we loved"

They turned their eyes mournfully toward Lester, who now sat with his hands over his face.

"And though it was all wrong,
The man we loved.
But when he came our way,
We did our best . . . to make . . . him . . . stay."

The crowd was obviously delighted, and I could tell that Les and Stacy were getting a kick out of it too, because Les had lowered his hands now and was watching, very much amused:

"We looked at him and smiled,
We freaked him out [more laughter]

'We love you so,'
He heard us shout.
We feared he'd get engaged
While all of us . . . were . . . underage."

A roar of laughter. Now Pam and Liz and Gwen turned imploringly to Lester, and he watched, arms resting on the table as the music changed tempo:

"Maybe we shall meet him someday,
Maybe later, maybe not.
For he's getting married this day
What a sad day, he was really hot."

Laughter rocked the room, and the girls hammed it up, leaning on each other for sad support:

"He's got a bed for two,
This man we love.
That's why we are so blue,
The man we love.
He'll never look our way,
We've lost . . . the . . . man . . . we . . . love."

They stood dramatically with bowed heads as the crowd burst into wild applause, then smiled and raised their arms to the audience. Before Les could get to his feet, they went to the head table and, laughing, kissed him on the cheek before going back to their chairs.

"Leave it to Alice," Les said, taking the mike. "I never know what my sister will do next. But thank you very much, Alice. I don't know when I've had so much fun. And to Pamela, Gwen, and Elizabeth, I'll see you guys on Broadway."

9

FOREVER TWENTY-ONE

Les and Stacy went to Costa Rica for their honeymoon, and when they came back, Les e-mailed me with tales of snorkeling and rock climbing, of zip lines and caves and jungles and sandy beaches in the moonlight.

Sigh, I replied. All I had was La Plata Beach, a big grassy area where students played Frisbee and soccer in nice weather and held impromptu snowball fights in winter.

When you're deep in statistical analyses and psychological theories, it's easy to compare your life with that of other people's who are living more adventurously than you, and I'll admit I checked on Patrick's Peace Corps blog more often than I should have:

Things are going great here—now I understand what people

mean by saying your second year is "the good part." Busy
with a U.N. food program grant to raise chickens, ducks, and
fish. Also trying to plan a camping trip in the forest for the
environmental club. Can you imagine me in the forest with
six teenagers? I've been working on getting a tree nursery
started and building a fuel-efficient cookstove. It's starting to
get hot as we go into our summer, and Thanksgiving came
and went. No kolokoloko *(turkey—my favorite word in*
Malagasy). But it's almost mango season.

I'm looking forward to Christmas (Krismasy here—there
are no c's in their language). It's really different. The kids
gather coconut tree fronds to decorate the church, pray all
night, then go out and walk the length of the town the next
morning, singing to wake the village. . . .

He hadn't updated his Facebook page in more than a year. It
was like Madagascar had swallowed him up. I wondered if he'd
even go back to the University of Chicago—if he'd come back to
the States at all. Which got me wondering where I would apply
for counseling jobs once I had my master's degree.

I have to say I was feeling more . . . complete? fulfilled? . . .
just by my job as registrar for SCOO—something that took me
out of the usual grind, something broader than the little world
on campus. I really enjoyed meeting the students who signed
up. I'd get their names on a posted sign-up sheet, and when
I'd call them to find out what skills or talents they had to offer,

we'd sometimes meet for coffee later, just to talk, and I think the committee members were right about some of the homesick freshmen wanting a connection. But we also had upperclassmen thinking about their own roles in the community a year or two later. It was just something I enjoyed that fit the person I was, and finding out who you really are and what you want out of life is one of the major goals of college, they say.

Valerie and I—and, to a certain extent, Abby—were *so* into it, but not so much Claire, and that was okay. We weren't out to twist arms, just to offer a chance to be more involved in the community. Claire, in fact, wanted us more involved in *her* life. What she wanted was for at least two of us to buy an assistantship in Magic Myst and make her rich, ours to come later. She'd already found one buyer but figured she needed three to support her.

"I'm sorry, Claire, I just can't afford either the money or the time," I told her honestly.

"Even if it means doubling or tripling your investment? The more you sell, the more you make from what your recruits sell, until finally you don't have to work at it much at all."

"And by then I would have failed most of my courses," I explained, and didn't add that as much as I relied on makeup, I just couldn't see trying to turn all my friends into Magic Myst models.

Abby heard us talking in my dorm room and came over.

"What happened to the half of a corned beef sandwich I had in my little fridge?" she asked.

"Oh. Was that yours?" Claire said, turning around.

"Duh . . . Yes? One room . . . two people? So if I didn't eat it, then . . . ?"

"Sorry. I guess maybe I thought you didn't want it and hadn't thrown it away yet," Claire said, avoiding Abby's eyes as she picked up her bag to leave.

"Claire, my Fritos are gone, and even the Mars bar I had on the window ledge."

"I'm sorry!" Claire said sheepishly. "Don't leave stuff lying around to tempt me."

I studied her more closely. She *had* lost some weight, and I didn't think it was intentional.

"Claire, don't you have any money left to buy food?" I asked.

"Hey, I'm doing fine," she said. "Just two more assistantships, and I'm set."

The leaf-raking event the last weekend of November was a big success too. Marcus and James rode around campus in the back of a pickup, holding rakes high in the air and shouting through a megaphone, SO COME ON OUT! Signs had been posted in all the buildings.

Students wearing SCOO armbands that we'd had made up descended on neighborhoods within two blocks of the campus—neighborhoods where there had been complaints before about drinking parties that lasted till three in the morning, street signs turned around and other stupid acts of vandalism to celebrate a winning game.

I was obviously enjoying being part of the initiative more than Dave was, but he gamely went along with whatever we assigned him to do. Meanwhile, the list of possible ways students offered to help the community lengthened: play chess, braid hair, wrap presents, wash windows, bathe dogs, tutor math, tutor English, help with income taxes, cook meals, play the trombone. . . .

"You know, we could turn this into a business once we left school," Valerie mused one night. "Like a matchmaking service for the community."

"Not you, too!" I said. "After claiming she didn't want the pressure, Abby says she's going to start one of those cupcake businesses and give those Georgetown shops some competition. What *are* you going to do after graduation, Val?"

"If I can't find work as a museum curator?" She stretched out her long legs the length of her bed until her pink painted toenails touched the frame. "I'd like to spend ten years doing a different job every year and see what I do best."

I smiled at the thought. "Yeah? And how could you manage that? Where would you get the experience?"

"I'd be one of those impersonators. You know, present myself as Dr. Valerie Robbins, horticultural expert, and the next year I'd be Val Robbins, nightclub singer. And then I'd be a tour guide around the Capitol or a taxi driver in Virginia, and—damn!—I'd be convincing."

"You would too. Just don't fly commercial planes, please."

Valerie sighed and turned over on her side. "What do you think we'll really do, Alice? I bet you'll marry Dave."

I was startled. "What even makes you think he wants us to marry?"

She gave me "the smile."

"What?"

"I just do. He wants to."

"He's just graduating. He doesn't even have a job yet."

"He will."

"You're crazy, Val. I've got two years of school ahead of me, counting my master's."

"Well, I've got only one, but after I finish my ten years of impersonations, I'd like to find myself at the altar with somebody."

"You'll find yourself in prison, that's what, and the newspapers will quote somebody saying, 'I never really believed she was a brain surgeon.'"

Dave and I were growing even closer, though. He drove me to Silver Spring once when I was helping out at the Melody Inn for the holiday rush, and afterward he picked me up and we went out to dinner with Dad and Sylvia. Another time we went to Cumberland on a Sunday to celebrate his folks' thirtieth anniversary.

"How's the resume going?" I asked him.

"I want to be ready to e-mail it by April, see if I can line up some interviews over the spring," he told me.

Meanwhile, Abby and Claire weren't hitting it off, and Claire had dropped one of her classes to devote more time to Magic Myst. We all suspected she was going hungry most days and didn't want to admit it, and she seemed upset with us too for not joining the select company of executive assistants, of which there were still only two for the whole U of Maryland campus.

Then one night she surprised us all by taking the three of us to dinner at Ledo's. She'd just recruited her second executive assistant and had received her bonus. We were celebrating.

"It's great, Claire!" Val told her. "Who's the girl?"

"A sophomore from Potomac," Claire said, indicating to the waiter that she was to get the check, and we all gave him our orders.

"I think Madison's furious that she didn't find Ashley first," Claire continued.

"Madison?"

"She's the senior, the other girl Sandra recruited. We were supposed to be best friends, combing the campus and sharing ideas, and instead we're competing all the time. It's like she thinks the upperclassmen are strictly her territory or something."

Someone's stomach rumbled and it wasn't mine. When bread was delivered to the table, Claire took the first piece before passing the basket around and spread olive oil on it before popping it into her mouth.

"Beautiful nails, Claire," I said, admiring the slim fingers that took another piece of bread and, this time, smeared it first with oil, then added a layer of cheese from the cheese shaker before eating it. "Any chance those fingers could help wrap presents next week? The U is paying for gift wrap and ribbons, and we're advertising that people in the immediate neighborhood can bring their gifts to us and we'll wrap them for free."

"Wow! I'm impressed! SCOO is really taking off," said Abby. "Where is this happening?"

"Adele Stamp," I said, which is the name of our student union building. "I doubt we'll get many guys, but we could be surprised."

"I'll think about it," Claire said as our entrées arrived, "but I'd love to recruit another executive assistant by then."

I think we talked about Lester's honeymoon over dinner, and Valerie's problems buying jeans for tall figures, and Abby's boyfriend falling asleep during movies, but finally we were all thanking Claire for a great dinner and persuading her to let us pay the tip, which wasn't a lot, divided among the three of us.

But strangely, when Val and I got back to our dorm room, I saw her writing some figures beside her desk calendar, and she said, "Alice, do you realize that this little celebration dinner, courtesy of Claire, cost us $37.95 a piece? Cost me that much, anyway."

"What?" I said, pausing there in the doorway, then closing the door in case Claire was listening. "How?"

"Five bucks each for the tip, and then we checked off the Magic Myst items we agreed to buy from the list Claire passed around just before the spumoni. Items at the top, prices at the bottom. Remember? I checked the moisturizer and the mascara, and my bill will come to $37.95, not counting tax. What was yours?"

I took the copy Val was holding and looked it over. I'd checked the loose powder for $19. Fortunately, the ice cream had arrived, and I'd passed the paper on. We'd been had.

"I hope Claire ate a hearty meal, because it's the last she'll be getting from me for a long time," I said. "But it's our fault. Always read the fine print."

Dave made a big deal out of my twenty-first birthday. Everyone did. Liz, Pam, Gwen, and I all celebrated each other's, no matter where we were. Liz sent flowers from Vermont, and Pamela sent a male stripper. I'd wondered about the phone call I'd received asking if I would be in my dorm at 4:45 p.m. for a special delivery. I asked Val to be there too, just in case it was a rapist or something, but when I answered the knock, here was this tall, broad-shouldered guy dressed to the nines, who handed me a bottle of wine and began singing a sultry version of "I've Got You Under My Skin" as he took off his jacket.

Claire and Abby heard him and came out of their room, and then a passing junior from down the hall stopped to listen and sent out a cell phone alert. By the time the singing stripper got down to his belt and lowered his pants, the hall was packed with girls and a few guys all watching the elegant way he stepped out of his trousers and flung them aside, then slowly removed his socks. Val and I sat cross-legged on her bed and giggled like fifth graders. I didn't know if we were supposed to tuck dollar bills into his red-spangled G-string or not, but that was about the time he ended the song.

And then, telling me he was only following instructions, he came over to the bed, excused Val, to much laughter, and then, taking her place, gave me one of those theatrically passionate kisses that drew laughter and applause from the hallway.

After that, professional that he was, he backed off, wished me a happy birthday, and with lightning speed, the pants were on again, the shirt, the jacket, the socks, and in a final tribute to twenty-one, he tossed me a red-spangled G-string. It could not possibly have been the one he'd been wearing, but the others gasped as though he'd magically removed his own somehow, and then he was gone.

My cell phone was ringing, and when I picked it up, it was Pamela.

"Happy birthday," she said, and we laughed together. "Just wanted to juice up your day a little. Wish I could have been there."

"You gave the whole floor a thrill," I told her. "Thanks for remembering, you big goof!"

That night Dave took me to the Four Seasons Hotel in Georgetown for a six-course dinner, including wine and cherries jubilee. Afterward we walked along Georgetown's waterfront, stopping often to kiss. I loved being wrapped in his arms—the warmth of them—and was glad he'd reserved a room for us there, so we wouldn't have to sleep in a dorm room that night. We lay in bed together, propped up on pillows so we could see the lights on the river below, the occasional boat going by, the lamps on the pier.

"Did you enjoy the evening?" Dave asked me.

"Very much," I told him. "Thank you, Dave. You know what a girl likes."

"Hope so," he said. "What *this* girl likes, anyway."

As I lay in that drowsy bliss just before sleep pulls you in, I revisited the events of the day. Twenty-one, the so-called magic number. I remembered that long-ago promise Patrick had made to me the summer before seventh grade—that he would call me, no matter where I was, on my twenty-first birthday, and if I wasn't engaged, we'd make a date for New Year's Eve. I wondered idly if Patrick even remembered my cell phone number, much less my birthday. Of course, no telling where he was now, or who he was with, and I drifted off to sleep, trying to figure out if the international dateline made my birthday yesterday or tomorrow in Africa. . . .

I had dinner at home the next night back in Silver Spring. Stacy was holding exercise classes for a weekend retreat, but Les drove in from West Virginia for the occasion. That made it really special.

"Wow!" I said. "Wish I could turn twenty-one every birthday."

"It's always good to have you here, honey," Dad said, giving me one of his bear hugs. "You'll never be too old for this."

Sylvia came out of the kitchen holding a six-layer cake she had made, and Les brought both wine and chocolates, so we were all set.

It was somewhere between the steak and the cake that the phone rang. Dad answered, and it was Aunt Sally. She and I used to talk much more than we did now, but Sylvia had told her I'd be here for dinner.

"We were just about to have our dessert, Sal, but we're only sitting around the table talking. . . . *Of course* you may. Here she is," Dad said.

I took the phone. "Hi, Aunt Sally."

"Oh, Alice." What a familiar, comforting voice hers was. But she must have felt the same about mine. "I declare, you sound more like your mother all the time. Marie would have been so pleased."

"Well, I am too," I said honestly. "How are you and Uncle Milt?"

"We're older—and we look it—but that's no surprise. I only hope that he goes first so he won't be left alone after I'm gone. None of our friends understand that. They think it sounds awful, but it's not."

Having just finished a funky course called Funerals and Fabrications in American Life, about the way commercial funeral establishments try to make us feel in order to buy their most expensive products, and the wide variety of emotions people can experience at the death of a loved one, I was perfectly able to see that this may well be a true expression of love and empathy.

"It doesn't seem that way to me at all, Aunt Sally," I said.

"And now you're twenty-one and a junior in college! Oh my goodness!" she said.

Here come the warnings, I thought—sex, alcohol, drugs, drinking, and how she's worried about Les and me all these years. I settled back in my chair while the others went about clearing the table, smiling my way.

"How I remember my twenty-first birthday!" she said. "I wasn't much of a drinker, you know. In fact, I'd hardly had anything more than a sip or two of champagne on New Year's Eve before that, but I went to a dance with a boy, and all my friends were at our table, and I had half a glass of wine, and we danced . . ."

Get ready, I told myself.

". . . and, Alice, I don't think I ever danced so well in my whole life!"

I blinked.

"I mean, it was like my legs were loose at the hips, but they knew just what to do, as though the floor were polished glass. I glided, I slid, I twisted, I whirled like nobody's business. When we got back to the table, I finished the glass of wine, and we danced some more. It was the most fabulous night on the dance floor, the night I turned twenty-one!"

Les saw the look on my face and paused with a bowl of green beans in his hands. Aunt Sally and I talked a little more, and after we said good-bye, I turned to Les: "I'm not the only one who's changing," I said, and told him about our conversation.

"Darn!" he said. "I miss the old Aunt Sally."

"Oh, I'm sure she's still around," I said. "You just have to press the right buttons."

Dad and Sylvia were excited about a trip to France in August and showed us brochures of all the places they planned to visit. I'd already promised to help out at the store for the two weeks they'd be gone.

"I love that you're getting away, Dad," I told him. "You need a break from the store."

"Well, I've never been to France, and Sylvia's always wanted to go back, so this seems like a good time to do it," he said.

After we feasted on Sylvia's cake, Dad and Sylvia insisted I wasn't to do dishes on my birthday, so Les and I sat on the back porch talking, our feet sharing the wicker hassock, each of us sinking low in a chintz-covered chair. Fireflies flitted here and there over the backyard, reminding me of the lights on the river the night before, lying there in Dave's arms.

"Got any big plans for this summer?" Les asked.

I played it cool. "Huge. I've got a part-time job in the public relations office at the U, believe it or not. Just collecting names and addresses for a database—people in the community who responded to our student outreach program, small-time donors, community leaders. . . . We're trying to expand the registry we started last September."

"They're paying you for this? Or is this still part of that volunteer project?"

"Low pay, but it's worthwhile, and of course I'll help out at the Melody Inn while Dad's gone."

Les was looking at me strangely. "And that's it? This is your summer?"

I couldn't hold back any longer. Just before dinner, I'd received an e-mail from Liz, and I'd been trying to figure out how to approach the subject with Dad.

"Okay, so there's one more thing—I'm going to California!" I said breathlessly, keeping my voice low. "Liz and Pam and Gwen and I made a deal that right after we graduated from college, we'd rent a car and drive to the West Coast for a vacation. Dad's promised me a car when I graduate, so if I could talk him into giving it to me a year early—"

"Whoa, whoa, and wow!" Les said. "And you're doing this a year early because . . . ?"

"Because Elizabeth's decided to take a year off after she graduates and teach in a rural school where only a BA is required, then enter a master's program later."

Lester continued to stare at me. "So? And this means . . . ?"

"This means that *next* summer she'll be interviewing for jobs, so she wants to take that long trip to California now, the minute classes are over at Bennington. I'm so psyched!"

Les settled down a little farther in his chair, as if knowing he was in for the long haul. "I take it you haven't asked Dad yet for the car."

"Actually . . . no. It would be a used one, of course. A red convertible would be perfect, and Pamela's offered to be the driver."

"Uh . . . I think the trip to California is a great idea, but you might want to rethink the convertible and the driver," said Les.

I crossed my arms over my chest. "I'm so ready for a vacation!" I told him. "With Dad and Sylvia preoccupied with Paris, I figure they'll be okay with me cutting loose for a while."

"Sounds good to me," said Les. "Where does Dave fit into the picture?"

"Well, he's graduating later this month and has some job

leads. I'm happy for him. But . . ." I avoided Lester's eyes. "I get the feeling that he's going to propose one of these days."

"Really! Guess you guys *are* serious."

I gave him a quick glance and looked away again. "And I'm not sure I want him to yet. I mean, how do you keep a guy from popping the question?"

"Have you tried anti-proposal spray? The heavy-duty kind you can use in the dark?"

Les always makes me laugh. I kicked his feet off the hassock. "Be serious," I told him.

"Okay. Whatever you do, though, be honest. If you want to wait, just say so."

"But maybe I don't. Maybe I want to get married already. And . . ." I reached for my glass of iced tea and sat jiggling it slightly, watching the shifting of the ice cubes.

"You might want to pay attention to those 'maybes,'" he said. And when I didn't respond, he added, "Al, you're only twenty-one. If you live to be eighty-four, you've lived only a fourth of your life so far. If you live to be a hundred and five, it's only a fifth of your life. If you live—"

"Okay, okay, I get it. Maybe I'll just go to California and stay there. Maybe the four of us will climb into that red convertible and ride off into the sunset."

"Well, if Pamela's driving, be sure your life insurance payments are up-to-date, and make me the beneficiary," said Les.

10
TAKING OFF

When Dad heard we wanted to drive to California, he freaked out. Sylvia, too. "It will take half your vacation just getting there and back," he said.

"Why don't you take a train out, so you can see the country, then fly back?" Sylvia suggested.

That appealed, actually. Amtrak had a special deal with an airline, so we bought our tickets and worked out an itinerary. All but Gwen. She had proven herself such a valuable lab assistant, that she'd been hired for the summer to work with a doctor researching the human placenta. Any med student would envy her the job.

"I wish you'd reconsider and come with us," I told her on the phone after my last class. I was standing out in front of the dorm with some of my stuff, waiting for Dad.

"I wish I could too, but from now on, my summers are booked till I get that 'MD' after my name. Send me a card from Big Sur, one of the places I've always wanted to see," she said.

I went to Dave's graduation and presented him with a neat desk set—a heavy, square acrylic paperweight and a letter opener with an acrylic handle. The clear acrylic had tiny parts of watches buried in it—little gears and wheels and springs.

"For the up-and-coming businessman," I said, kissing him on the cheek. He pulled me closer, and we had a real kiss.

I didn't spend the night with him because his parents were taking us out to dinner. Also, I was getting up early the next morning to finish packing for the train ride.

Our good-bye kiss away from his parents said it all, my body molded into his. He made me promise to spend a weekend in Cumberland with him as soon as I got back.

"Alone," he added. "No girlfriends." He grinned. "Have a good time, now. Two weeks is all you get."

Pam and Liz and I boarded the train as excited as we'd been years ago when we took Amtrak to visit Aunt Sally in Chicago. This time we had two economy sleepers across the aisle from each other. Each had two armchairs, facing each other, which joined to make a bed at night, and a top bunk that folded down from the ceiling. Since we needed only three beds, we dumped all our extra stuff on one of the top bunks. We decided to take turns sleeping in the room with the extra bunk. The shower and toilets were on the lower level of the car.

As we pulled out of Union Station, all three of us squeezed in one of the rooms, Pamela said, "Remember our last train trip, when those guys were horsing around outside the window, trying to see in?" We all laughed.

"And we'll *never* forget the man you picked up, Pamela, who tried to get in your room later," Liz teased.

"Tried to get in her pants!" I added.

"*He* tried to pick *me* up! I only agreed to have dinner with him," Pamela argued.

"And Aunt Sally almost passed out when we told her," I said, and we laughed some more.

An attendant came by to make sure we knew how to use all the room amenities and ask if we needed a wake-up call the next morning. Then, after the conductor had taken our tickets and someone had come by to make our dinner reservations, we were free to move about the train.

In the dining car we were seated across the aisle from five guys who were all trying to cram in at one table.

"Now, you three lovely ladies wouldn't object to having one of these fine gentlemen at your table, would you?" the chief dining room steward asked, smiling at us, and Pamela instantly moved over to make room.

We introduced ourselves.

"Tom, Dick and Harry, Moe and Joe," said the blond guy sitting opposite me, giving fictitious names to himself and his friends. We went along with the joke because it was easy to remember.

Four of them, it turned out, had just graduated from Georgetown University, the other from American, and they were giving themselves a cross-country train trip as a graduation present: Washington to San Francisco, then up to Seattle, then back east again, making multiple stops along the way. They were traveling coach class, which meant they had reclining seats instead of beds, no showers, and they had to pay for their food. We sleeping-car passengers had meals included in our fare.

So we told the guys they could have our desserts, and we ordered cheesecake for the three of us and gave it all to them. Afterward we sat in the lounge car and talked—their real names were Drew, Andy, George, and Kyle, though "Moe" for Moses was authentic. As the train went through the Cumberland Gap, I thought of Dave, and when it was too dark to see out, we found two tables on the lower level and played gin rummy and drank beer until eleven.

"Gosh, they're nice!" Liz said after we got back to our sleeper. "Moe is so *funny!*"

"We lucked out," said Pamela. "We get them the whole way to San Francisco."

Our agreement was that Pamela was to sleep solo the first night from Washington to Chicago, where we changed trains. Then Liz would get a room to herself from Chicago to Denver, and I got to have it from Denver to San Francisco.

Elizabeth decided to take her shower at night in case there was a waiting line in the morning, so she picked up her shampoo and robe and towel and headed downstairs while the attendant finished making up our beds. Almost immediately, however, she was back upstairs and collapsed on the lower bunk of our compartment, her face as pink as her T-shirt.

"Now what?" asked Pamela.

"All I did was open the door, and there stood a middle-aged man completely naked!" she gasped.

"What was he? A flasher?" said Pamela.

"No! He was drying off. He was as startled as I was. I am *so* embarrassed!"

The attendant returned with more sheets and smiled as he said, "What you have to remember, ladies, when *you're* in the shower, is to push that lock all the way. We get at least one surprise per trip." He grinned as he put a chocolate on each pillow before he wished us good night.

Elizabeth covered her face. "One of you come down with me and guard the door while I'm in there!" she said.

Now she was sounding like the old Elizabeth again.

"That's like your opening the wrong door at the Gap the summer you moved to Silver Spring," Pamela said to me. "And there stood Patrick Long, in all his glory."

"Not quite," I said. "He had his Jockeys on."

"Please!" Elizabeth begged. "Somebody go back down with me and see if that man's out of the shower. What'll I say if I meet him in the dining car tomorrow?"

"How about, 'Nice legs'?" Pamela suggested.

"Or, 'Sorry, I didn't recognize you with your clothes on,'" I said.

"You guys are no help," Elizabeth said, but she finally went back down alone. Pamela said good night and went in her room, and I climbed up on the top bunk of ours and settled down. When Elizabeth came back up, she had a clean, soapy smell, and her dark hair glistened as she toweled it dry. I had my light off, but I could see her reflection in the mirror on our wall as she thoughtfully combed out the tangles. It came to me then that she finally looked happy. She wasn't bone skinny like she used to be.

"I wish all guys were like those five we met at dinner," she said. "Do you realize that not one of them swore the whole evening? Nobody got sloshed, no one was crude."

I propped up my head on my hand. "I think that when guys get more mature, they don't try to show off so much. Girls are the same way. After you start working toward a career, you let other things define you."

"I guess that's it," said Liz.

We heard the train whistle in the dark, and then it started up again after its stop in Pittsburgh. I lifted my shade once in the night to see a full moon over the silhouette of trees, and then I let the train rock me back to sleep.

The guys looked pretty sleepy the next morning, especially Moe, who, being the tallest at six foot three, hadn't slept all night.

"*Look* at them!" Andy grumbled to George at breakfast, casting a scornful glance our way. "Hair combed, bright-eyed . . . Don't they make you sick?"

"That's 'cause we're *rich*!" Pamela teased. "We *saved* up our money for a sleeper."

"Lucky you," said Kyle.

At that exact moment a middle-aged man came up the aisle and stopped at our table, and Elizabeth's face instantly turned bright red. As the guys gawked, the man looked at Elizabeth and, with a twinkle in his eye, said, "Well, now that you know me intimately, I guess I should wish you a pleasant trip." And he went on his way.

"Whaaaat?" asked Drew, leaning forward and staring at Elizabeth, who was laughing now but hiding her face in her hands.

"Oh, she just picks up stray guys," I said.

"Like puppies, you know. Can't resist them," Pamela said. Then she added, "They were in the shower together last night."

"Well!" said Moe. "This is going to be *some* trip!"

On our five-hour layover in Chicago, the guys headed off for a museum. They invited us to come with them, but we were having lunch with Aunt Sally and Uncle Milt, so we just said we'd see them back at the station when it was time to board the California Zephyr.

We had a little time before lunch, so we walked over to the Sears Tower and took the elevator to the observation deck, where we could see out over Chicago and Lake Michigan. It was impossible, of course, not to think of Patrick and my visit to him at the University of Chicago. I could see its Rockefeller Chapel as well as the beach below us where Patrick and I had walked that first day. *He's on the other side of the world now,* I told myself. That part of my life was over.

When we got back to the train station, Aunt Sally and Uncle Milt were waiting with outstretched arms. Aunt Sally almost squeezed me to death.

"Young ladies, that's what you are!" she kept saying, grabbing each of us by the shoulders and looking us over.

"It's been too long, Alice," Uncle Milt said, giving me a big hug.

They took us to a Japanese restaurant that Carol had recommended, and we talked as fast as we could, describing Lester's wedding, catching up on each other's lives.

"I still remember our last visit here—how Carol took us to all those fantastic shops and we tried on hats," Elizabeth said.

"And you were so upset, Sally, about the man who tried to get in my room on the train," said Pamela.

"Oh, I remember *that* like it was yesterday!" Aunt Sally said. "You girls were so young, *anything* could have happened."

As we talked, I studied my aunt and uncle. They definitely looked older than when I'd seen them last. Aunt Sally's hair was all white now, not just white in places, and Uncle Milt was a lot thinner.

I didn't like seeing them growing older. They were the only relatives I really knew well. When they drove us back to the station, Aunt Sally gave me an extra hug. "I love you, dear," she said. "And your mother loved you too."

* * *

After we'd boarded the train to California that afternoon, we went through the coach cars looking for the guys, since coach passengers aren't allowed in the sleeping cars, and found them looking somewhat refreshed, all but Moe and George, who had reclined in their seats as far back as they could go but who still, obviously, were not sleeping.

We asked for a "table for eight" in the dining car that night and were given two tables across from each other, Kyle sitting with us this time. The guys told us about their morning at the Museum of Science and Industry, but halfway through dinner, we saw Moe leaning against the window on their side of the aisle, eyes closed. And I couldn't believe my ears when I heard Elizabeth say, "We've got an extra bed, Moe. Do you want to use it?"

Pamela and I stared. Elizabeth? *Elizabeth* said that? I realized it was her turn to sleep in the room with the extra bunk that night, and it was hers to do with as she pleased, but I never would have expected that.

Moe opened his eyes. "You mean it?"

"Hey, *I'm* sleepy too!" said George.

"Me too!" chimed in Drew and Andy.

"You don't take her up on it, I will," said Kyle.

"Is it allowed?" Moe asked.

Elizabeth shrugged. "I don't know," she said, lowering her voice, "but we could smuggle you in."

That became the evening's project, to somehow smuggle six-foot-three Moe into the spare bunk without the attendant knowing.

"We could always dress him up as a woman, Elizabeth, and then if the attendant saw him in your room, he wouldn't be so shocked," said Pamela. We were in the lounge car now, even though it was too dark to see out.

Moe rolled his eyes. "That was a Marilyn Monroe movie, wasn't it?"

"I've got an extra pair of pajamas," said Elizabeth.

"They just might reach his knees," said Drew.

"Wig?" asked George. "Anybody got a wig?"

We knew that the train attendants had probably seen everything there was to see, but we didn't want Moe to have to pay extra for the bed. So after the attendant had made up our beds for the night, we took all the stuff we'd stored on the extra bunk and crammed it under the lower bunks.

Elizabeth stayed in her room with the curtain closed, Pamela kept watch down the hall, and as soon as the attendant went to the lower level to make up a bed down there, I went to the observation car and got Moe, and he ducked into Elizabeth's room. Then Pamela and I dived in after him, and we closed the glass door behind the thick blue curtain.

Pamela, Elizabeth, and I had to crawl onto the bottom bunk to leave room for Moe to move. We were giggling like grade school kids.

He had changed into sweatpants and a T-shirt and was in his stocking feet. He bent down so he could see us. "Hey, I really appreciate this," he said, and put one hand over his heart. "I solemnly swear to keep my hands to myself and stay in the top bunk." He looked at Elizabeth. "You can even keep the curtain open a little so your friends can check up on me, if you want."

"We trust you," said Elizabeth. "I'll just ring for the attendant if you molest me." She pointed to the round yellow button on the wall by her bed.

"You've got a call button up there too," I told him.

"You mean if Elizabeth molests *me*, I can call for the attendant?" Moe asked.

"For tonight, you're at the mercy of Elizabeth," Pamela told him.

"Lucky me," said Moe.

I was the first one awake in the morning. I snapped on my light long enough to see that it was 6:57, but I wasn't quite ready to get up yet, so I turned off the light again and nestled down under the blanket. I could hear a door sliding open now and then from out in the hall and the attendant's cheery, "Good morning!" Suddenly I bolted straight up. I remembered that we had requested a wake-up call at seven.

Why on earth had we requested wake-up calls? Liz, I think, had said she didn't want to be the last one straggling down to the restrooms with all the other passengers staring at her, and Pamela had said, "Whatever." A wake-up call didn't mean you had to get up.

The attendant was going to be knocking on our doors, though. Would he come in the rooms or what?

I leaned down and peeked out one side of our curtain to see if

Elizabeth was up. Then I gasped, because the curtain across from us was askew, and a man's huge foot was plastered against the glass.

"Pamela!" I cried.

There was a murmur from below. "Huh?"

"Moe!" I said. "His foot!"

"*Huh?*" Pamela said, more loudly. I heard her sheets rustle.

"Oh, cripes!" she said, reaching out and fumbling with the lock. She had just slid the door open a couple inches when the attendant appeared outside, his back to us and his hand up, ready to knock on Elizabeth's door. He paused, looking at the man's foot. Then he knocked.

We didn't know what to do, so we didn't do anything. Just froze.

There was a pause, and the attendant knocked again. Then the door slid open and Elizabeth's face appeared. Only she too was staring up at Moe's leg dangling down from the upper bunk, his foot against the glass.

"Seven o'clock!" the attendant said, smiling.

"It's not what you think!" Elizabeth choked. "He was just so tired, and he promised he wouldn't do anything, and . . ."

"Oh, Elizabeth, shut up, shut up!" Pamela muttered from below.

The foot suddenly disappeared from the window.

"Miss," said the attendant quietly, leaning into Elizabeth's room so as not to be heard all up and down the hall, "you paid for this room, and you can do whatever you like in it, as long as you don't disturb the other guests."

Pamela and I fell back on our beds in silent laughter.

"Coffee and juice down the hall," the attendant said. Then he knocked on our door. "Seven o'clock!" he said cheerily. I couldn't see his face, but I could hear the smile in his voice, and then his chuckle as he moved on down the hall.

It was a trip we'd never forget. We were in Denver just after breakfast and spent almost the whole day in the observation car with the guys as the California Zephyr slowly climbed toward Winter Park, through Fraser Canyon, Granby, and Glenwood Springs, where the Roaring Fork River met the Colorado. We cheered when a raft-load of guys all stood up and mooned us and cheered again when a load of female rafters bared their breasts at the train. "See that a lot on weekends," our attendant told us later.

Having left peach orchards in Maryland we were now seeing patches of snow up in the mountains, and snow-covered peaks in the distance. Most of the wildlife appeared in the early morning or at dusk.

"What's that dog doing way out here?" I mused, watching a lone creature slink across a barren hill some distance from the train.

"That's not a dog, that's a coyote," Kyle said, giving my ribs a poke.

"A coyote! I just saw a coyote!" I exclaimed, fascinated.

And a few minutes later Elizabeth cried, "Deer! A whole pack!"

"Those aren't deer, they're antelope, and it's not a pack, it's a herd," Moe said. "Don't you city girls know *anything*?"

Sometimes we sat on the guys' laps to make room for other passengers in the observation car or took a break and went to our compartments to nap. George, it turned out, had his guitar with him, and when we came back once to the lounge, he was softly playing, some of the passengers singing along. There was a movie in the lounge that night, but again we played cards on the floor below, and then it was my turn to have our second bedroom. This time I let George have the top bunk. The attendant didn't blink an eye when he discovered our new roommate, and I didn't feel the need to explain.

The eight of us stuck pretty much together the rest of the trip, eating our meals at adjoining tables and hanging out in coach or in the observation car. We talked about college and jobs and plans, and when we reached San Francisco, the guys insisted on taking us out to dinner at a great restaurant on the Bay as thanks for sharing our room and our desserts.

We exchanged names and addresses, and when we parted at last, we gave each of the guys a kiss and a hug. I couldn't tell if they seemed more like boyfriends or brothers. Just friends, I guess, and it felt good.

That night, in a Holiday Inn, Elizabeth said, "Well, now I can say I've slept with a man!" and laughed. But I noticed she looked particularly pleased.

We rented a sky-blue Honda and, with a map from AAA, set off for Yosemite, where we hiked until our legs would take no more. After a night in a lodge, we headed down to Sequoia

National Park and stayed even longer than we had planned. There was something about the huge trees—big enough to drive a car through, to *live* in, actually—something so fatherly about their age, so grandfatherly, that we almost felt we ought to hug them before we took off again.

"Doesn't it make everything else seem small?" said Elizabeth. "I don't mean in size, I mean in importance. All that these trees have lived through, yet here we are, worrying about grades and guys and weight and . . . and life. Trees don't worry. They just go right on being trees."

"Very profound, Liz, except you're not a tree," said Pamela. "You can't just stand in one place and be fed through your roots. You do have to earn a living eventually."

"And you can't reproduce just by standing there shedding acorns or something," I told her.

"Why is it that no matter what we're talking about, you two always bring it back to sex?" Liz asked, and suddenly we all started to laugh. For just a minute the old Elizabeth was back again, and we were sort of glad to have her.

The next day, after we had called home to let people know where we were, we made the long drive to L.A., where we did Universal Studios and the tour of movie stars' houses—even a day at Disneyland and a little shopping on Rodeo Drive, just to say we'd been there. Then we headed back up the coast to Hearst Castle and, after some time there, started our long-awaited drive up Highway One through Big Sur toward Carmel and the Monterey Peninsula.

It was an amazing drive, with the ocean to our left and the towering rocky wall on our right. We let Pamela do most of the driving because she enjoyed it more than we did and was good at it. It wasn't quite fair, because we got to see a lot more of the scenery than she did, but we all were having a fantastic time.

And then . . . a tire blew.

Elizabeth, of course, screamed, but all Pamela said was "Dear God." It was the closest I'd ever heard Pamela come to praying. There was scarcely any shoulder on the road at all, neither rock side nor cliff side, but Pamela carefully edged the Honda over as close to the wall as she could get and turned on the emergency blinkers.

The problem was that we were on a curve, and any car coming along the narrow road from the south, if the driver was going too fast, might plow into us from behind. I think we all had visions of being rammed at seventy miles an hour and sent hurtling through the air and over the cliff.

"We're going to die!" came a soft wail from the backseat.

"Elizabeth, will you shut up!" I snapped, only because she'd said what we were all feeling. "Does anyone know how to change a tire?" I sure didn't, and I doubted that Elizabeth did. I looked hopefully at Pamela. She shook her head.

Now I began to panic.

A car eased past us from behind and went on. Nobody going in the opposite direction stopped to help because there was no good place to stop.

"We're going to get hit!" Elizabeth said shakily. "It's only a matter of time."

"Then get out of the car and stand back there at the curve and wave your panties or something," Pamela said irritably.

I began to wonder too if it might be safer if we all got out of the car. I had helped pack the trunk and hadn't seen any emergency flares.

Just then a car pulled up behind us, and we all turned to see two men sitting in the front seat, talking to each other and looking at us. One of them got out and came along Pamela's side. He had on jeans and a Heineken T-shirt, about thirty, I guessed, with tattoos up and down both arms.

"Keep the door locked, Pamela," I warned her. "Just lower the window a couple of inches."

Pamela started the engine long enough to roll down the window slightly, then turned the key again.

The man was looking us over. He put his face to the back window and studied Elizabeth, then grinned at Pamela and me. He also grinned at the second man, who was getting out of the car now and coming up behind us.

"P-Pamela!" Elizabeth bleated.

I slowly pulled out my cell phone and pressed 9-1-1.

"Looks like you girls got trouble," the man said.

"I'm afraid so," Pamela said. And, noticing my cell phone, she added, "We're calling Triple A."

I nudged Pamela and tilted my cell phone toward her. *No signal,* it read.

The man gave a short laugh. "She's calling Triple A," he said to his friend, and the friend laughed too. And then, to us, he said, "Well, they'll be here in about three or four hours, I'd guess. You're a long way from the nearest garage, sweetheart."

I heard Elizabeth whimper from the backseat. I tried to swallow, but my throat was dry.

"Why don't you let us take you to wherever you're going?" the man said. "You can leave your blinkers on and the key behind the sun visor. Just tell Triple A to bring an extra man to drive the car on into Carmel."

"No," said Pamela. "I think we'd better stay with the car."

The men turned away from us and started whispering to each other as another car slowly made its way around us from behind.

"Don't open the door, Pamela," I repeated.

"Oh, God!" Elizabeth wailed softly. "I'd rather go off the cliff than be murdered or raped."

When both men turned toward the car again, I leaned across Pamela and said to them, "We were hoping someone would offer to change the tire for us. We'd be glad to pay."

"Be happy to, sweetheart, but we'd need your spare. Why don't you give us your key and we'll see what kind of jack you have. Might need a hydraulic."

Pamela looked at me. "They don't need the key," she whispered. "I can unlock the trunk from in here. Should I?"

I thought it over.

"Well, we're sure not giving them the key or they could get in here," I murmured. "They could also drive away with the car or force us to go with them. And if you open the trunk, they could steal everything we own. Better not."

"No, thanks," Pamela said to the man. "We'll wait for Triple A."

"You could get yourselves killed," the first man said. "What'sa matter? You scared of us? You better let us take you somewhere. Best chance you got."

"No!" said Elizabeth. "Just go away!"

"Suit yourself," the man with the tattoos said, and they walked back to their car. With a roar of the motor, they raced past us, almost sideswiping our car.

"What are we going to *do*?" said Elizabeth.

"The question is, what are we *not* going to do, and handing over the keys to some strange guys isn't one of them. But somebody's got to be able to get to our spare," I said. "I'd better go stand at the curve and warn cars that we're here."

"I wish we had flares. Be careful, Alice," Pamela warned.

But before I could open the door, a second car pulled up behind us. A van.

"Oh, God!" Elizabeth cried.

We turned to look as a man of about fifty got out. There was a woman sitting in the passenger seat. He came carefully up to the window, watching for cars coming around the curve.

"Not a very good place for a flat tire, is it?" he said through the window.

"No," said Pamela.

"I've got a hydraulic jack. You have a spare, I presume?"

"Yes, it's under our bags in the trunk," Pamela said.

"Well, I'd better put out a couple of flares. Then, if you girls will get in the van with my wife, it'll lighten the load and I can change your tire. 'Less you want to stand back there by the wall. Sure don't want you here on the road."

We looked at the man, then at his wife, then at each other.

"Name's Gerald Gray, and I'm a retired school principal, if that'll help," he said.

We decided we had to trust somebody, so we got out of the car and gave him the key. Then we climbed in the van with his wife, who offered us each a slice of homemade banana bread and asked us about our trip. By the time she'd told us all the places they'd been and shown us pictures of her grandchildren, Gerald Gray had changed our tire and was back with the key.

"What you need to do is get to a gas station when you reach Carmel and have them repair the tire. That spare's only a temporary. Good luck, girls," he said.

"You have no idea how much we appreciate this," I told him.

"Could we pay you for your trouble?" Pamela asked. "Really, we'd be glad to!"

Mr. Gray only smiled as he got back in the van. "No, just pass the favor along when you come across somebody else in need," he said. And I vowed to save that little piece of philosophy for Lester when I told him about our trip.

* * *

When we finally got back to San Francisco, after two gorgeous days on the Monterey Peninsula, we checked into the same Holiday Inn where we'd rented the car—the only motel on our itinerary that we'd reserved in advance—and found a note waiting for Elizabeth.

As soon as we got to our room, she opened it.

"From Moe!" she said, her cheeks beginning to flush.

You told me you'd be staying here your last night of the trip, so I hope you get this. I'll always remember you for the best night's sleep I ever had. Can we stay in touch? You've got my number.

Moe

"Yes!" breathed Elizabeth when we'd read the note.

We looked at her.

"Yes, we can stay in touch," she said, smiling.

11
THE SUMMER OF DAVE

When Dave met us at the plane this time, he swooped me up in his arms and kissed me and we didn't hold back.

"Missed you!" he said. "You have a good time?"

"A great time!" said Liz. "She slept with another man."

Dave didn't stop smiling as he reached for my bag at the baggage pickup. "Yeah?"

"In separate bunks," I told him. "You'll hear all about it."

"Can't wait," said Dave, and kissed me again.

It was the start of a diversified summer. I was working part-time on the SCOO database for the university. Devon and Samantha had proposed more ambitious things that the U might sponsor in the future: fall barbecue, a clothing drive, a shredding truck to cruise through the neighborhood on some designated Saturday, a pet-washing Sunday—the ideas kept coming. Marcus took me along to a meeting of a new political organization formed of both Democrats and Republicans trying to get more agreement in Congress and to persuade college students to vote.

Dave was still interviewing for jobs in the insurance industry, where he hoped to become an actuary. He was staying at his parents' home in Cumberland but was frequently down in the Washington area for interviews.

And so it began: "The Summer of Dave." We did everything together that we possibly could. Washington, DC, is full of summer festivals, and in June alone, after I got back from California, we went to the Smithsonian Folklife Festival, the gay pride parade with Marcus and Devon, and the Capital Jazz Fest, as well as a wine tasting over in Virginia. For the Fourth of July, though, Dave got a room for the weekend at a hotel in Crystal City where we could watch the fireworks from our private balcony.

Just another thoughtful touch from a very thoughtful person, and as I lay back in his arms, sharing the chaise longue, feeling his body warmth against mine, I thought, *This must be love— lying in the arms of a strong, considerate man.*

We watched the starbursts in the sky beyond the river, listened for the distant boom, watched the waterfall bursts, the little explosions that reminded me of a weeping willow, and Dave's favorite, when several rockets were fired at once and the bursts were more like a bouquet—a flower here, a flower there, bursting into bloom, then disappearing until a final explosion, everything at once.

"Alice," Dave murmured in my ear, "I want our life to be like this forever, one happy surprise after another, and I think we can make it happen. Will you marry me?"

I said, "Yes."

Then we kissed, because there and then, everything seemed possible.

It was like the replay of a scene I'd already acted out, and I guess I had—in my head. All I could think was, *Why not?* We couldn't go on like this forever, just hanging out. Dave had already turned down one job offer in Missouri, to stay near me, and now he could start planning the rest of his life.

It was a beautiful evening. He slipped his grandmother's ring on my finger while the moon was still visible from where we sat—a too-heavy ring with a sapphire in the middle, a tiny diamond on each side. Dave said that would have to do until I could decide on a ring myself.

The next morning I just had to tell someone. I called home and Sylvia answered. I could hardly contain the excitement in my voice, but I really wanted to tell Dad.

"Is Dad home?" I asked.

"No, he went out for gas and a few groceries," she said. "How are things with you? Are you having a nice Fourth of July weekend?"

I had to tell her. "Oh, yes! Dave and I. And guess what? We're engaged!"

Sylvia gave a little gasp. "Why . . . you *are?*"

"Yes. I've even got his grandmother's ring. You're the first person I've told."

"My goodness!" There was a pause. "What news, Alice! Ben will be so surprised!"

"I hope he'll be happy about it," I said tentatively.

"If you're happy, your father's happy. So—any thoughts about the date?"

"Next June, maybe. After I graduate."

"That's exciting! Oh, wait a minute. I hear Ben's car in the drive. . . ."

Dad was a little out of breath when he came to the phone. "Al? What's up, honey? I thought you were in Virginia this weekend."

"We are. I just wanted you to be the first to know: Dave and I are engaged."

There was complete silence from the other end of the line.

"We're planning to get married next June." And then I added, still waiting for his response, "Just before I start grad school."

"Well! Sweetheart!" he said at last. "Congratulations are in order, then! I guess I didn't realize you two were that serious." Another pause. "Is this something you've been talking about? You've taken me by surprise, that's all."

"The engagement was sudden, but we love each other. And Dave needs to know so he can plan. As you know, he's been job hunting, but he wants to stay in the area until I get my master's."

"Well, well, that sounds sensible. We'll have lots to talk about the next time you're home. Love you, Al."

"I love you too, Dad."

For some reason, I delayed calling Les and Stacy. I didn't want to tell Stacy until I'd told Les, and there was no guarantee I'd get him if I called. So I tried Elizabeth's number. She didn't pick up. I called Pamela.

"Wow! Alice! That's so great!" she said. "Where were you when he proposed?"

"On a hotel balcony in Crystal City, watching the fireworks on the Mall."

"Wow!" she said again. "Now, *that's* creative! Have you told Liz or Gwen?"

"They're next. I'm going to ask my cousin Carol to be my maid of honor, but you and Liz and Gwen are bridesmaids, if you'll do it."

"Of course we will! You know that!" she said.

Liz had the same response.

"During the fireworks celebration? Oh, I love it! I'd love to be a bridesmaid. When's the wedding?"

"We're talking about June. I've got to call Gwen."

Gwen's response was more like Dad's. "*Really?* You're serious? I knew you guys were in a relationship, but I didn't know you were talking marriage. You're still planning to get your master's?"

"Oh, definitely. Nothing's changed there. And, Gwen, you'll be a bridesmaid, won't you?"

"Absolutely. Tell Dave he's chosen the second most wonderful girl in the world."

"Okay . . . Who's the first?"

"Me, of course. That's what I keep telling Austin, anyway."

I also invited Val and Abby to be bridesmaids, which made six, counting Carol, and she said to give her a definite date and she'd put it on the calendar.

"Think you can come up with six groomsmen?" I asked Dave as he drove me back home after the holiday weekend.

"Hmmm. Let's see. My best beer buddy, my poker buddy, my wrestling buddy . . . ," and he kissed me.

Moses Woodword lived in DC, and after our Great Amtrak Adventure out west, he and Liz started going out a lot. As soon as she heard that Dave and I were engaged, she arranged for the four of us to get together, and we spent a long evening at a rooftop restaurant overlooking the Capitol, one of Moe's favorite spots.

Liz and Moe were crazy in love—could hardly keep their eyes off each other. She wanted us to get together with Gwen and Austin, too, and I had to tell her that they'd just broken up, surprising us all. Austin had taken a job in North Carolina and decided he was moving on.

"I wish we could just collect all the people we've ever loved and stay together in one big happy family," Liz said, pulling her sweater around her shoulders as a breeze swept the terrace.

Moe put one hand over hers. "But the circle keeps growing,

and you'd want that, wouldn't you? Otherwise, I'd never have been a part of it."

So true, yet we all had liked Austin.

"I know," Liz said. "At least I've got you guys. I'm so *excited* for you, Alice! Tell me how I can help, and I will."

All I really had to do for Lester's wedding was show up. But for the bride, or the bride and her stepmom, there's a to-do list that never stops. The first thing to do was reserve the church, and I was astonished to discover that our date was already taken, unless we wanted to get married in the morning instead of the afternoon. We didn't. So Sylvia and I made it June 16, after checking with Dave, and the church receptionist pleasantly informed us that we might want to reserve the reception site next, because many of those are booked a year or more in advance, and we were already a month behind. We booked a hotel.

"If we have to reserve a florist a year in advance, we're going to have dandelions," Dad said that night at dinner, and that made us all laugh. You should never get married if you have no sense of humor, I decided.

Quite naturally, Sylvia wanted to get as many of the arrangements nailed down as possible before they left for France. I hated the feeling that I was on an assembly line, but for her sake, we signed on with a caterer and made a deposit. Then I felt we could coast for a while.

We all went up to Cumberland to have dinner with Dave's parents so the four parents could meet each other. Dave's mom was as thoughtful as he was, and Dave's dad, though hard of hearing and sometimes misunderstanding what we said, was jovial and made us feel welcome.

"Well, that's that," Dad said on our way home again. "What else is on the list?" Dave had stayed behind to spend the weekend with his parents.

"The only thing you have to do is get measured for a tux," Sylvia told him enviously. "The only things Alice and I have to do are to shop for a gown, choose the flowers, buy gifts for the bridesmaids, decide on the menu, the cake, the invitations and favors and bridesmaid dresses and—"

"Whew!" said Dad. "The sooner we get to France, Sylvia, the better."

Dave and I house-sat for them while they were away and got the feel of being a married couple. We slept in my old bedroom, now another guest room, and Dave left for his interviews and came back to the house for the night. Usually he picked me up at the Melody Inn, and we ate out or met some friends, but Dave cut the grass for Dad and I cleaned up inside when needed.

I wouldn't say that a couple should live together before they marry, but it does alert you to a few things you hadn't noticed before. When Dave picked up the newspaper, for example, either to read with his morning coffee or after work, he seldom bothered to read the front section or the editorials but went right to the sports or business section, and I realized, thinking back, that whenever our gang, sitting around my dorm room, discussed a political or controversial subject, Dave never, that I could remember, contributed to the conversation.

I walked to the kitchen doorway, still holding the celery for a salad, and watched him surfing the TV channels, skipping over the evening news and going to ESPN. "I heard on my car radio that there was another uprising in the Mideast," I said.

"Yeah?" Dave said, and found the baseball scores he wanted.

I frowned as I chopped the veggies for the salad. What did I have, a case of the premarriage jitters? Weren't most guys interested in how the Nationals were doing? He'd come back from an interview that hadn't gone too well. If it had been me, would I then want to listen to a newscast about revolts and massacres? I don't think so. . . .

He nuzzled my neck as we were both waiting for the microwave to ding.

"Been waiting all day for this," he murmured.

"What? The microwave to ding?"

"No. Nuzzling your neck and what comes after."

"Well, that's something we agree on."

He looked at me quizzically. "Meaning . . . uh . . . ?"

I tried to make a joke of it. "Just that you don't seem too interested in what goes on in the rest of the world."

Dave pondered that a bit as he took a pot holder and lifted a plate from the microwave.

"No, I guess you could say I don't. It's not that I don't care what goes on, it's just that I've got all I can handle right here in my own little space. If I can tend my own garden, so to speak, and everyone else tends theirs, we'd get along fine in the world."

I gave him my "incredulous, astonished, can't-believe-this" look.

"Dave, that's so simplistic. I mean, the problems are so complex, with so many different countries involved. . . ."

"Exactly," he said. "That's why I keep out of it. Too many folks already putting their oars in the water. Now, turkey tetrazzini, anyone? Courtesy of Stouffer's?"

We had the house clean and the grass freshly mowed when Dad and Sylvia came home, looking relaxed and delighted with their trip.

"If you haven't decided on a honeymoon location, let us suggest Paris," Dad said. "Absolutely wonderful."

"I'm so glad you had a good time, Dad," I told him. "No big problems here or at the store." And we all went out to dinner so they could tell us the highlights of their trip.

Dave finally got a job with an insurance company, at a branch office in McLean, and things were different now that he was working and I was back in school. We were used to being together in a crowd, the little group we'd hung around with as undergrads, where we were more or less defined by the group: Dave, the genial guy who pretty much stayed on the sidelines but was up for whatever the gang wanted to do; and Alice, the practical, sometimes funny girl who never met a question she didn't ask—something like that.

But now, away from the group, when we were together on weekends—just the two of us—it seemed we didn't have much to talk about, and this unnerved me. I felt that we should have more. We spent a lot of time talking about where we'd most like to live (somewhere in the DC area), rent or buy (buy), number of children (two or three)—all important topics; our parents got along okay; and Dave said our church was fine with him. But he didn't seem to care for the same movies I did. Drama bored him. He liked action movies. Big problem or little problem? I liked to talk about what I read in the paper, but if it didn't affect us directly, Dave wasn't much interested. Big problem or little problem?

How did we get so far as a couple and not really know what the other cared about? I wondered. Up until now, I guess, our differences were masked by the crowd, but now they stood out, and they were more at odds than I'd expected. It didn't seem to bother Dave, but it bothered me. I was rooming with Val again my senior year, so Dave and I often spent weekends at the little apartment he'd rented near work, and if we couldn't agree on a movie or couldn't decide between a play and a hockey game, we generally spent the evening in bed. That was fine with Dave, but we couldn't spend our lives in bed. Sometimes I even wished we'd gone out with the gang instead of opting to be alone together.

It was hard to concentrate on my coursework. No two people were completely alike, I told myself. Wasn't this simply the normal give-and-take? Isn't this what the engagement period was supposed to do—offer a sort of shakedown period when you learned the fine art of compromise?

In a course I was taking on marriage and family life, the instructor drew two overlapping circles on the blackboard during one of his lectures. Each circle represented the interests and concerns of a spouse—one for the husband, the other for the wife. The larger the area of overlap, where they both shared the same, the greater the compatibility.

I sat down once and drew those circles. In my own circle I wrote all the things I loved or was interested in: the prospect of being a counselor, children, my family, doing things with friends, theater, animals, hiking, documentaries, human rights groups, peace organizations, sex, Christmas, Greek cuisine. . . . And the next time Dave and I were together, I took out my circles and asked him what he loved most. I was making a chart, I told him. He smiled.

"Sex," he said.

I smiled and wrote that down in the overlapping space.

"You," he said, and I blushed as I realized I hadn't written down his name at all in my circle, so I hastily inserted his name.

"Watching football on TV," he said. "Baseball, not so much."

I wrote down football in the space that was solely his.

"The stock market, the promotion I hope to get . . . ," he went on. "Uh . . . sushi, sailing . . ." He shrugged. "That's about it, I guess."

"Children?" I asked. "I thought we'd discussed this—that we both wanted kids."

"Sure, if we have any," he said. "I'm happy either way."

"Animals?"

"No. No pets."

"Movies?"

"Action movies."

"Documentaries?"

"No."

"Live theater?"

"God, no."

"Christmas?"

"Sure."

"Music?" I asked. Even though I was tone-deaf, there was music I loved. "Do you love Gershwin? 'Summertime'?"

"I don't know it." He was looking at me quizzically.

"What organizations do you belong to, Dave? I mean, which ones interest you?"

"You mean like investors' clubs? I belong to one of those."

"Human rights? Environment?"

"Any organization that wants a buck, no." He pulled me to him. "Well, I take that back. The Sierra Club. What is this? The third degree?"

"Just trying to see how well we match up."

"The main thing is that we love each other," Dave told me. "You do your thing, I do mine, we're both happy."

12
SAYING GOOD-BYE

Val and Colin had broken up after he graduated, and she was going out with a new guy now. Sometimes, when she wanted to be alone with him in our dorm room, I'd spend the night with Gwen, and I liked that. She was invariably studying, but I'd happily camp out on her floor in my sleeping bag, glad that she didn't have time for long, heartfelt discussions about my love life.

I kept myself as busy as possible because the more free time I had, the greater the anxiety grew inside me that I had said yes too soon to Dave, and the heavier his grandmother's ring felt on my finger.

I invited him to a congressional debate on campus about immigration, but he turned it down. He wanted me to go to a Capitals game instead, and I finally gave in, but then I was sullen all evening. This wasn't fair to either of us.

"Things will get better," he told me. "Once we're living together, it will be easier."

"You'll have your actuarial exams," I said, "and I'll be doing grad work. If I decide not to do a thesis, I'll have to take extra courses. I might not be able to get it all done in a year."

"But we'll have each other," he replied.

The point was, we "had" each other now, but we weren't in it one hundred percent. At least I wasn't. *What do I want?* I kept asking myself. No two people were exactly alike. Dave was kind, considerate, patient . . . All he wanted in life was to settle down somewhere with me, each of us doing our own thing, raising a family . . . What else was there?

I'd always thought I wanted to be married in my mom's wedding dress, but for some reason, I couldn't bring myself to go home and get it from the attic. I liked the dress from the pictures I'd seen of it, but I couldn't seem to make myself take that step.

Partly, I was working really hard at school. I loved my courses this semester, but the professors expected more of us in our senior year than they ever had. I told myself that I would definitely sit down at Thanksgiving and finish making my wedding plans. In addition to deposits on the hotel and the caterer, Sylvia and I were deciding on a photographer, and there were dozens of other details to work out—the invitations, the cake, the seating arrangements, the décor, the band, the honeymoon. . . . I had to remind myself that I couldn't behave like a college girl forever—I would be a married woman soon and had to start thinking like one. But when Thanksgiving came, the wedding stuff just seemed too overwhelming.

Overwhelming, and the truth was that sometimes I just felt bored with Dave. Maybe it was lack of imagination, I thought, but he never seemed able to think of anything to do besides watching movies, having sex, eating out, and checking the stock market. Sometimes hiking, and I liked those things too. But if our life together was going to be "one happy surprise after another," it seemed they'd have to come from me.

I started going back to church on Sundays simply because I longed for people who talked about the same problems I was interested in—world problems, social problems. It was a whole new bunch, of course. The high school kids I had known had either moved away or were now part of the singles group for twenty-somethings, and I wasn't sure, being engaged, that I belonged there.

Les and Stacy came for Thanksgiving and were staying till Sunday. Friday morning Dad and Les went shopping for a new computer, and Stacy was still in bed. Sylvia and I were lingering over a late breakfast. I toyed with the sapphire on my finger.

Outside the windows, the tree branches, bearing only a leaf or two, formed a motionless web across the gray sky. Not a twig stirred, as though my inertia were contagious.

"So how are the arrangements coming?" Sylvia asked. "Anything I can do?"

"Not really," I told her.

We each picked up our cups in unison and sipped quietly, but Sylvia was the first to put hers down. She sat there in her blue robe, studying me with her blue-green eyes, and said finally, "You're just not sure about this, are you?"

I stared at her in surprise. "Of course I'm sure! We're engaged. I told him . . . I *love* him . . ." And suddenly I began to cry. "No," I sobbed. "I'm not sure and I don't know why. That's the awful part. I don't think I'll ever be sure."

"Oh, sweetheart." She reached across the table and put her hand over mine. "Have you told Dave how you feel?"

"No! He'd hate me! He's a perfectly nice guy, but I just . . ." I looked at Sylvia imploringly. "Were you ever around someone who made you feel lonely? Not all the time. But . . . a lot of the time?"

"I think I know what you mean. Yes, I felt that sometimes with some of the men I dated."

"It's like . . . like he's not really a part of my life. Or maybe I'm not really a part of his. I try, I really do try, but . . . How can you break up with someone just because you don't like the same things? He's a such a decent guy, Sylvia, but . . . I don't feel like I can honestly be myself with him."

Sylvia looked at me earnestly. "Then don't do this. Don't marry him."

"But . . . but . . . the ring! We're engaged!"

"Give it back."

"We've already looked at apartments! We've already made some plans."

"Plans can be changed."

"It's so unfair to him, Sylvia! Where does it say that a husband has to be interested in the same things his wife is? He'll be so hurt!" I wept.

"It's nothing compared to the way he'd feel if he found out he'd married a woman who wished she hadn't. Give the ring back and tell him you want more time to think about it, if you need to."

"He'll hate me," I said again. "And I really do think I love him."

"Then you'll care enough for his feelings not to marry him till you're sure."

"But how will I ever *know*?" I sobbed. My face felt hot and swollen. "I don't think I'll ever know. What if I'm looking for the perfect man, and he doesn't exist?"

Sylvia got up and came around the table, and I buried my head against her stomach. I remembered how Sylvia herself had gone to England for a year because she couldn't make up her mind whether to marry Dad or Jim Sorringer. Maybe I'd have to go to Australia. The Barrier Islands! Somewhere far away where no one could reach me. Maybe I should be psychoanalyzed or hypnotized to see how I really felt.

"When you find the right man," Sylvia said, combing her hands through my hair, "he won't be perfect. But you'll know. You'll just know. Maybe not right away, but in time."

I'd stopped crying by then, and she gently pulled away as

my breathing slowed. Then she sat down in the chair next to me, one arm resting on the table, and just listened.

"I certainly admire Dave," I told her. "He's going to make a good actuary. He'll make a good husband . . . for someone. But sometimes I just feel like we're . . . we're magnets of the wrong polarity. Instead of sticking together, we sort of . . . repel. No, not exactly. Not all the time." *Oh, God,* I thought, *she used to be my English teacher.* What kind of a simile was that?

"If Dave's the right one, you can't imagine not spending the rest of your life together," Sylvia said finally. "When you've found the right one—when you see him, when you're with him—you'll feel like you're coming home."

Stacy came down in her robe, a towel around her wet hair, just as Dad and Les walked in. I didn't even let them take the new computer out of the box, because I knew that once they started setting it up, they probably wouldn't even hear me. Dad sat down slowly on a chair in the living room when I told him about my decision.

"Al, are you sure about this now? Not just the usual pre-wedding jitters?" he asked.

"No, but it feels more right to break the engagement than it does to go ahead with it," I said, my nose still clogged. My voice was weak, like all my strength had gone out of me and it took all I had just to make this confession.

"Then you've got to call Dave and tell him, and the sooner the better."

My eyes teared up again. "But . . . we've reserved the church,

Dad! You've put a deposit on the hotel and the caterers! How can I—?"

"How can you go through with something you're already feeling might be a mistake? That's the real question," said Dad. "I don't care if we'd already ordered the food and the invitations. I don't care if you got all the way down to the altar, honey, and then changed your mind. It's your future we're talking about here, and if you're not sure, then now's the time to say so."

I could almost feel the relief washing over me. "Dave's coming to see me tomorrow," I said. "I want to tell him in person. I owe him that much."

Dad nodded. "Yes."

"You and Dave have your whole lives ahead of you," said Stacy. "Six months from now, you could both be involved with other people. Really."

But it was Lester I wanted to hear from. So far he hadn't said anything, just looked thoughtful. After he and Dad had set up the computer in Dad's office, they discovered they needed another connector cord, and Les offered to drive to RadioShack to get one, so I rode along.

He reached over and put one hand on my knee, giving it a quick squeeze. "It's tough, isn't it?" he said.

My chin wobbled a little. "It's . . . it's awful, Les! Dave's driving down from Cumberland—he spent Thanksgiving with his folks—and he's going to be so sad!"

"You don't think he might have guessed? It might not be as big a surprise as you imagine."

I glanced over at him. "Why would he guess?"

Les shrugged. "I don't know. Some guys are more percep-
tive than others. It just seems . . . well, to me, anyway, and what
do *I* know? . . . that something's missing between you two—on
your part, anyway."

"That's exactly how I've felt too, but what is it? Dave's kind,
he's attractive to me . . ."

"Joy," said Lester.

"What?"

"Do you remember Dad and Sylvia's wedding ceremony? I
do—something the minister said, about the three components
of love: passion, tenderness, and joy. I've never forgotten."

I remembered it now and thought about Dave.

"I *do* feel passion for him," I said. "When we're—"

"Never mind! You don't have to spell it out."

"And I certainly feel tender toward him a lot of the time. . . ."
I hesitated. "That's why I feel so awful now."

"And joy?" Les prompted.

I thought about it. Could I really say I was joyful? Did I
greet Dave with joy? I was always happy to see him. But when
I thought of our future together, tried to picture my role in his
life . . .

"No," I said at last. "That's what's missing. Joy and antici-
pation. The feeling that this is the right man for me, that I
just can't wait to be his wife and experience all that's coming
next."

"Then there you have it," said Les.

* * *

I don't know how long I stayed in the shower that evening, my refuge from worry and indecision. I stood with my back to the spray, arms hanging motionless at my sides, as I watched the water run down my arms, my hands, and finally, in a thin stream, off the ends of each finger, like claws. As though I were about to inflict pain, was capable of causing injury.

I was back at my dorm room Saturday when Dave drove up. I went right out and got in his car before he could come inside.

"Well, what's this?" he said, as though I had a surprise for him, and gave me a quick kiss on the cheek.

"I just want to go for a drive—I need to talk," I said.

He looked over at me uncertainly. "All right," he said. We drove down into Sligo Creek Park, and he stopped the car along the water. "What's up?"

I wanted to get out and walk, but he didn't. He was beginning to look uneasy and said he'd rather stay in the car. I'll admit it wasn't exactly walking weather. It was drizzling and the sky was as gray as I felt inside.

I sat hugging my elbows in my bulky green sweater. "This is so hard for me," I told him, "and it's going to be even harder for you. I'm just so sorry, Dave, but I have to give your ring back."

His eyes had a look of disbelief. "Alice!"

"I've thought and thought about this, and I do love you, but—"

"Alice, how can you love me and do something like this? What's the matter?"

I'd been afraid he might gather me in his arms and tell me that he wanted my happiness most of all, and if I wasn't sure . . . the way I'd imagined my dad behaving when Sylvia first told him she needed time to decide between him and Jim Sorringer. Then I might have waffled, might have ended up keeping his ring after all. But Dave didn't do that. He just sat there, turned toward me, staring.

"Dave, I just don't feel we share enough."

"Come on! We have a good time when we're together, don't we? Is this about that play you wanted to see and I didn't?"

"You have every right not to like the things I do."

"Then . . . ? I'll go! I'll go! Anything to make you happy."

I shook my head. "That would get old after a while, and it wouldn't be fair to you. We both know that. Neither of us should have to do so many things we don't really enjoy. We'd start out okay, but then we'd resent it."

"What's happened? You meet another guy?"

"No. This is about us, Dave. I love you, but it doesn't seem enough. I guess I thought that with time, everything would come together—but it just hasn't happened. What I'm missing is joy."

"You expect the moon, that's what," he said, his back against the door, arms folded across his chest. "You've got some pre-ordained notion of how you're supposed to feel. You're in love with an ideal."

"It's not just idealistic, but you're right. I *do* have an idea of how I should feel, and I don't feel that way. Not enough of the time, anyway. I . . . I just want to postpone the wedding and think some more about it." My heart began to pound. I was waffling already. I took the ring off my finger and handed it to him.

"Alice," he said, taking it reluctantly, and his eyes were pleading. "Don't do this."

My eyes filled with tears. "It's the hardest thing I've ever done in my life, Dave. Please let me think about it."

Now he shook his head, staring out the window a brief moment, holding his breath. Then he looked at me again. "No, it just prolongs the sadness. I guess maybe . . ." He looked away. "Maybe I've suspected, I don't know. I've seen how you come alive sometimes with other guys when the gang's all together. . . ."

I started to protest, but he said, "I don't mean you're hitting on them, but you enjoy all the talk, all that discussion, all the stuff you think of to do. I can see that . . . in some ways . . . we're going in different directions. But if you didn't love me enough when I proposed to you, you shouldn't have accepted."

"You're right," I said. "I just didn't know."

He closed his eyes. "I really thought we were meant for each other." Opened them again. "That we got along so well."

"So did I, for a while. And we had some wonderful times together. Really. You'll find a girl who's absolutely right for you. But I have to go into marriage with my whole heart, Dave, and I've just got too many reservations. Try to forgive me."

"I'll try," he said.

He squared himself behind the wheel and turned the key in the ignition. We rode silently back to campus.

When he stopped the car, he said, "I really did love you, Alice," and I was almost glad it was past tense.

"I know," I said. "I loved you too."

And then, knowing he would not call or write me again—and knowing with certainty now that I did not want him to—I said, "Good-bye, Dave."

He leaned forward and kissed me lightly on the forehead. "Good-bye," he said.

Once I had got out and shut the door, he drove away and didn't look back. I stood on the sidewalk watching him leave and knew I had made one of the best, and the most difficult, decisions of my life. I was alone again, but I wasn't lonely.

There were serious things to think about now. I was determined to repay Dad the deposits he had made for my wedding. With Dave out of the picture, I had more time to concentrate on my studies, but it was going to be a very different Christmas from what we'd thought. We had planned to get together with Dave's folks—his and mine—and of course that wasn't happening. And to top it all off, Elizabeth called with the news that she and Moe were engaged.

"Oh, Elizabeth!" I said. "I'm so *happy* for you!"

"And he'll be taking his bar exam soon."

"That is so great!" I told her. "We all love Moe!"

"We haven't set a date yet. I want to get you through your wedding first before I start planning mine."

"No," I said, and didn't want her to feel sorry for me. "It's over with Dave. I broke our engagement."

"*What?*"

"It just seemed right. I wasn't sure. But you know, I feel so much better. . . ."

"Oh, Alice!"

"Really, I'm okay," I said, and meant it.

13

UNBELIEVABLE

The next month was one of the worst and best I could remember. Sometimes I thought I might be schizophrenic, because one day I felt free and ready to explore the world, and the next I wanted to cuddle up in my decrepit beanbag chair, far too small for me, sure that I had given up the most loyal man who would ever love me. The *only* man, perhaps, I thought when I was most despondent.

I wished Dave had been mad at me. Railed at me. Driven off at ninety miles an hour, and I could have thought, *Good riddance.* Instead, he'd kissed me on the forehead. Maybe I should call him. Text him. Say I was a fool and wanted him back. Maybe joy would come, if I gave it time.

Then, one day in class—a class titled Old Philosophers,

New Age—we were discussing Emerson's essay "Self-Reliance," and this line from it seemed to be written especially for me: *Trust thyself: every heart vibrates to that iron string.*

Yes! Except that some days the iron string felt weak and wobbly and I could scarcely hear it at all. Other times it was loud—loud enough to propel me out of bed some mornings as if to say, *Get up and go be the person you want to be!*

Still, I dreaded Christmas. The fact that the rest of the world seemed happy and filled with the holiday spirit made my sadness worse. I dreaded seeing my friends and hearing their happy news, having to explain, over and over again, what happened between Dave and me. I knew they'd only want to comfort me, not judge, but somehow I felt that nothing they could say or do would make me feel better. It had to come from inside, and sometimes it was there, sometimes not.

I've heard that the best thing to do when you're feeling low is to concentrate on someone else's unhappiness, work to make someone else feel better, and when Sylvia told me that Aunt Sally and Uncle Milt were virtual shut-ins, due to Milt's failing health, I decided to spend a few days after Christmas with them.

"They'd be delighted, Alice. A wonderful thing for you to do," Dad said.

Valerie had applied for a job as curator of a small new museum that was being built in Oklahoma City, and she'd been more or less accepted for the job if she wanted it. She was going down after Christmas to look the place over, talk with the foundation that was building the museum, and see how she felt about living there after she graduated.

Oklahoma? I thought. Was she serious?

"Come with me," she had offered. "Maybe you'll like it so much, you'll want to move there after you get your master's."

I doubted that, but because it would be new territory for me, a new experience, I told her I'd join her for a few days after I visited Aunt Sally in Chicago.

My next bank statement, though, confirmed what I'd already suspected—that I had about reached the bottom of my savings. All these years, through high school and college, I had faithfully put money aside from everything I earned, knowing that while Dad would pay for my tuition and books all through college and grad school, everything else had to come out of my own savings. That trip to California had almost wiped me out. I would have to live a Spartan life till I graduated, and I still owed Dad for the wedding-that-never-was. Okay—Oklahoma was my last hurrah. Was that depressing or what?

I've been lonely before and it didn't kill me, I told myself on Christmas morning when I sat down with Dad and Sylvia to open presents. Les and Stacy were with her parents this time. Dad did his best to keep things cheerful. He played only light music on CDs, gave me funny presents in my stocking. He and Sylvia kept me busy in the kitchen, and neighbors came by later to share the holiday spirit. But there's a certain loneliness that comes from having no one special in your life, and I was feeling that acutely.

* * *

This was a mistake, I thought, when I got off the plane in Chicago. I wondered if I would ever be able to go there again—pass through it, even—without feeling depressed. Two relationships hadn't worked out now, and being reminded of the first made it all the more painful.

But I found I liked being with Aunt Sally and Uncle Milt, because no one tried to make me feel jolly, so I didn't disappoint. I brought them a framed photo of them with their daughter, Carol, that they probably never realized Dad had taken at Lester's wedding, a large magnifying glass with a light, and DVDs from Les and Stacy. Aunt Sally had perfected the art of seeming delighted no matter what you gave her, but I didn't even have to pretend: When I opened their gift for me and found a used copy of the book *The Prophet,* with Mom's name on the inside cover, I was really delighted.

"It was all the rage back in the seventies," Aunt Sally explained, "and Marie loaned it to me when she'd finished, but I never got around to reading it all. Then I was cleaning out our bookshelves a few months ago and found it. I thought you might like to have it, since your mother was so fond of it."

"What a perfect gift!" I said, gently turning the pages. "Anything of Mom's is a real treasure to me."

Uncle Milt didn't beat around the bush. "Your dad tells us your engagement's off, sweetheart. You just take your time. Our little Alice deserves the best, and if a fella doesn't measure up, you forget him."

"It wasn't a case of not measuring up, Uncle Milt," I told

him. "We were just too different, and he'll make a great husband for someone, just not me."

"Well, I dated a lot of boys who were too different from me before I met this one," Aunt Sally said, stroking the back of Milt's head, letting her fingers slide down the collar of his shirt and up again. "And I'm glad I waited, because I got the best."

I smiled, loving that they were still so close. "I'm in no hurry," I said.

Alone in their guest room later, I gently turned the pages that my mother's fingers had turned, and various phrases by Khalil Gibran leaped out at me: *Let there be spaces in your togetherness / And let the winds of the heavens dance between you.* Didn't that refer to Dave and me? Wasn't that an admonition not to be too much alike? But just when I felt that old familiar panic begin, I read this phrase: *No man can reveal to you aught but that which already lies half asleep in the dawning of your knowledge.* That meant not even the prophet himself could tell me what was best for me—I needed to trust that I made the right decision.

I stayed only two nights, helping Aunt Sally sort through some old photos and playing hearts with Uncle Milt. We watched *Masterpiece Theater* together, and the next day, with my plane leaving for Oklahoma City at 4:15, I could tell that they both could use a nap. So I told them I wanted to get to the airport early—that I needed to find a gift for Val—and they were happy to let me go, with hugs all around. Milt had insisted on driving me to O'Hare, but Sally had wisely arranged for a neighbor to take me, and I was glad. It was a miserably cold day with sleet coming down, making the walk from Aunt Sally's out to the car slightly treacherous, and I huddled in the passenger seat, wishing the neighbor would turn the fan up a couple notches to get the heat to my legs. At the airport I was in such a hurry to get inside, where, I hoped, it would be warmer—fat chance—that I awkwardly offered the man a twenty-dollar bill. This delayed my exit even longer as he described the many favors Milt and Sally had done for him and refused to take any money.

Inside the terminal at last, I shook the sleet from my hair and wheeled my carry-on over to the departure board, only to discover that my plane would be leaving an hour and a half late. I was already two and a half hours early, which meant I had four hours to buy a Christmas present for Val, where every shop in this airport charged twice as much for everything as it would cost somewhere else. Besides, I'd already bought a cute little wool cap for her, so I didn't really need anything more.

I sighed and tried to figure out which waiting section looked the most comfortable for the next four hours since I really didn't want to go through security yet. I was walking past a luggage shop, hoping to find a bookstore, when I saw a tall man coming toward me, wheeling a large duffel bag behind him, a smaller bag over one shoulder. He had a two-day growth of stubble on his face, and a lock of hair had fallen down over one eye. There was something familiar about him, and then . . . And then . . .

He stopped about ten feet away, and so did I.

Was it possible?

I took a few steps closer.

"Patrick?"

"Alice!"

One hand went to my chest to restart my heart, and this time he took a few steps forward. We continued to stare at each other in shock and wonder.

"What are you . . . ?" we said in unison. Then we both began to smile at our awkwardness.

"What are you doing in Chicago?" Patrick asked first.

"Heading off to explore the world," I joked lamely, gazing at the hair that was a darker red now, a reddish brown. His eyes were lined beneath, as though he hadn't slept for several days, probably because he *hadn't* slept for several days, but I'd know his smile anywhere. "What are *you* doing here?"

"Coming home," he said. "Heading to Union Station for a train to Milwaukee."

"I can't believe . . . ," I said.

And then . . . I don't know if it was some small gesture he made, but when he had let go of the duffel bag beside him, we were both moving forward at the same time, and I was in his arms, my cheek against his chest, drinking in his scent, his breath, his heartbeat—all so familiar to me.

People walked by, and we didn't care. Someone could have wheeled our luggage away, and we probably wouldn't have noticed. When we finally backed away, we kept clutching each other's sleeves as though we couldn't let go.

"Where are you going, really?" Patrick asked.

"Oklahoma City."

"Oklahoma!"

"To visit my roommate. She signed on for a job there after she graduates. She wanted me to come look it over, help her decide."

"Then you're still in school?"

"Yes. I'll be starting my master's after I graduate in June. What about you?"

"Coming home to have a serious talk with the U. See how much credit they'll let me have for my study abroad and my two years in the Peace Corps." He gave a sheepish laugh that sounded so much like the old Patrick. "Actually, what I was looking for right now was a Big Mac. I promised myself that as soon as I set foot on U.S. soil, I'd treat myself to the biggest burger I could find."

"Could I go with you?" I asked.

His face lit up like a neon sign. *"Can* you?"

"I've got time."

He reached for his duffel bag, but he didn't take his eyes off me. "I still can't believe this," he said as we walked a few feet more.

"Neither can I. That we'd be in the same concourse, even." I finally remembered that Patrick's parents had moved to Wisconsin after Patrick started college. "What time's your train?"

"It's a commuter; I could go any time. All my folks know is that I'm coming this week. What about you? When's your flight?"

"It was delayed until six forty-five."

"That's terrific! Great!"

We found a hamburger place. I don't even remember the name of it. I just remember sliding into a booth across from Patrick and watching him eat two burgers while I ate one and shared his fries.

"Isn't this unbelievable?" he said. "What are the odds, do you think?"

"Ten million to one?"

"So fill me in on everything. And if I start to doze off, it doesn't mean you're boring. It's just that I've probably slept only an hour or two in the last forty-eight."

"Oh, God, Patrick! You need to get home and collapse," I said.

"Not as bad as I need these burgers," he told me. "Oh, man, these are really good."

"When did you eat last?" I asked curiously.

"Uh . . . two days ago? I'm not sure."

"What did you have?"

"Rice."

"And before that?"

"Some kind of rice."

We both laughed.

"No, there was food on the plane, but not much. So what about you?" he asked. "Where did you spend Christmas?"

"With my parents. Then I came to Chicago to visit Aunt Sally and Uncle Milt. I was on my way out."

Patrick grew quiet, but his eyes were still fixed on mine. "When I was in Madagascar . . . whenever I visited the capital . . . I checked Facebook, and the last I read, you were engaged." He glanced at my left hand and back again.

"I called it off at Thanksgiving," I said. "We're not seeing each other anymore."

"Oh." He stopped eating—stopped smiling—and looked at me intently. Those eyes . . . God, I'd missed his eyes! "I'm . . . sorry?" he said. "No, actually, that's a lie. That's about the best news I ever got."

I felt my heart leap inside me. It actually thumped against the wall of my chest.

Patrick reached across the table and squeezed my hand. "You don't know how great it is to see you again. There were times in Madagascar I wondered if I ever would."

I smiled. "Then how do you know I'm not an illusion? Maybe you're so tired, you're hallucinating."

"That's what worries me," he said, and his thumb caressed mine. "You feel real. Let's see if you can pass the reality test. Who was your sixth-grade teacher?"

I laughed. "Mrs. Plotkin."

"What was the name of our high school newspaper?"

"*The Edge.*"

"What did I promise to do on your twenty-first birthday?" Those eyes again. He had stopped smiling now, and his face was more serious.

"You were going to call and make a date for New Year's

Eve." I guess I'd stopped smiling too, but he was still holding my hand, his thumb still caressing.

"Providing you weren't taken by then," he said. "But according to Facebook, you were in a relationship, and I didn't want to interfere."

"I wish you had."

"Do you mean that, Alice? We've been apart a long time. Met other people . . ."

"I know."

"Then maybe *I'm* an illusion," he said, grinning. "No, here, feel my cheek." He pulled my hand over so I was rubbing his stubbly skin.

"It's real, all right," I said.

We had each finished our food. I had, anyway. Patrick rested his head in his hand, and his eyes were half closed. "Dessert?" he murmured. "I need one of those fried apple pies." His head began to nod, and he jerked upright.

"Another few minutes and your head will be in your plate," I laughed.

"Then maybe I'll just take some to go." But he made no move to get up. "Do you really have to catch that plane?" he asked.

"Well, I . . . I could ask about the next flight." Now he was leaning forward, arms on the table, both hands holding mine. "Or . . . tomorrow, maybe?" I said. "Or . . . the day after?"

If my head was doing rapid recalculations, my heart had already decided for me. As soon as we were on our feet, I was in his arms again and we were kissing right there in the burger place. It seemed as though his lips were my lips, his breathing my breath. And when at last he let me go, everyone around us was smiling, and a couple of sailors gave us the thumbs-up.

When Patrick stopped at the counter on our way out and asked for the fried pies, the man handed them to him and said, "It's on us."

I can't even remember how we got to the hotel—the airport shuttle, maybe?

As soon as we were in the room, Patrick turned to me, his face serious, and kissed me, a long, intense kiss, his hands running through my hair, pulling me close to him, and when he stopped once to look in my eyes, he kissed me again.

"I'm going to lie down for a quick catnap," he said. "You can crawl in beside me. I just need fifteen minutes or so."

"Sure," I said, and Patrick took off his shoes. We stacked the decorative pillows on the desk and folded back the heavy duvet. Patrick lay down, fully clothed, and promptly fell into a deep sleep, lying on his back, his mouth half open, his hands turned palms up beside him. I gently covered him with the sheet and two blankets, and his breathing became slow and deep. I sat on the edge of the bed, my hand caressing his forehead, brushing the red hair I loved so much back away from his eyes.

Was I just setting myself up to be hurt again? He had already broken up with me twice, but then, I was the one who almost married someone else.

I'm not sure how long I sat there just watching him breathe, sleep. He didn't wake in fifteen minutes, of course, and I didn't try to raise him. How was this possible that we had met this afternoon? If I had gotten to the airport five minutes later . . . If he had not detoured after coming through customs to find a Big Mac . . . If I had stayed at Aunt Sally's another hour . . .

We probably would have contacted each other eventually. Once Patrick was back in the States, someone would post the news on Facebook, whether he did or not. But to meet him here . . . to have had the time, both of us, to spend with each other . . . Maybe I believed in magic after all, and I couldn't stop smiling.

I got up finally and went over to the desk. Taking out my cell phone, I called my airline first and changed my reservation—not to the next day, but the day after—then I tried Elizabeth's number. No telling where anyone was since it was winter break for everybody but Pamela, and she was probably on a job. The phone rang six times, and then Liz picked up.

"Alice!" she said. "How's Oklahoma City? How's them broad-shouldered, bowlegged, terbaccy-smokin' cowboys?"

"I don't know," I told her. "I didn't go. I'm in a hotel room in Chicago."

"Oh, my God! What happened?" And I heard her say to someone, "She's in Chicago!" Then to me, "You won't believe this, but Gwen and Pamela are here at my house, and we're having a blast. What happened to your plane?"

"Nothing. I missed it. You won't believe this, either, but I met someone."

A shriek from the other end as she relayed my message.

". . . a hotel room with somebody. . . ." A fumbling sound, then Pamela had the phone.

"Okay, who are you with? Male or female?"

"Twenty questions. Male."

"Twenty questions, my foot. *Who?*"

"Patrick."

"Patrick!" she screamed at the others, and then I heard Gwen and Liz screaming too.

Now it was Gwen's turn. "Alice, tell us: Did you plan this all along?"

I told her about meeting up with Patrick at the airport.

"Is he there now?"

"Here in the room."

"Let me talk to him. My God, this is wonderful! He's back!"

"He's asleep, and I wouldn't wake him for the world. He hasn't slept for forty-eight hours, and I'm just watching him breathe, as happy as I can be."

Then I told them about how he'd planned to surprise his parents and how I wouldn't be going to Oklahoma for two more days. We talked until the connection got lousy and my battery ran low.

"Sweet dreams, girlfriend," Gwen told me. "You deserve them."

"Kiss him for me, Alice," said Pamela.

"This is the second most wonderful thing that's happened this week," said Liz.

"What was the first?" I asked.

"Mo and I set the date for our wedding. A year from now, right after Christmas."

"That's wonderful, Liz," I told her.

I had to call Valerie and tell her what happened, and she was as excited as I was. I said I would let her know when I was coming, and her final words were, "Take your time."

Patrick moved only once in the next two hours, and that was to turn on his side, but his breathing scarcely changed—deep and slow.

Now what? I asked myself. In all my fantasies of making love with Patrick for the first time, none of them went like this. Patrick zonked. Me with my clothes still on. Sleet coming down again outside and hitting the window. Here on the tenth floor, I could hear the whistle of wind through the air ducts. And me, happy as a clam.

I got the charger from my suitcase and plugged in my cell phone. Around eight o'clock I ate one of the fried apple pies. Then I went in the bathroom and took a hot, steamy shower to warm up. There was a silly nightshirt in my suitcase with a terrapin on the front that I slipped on. I brushed my teeth and took my pill. I'd been good about taking my birth control pills, knowing it was part of my life now. Then I turned out the light and crawled into bed with Patrick.

My feet were freezing. I'd turned the thermostat up, but I think it was probably there for decoration, because it didn't seem to make any difference. Then, carefully, I inched myself over until I was spoon shaped in Patrick's arms. Both of us lay on our sides with our knees bent, and I gently lifted Patrick's arm and pulled it forward across my body. He simply took a deeper breath and went on sleeping, and after a while I slept too.

I woke sometime in the night—I wasn't sure when—and I could tell by the way Patrick readjusted his arm around me that he had wakened too. "Alice?" he whispered behind me.

"Yeah?" I didn't want to turn around, because I'll bet my breath was horrible.

"Just wanted to make sure it was really you," he said, and pulled my body even closer to his. And then, "What do you have on?"

"My terrapin nightshirt," I said, laughing.

"I'm still drained."

"I know."

"Do you care if we wait till tomorrow?"

"No, I'd rather."

"Let's make it a date. I'll shave, brush my teeth . . ." And then his voice trailed off, and he was gone again.

I was awake and dressed before he got up the next morning. I think he'd slept eleven hours straight. When the housekeeper knocked on the door, I told her we didn't need anything, and she disappeared.

Patrick lay with his arms behind his head, smiling at me from his pillow.

"Ah! The man awakes," I said. "Should I order room service?"

"Why not?"

I found a menu in the drawer and kissed him. "What do you want? Rice cakes? Rice pudding? Chicken soup with rice?"

Patrick ordered pancakes with scrambled eggs and sausage, and dared me to kiss him again with fifty-nine-hour-no-brush breath. I agreed it was horrible, but kissed him anyway, and then he got up, went in the bathroom, and showered.

When he came out at last, sweet breath and body, a clean shirt with a pair of wrinkled trousers, we couldn't seem to stop kissing, and then we settled down at the little table the room-service guy had wheeled in for us and talked.

I told him about Dave—what a really nice guy he was, but I simply didn't feel that we had enough in common.

Patrick just listened and nodded.

"So tell me about Jessica," I said when I finished.

Patrick buttered another piece of toast, then set it aside and sipped his coffee. "I did like her a lot at first. We'd both joined the Peace Corps at the same time, and she was in a neighboring village, but . . . I don't know. When we met at the capital, all of us together, and had our meetings, she just seemed to have a different attitude—approach, maybe—to the Madagascan people, a bit too paternalistic, I guess you'd say. Not the way I saw them at all. And then, even more of a deal breaker, she fell for another volunteer. Which made the breakup easier—a lot easier."

"I'm glad."

"About . . . ?"

"That you fell out of love with her."

"Before that there was Amanda. . . ."

"Oh."

"I fell for her when I was still in Barcelona. That's when I e-mailed you about other women in my life. We had something going for several months, and then, just as suddenly, it was over. I never quite figured it out. Something she said, something I said, it never got untangled, and after a while we just didn't care, so I figured it was a good thing it was over."

"Somehow I got the idea you might be staying on after your Peace Corps commitment was up," I told him.

"Yeah, I was thinking I might volunteer for one of the non-governmental organizations, Population Services International or something, and I did for a few months. But the more I thought about it, the more I wanted to come back. I missed home, and I decided that I'd better straighten things out with the university, see how much credit they'd give me, and work on my degree. That I could probably do more with my life if I had more credentials. What about you?"

I told him I wanted to have my master's by a year from June. Start my counseling career.

"Where did you have in mind?"

"I don't know yet. I was off to explore the world when I ran into you," I said, smiling, and ran my toes over his stocking feet under the table.

"Any reason you couldn't explore it with another person?" he asked.

"None that I know of."

We wheeled our table and dirty dishes back out into the hall, and Patrick put the Do Not Disturb sign on the door handle. Then he pulled the shades on another gray January day and found some music on the clock radio. We danced slowly around the room, my head on his shoulder, my arms around his neck, until after a while we weren't dancing at all, just holding each other close, closer than we'd ever been before, and then we moved toward the bed. Patrick helped me take off my clothes, and I helped him take off his.

It was mysterious and wonderful, having known each other all these years, that this was the first time we had seen each other completely nude—the red hairs on Patrick's body, the blond hairs on mine. Patrick's frame was more muscular than I'd remembered it, but he was gentle.

"I don't have condoms," he told me.

"I'm on the pill," I said, but, just to be completely safe, I found the pack Planned Parenthood had given me, tucked down in one corner of my travel kit. Dave had always used his own.

Then I slid into bed and into his arms. We explored each other—slowly, lovingly, taking our time—something we had imagined doing for a long, long time. I loved the tender way our hands touched and stroked and our mouths searched each other's out. . . .

"I love you, Alice," Patrick said.

"I've always loved you," I told him.

When he entered me at last, in the same loving way, I didn't care that he came almost immediately because I knew there would be another time, and another, and another.

We didn't go outside until late afternoon, and then it was just to the drugstore to get some acid pills. Patrick wasn't used to the gigantic breakfast he'd eaten and knew he'd have to go easy at dinner. We ate in the hotel dining room, but we disappointed the waiter by ordering only soup and salad. And then we were in our room again, in the bed again, and after we made love, we talked until late into the night about past and future and now and everything.

"You don't know how much I've missed you," he said, tilting his head back so he could see my face, brushing my hair back off my forehead. "*I* didn't know how much I'd miss you till I was half a world away."

"You liked being in the Peace Corps," I reminded him.

"I did. And I felt that's where I needed to be. But I also felt I was missing someone really important to me, and then I read that you were engaged. It really hit me hard."

"You never felt that way about Jessica or Amanda?"

"No. Not in that way."

We stayed one more night, and then I told Val I'd be down for a few days, and Patrick called home to tell his mom he was on his way.

As we lay together for the last time, Patrick said, "I'll be at your graduation. Could you come to Chicago over spring break?"

"Of course," I answered. "I'll tell the whole gang I'll be with you."

"Aren't you going to call Liz and Pamela?"

"I already have."

"When?"

"While you were sleeping yesterday."

"I didn't hear?"

"You were dead to the world, Patrick. I picked your pocket, stole your credit cards, checked your iPod—I was one busy girl."

He smiled and studied my face before kissing me again.

"Man, it's good to be home," he said.

14
SUMMER NIGHTS

In Oklahoma City, I rode around with Valerie in her rental car, but all I could see was the inside of O'Hare Airport and Patrick standing there with a bag over one shoulder, looking at me in that surprised, delighted way. I listened to her chatter about the building that was being remodeled for the museum, and all I could hear was sleet hitting the tenth-floor window in the hotel as Patrick and I snuggled beneath the covers. Val and I ate lunch together at a new Indian restaurant, where she raved about the mango lassi, and I smiled, remembering the plate of chicken wings Patrick and I had shared just before I caught my flight.

"Alice, have you listened to one single word I've said since we sat down?" Val asked, slowly waving one hand in front of my face.

I snapped to. "I'm sorry. Really. I just . . . I'm—"

"In love," said Val. "I can see it in your eyes, your face, the way you move, the way you walk."

"I know," I said, smiling. "I'm being held captive by everything he said, he touched, he . . ."

"So what happens next? You're going to finish out the semester, aren't you?"

"Of course. I'm going to try to see him over spring break. And he's coming to my graduation. The problem is that I'm broke—almost. If I don't eat any meals or see any movies off campus from now till May, I could make it. But that's all. Patrick paid our hotel bill in Chicago, and he said he'd pay my plane fare back and forth to Chicago, but . . . look at me! I'm a grown woman and I've been dependent on my dad practically my whole life, then Dave, now Patrick . . ."

"And you feel like a 'kept' woman? Is that it?"

"Exactly."

"I can think of worse. If I had just reconnected with a man I love after all these years and he was loaded, I'd be tap-dancing down the hall."

"Be serious, Val. I want my own income."

"And you're going to have it, sweetie, as soon as you get your degree and get the hell out of here! Be patient! Enjoy! Where does Patrick get his money, anyway? Wealthy family?"

I nodded. "His dad pays for his schooling—same as mine. But Patrick's grandfather set up a trust fund for him that kicked in when he reached twenty-one. Gets so much a month, I think. Not a lot . . ."

"How much money in the trust?"

"I don't know. Sorta not my business."

She slowly shook her head. "And I'm stuck with you as a roommate till May. The woman who isn't there."

The University of Chicago is on the quarter system, and there was only one day of my spring break that overlapped with the break Patrick had between quarters. As the most expensive trip ever, I skipped a day of school for those two days and two nights, and there were only a few moments when we weren't together, physically touching. It was worth the plane fare, Patrick said.

He claimed he couldn't wait for my graduation to see me again, and so for one mad weekend, he flew back to Maryland, and I brought him home to see Dad and Sylvia. I'd finally told them about meeting him in Chicago after Christmas, almost afraid that if I let them in on my joy, the dream would pop. Or that they would suspect I might have got him on the rebound, after my breakup with Dave.

But there we were on a surprisingly cool April day, coming through the doorway together, me in my thin white sweater and chocolate-brown pants, my hair blow-dried in a new careless way, curled up at the ends, and Patrick in a blue henley, a small U of C emblem on one side. When Dad came down the stairs, his own happiness taking over his whole face, I knew right away that he was delighted.

"Patrick! How good to see you!" he said, clapping him on the shoulder and simultaneously shaking his hand.

"It's wonderful to be back. It really is," Patrick said.

Sylvia came in from the dining room. "Well, look who's here!" she cried, coming over to give him a hug. "Patrick, I'd recognize you a mile off. That hair gives you away every time."

I generously let them have their fill of him, as we sat around talking about his two years in the Peace Corps, and how he had worked it out with the University of Chicago to let that, and a few additional courses, count as a year of study, so that he had only one more year to go for his undergraduate degree. (First time in my whole life Patrick was behind me in anything.)

As I listened to Patrick relate some of his experiences in the PC, I realized that these were things I knew nothing about, but they were the things that made up the Patrick I loved. And I loved this man—that I *knew*. Every detail fascinated me—the hedgehog he'd saved from drowning in his well; celebrating Easter by eating fish with his Malagasy family under a cashew tree; and the smaller children who had followed him about and regularly invaded his living quarters, who could not understand why he was leaving, never to come back. Not only was I interested in the life he had lived overseas, I cared.

We talked for another half hour, and then Dad said, "Well, we know you have only a short time to visit this weekend . . . ," and this gave us our chance to say our good-byes and leave.

We stopped in at the Stedmeisters' for another hour, another round of hugs, and then I drove him out to Great Falls, and we stood on the overlook watching the rush of water over the rocks. I leaned back against him and he wrapped his arms around me, chin on the top of my head. I decided that if I could be anywhere in the world at that moment, it would be just where I was then.

That evening, after a long, candlelit dinner at the Anchor Inn, we lingered at the table in front of a crackling fire and talked. The more I saw of Patrick, the more I noticed that he was the same and not the same. He was quieter, for one thing— more thoughtful. He'd seen a lot more of the world and wasn't so quick to have an opinion on everything. He said I'd changed too, and not just my hair.

"What exactly?" I asked.

"Well, for one, you don't react to little things that would have embarrassed you before," he said. "Like lettuce between your teeth."

"I've got lettuce in my teeth?" I cried, running my tongue around inside my mouth.

"Oops. Spoke too soon," Patrick said, grinning.

"Okay. What else?"

"You're prettier."

"Really? Well, you're handsomer too, but that's only one of your many qualities."

"What qualities would those be?"

"I thought we were talking about *me*!" I told him.

"We are. We're talking about us," he said.

I liked that even better. And then we got down to the serious stuff. Holding hands, I told him more about Dave, and he told me more about Jessica.

"What did she look like?" I asked.

"A little like you, only heavier."

"What went wrong? Really."

"We just argued a lot. Big things. Little things. Both control freaks, I guess. I figured if we were arguing that much then, it would get even worse the longer we stayed together. Not that we were engaged or anything. Part of the attraction, I guess, was that we were both far from home, a little lonely, and she—we— we were available. How about you and Dave?"

"He was, and still is, a nice guy, Patrick. But he wasn't you—and you were away . . . ," I said. "We simply cared about different things."

What we wanted, I guess, was to be sure there were no lingering doubts, regrets—no troublesome baggage coming along into our new relationship. And when the flames had died down in the fireplace and it didn't appear as though the management was eager to get them going again, Patrick paid the check and drove his rental car across the river to his hotel near the airport, and then I was in his arms again, and we stood for a long time in the embrace.

Lovemaking is different with every man, I suppose, and Patrick was different from Dave. Dave had been considerate, gentle, wanting to please me, and so was Patrick. But Patrick's lovemaking was more urgent. He took a longer time getting me aroused, and every gesture seemed to have meaning for him.

"You're beautiful," he said of my breasts, cupping them in his hands.

I ran my hands over his chest, the fine red hairs like peach fuzz, and thought how lucky, how really lucky, we were to have found each other again.

When I graduated, Patrick had only that weekend to be with me, but we made the most of it. I don't know—both graduations, high school and college, seemed more like beginnings than endings to me. Like I should be celebrating what was to come, not what had been completed. The minute high school graduation was over, my friends and I had made that mad ride to Baltimore to join the crew of the *Seascape* for the summer, and now I would immediately be starting courses for my master's degree, so school wasn't over for me, not at all. But Dad and Sylvia saw it as a celebration, so I joined in the mood for the day, actually more happy to see Patrick than to walk across the stage in that hot gown and accept a diploma.

Dad's gift to me was my first car, a copper-colored Subaru—used, of course—all polished up with a big bow attached to the steering wheel. I knew I was getting a car and had given him an idea of what I wanted, but actually seeing a car that belonged to me—holding the keys in my hand—was a feeling I couldn't have anticipated. The ability to just get in a car and *go*—anywhere at any time. No more bus and Metro schedules, no begging friends for a ride, no calling home to see if someone could come get me.

"Dad, you're the greatest!" I said, giving him the kind of bear hug he gives me. "I *love* it, love it, love it!"

"Glad you like it, sweetheart," he said. "And I would be lying to you if I said that Sylvia and I weren't delighted to know that we officially have the full use of our own cars again."

They had let me use theirs on and off all through high school, and occasionally during college, but now my Subaru would have its own place in the student parking lot, and I'd get a U of M sticker to put on the window. Sylvia took a picture of me in it to send to Aunt Sally.

Les and Stacy were there for my graduation, of course, and after I'd sat in my Subaru and stroked the seats and the dashboard, Les gave me his graduation present: A road atlas and a set of flares. And then, grinning, he handed me a book of coupons for two hundred dollars' worth of gas. "No excuse now not to come visit Stacy and me," he said, and I promised.

"You don't know how much I appreciate this, Les," I said, thinking of my near-extinct bank account. "You *really* don't know!"

Moe and Liz had attended my graduation, and Gwen now had a new boyfriend. She'd started going out with a chem major named Charlie, who was studying pharmacology, and they made a good pair. He was funny and full of life, and crazy about Gwen, I could tell. It was good to see her taking time out of her overbooked schedule to cut loose a little.

The six of us drove into Georgetown that evening and ambled along the streets, looking in the windows of funky little shops. We stopped in one so Liz could buy a toy for her younger brother, and each of us bought one of the little horns we found in a bin. Gwen and Patrick and Moe discovered that theirs, blown together, made a minor chord, but when I added mine, it ruined it all.

"Gosh, Al, even your horn is tone-deaf," Liz teased.

At one point in the evening, Liz, Gwen, and I were walking ahead of the guys, arms around each other, and suddenly Gwen said, "Alice, I've been meaning to tell you. Charlie and I were eating at the Noodle House in Rockville and saw Dave there."

"Really? How is he?"

"We didn't get to talk to him. He was with someone, a short brunette. We were just getting settled and they were getting ready to leave."

"His girlfriend, you think? I hope?"

"Seemed to be. He was teasing her about something and they were pretty affectionate. He looked happy."

"That's the best news I've heard all week," I said. "Now *I'm* happy."

We had dinner in one club, and later stopped in another to listen to a guitarist, a nice mellow end to a great evening together. And then Patrick and I were back in his hotel, in each other's arms, and only the occasional muted hum of a plane beyond the window interrupted.

Both Patrick and I were in school over the summer. We had to be in order for me to get my master's degree by the following June and for him to get his undergraduate degree from the U of

Chicago around the same time. I had applied for, and received, an efficiency apartment in the building reserved for grad students, and I was able to have it all to myself. Not only that, but I answered an ad from one of the physics professors to clean her house on Tuesday evenings when she was at the gym. I found I actually enjoyed the job. It gave my brain a rest and my body a workout, and I'd grown up knowing how to scrub a bathtub and use a dust mop. The seventy dollars provided some desperately needed pocket money for the week.

It was as though our two schools, Patrick's and mine, conspired to keep us apart, however. My spring term ended May 17, and the summer term began May 28. Patrick's spring term ended June 15, and his summer term began June 18. The only times both of us had free were weekends, which meant a mad dash to the airport after a last class on Friday and usually the last flight back on Sunday night—with no studying in between, of course—which meant we couldn't afford many of these weekends.

But we squeezed in every minute of fun we possibly could, and we even persuaded Lester's old roommate, Paul Sorenson, to take us out once on his sailboat, *Fancy Pants*, then treated him to a crab dinner on the Chesapeake Bay.

In late summer, however, there were actually four days that both Patrick and I were free, and this time he rented a condo for us in Ocean City. Off we went in my Subaru, and I let him drive. As we crossed the Bay Bridge, Patrick's hand on mine, we both looked at each other and started to laugh.

"You remember the last time we were here?" he asked.

"The *only* time we were here, Patrick," I said. "Together, I mean. I still have that picture in my scrapbook."

"We should take another," he said.

"Uh-uh. With fifty cars behind us and security at both ends? But, you know, they have the Chesapeake Bay Bridge Walk every year—close one of the spans to car traffic and crowds of people walk across. We should do that sometime," I suggested.

Once we got in the condo and put our bags down, I went in the bathroom and put on my bikini. The day was gorgeous, and we'd talked about getting all the swimming in that we could, since rain had been predicted for later.

When I came out of the bathroom, Patrick was on the balcony, still wearing his shorts and T-shirt. I squeezed onto the chaise lounge beside him, my bare legs draped over his, running one foot over his calf. He caressed my thigh as we looked out over the water.

"Remember when you came to the beach, Patrick—the summer between sixth and seventh grades? When Elizabeth and Pamela came with Dad and me, and Lester drove you over later?"

"Sure, I remember," he said. "The summer Pamela lost her bikini top in the ocean. How could I forget?"

"Everything was so new then," I said.

"It still is," Patrick said, and kissed my shoulder. "I remember the bathing suit *you* were wearing too."

"You do?"

"Bows at the sides—sort of an iridescent green."

I looked at him in amazement. "I didn't think guys

remembered things like that. I'll bet you also remember how Pamela planned to climb into bed with you as a joke to make you think it was me, but she got Lester instead." That made us both laugh.

"Should we go down on the beach while we've still got some sun?" I asked.

"Maybe," Patrick said.

I went back inside to find my sunblock, but when I got it out of my bag and turned around, Patrick was standing in the balcony doorway, smiling at me. I went over and put my arms around him and we kissed. And the way we kissed, the way we pressed our bodies together and he caressed my back, I knew that the beach didn't matter that much anymore.

For a long time afterward we lay, just caressing each other, the briny smell of the ocean blowing in on the breeze around us, the noise of the surf and swimmers from below. I traced his forehead and nose and lips with one finger, and we kissed again. Once in a while I felt a pang of jealousy, wondering how he and Jessica had made love, but then it passed.

"Do you ever wish you'd been the first, Patrick?" I asked finally.

"Oh, maybe on some level I do, but it doesn't matter, because I'm in love with every part of you, not just that. And I wouldn't have wanted to hurt you. The first time can't have been all that pleasant."

"Well, it did hurt."

"I'd just like to think I'm more unique and fabulous," he said.

Then he asked, "Do you wish you had been the first for me?"

"A little." I paused. "Okay, not true. A lot!" He laughed and pulled me closer.

When we finally got out on the beach in the late afternoon, most of the swimmers had left the water. We swam awhile, stood and jumped the breakers as they came in, and finally walked ankle-deep in the surf, arms around each other, occasionally stopping to kiss. But when we reached a concrete breakwater extending up onto the sand, Patrick sat down on it, facing the ocean, and I sat in front of him, between his outstretched legs. He put his arms around me, his chin resting on my shoulder, and we watched the gulls circling and diving above the water.

"I love you, Alice," he said.

"I think I've loved you all my life," I told him.

"Marry me, then?" he said. "After you finish grad school?"

It wasn't the way I had imagined a proposal. It wasn't a candlelit room with wine and roses and Patrick down on one knee. But it was exactly right. What I felt was complete and utter joy.

"If you can wait that long," I said.

"I'd wait for you forever," he told me.

"Oh, Patrick," I said. I lost myself in his embrace, and I felt like an amoeba, my body melting into his, his into mine.

"I don't have a ring for you yet," he whispered. "I wanted you to be able to choose it yourself."

"Let's choose them together—matching bands," I told him. "I don't want a diamond."

"You sure? You can have both, you know. And Mom's got a diamond she wants you to have."

"No. I don't want something I have to take off every time I do the dishes. I just want a ring you can put on my finger that stays there forever, Patrick."

"Then that's what you'll have," he said.

When we came back two days later, we stopped at my house first. Dad had been reading the paper on the front porch and was just going back inside. I jumped out of the car and ran like a crazy person up the steps behind him, then threw my arms around him when we got inside. Patrick followed, grinning.

"Well!" said Dad, hugging me back. "I take it you two had a good time."

"Oh, Dad," I said, "we're engaged!"

Dad beamed and turned to hug Patrick, too. "Congratulations!" he said. "I couldn't ask for anyone finer. Sylvia!" he shouted out. "Come hear the good news!"

Sylvia came out of her study, glasses in hand.

"We're engaged!" I told her happily.

Sylvia threw her arms around us both at once, and I felt almost like a kid again, I was that happy. Happy and joyful and . . . And there it was. Passion, tenderness, and joy.

We called Patrick's parents and got the same reaction from them.

"Have you given any thought to the date?" Sylvia asked.

"We're thinking October of next year," I said, "and we'll do as much of the work we can ourselves."

Patrick stayed for dinner, and the four of us talked until eight o'clock. Then I drove him to the airport, and we had one long, lingering kiss. I drove back to the house because I wanted to use our washing machine to get the sand out of my suit and towel. And even though it was late, I had this tremendous urge to go up in the attic and find my mother's wedding dress. It would undoubtedly have to be altered some—she had been taller than I was, Dad told me—but our shoulders and waists, he thought, were about the same size.

I found the large cardboard storage box labeled MARIE'S WED-DING DRESS. The sealing tape was still in place—almost baked to the cardboard by now—making it difficult to pry the box open.

Once again, I worried that the dress had discolored or that insects had gotten to it, so I tried to brace myself for whatever I found. When I got the lid off at last, I found the dress wrapped in blue tissue paper, with more tissue stuffed in the bodice and sleeves. I removed the paper and held the dress up, a light ivory-colored taffeta, beautifully cleaned and preserved. It had a round neckline, three-quarter-length sleeves, a fitted bodice, and the skirt fell in gentle folds. Just knowing that Mom had worn it made me hold it close, and I knew that no matter what it may have turned out to look like, I would have worn it and loved it, simply because it was hers.

I was just about to fold it up again and gently replace the tissue paper when I saw a note card, folded in half, lying in the box. The name of the consignment shop where she'd bought it, I imagined. But when I picked it up, I saw my name on the front. I sucked in my breath, my eyes huge, and unfolded the card.

There, in my mom's handwriting, I read:

I know I would have loved him too.
Mom

15
SNAKEHEADS

Elizabeth, however, was the first of our crowd to marry. The ceremony took place in Our Lady of Lourdes Church a few days after Christmas, and she was the most beautiful bride I'd ever seen. Small strands of pearls and baby's breath had been woven in her dark hair, and she wore a Victorian gown with a high lace collar. She was simply so spectacularly beautiful that I saw Moses suck in his breath when he saw her coming down the aisle on her father's arm.

She had chosen a cousin to be her maid of honor because, she said, she couldn't choose between Pamela, Gwen, and me, so she made us all bridesmaids. Pamela, however, broke her leg in a skiing accident, so it was just Gwen and me, with Pamela looking on from the pews. Gwen and I wore mauve gowns and matching shoes. Nathan, who was ten now, served as altar boy, and Drew, George, and Kyle—three of the other guys we'd met on the California Zephyr—stood up with Moe.

"Well, Liz," I said in the restroom later, when we were touching up our makeup for the photographer, "who would have guessed that you'd meet your future husband on Amtrak?"

She laughed. "Isn't Moe great?" she said. "Isn't he wonderful?"

"He's one of the best," I told her, and I truly believed he was the best guy on earth for Elizabeth.

They went to Italy for their honeymoon and came back to buy a town house in the District. Moe had been hired by the Justice Department, and Liz would be teaching at a private school in Virginia while she worked on her master's degree.

A number of our old gang had come back to town for Liz's wedding, but we'd lost track of both Penny and Brian. Karen was in Philadelphia, Jill and Justin in Baltimore, Lori and Leslie in Seattle. It's sort of sad, you know. When you're in high school, it's like one close community, and you imagine that your little circle of friends will keep in touch forever. You believe that everyone will continue to get together every chance they can, and for a while they do. But then not everybody comes home for the holidays, and later on you find out that while some of them came back, they didn't bother to call. People just drift away. What you do, I guess, is see who still writes to you ten years after you've graduated, and *those* are your real friends.

* * *

Pamela, meanwhile, was still living in New York and had dated a number of men. We thought she might be serious about the one who helped her through recovery after her accident, but nothing came of it. She was working for an advertising agency full-time now and loving her job.

Patrick and I went up one weekend to visit and met her after work for dinner. She arrived in a svelte black suit, stockings, and heels, a silk scarf of black and white geometric shapes at her throat, the epitome of a New York businesswoman climbing the corporate ladder.

"Look at you!" I cried. "You look like a commercial for AT&T."

She chose the restaurant, a new one near the theater district, that had the most heavenly risotto I'd ever tasted.

"How do you find all these wonderful places?" I asked as we waited for our coffee. "If I lived in New York and ate out all the time, I'd weigh a ton."

"Guys," she said. "I don't discover them on my own. I remember the menus, though, even though I don't indulge."

And of course I understood, but Patrick looked at us quizzically, and we exchanged amused smiles.

"It's like this, Patrick," Pamela said. "When I'm out with a guy, I want to be attractive, so I may be starved when I pick up the menu, but while I tell the waiter, 'Watercress salad with mandarin oranges, please,' my stomach's saying—"

"Sirloin steak with fried onions and mashed potatoes," I finished, and we giggled while Patrick stared.

"I may have spent two hours in the gym before I showered and met my date, and then I order fillet of flounder with broccoli while my stomach says—"

"Country-fried chicken and biscuits," I offered, and we giggled even louder. People around us looked over.

"Asparagus spears and hold the dressing," Pamela said, in her most movie-star voice.

"Macaroni and cheese and two corn dogs to go!" I exclaimed in a nasal twang, and that broke us up.

Suddenly the waiter appeared at our table, looking at us hesitantly: "Might I interest the ladies in some dessert?" he asked.

Pamela and I tried to stop laughing.

"I'll have the mocha crème cake à la mode," Pamela said.

"Make that two," I added.

"Make it three," said Patrick. "And could you bring some mints along with the check, in case my guests get hungry later?"

I still hadn't been to see Les and Stacy's place in West Virginia, and in early May, Dad called one Friday and said that he and Sylvia were driving down the following day, just for an overnight visit to Lester's. Did I want to come along?

Yes! Dad let me have the backseat to finish an assignment for a class on Monday, and we set out, glad that there wasn't much traffic on a weekend. Even before we reached the state line, however, I put my books away and concentrated on the scenery. Spring in West Virginia is gorgeous, with feathery green in every shade, dotted here and there with dogwoods. I could only imagine what the hills would look like in fall.

"Isn't this glorious, Ben?" Sylvia kept saying. "I can truly understand why Les has fallen in love with the state."

Dad was intent on his driving, however, and there didn't seem to be a straight stretch of road anywhere. It curved one way, then the other, switchback after switchback.

"Can you guess what these roads are like in winter?" he said, hunched over the wheel. "I hope they live close to their work. I'd hate the thought of driving over ice on these curves."

But Sylvia and I were entranced with nothing but trees, trees, trees on either side, like tall parental figures, holding out leafy arms to embrace us. To transport us away from all the cares of city life.

"I think this getaway is just what we need, Alice," Sylvia said. "Every moment we've had together seems devoted to the wedding, and it's just nice to clear our heads for a few days, isn't it?"

I agreed.

Les and Stacy were renting a town house in a small community a mile from the center where they worked. Les was in their little patch of front yard, watering the shrubs, when we pulled up in front. He grinned and turned off the hose.

"Your Honda make the hills okay?" he asked, coming over to give us each a hug as we climbed out and stretched.

"Of course!" said Dad. "It's only seven years old. What did you think?"

Les scooped me up in his arms. "Finally got you away from books and bridal magazines, huh? Come on in, everyone."

Stacy was putting lunch on the table, but she stopped to give us a tour of their home, everything sparse and sleek—Z-bar lamps with LED lights by the chairs and on desktops, geometric prints on the walls and sofa cushions, bright and modern and attractive.

"You've done a fantastic job! I love it!" I told her. It was fun following her from room to room, pretty in her jeans and peasant blouse with the untied ribbons at the neckline.

"We had a budget and followed it to the penny," she said. "Amazing what you can do with IKEA and a few yard sales thrown in."

After lunch Les took us on a tour of the convention center. His office had a wide window looking out on the woods, and we exclaimed over the indoor Olympic-size pool where Stacy taught swimming and exercise classes.

"Anything particular you wanted to do while you're here?" he asked us. "I can even round up a few horses if you'd like to ride. What about you, Alice?"

"Fishing," I said.

Everyone looked at me.

"Fishing?" said Les.

"I don't think I've ever been fishing in my life. I want to be able to say I tried it."

Les looked at Stacy. "We've got the rods and the tackle. If we got up early tomorrow and caught anything, could we add it to tomorrow's lunch?"

"Absolutely," she said. "But I won't count on it."

So he took us to see the river, himself in the lead, holding branches out of the way as we followed the path.

"Snakes are beginning to come out of hibernation and sun themselves, so watch where you step," he warned us.

I paused with one foot two inches from the ground. Snakes and mice and roaches are all on my wipe-off-the-face-of-the-earth list, and suddenly I began seeing snakes everywhere. Every branch on the path, every twisted root of a tree, brought a gasp or a yelp from me.

Finally Les said, "Al, you want me to get some Prozac or something?"

"No, I want you to carry me piggyback all the way to the river," I bleated.

"If there are any snakes on the path, Les will come to them first, Al," Dad assured me, bringing up the rear, his sunglasses moved up on his forehead to see through the darkness of the trees. "If they're off in the brush, they're not going to bother you unless you bother them first."

"Or look at them," Les said. "If a snake is staring right at you, stop and look away."

Now I came to a dead halt on the path. "Really?" I knew that applied to dogs and bears, but . . .

"Of course. Haven't you ever heard of 'snake eyes'?"

"Is this true, Les?" I demanded.

"Absolutely," said Les, keeping a straight face. "And after you yield the path to a snake, keeping your eyes averted, you're supposed to give a little bow and say, 'After you.'"

Dad chuckled, and Stacy swatted at Les from behind.

"You're no help, Lester. If we were lost in a jungle together, we'd get eaten by the first thing that came along," I told him.

The river was beautiful with the reflection of the afternoon sun on the water. There was a homemade dock at the water's edge and a rowboat tied to a post.

"Whose boat?" asked Sylvia.

"Bill, our neighbor's," said Stacy. "He'd be glad to let you use it."

"Sure you're up to this, Al?" Les asked. "We'd need to get up really early, when the fish are biting."

"I'm fine as long as we're in a boat," I said.

We enjoyed Stacy's chicken divan that evening and Lester's homemade wine. As darkness closed in, we could hear the night sounds in the woods, and I began to feel more relaxed than I had in a long time. We all retired early, Dad and Sylvia in the guest room and me on a daybed under a handmade quilt, in the little home office off the living room.

Les tapped on my door about five the next morning.

"Al? You still want to go fishing, or would you rather sleep?" came his voice from outside the door.

My eyes opened a slit. Surely it couldn't be morning already.

I felt myself sliding back into sleep, but he tapped again and stuck his head inside. "If we want to catch anything, we've got a better chance if we go now. Bill says the fishing's best between five and seven."

"I'm up, I'm up," I said hoarsely, willing my eyes to open.

And finally I was in the kitchen in my jeans and sneakers and an old sweatshirt of Stacy's, my hair in a ponytail, nothing but ChapStick on my face.

"I made us a couple of peanut butter sandwiches and dug up a can's worth of night crawlers for bait after you went to bed last night," he said. "I think we're set."

He handed me the bait can, a bucket, the sandwiches, and a thermos, while he carried the rods, the tackle box, and a flashlight.

I didn't worry about snakes this time because no snake would be trying to sun itself yet. Something scurried across the path—a chipmunk, I think—but I kept my eyes on the beam of the flashlight ahead, and finally we were at the dock. Les held the rowboat steady while I climbed in.

There was something special about being out on a river before dawn with my married brother—watching the slow current make its way around the boat, the trees barely visible, birds calling from shore to shore.

"Right about here," Les said, maneuvering the boat to a point almost even with a fallen tree on the opposite bank. "This is where Bill suggested we try our luck."

I wanted Les to know I could do whatever he could do,

so—in the early morning light—I watched how he baited a hook and practiced tossing my line in the water. I never got it as far out as he wanted it to be, but he said that would do, and we settled down to eat our sandwiches and watch the bobbers moving slightly up and down on the water. I was glad that Stacy had suggested I bring a box of wipes along. Never eat a peanut butter sandwich right after you've baited a hook unless you have some wipes.

"I think married life's agreeing with you, Les," I said. "Stacy, too. You both look great. What's it been now—three years?"

"Coming up on four," Les said. "Yep, we're doing fine. I can't say I'll stay in this job forever, but for now we both like living here a lot."

I saw that his bobber had gone under, but when Les reeled his line in, the hook was empty.

"Took the bait and got away," Les said, and dug another night crawler out of the can.

We weren't having much luck. Les picked up the anchor once and moved to a different location, but we got only a few nibbles and lost a lot of night crawlers.

When the sun had risen full, reflecting off the water, we passed the sunblock back and forth for something to do. The minutes ticked by, and I began to feel that I was being hypnotized by the bobber and that if Lester were to chant *You are sleepy, you are sleepy*, I'd probably topple over.

Suddenly my bobber went under, and I felt a tug on my line.

"I got something! I got something!" I cried excitedly.

"Okay, easy now. Don't let the line go slack," Les said, standing up as my line moved in the water. "Keep it taut while you reel it in, and not too fast."

The line was heavy, and the rod was slightly bent.

"Got a big one, Al. Want help?" Les asked, taking a step toward me. Even he was excited.

"No! I want to do it myself!" I cried, sounding like a four-year-old. "Is the bucket ready? Do we have a net?"

"No net, but the bucket's ready. Just keep pulling it in . . ."

The line kept jerking. The fish was obviously trying to get away, but the closer it got to the boat, the heavier the line felt. I was afraid it was going to wriggle loose of the hook, the rod bending farther and farther, and finally I flung the line backward, and a long, silver, slithering something landed flopping and twisting in the rowboat.

"A snake!" I screamed, and fell backward, down into the bottom of the boat.

"Al!" yelled Les.

"A snake!" I shrieked again, letting go of the rod, and suddenly the creature was on top of me.

"Get it off! Get it off!" I screamed.

"It's an eel," Les yelled back, trying to grab the line and steady it, but the slithering thing flipped around on top of my chest until finally Les grabbed it with both hands and threw it back in the water.

He stood there looking down at me, and I could see he was trying not to laugh. "You okay?" he asked.

"You didn't tell me there were snakes in the river!" I chided, struggling to get up again.

"It was an eel, Al."

"It was a snake. A water snake! A water moccasin or something!"

"E-E-L," he spelled out, reaching down to pull me up.

"Prove it."

"I can't. I threw it back. It was too big for the bucket, and I couldn't subdue you both. If I'd had a net, though, I would have put it over you." He steadied the boat, a hand on either side, as I awkwardly pulled myself back onto the seat.

"Sure you're not hurt?" Les asked.

"We might have both been bitten and poisoned," I said, rubbing my shoulder. "It was at least four feet long."

"Three, maybe." Les grinned. "Ready to go back and get some breakfast?"

"Yes." I was more civil now. "And thanks for the fishing trip, Les, even though you live near a snake-infested river."

"Eel," said Les, picking up the oars and turning the boat around.

"Full of water moccasins and snakeheads," I muttered.

When we got back, Dad and Sylvia and Stacy were having coffee.

"How was the fishing?" Dad asked.

"We had a nibble or two, but nothing we could bring back," said Les. "The fish just weren't biting much this morning."

"All except the snakeheads," I said.

"Snakeheads?" Stacy paused, holding the coffeepot. "Did you see a snakehead? We're supposed to report them if we see any. Fish and Wildlife Service is trying to keep them out of West Virginia rivers."

"Yeah, I'll file a report," said Les, and I could see that he was struggling to hold back a grin. "I'll tell them there was some weird thing out on the river this morning . . . couldn't quite make out what it was, but it was wearing one of my wife's old sweatshirts and was definitely new to West Virginia waters."

It was hard to leave Les and Stacy and their little home in the woods. They seemed so content with each other, and I wanted Patrick and me to be as happy as they were.

After breakfast, and then lunch on their screened porch, Les walked our bags to the car.

"So what's the secret of a happy marriage, Les?" I asked.

"Hmmm," he said. "Always say yes."

"C'mon. Really."

"It's something every couple has to work out for themselves, Al. I can't give you a formula. To live together with anyone takes adjusting, you know that—even roommates."

"Okay, but what works for you and Stacy?"

Les opened the trunk of Dad's car and put the bags in. "Number one, listen. Number two, always be honest. Three, never take your company fishing."

I poked him in the ribs. "I had a good time anyway, Les. I guess we'll see each other at the wedding, if not before?"

"October it is. Got your wedding present all wrapped and ready."

"Really? What is it? Tell me now!" I begged.

"A tackle box and bait bucket," he said.

I got my master's degree in June—just a plain old MA, no frills, but I was pleased and so was Dad. Patrick gave me a small gold heart on a gold chain for a present. He graduated too that summer from the University of Chicago—summa cum laude, of course—bought a car, and moved to Maryland when he was hired in about two minutes by a think tank in DC studying health and food production in developing countries.

Since I'd be living at home temporarily, the Stedmeisters invited Patrick to stay with them till the wedding. He and Mark had been good friends, and this helped them feel that they were still part of Mark's life. They gave Patrick a key to the house and told him to come and go as he pleased, and we were grateful. Even though Montgomery County had no openings for a counselor at this time, we went apartment hunting, and we finally found one in a new complex in Bethesda. It would be completed about a month before we married.

We had set our wedding date for October 18, in the church on Cedar Lane where Dad had taken Sylvia to the Messiah Sing-Along, where he and Sylvia had been married, and where Les and Stacy, too, had said their vows. I promised myself our wedding would be as easy on our relatives and guests as possible. I would not ask them to travel to some distant location, would

let my bridesmaids help choose their dresses, and most definitely would request, in the program, that guests remain seated
when the bride came in. I hate the way everybody rises, like
she's royalty or something.

In fact, Abby, Valerie, and I used to wonder where that old
idea came from that this is *her* day—like everything has to be
exactly the way *she* wants it.

Claire saw it differently. "But it *is* her day! It's the day in
her life she's the most beautiful. She's *giving* herself to her new
husband."

"*What?*" I cried. "What is she, a loaf of bread? He's giving
himself to her too, remember."

"It's not the same," Claire said.

"It's *their* day!" we argued. "The bride's *and* the groom's."

"Nobody looks at the groom. *Everyone* looks at the bride,"
said Claire, and there was no reasoning with her.

In any case, although I was as anxious as anyone else to be
beautiful on our wedding day, I sure didn't want a trumpet-style
entrance when I came down the aisle.

Like Liz, I couldn't decide which of my friends should be my
maid of honor. I could have chosen my cousin too, and Carol
would have been the perfect choice, but she was in Pennsylvania
now and had just started a new job, so it wouldn't be fair to
saddle her with all the duties that go along with it. Same for
Stacy in West Virginia, Pamela in New York, and Gwen in medical school now, not just premed. Valerie was in Oklahoma, and
Abby had moved to Oregon and gone into partnership with her

aunt. Maybe there's something to be said for getting married while all your close friends are still around you!

It was easy, then, when both Gwen and Pamela suggested that I ask Liz to do the honor, since she was a teacher now and had the summer off. Liz said she'd be thrilled. And Stacy simplified things when she asked if she could be in charge of the guest book, as I'd done for her. So I had my cousin and five best girlfriends in the wedding party, and Patrick said he'd come up with five male friends too, plus Lester. Whew. I figured the hardest part was over.

There was a similar discussion about a bachelorette party and a shower. Pamela was determined there should be some kind of a night out for the gals, but it was hard enough getting people together for even one night, much less two.

And then I got a phone call from Mark's mother.

"Alice, I would like very much to give you a bridal shower," she said. "I'm not sure if young women have such things any-more or if they're anything like the ones I remember when I was a girl, but I'd like to try. It's been so much fun having Patrick stay with us while your apartment building is being finished, and . . . well, I would just like to do this, too."

"Mrs. Stedmeister, that would be lovely," I said. "And I hope it will be just the kind of shower you remember, because that's the kind I want."

When I called my bridesmaids and told them, Pamela's reaction was, "At the Stedmeisters'? We're going to have a fifties-style shower?"

"They're not that old," I said. "And whatever she plans will be fine with me."

And it was. I had given her my guest list for the wedding. Her name was on it, of course, and Sylvia's, and we chose the women who were my own special friends, excusing both Val and Abby, whom I wouldn't expect to fly in just for a shower. I wanted to include Marilyn, who had worked so long for Dad at the Melody Inn, and Claire and my friend Yolanda, and whomever else Mrs. Stedmeister would like to invite.

Les had driven in with Stacy for the weekend, and he and Patrick and Moe said they were going out for the evening, a little bachelor party, they told us—*wink, wink*—and alluded to a night in Baltimore, known for some of the racier clubs. When I arrived at Mrs. Stedmeister's, however, and remarked on what a beautiful evening it was, she said, "Oh, isn't it? And a perfect night for a ball game, too."

The Orioles! I thought. Those guys had known all along they were going to Camden Yards to watch the Orioles play, but they liked to torment us with thoughts of a strip joint.

"Was Mark a fan?" I asked.

"Indeed he was, and Patrick was even wearing Mark's Orioles cap when they left. In fact, Ed's back there watching the game right now." She nodded toward their study. "I told him to keep the noise down."

I exchanged smiles with Liz, and we went on into the living room, where I was met with the welcoming faces of so many women I loved.

"Marilyn!" I said. "I haven't seen you in ages. And Carol!"

The room was full of happy chatter as introductions were made, and I was surprised to find that Mrs. Long had come all the way from Wisconsin. Patrick's dad was having dinner with a friend from their days in the State Department.

"Edith Stedmeister and I were friends even before we realized we had two sons in the same grade," Patrick's mom told me.

"Yes, Virginia and I were in the Republican Women's Club, and we've been friends ever since," said Mrs. Stedmeister. "Just another reason I'm glad to have Patrick stay with us until the wedding."

It was a night right out of a bygone age—for me, anyway. Mrs. Long had been given the honor of presiding over the silver tea service in the dining room, and as we each passed the table, having filled our china dessert plates with bonbons and pastel-colored tea cakes, she handed us a cup and saucer, with exactly the right number of sugar cubes on the side and a slice of lemon.

Back in the living room, gifts were presented to me one at a time by Mrs. Stedmeister, who read the inscription on each card and remarked on the beautiful wrapping paper, and what a lovely bow. And it was amazing how each of my friends morphed into the atmosphere, as though we were all cast in a movie of decades past, modulating our voices, censoring some of our expressions, and sitting upright with knees together, balancing a teacup on our laps.

I exclaimed over each gift—the electric frying pan, the

blender, the set of silken sheets, the fluffy blanket, the flatware set—and I was glad to get each one, because Patrick and I were starting out with nothing, nothing except a mini fridge, a microwave, some clothes hangers from college, and a very modest trust fund from his grandfather. The Longs, wealthy as they were, believed that once a child had graduated, he had to make his own way in the world, and we agreed. Few children were left trust funds from their grandfathers, it's true, but until Patrick reached twenty-five, his was only enough to cover car expenses for a year, if that.

"I love you guys," I told my friends, holding the soft new blanket against my cheek. "I'll think of you every time I crawl into bed."

"That will be the last thing on your mind," Pamela said, and that got a laugh from even Mrs. Long and Mrs. Stedmeister.

At the end of the evening, after I had thanked all my guests, Mrs. Stedmeister stood up to make a little speech—things she remembered about me: my freckles, which grew more prominent in the summertime; my laughter, which she could always distinguish from the others. . . . And as I studied this tall, thin woman with the angular face, only her hair seemed to have changed from the short salt-and-pepper look she used to have to the almost white hair it was now. I could still see her standing uncomfortably at one end of the Stedmeisters' swimming pool the afternoon she announced that there would be no drinking or pot smoking at their house.

What courage that must have taken for this shy woman

with the soft voice, looking out over the wet heads of us swimmers, who had all gathered at the side of the pool to stare up
at her. The gracious woman who had, week after week, put
out refreshments for us on their picnic table and then disappeared, who had allowed us to leave puddles in her bathroom
and stray towels and parts of bathing suits, which we would
find laundered and neatly folded the next time we came. I felt a
special love for this woman who had suffered a tragedy I could
only imagine, who was somehow softening it by treating Mark's
friends as her own.

She was talking now about my former fear of the deep end
of the pool and how I had finally conquered that, of how pretty
I'd looked in a new bathing suit, and I realized that she knew
far more about us than we had ever guessed, she and her short,
pudgy little husband who had spent so much time working on
cars in the driveway with Mark.

"I'll always be grateful to you both," I said when she'd finished and had presented me with a beautiful little box of thank-
you cards. "You and your husband put up with more than we
expected or deserved, and if there were a badge of courage for
that, the Stedmeisters would have received it."

I kissed her on the cheek and hugged her to me, then said
good night to Mr. Stedmeister, who emerged from the den to
"say hello to the ladies" and announce that the Orioles were
ahead three to one in the ninth inning.

My bridesmaids helped carry my gifts to the car, and we
said good night to Mrs. Long, who was staying in a hotel, and

Marilyn, who had to get home to her children, and Sylvia, who said it was past her bedtime. That left eight of us there on the driveway, including Yolanda and Claire.

"It was like being in a time warp!" Gwen breathed.

"Awesome!" said Yolanda. "Like a contest, to see who could sit all evening without spilling tea in her lap!"

"So what do you girls do for fun down here?" Carol asked. "Now that your guys are out on the town?"

"Are you kidding?" said Liz. "Do you know where they went?"

The others turned our way. "Where?"

"An Orioles game!" I said. "They hinted that it was some forbidden nightclub, and all the while they're at a ball game!"

"So what are *we* going to do with the rest of the evening?" asked Stacy, tilting her watch toward the house so she could read it in the light from the windows.

"It's only ten. I think the guys need to be taught a lesson," I declared. "Any ideas?"

Pamela lifted one finger in the air. "Hold on!" she said. "Let's see if he's working tonight."

"Who?" I asked.

"Someone who owes me a favor," she said, and got out her cell phone.

We waited there in the moonlight while Pamela made a call. I could tell by her expression that she'd reached the person she wanted, but there were obviously negotiations going on. Finally her face broke into a smile and she nodded in our direction.

"Got it!" we heard her say. "Okay . . . in about twenty-five minutes."

"Where are we going?" I asked as she slipped her cell phone back in her bag.

"To the Source nightclub in DC," she said. "We are the 'Sullivan party of six,' only we've added two other guests and hope they won't mind," and she gave us the address. "Let's go."

"That's someone's reservation?" Stacy asked.

"Yep, but they aren't due until eleven, my friend says. If they show up, I'll think of something."

"Whoopee!" Carol exclaimed.

"Pamela!" I cried. "How will we—?"

"C'mon, live a little. If the Sullivans show, we'll claim we said the 'Solomons' and made the reservation five days ago." Pamela dug around for her car keys. "Relax. I know this guy from theater arts. He got this great job helping design the place."

We gasped and giggled, and when my car was full, the four others got in Gwen's, leaving the remaining cars out on the street till we got back.

16
FOREVER

We left our cars with the valet, and Pamela announced the Sullivans at the door. The doorman, also bouncer, looked us over, checked off the name, and we were escorted inside to an ultratech room of lights and sounds and furniture that resembled seats inside a spacecraft. There were headsets lying about.

Pamela apologized to the maître d' for having added two more guests to our party but said she hoped he could accommodate us, and he icily pushed two tables together.

According to the menu, we were in the Voyage Room, and by manipulating the controls at the end of our table, something like those on old jukeboxes, we could select our particular spaceship and individual route, which sometimes had us hooking up with one at a neighboring table. A rather sophisticated icebreaker.

"What are we supposed to do with these?" Liz asked, picking up one of the headsets, and in answer to her own question, she put it on her head. We watched as her face became more intent, obviously following recorded directions, and she motioned to the screen at the end of the packed room, where it appeared we were all in space heading toward a distant planet. Three men at a corner table were looking our way, and suddenly another spaceship appeared on the screen at the end of the room. Liz yanked off the helmet, and her face got that old familiar Elizabeth blush that made us laugh, and the men also.

I was handed the drink list, and when I saw the twenty-dollar service charge per person at the bottom of the paper, I almost choked. The drinks themselves were beyond pricey. You could buy two six-packs of Bud for what one glass of wine cost here.

"What are we going to do?" I whispered to Stacy, one finger sliding down unobtrusively to the cover charge.

"Charge it to the guys' credit cards. Serves 'em right for trying to upset us," she said. "Wild night, my foot!"

"Amen!" I said. "Champagne, anyone?"

We each ordered a glass of wine. The room was so noisy, we almost had to shout to be heard.

"What did you have to do to get us in, Pamela?" Claire asked her.

"Nothing. It's a guy from my theater arts school," Pamela yelled back. "I spent a weekend helping him film a vignette. He owes me one."

Gwen was looking at a descriptive card about the club that read: *By invitation, guests are welcome to explore the Temptation and Source Rooms, by taking the hidden stairway beyond the purple curtain.* "What the heck kind of club *is* this?" she asked.

"Don't worry. It's mostly 'sophisticated suggestiveness,'" Pamela said. "After Antony got hired here, he came back and gave a lecture on 'The Atmosphere of Desire.'"

"On what?" yelled Yolanda from her end of the table.

"Sex," Liz yelled back.

I could hear my cell phone chime, but just barely. "It's Patrick!" I told the others, reading his text. "Says they're on their way back, had a 'spectacular' evening, and wants to know if I'm home."

The girls all hooted. "What are you going to tell him?" asked Claire.

"Out with the girls," I said, my thumbs sending the message.

"I feel so matronly in this dress," said Carol, looking down at the navy-blue sheath with the white collar and cuffs. "I feel like an airline attendant or something."

"Hike it up about five inches," Yolanda suggested, so she did, showing a shapely expanse of leg.

On the large screen someone's spaceship had landed, and we seemed to be going back in time, not forward. A wild garden of some sort. I put on the headset and heard a loud cacophony of parrots.

At that moment a thirtyish man dressed in silver lamé, something between a tuxedo and a spacesuit, emerged from the crowd and leaned over Pamela, then just as suddenly disappeared.

"Antony says the Sullivans just arrived. We've got to give them our table and go up to the Temptation Room."

"Already? All *right*!" said Yolanda.

"And bring our wine with us," said Gwen.

Elizabeth's and Stacy's cell phones were both dinging now, and they were laughing before they even checked their screens.

"Moe wants to know when I'll be home," Liz giggled, reading his text.

"That's what Les is asking too," Stacy said.

"What are you going to tell them?" asked Gwen.

Liz thought for a minute. "Don't wait up," she said, and we shrieked with laughter.

We made our way to the high purple curtains at one side of the screen, then up the winding staircase to a door at the top that looked like the entrance to a cave.

It appeared to be the restaurant part of the nightclub and, at this hour, wasn't as busy or noisy as the floor below. Inside, we found artificial trees and fake fruit hanging from the branches, two live parrots squawking at each other. The wait staff wore nude-colored bodysuits with fig leaves placed appropriately. The spacecraft below had supposedly delivered us back to the beginning of man.

The maître d' took us to a round table for eight. The chairs seemed to be made from twigs and branches. I avoided the snake dangling from a tree with an apple in its mouth and let Pamela have the honor of it looking over her shoulder.

"I'm afraid we're no longer offering dinner this evening, but would you care for fruit or a dessert? An aperitif, perhaps?" the man said.

"Perhaps," said Pamela, and the maître d' nodded toward a waiter, who came over with a small card listing pears and cheese and caviar and a "chocolate volcano" dessert. Valerie ordered the volcano and asked for eight spoons. We had already racked up a considerable tab, and some of the others asked for more wine.

Liz asked for Perrier. "Somebody has to drive," she said.

"Good thinking," said Stacy. "I'll do the same."

We could hear each other a little better here.

"What part does your friend have in all this?" Carol asked Pamela.

"Design and décor. He'd already had two years in design school before he came to my theater school. A friend recommended him to a man who had this idea for a nightclub, and Antony came on down."

We were enjoying the waiters in their bodysuits, imagining them without the fig leaves, and had almost finished our chocolate when Antony appeared once again to Pamela's left.

"The Sullivans are on their way up, and the doorman is looking for you," I heard him tell her. "Take the service elevator up to the Source."

When the elevator came, the doorman was on it.

"Sullivan?" he asked suspiciously as we boarded.

"Solomon," Pamela told him. "I'm afraid someone got our names mixed up and thought we were the same party."

He didn't seem to be buying this, but just in case we were being truthful, he didn't protest as we got off on the next floor, and he stayed aboard as it went back down.

We heard the music even before the elevator door opened. We had expected to enter something even more primitive than the Garden of Eden, and in a way we did, because the walls were covered with a mural of dinosaurs and exploding volcanoes, but the activity was anything but. A band was playing and couples were dancing the Dougie there on the floor.

"I don't get it," I told Pamela when we were seated at three small cocktail-size tables.

She looked it over, her slim arms still bearing a trace of a mild summer tan.

"Life," she said finally. "The source of all this that came after, something like that—the dancers as evidence."

"O-kaaay," I said finally.

"They probably wanted a high-tech atmosphere to draw people in, a restaurant, and a nightclub dance floor, all in one club, so it's the Voyage, the Temptation, and the Source."

It didn't quite work for me, but it obviously did for the club, because the place was in full swing. Maybe you weren't supposed to think too much about it.

But twenty minutes later the doorman himself came to our table:

"Miss . . . uh . . . Solomon?" he said curtly, addressing Pamela.

Pamela put on her best act. "Yes?"

"I believe it's time for your party to vacate," the man said.

"Excuse me?"

"There are three gentlemen at the door, Madam, asking for you. Your husbands, I presume."

"How can that be?" Pamela asked. "Our husbands are attending a board meeting in New York."

"Perhaps so," said the doorman, his voice thick with sarcasm, "but right now they are there at the door in baseball caps. And your bill, Madam . . ."

He gave Pamela the bill, but Stacy was already handing him her credit card. "We'll settle up outside," she told the others.

Lester, Patrick, and Moe were standing just inside the entrance, and they looked at us quizzically when we got to the door. We waited till we were outside, then cut loose in an explosion of laughter.

"What a blast!" cried Carol. "This has been one fantastic evening!"

"Yeah?" said Les. "I thought you women went to a shower."

"And *you* guys told us you'd gone to a strip club to try to get us all upset," Stacy said. "What's good for the goose . . ." They laughed too.

"Well, just so everyone had a good time," Les said.

"Oh, we did," Stacy told him, and handed him a copy of the bill. "You guys can split it three ways."

* * *

Though we had rented our apartment from the first of October, the workmen didn't finish painting it until just ten days before our wedding. Patrick's parents and mine, as their wedding gifts to us, gave us checks to buy our furniture, and I was at the apartment the day the living room couch was delivered. Patrick was with me on Saturday when the table and chairs and a rug arrived. Bit by bit we watched our little one-bedroom apartment turning into our first home.

There was a small study off the living room that would serve as an office, and Patrick had inherited an old desk of his father's. Somehow—with a few end tables of Sylvia's, a bookcase, and a dresser that I loved—the apartment grew smaller and smaller the more we put into it.

Nothing really matched—we had bought each piece separately and that's the look we wanted. And we were happy.

We had already decided we wouldn't spend the night there until we were married. We wanted to come back from the honeymoon to a brand-new place, a new beginning. We'd reserved Sunday to bring in most of our personal things—clothes, books, desk supplies, DVDs, all the miscellaneous stuff of life—and that's when Patrick and I had our first big argument.

I'm not sure what it was all about, because so often you seem to be arguing about one thing when the real problem is something else. We'd agreed on most things, even a honeymoon in Ireland. But there had been a lot of tension, too—mostly

happy tension—about all the wedding details, finding the apartment, moving, Patrick's new job, my lack of one, starting a new
life together. . . .

We had a lot more room than what we'd had at college, but
without all the closets and attic and basement space we'd had
back in our homes. We'd talked about not bringing a whole lot
of stuff with us. Patrick was crazy about streamlined living, but I
felt as though I had cluttered up the closets at home long enough.
That Dad and Sylvia should be able to call the house their own,
and this was my home now; I wanted everything near and dear
to me right here. So, with the exception of some toys and books
I'd had as a child that Dad wouldn't let me give away even if I'd
wanted to, I brought almost everything else with me. Except my
old beanbag chair. I finally put that out in the trash.

It started with Patrick getting frustrated at how many boxes
we were carrying in. When you're living abroad, you get used
to doing with very little and traveling light. And when I arrived
with still another load, the last one, he lost it.

"What *is* all this stuff, Al?" he said. "Did you sort through
any of it, or did you just dump all your things in boxes? I hate
clutter." We were both feeling tired and hot. We didn't have the
air conditioner on because the door was open.

"I *did* sort through it, Patrick. I just have a lot of things I
want to keep," I said.

He kept opening box after box in silence, shelving my
books, putting boxes of clothes in one area, personal items in
another. I'll admit I probably didn't need to keep a videotape of

Gone with the Wind or a fifteen-year-old road atlas. I didn't need to keep my favorite dresses from high school and a dozen or more copies of each issue of *The Edge*. But it was when he got to a photo album, half filled with pictures of Dave, that he turned on me.

"So what's he doing in our apartment, Alice?" he asked, holding the album out away from him as though it were contaminated.

I shrugged, but I could feel a storm brewing. "He was part of my life for a while, Patrick, just like Jessica was a part of yours."

"I didn't keep her e-mails. I didn't even keep her pictures."

"Well, you kept at least one. You showed it to me."

"Okay, so I kept one. I didn't keep a whole album that would take up three inches of shelf space."

"What are we arguing about here, Patrick? It's only one inch wide. Is that really worth having a fight about?" I said. I'm not sure that was all that bothered me, though. What I sensed was an element of control in Patrick's voice, what I could and could not have in our home. Which memories were allowed and which weren't.

"We don't have enough shelf space as it is! *Look* at all this junk!" Patrick said.

The word *junk* set me off. "So I'll keep it under the bed, okay?" I snapped, grabbing the album out of his hands.

Patrick sat back on his heels. "That's great. Under our bed. Dave's in *our* bedroom."

"Oh, Patrick, grow up!" I said, and instantly wished I hadn't.

I remembered what the minister had said to Stacy at Lester's wedding: *Inside every man is a little boy. . . .* Patrick glared at me for a long moment, then stood up and clomped out to the kitchen. I heard him slide a bottle out of the fridge, then slam the door. Hard. I heard the sound of a cap being taken off a bottle, and for several minutes Patrick stayed in the kitchen while I continued unloading a box.

When he came back in with a Pepsi, he said, "I hate clutter, and I hate stuff taking up every available inch of space, and I particularly don't enjoy starting our life together with a photo album of an ex-boyfriend around the place."

"Patrick, you can't tell me what I can keep and what I can't," I told him. "I'll try to keep the clutter down, and I'll sort through my stuff even more. But Dave was a part of my life for a time, and while I'm not putting the album on the coffee table for all to see, I'm not going to throw it out, either."

He didn't answer. He simply picked up his car keys and left.

I wrapped my arms around my ankles, put my head on my knees, and cried. If Patrick was going to walk out over pictures—mere pictures—of a former boyfriend, what would he do when *real* problems came along? Maybe I should have taken the album to my house and left it in the attic. But then it would always seem as though there was something too dangerous to have around.

I thought of how childish Patrick was behaving, and then I remembered: *Inside every woman is a little girl.* Maybe *I* wasn't acting very grown up either. If it were an album of Jessica we were arguing about, would *I* want it under our bed? I wouldn't. In fact, I had to admit, I'd react exactly the same way.

A key turned in the lock and Patrick came back inside. He hadn't gone anywhere.

"Patrick, I . . . ," I began, looking up.

"I'm sorry," he said.

"No, *I'm* sorry. I'm being childish too."

"Okay, so you are." He knelt down beside me and we kissed.

"I'm going to take it back home and put it up in the attic with my books and toys and all the other relics of my past life," I said.

"Fine with me," said Patrick. He gently nudged me back on the floor, and the argument was soon the least important part of our day.

Uncle Milt and Aunt Sally insisted on coming to our wedding, though Milt wasn't well. They were staying with Dad and Sylvia too, in Lester's old bedroom. Carol and her husband were at a nearby hotel. So were Mr. and Mrs. Long. We had all got through the rehearsal dinner in fine shape. Everyone from out of town had been included, which meant quite a crowd. I was delighted to see Abby and Val again, but I spent extra time with Patrick's parents.

Mr. Long didn't look as healthy as I'd remembered him last—Patrick and I had visited them in Wisconsin not long after he'd proposed—but Patrick's mom was as elegant as ever, thinner but charming.

"This makes me so happy, Alice," she confided. "Somehow

I just knew this day would come. When Patrick got back from Madagascar and said he'd met you in Chicago at the airport . . . the expression in his eyes when he said it—I just knew."

I hugged her, even though I wasn't sure she was the hugging type, and though for a brief instant I could tell she wasn't, she suddenly returned my hug as though it were something she had been hungering for, for a long time.

After everyone had gone back to their hotels later, and Milt and Sally were in bed, I was sitting on the floor of my old bedroom with one suitcase on the floor in front of me, the other up on the bed, packing for the honeymoon. My door was ajar, and after a soft tap, it opened and Dad stuck his head in.

"Still up? Big day tomorrow, honey," he said, as though I needed reminding. He stepped inside. "Care if I come in for a minute or two?"

"Of course not, Dad. Come in! Sit down, if you can find a spot."

He stepped over my suitcase and sat down on the bed.

"Well!" he said, looking around, the smile never dimming. "I couldn't be happier, Alice."

"Me either," I said, and gave his legs a hug. And then I drew back and looked up at him.

He understood. "Remember the last time this happened? Me sitting on this bed, you hugging my legs?"

I rested my head against them again, smiling. "Yes, I was in ninth grade, and Patrick and I had just broken up. I thought my world had ended."

"And it was impossible to tell you then that it hadn't. You just had to live through the pain."

"You didn't try to tell me that Patrick and I would get back together again."

"Because who could promise that? Or whether it was even the best thing to happen?"

"You just listened and let me cry."

"Sometimes that's the only thing to do. And now . . . !"

I gave his legs another squeeze. "And now the best dad in all the world is going to bed because *he* has a big day tomorrow too!"

He leaned over and kissed my forehead. "I'll sleep on that," he said. "Good night, sweetheart."

On Saturday, on one of the most beautiful fall days in the world, I waited in the bride's room of the church, listening to the organ playing the prelude as guests arrived.

Two large arrangements of white chrysanthemums, purple and white orchids, and sprigs of green ivy adorned the front of the sanctuary, and a few white chrysanthemums, tied with green and purple ribbon, greeted guests at the front of each pew. Outside the two glass walls, each made of hundreds of smaller panels of tinted green and yellow glass, the trees were blazing with October colors—deep purples, tangerine, forest green, and buttercup.

The day before, my bridesmaids and I had all had manicures and pedicures, and this morning the whole house had been given over to makeup and hair sessions. Les and Stacy helped out by taking Milt and Sally to a long brunch, and they didn't bring them back again till they got an all-clear signal from us. Gwen's tiny five-year-old niece was my flower girl, and she sat demurely on a stool, waiting for her turn down the aisle, her lavender and green floral dress covering a skinned knee and her patent-leather shoes shined to a mirror finish beneath her lace-trimmed socks. Gwen had woven green and lavender ribbons in her braids, and she sat stone still, as though any movement might dislodge them. I smiled her way, and she returned a big one, two big dimples dotting her cheeks.

The bridesmaids moved about in their green satin dresses, wearing their gold earrings, a gift from me, and checked the windows to see if last-minute guests were arriving. We had selected a simple style that would suit them all: cocktail-length dresses with round necklines and three-quarter-length sleeves, each carrying a bouquet similar to mine.

"Les looks so elegant in his tux," Pamela whispered as she watched my brother ushering people to their seats. "He'd look hot in anything."

Stacy was handling the guest book, and she was the one we were watching. When she took her seat, meaning that the guests were all seated, Les would check with us, then give the organist the signal, and the music would change to the bridal procession.

"One last pee," I told my bridesmaids. "Sorry, but my bladder's working overtime."

"Be careful of your dress, Alice. Let me hold it up for you," said Liz, and we went in the restroom together.

It was a rather complicated procedure. Even using the larger stall for the handicapped, Liz had to lift the back of my dress practically over my head and hold it for me so I could find the toilet. Afterward, when I finally got rearranged, I went back out to the sink and washed my hands. Liz was in another stall, and I thought I heard gagging.

What was going on? I wondered. Could she possibly be bulimic? Surely Liz wasn't going through that again.

"Liz?" I called.

She came back out, carefully wiping her mouth.

"I'm okay," she said, and filled a paper cup with water. And then, more softly, sheepishly, she said, "I think," and rinsed her mouth.

"Are you *sick*?" I asked. I couldn't read the expression on her face. Guilt? Embarrassment?

And then a smile took over her whole face, and she whispered, "I'm pregnant!"

"Liz!"

"I just found out Thursday, but I didn't want to tell anyone, so please don't!"

She needn't have worried about that, because I was speechless.

"I decided I'd really rather start a family than go for my master's. Is that so awful?" she asked.

"No, Liz! of course not. That's wonderful! But . . . ?"

"I'm deliriously happy! Don't worry. There's absolutely nothing in my stomach, because I didn't have any lunch. I just popped a mint, and that usually lasts me about forty minutes before I feel like gagging again, so I'm safe."

"Oh, my God! Are you sure?"

"I think so."

We hugged, then picked up our bouquets again.

"Listen, Liz, you don't have to go down the aisle," I said. "It's okay if you don't feel up to it."

"No, I think I can do it. I wouldn't try it if I thought I couldn't."

And then we heard Lester's voice at the door.

"Alice? What's the deal?"

"Coming," I said. "Give the signal."

The music changed, and we lined up—Abby, Val, Carol, Gwen, Pamela, and finally Liz. Then the flower girl was starting down the aisle, and we could hear little oohs and aahs as she made her journey.

I had stood before the mirror that morning in my mom's gown that a dressmaker had altered and restyled just for me. I wanted a dress with a little more "Ah!" factor, and because it was plain, this was easy to do, the dressmaker had assured me. We worked together, and to the waist of my taffeta gown, she had added a cummerbund-type sash a slightly darker shade of ivory, made of satin. And because the dress was too long, she had pinched the fabric together in little tucks, placed randomly here and there on the front of the skirt, shortening it just enough to cover the ankles, so that the hem would then fall into a lovely natural short train in the back. And at each little tuck she had placed a small fabric rose, of the same ivory satin. I wore a shoulder-length veil of ivory netting, held in place by a matching roll of satin fabric on the crown of my head. And around my neck, the little gold heart on a chain that Patrick had given me at my college graduation.

"Love you, Mom," I had whispered to my reflection in the mirror.

Now I was moving out of the vestibule with my bouquet of white orchids and small trails of green ivy, toward my dad. He drew back for an instant when he saw me, as if he recognized someone else. Then his eyelids crinkled in a wide smile and he extended his arm.

As we made the turn onto the white carpet, I could feel my father's arm tremble, and I turned to look at him.

"Like me?" I whispered, playing our old childhood game that didn't make a bit of sense to anyone but us.

His eyes misted over. "Rivers," he whispered back.

"Love me?" I asked.

"Oceans," he answered.

"I love you oceans too," I said, and squeezed his hand.

And there was Patrick waiting for me, tall and splendid, his red hair looking auburn in the light, and his smile was so infectious that he had everyone smiling. I think what I remember most about our wedding were the smiles. Everyone seemed so happy for us—Sylvia, Lester, the Longs, my friends, but especially Dad. The best man, a friend of Patrick's from the Peace Corps who had flown in the night before, just in time for the rehearsal dinner, stood beside him now, along with the other five groomsmen: two of Patrick's friends from the University of Chicago, Moe, Charlie, and Lester.

I kissed my dad when he let go of my arm, and he patted my hand. Then I turned to Patrick. It was as though his eyes were speaking to me, like they were taking me all in, swallowing me up, and mine were promising him my life.

The minister smiled at us affectionately, and among his remarks he said, "Everyone here is wishing you a happy and successful marriage, and what you should remember about this day—above the dress, the cake, the music, and the flowers, lovely as they all are—are the things that brought you together in the first place, the things you love about each other that made you want to spend your lives together. Let those be your talisman, your rock to hold on to when the waters get rough."

When it came time, we slipped the mixed white and yellow gold bands on each other's fingers, and Patrick's hand was strong and steady beneath mine.

"And now, Patrick and Alice," the minister said, "I pronounce you husband and wife. Patrick, you may kiss your bride."

Patrick took me in his arms and whispered, "It's forever, Alice," and embraced me for a long and tender kiss, and his eyes followed me even after we moved apart. And then, arm in arm, the organ pealing out the processional, we walked happily back up the aisle, drunk with love.

* * *

The only way to describe the reception was "wonderfully happy." For me, Elizabeth's secret gave the atmosphere a special feel, and I couldn't help looking her way, smiling at her and Moe as he brought her juice when she turned down the champagne.

Patrick and I had chosen the song "You" for our dance, and it was perfect, sung by a male singer:

I've wandered,
I've traveled,
I've searched as I roam,
But no one has felt
Like a haven, a home.

Then I found you,
I've loved you,
My dreams have come true;
My journey is over,
My heart's home is you.

I danced with everyone, even Elizabeth's little brother. Dad squeezed me tight as we danced, and I could see Mrs. Long stroking the back of Patrick's neck with one finger as he moved her about the dance floor.

I expected a sentimental toast from Dad. He didn't quite say, *She'll always be my little girl,* but he did say that raising me without a mother took all his creativity and wisdom but gave him some of the happiest moments of his life.

There couldn't be a better moment. I stood up then and took the mike. I said that I wanted to toast my father, a man who had to raise two children while grieving his wife. "He wasn't a good cook," I said, "but he learned. He didn't have all the answers, but he listened. And when things happened that no one could change, he was there for me to lean on, and he loved me." My voice quavered a little as I lifted my glass and turned to Dad. "To my father, who is all a girl can ask for in a dad."

There was a resounding cheer as I went over and hugged him, trying not to tear up, but I didn't care if my mascara smeared a little.

Aunt Sally got to her feet then to say that Marie would have been so proud of the way I turned out, and Pamela, of course, had to say something crazy, to the effect that Patrick had better treat me right or there would be a posse of women on his tail.

But it was Lester's toast that surprised me. I figured he'd been planning something clever and funny for weeks, but instead, he lifted his glass and said, "To the happy couple: I wish you a lifetime of passion, tenderness, and joy. And to my little sis, I want to say, wherever you find yourself, just remember, I've got your back."

17
STARTING OUT

Patrick and I went to Ireland for our honeymoon. As luck would have it, one of the counselors in Montgomery County resigned mid-semester for health reasons, and I was told I could take her place. I explained that I was getting married, and we had hoped to take a two-week honeymoon in Ireland.

They congratulated me, of course, but let me know that I *was* on the waiting list for a full-time position, that there *were* other counselors available, and if there was *any* way we could reduce that honeymoon to one week instead of two . . .

"We'll do it," Patrick said, knowing how much the job meant to me. "We'll do half of it now and go back on one of our anniversaries."

We hit Dublin, of course, the National Museum and the

pubs, and we loved the performers on Grafton Street. I most wanted to visit Dublin Castle, and Patrick wanted to see Trinity College. After that, we focused on southeast Ireland and the countryside, so that Patrick could see Newgrange—a 3200 B.C. grave site.

"I hate to go," I told Patrick when our week was up, and we left the lovely town of Kilkenny.

"Well, they always say to leave when there's more to see, and that means you'll come back again," he said.

And so the day after we got back from Ireland, I began my work as a middle school counselor. My first job, I discovered, was to make friends with the students informally so they would feel comfortable coming to me when they had a problem, and, as I told Patrick later, I felt a little as he must have felt in Madagascar, making friends with the natives while barely speaking their language.

Marsha Sims, the principal, assigned me to lunchroom duty every day for the first two weeks, where I chatted up tables of girls sharing each other's makeup, tried to carry on conversations with students who were sitting by themselves, and wore my Redskins T-shirt before a big weekend game to get the approval of the boys. I chose a wardrobe I hoped was neither the latest fashion nor "middle age," as the girls called any outfit that was too matchy-matchy or otherwise didn't meet their approval. Sometimes I asked the girls' opinion on which earrings looked best with what sweater, and I couldn't tell if they were humoring me when they answered or if they relished giving advice. But eventually a student or two would call out, "Hey, Mrs. Long," in the hallway, and then I began to feel I was in.

A few girls came to me tentatively to ask questions about whether they had to take algebra, when what they really wanted to know, their second visit revealed, was whether it was true that guys didn't have to use a condom if they were circumcised, the latest bit of misinformation being floated around by the boys, evidently.

Patrick was liking his job as well, but—in typical Patrick fashion—he was already wanting something more challenging. The pay was low, but for now we each had a job we enjoyed, we were decorating our new apartment, and we weren't too busy to devote the weekends to each other.

When Elizabeth was eleven weeks pregnant, she miscarried.

Moe called and told me the news. "Her mom's been here to see her, Alice, but I think it would help if you came by," he said. "She just can't stop crying."

I will always remember this as one of the saddest times Elizabeth and I shared.

I drove immediately to their town house, tears streaming down my cheeks. As I made my way down Massachusetts Avenue, I tried to think what I could possibly say that would comfort her. All the obvious things sounded wrong—like how she could try again, would undoubtedly carry to term next time; that it probably wasn't as bad as losing a full-term baby; or maybe the fetus wasn't normal, and nature took the right course. . . . How could I possibly know any of this? Why would any of it make her feel better? She had lost *this* baby, her first one, and this is the one she wanted.

I decided not to think but to feel for the right words, and when Moe let me in and I found Elizabeth on the couch, her face thin and drawn, I just put my arms around her and rocked her, and we cried together. She was in her second year of teaching, a third-grade class in a rural county, and had planned to take maternity leave in April.

My shirt was soaked with her tears, and she clung to me as though somehow I could say the right thing, the comforting thing, and I never felt so helpless in my life.

"I can't possibly know how you feel, Liz, but I'm so terribly sorry," I said, and let her sob.

Moe sat miserably on a chair across from us. I listened to Elizabeth tell me how only a week before, she and Moe had painted the baby's room a soft yellow, with a border of little ducks around the ceiling. She was weeping again.

"It's awful, Liz—about the worst thing that's ever happened to you, and nothing we can say will change it," I told her.

"I thought I had d-done everything right," Liz said. "I never lifted anything heavy, I gave up wine and b-beer . . ."

"I know. I saw you refuse champagne at my wedding. And you told me you were taking prenatal vitamins."

"She was great—did everything the doctor said," Moe offered.

Pamela had called, Liz told me, and Gwen was coming later.

I knew we all wanted to do and say the right thing, whatever that was. I gently rubbed her back.

"Maybe we shouldn't have tried to p-paint the room. Maybe it was paint fumes that affected the baby," Liz said anxiously.

"Liz," Moe interrupted, "the doctor said that wasn't it."

But I let her talk on, exhausting all the things that might have caused the miscarriage, and now she changed course still again:

"I was doing so well," she wept. "I felt good and every-thing, and that's what's scary." Elizabeth's nose was so red, it looked almost raw, matching the acuteness of her pain. Her face scrunched up, and for a moment she looked like the little girl I knew back in sixth grade who cried when she fell off her bike. "If I did all the right things this time, and I still miscarried . . ."

Moe got up and left the room, one hand over his eyes.

She buried her head against me again, sobbing, and I stroked her hair. "And if you asked your obstetrician, I bet he could tell you about dozens of women who miscarried the first time, just like you, and went on to have a whole houseful of children," I said.

After a long time her sobs subsided, and at last she pulled away from me and leaned back on the cushions, staring up at the ceiling.

"Well," she said finally, "maybe God had a reason. Maybe it will teach me to be more patient and humble. Or when I *do* get pregnant again, maybe it will make me love that baby all the more. I'll just have to accept it."

This time there really *wasn't* anything to say, because religion is so personal, and it's different for every single person. But it occurred to me that God gets the blame for a whole lot of stuff that "just happens," and if he wanted Elizabeth to be more patient and humble, he could have thought of a better way than that.

"It's possible, Liz. It's also possible that—like rain—it just happens and has nothing to do with humility." And then I added, knowing that sometimes the best way to work out grief is to concentrate on someone else, "But remember that Moe's sad too. You told me he wanted a large family. There's someone else around here who needs comforting."

And that seemed to be the right thing to say, because she stared at me for a moment, and suddenly she swung her legs off the couch. "You're right," she said. "I've been thinking only of myself. Oh, Alice . . ." She hugged me. "You're the best friend I've ever had."

I knew that was my signal to leave, because her feet were pointed toward the kitchen, where Moe was silently drinking a cup of coffee.

This wasn't a magic bullet, nothing that would stop the next round of tears or the sleepless nights to come and the endless worries, but Moe was like a tree in a storm, something strong she could cling to, and I felt he'd see her through.

I loved being married. When Patrick and I got home each day, we liked to just stretch out on our bed and talk. Cuddle and talk. Sometimes I rubbed his back, sometimes he rubbed mine. Once in a while we even made love before we made dinner, but mostly, it was just a close, sharing kind of time that set the tone for the evening.

He'd tell me about a difficult issue they were studying at work—trying to find the research on it—and I'd tell him about a difficult student. We never solved the problem by talking about it, but it helped clarify it and—whether because of the talk or the back rub—we always felt better afterward.

"What did I ever do without you?" I murmured against his neck.

"Got through college, for one thing," Patrick said, and kissed my nose.

"You know what I was thinking the other day?" I continued. "That it's nice being in between."

"As in . . . ?"

"Liz wants a baby so badly, and Pamela wants just as badly not to have one. We don't want children yet either, but if I did get pregnant, we're ready to care for it and love it."

"And you're telling me this now because . . . ?"

"Because I'm happy."

"You're not off the pill, are you?"

"No. And we'd have talked about it first, if I was."

But having a "Mrs." in front of my name didn't change much outside the apartment. For some reason, I'd thought that not only would the world treat me differently but that *I* would be transformed somehow. I was now a "married woman."

But salesclerks didn't wait on me any faster or more courteously because of the ring on my finger. I had just as much trouble making omelets. My hair still looked awful in humid weather, and my face still broke out if I ate too much chocolate.

Worst of all, I still did such stupid things. *Said* stupid things. There was a bad leak under our bathroom sink, for example, and the apartment manager said that a plumber would be coming at eight o'clock Saturday morning to fix it.

"Oh, not before eleven!" I told him. "My husband and I like to sleep late on weekends."

And he said, "Mrs. Long, do you want your sink fixed or not?"

Even after we'd been married a year, I hadn't seemed to learn much. On our first anniversary, even though we'd already agreed to celebrate a few days later when it was more convenient, I made a candlelit dinner, with steak and chocolate pie, I put on a sheer dress Patrick particularly loved, and there I was, waiting for him when he came home from work.

First of all, he was tired because there had been all kinds of complications on the job. Second, he was late because he'd had to work overtime, and I'd put the steaks under the broiler as soon as I heard his car. And third, he'd grabbed a sandwich from a vending machine, so he wasn't particularly hungry, whereas I was ravenous. To make matters worse, I got salad oil on the dress I was wearing, and finally, true to form, I started to cry.

Patrick tried to be patient. "I thought we'd agreed to celebrate this weekend, hon," he said. "How was *I* supposed to know you were making a special dinner?"

"I wanted it to be a surprise," I wept.

"Well, I'm not a mind reader," Patrick said, pulling off his tie. "I'm hot, I'm tired, and I need a shower." But he came to the table anyway and ate half his steak. He said he'd have the pie later after he'd cleaned up. Instead of a shower, however, he sprawled out on the couch and fell sound asleep. And that was my first lesson in learning that I wasn't made of glass and that there were a lot of things Patrick couldn't possibly know unless I told him.

Elizabeth, Pamela, and I were all working full-time. Since her miscarriage, Liz seemed to throw herself into teaching. She was good at it, according to the many notes she received from parents, and she and Moe were planning a trip to Greece sometime in the future.

We saw very little of Gwen, now that she was in medical school, but Pamela was doing remarkably well in the advertising business, seeing as how her training had been in theater. She'd broken up with the man who first hired her, though, and was working for another company, but Pamela always seemed to land on her feet.

Meanwhile, Patrick was working days and taking night courses a few at a time for his graduate degree at American University, and sometimes it was hard to find time for each other.

"Being married is actually work," Elizabeth said once when we were comparing notes. "It's not as though, once you've made a commitment, you can take the other for granted and things will be fine. You have to *work* at making a good marriage."

Amen to that.

"But you know what helps?" she continued. "Whenever I think I can't stand one of his habits one minute longer, I force myself to remember something I've done or said that really ticked him off, and suddenly they seem to cancel each other out."

One spring Saturday, Patrick was out of town, and Elizabeth drove over to spend the afternoon. We had just come back from the garden store with pots of flowers to be arranged later on the apartment balcony and were taking time out for a beer.

Liz sat down on the couch, moving a pillow to make room. "What's this?" she asked, reading a note taped to the back of it: *Wish I were here in your lap.*

I instantly colored. "Patrick and I leave each other notes from time to time, especially when he goes away. I put notes in his suitcase, and . . . he leaves notes all over the house. When we watch TV together, he likes to lie with his head on my lap on that pillow." Elizabeth looked at me rapturously, and I continued: "*Also* in the refrigerator, under my towel, taped to the toilet seat . . ." We laughed.

"Moe and I celebrate all our firsts," Liz said. "The anniversary of our first kiss, the night he proposed—things like that." She sighed, smiling. "I hope we can stay in love forever. I hope that what we have now is the real world, because—except for losing the baby—I like things just the way they are."

It was at my job that *I* felt most in contact with the real world, because I realized just how sheltered my life had been up to that point. The only place I'd ever worked for any length of time was the Melody Inn, with my father as my boss. Now I was a member of a faculty, and Principal Sims was an attractive dark-haired woman who reminded me a little of Snow White's stepmother.

It wasn't that she was cruel or malevolent. It was her perfectionism and the way she gave orders that got to me—and the fact that I was in no position to object.

"Is that understood?" she often said after she'd explained how she wanted something done. Or, after giving each of us a task for the coming field day or student talent show, she would say, "Now, Steve, what are you going to do?" or "Alice, your job is . . . ?" and then wait for us to parrot it back to her as though we couldn't be counted on to remember. The rest of the faculty sort of humored her, smiled behind her back, and let it roll off, but for some reason, it really rankled me, perhaps because I felt I got the brunt of it much of the time.

The students, however, were fascinating.

"Were we ever that awkward?" I asked Patrick. "Honestly, when the bell rings and kids surge out into the hallways between classes, you take your life in your hands just to be out there! They charge around corners, arms flailing, and a lot of the boys are as tall as the gym teacher. Were *we* ever like that?"

Patrick took the salmon out from under the broiler and sprinkled it with lemon juice. "Of course not. We were agile and intelligent—responsible with our money and kind to little old ladies and dogs."

I wasn't surprised that girls came to me more readily than

the boys did. When I saw boys in my office, they were generally sent there because they'd been disciplined by our assistant
principal, and I was expected to do the follow-up, see what was
causing the problem.

I got along with most of the students. I liked to collect
funny posters for my walls to help the kids lighten up—like
the old photo of the little kitten clinging to a tree, with the caption HANG ON, IT'S FRIDAY! A lot of the kids could sure have
used some lightening up. Many led such complicated lives and
had experienced far more than I had—abuse, drugs, alcohol, an
abortion, even.

"There are so many of them, Patrick," I said. "For every student I counsel, there are probably ten more I never see, with
awful things going on in their lives. There are backup cases for
the psychologist too. It all seems so hopeless sometimes."

"We felt that way in the Peace Corps," he said, "until someone told us the starfish story."

"What's that?"

Patrick put down his fork. "A man goes out on the beach
and sees that it's covered with starfish that have washed up
in the tide. A little boy is walking along, picking them up and
throwing them back in the water.

"'What are you doing, son?' the man asks. 'You see how
many starfish there are? You'll never make a difference.'

"And the boy pauses thoughtfully, picks up another starfish,
and throws it back into the ocean. 'It sure made a difference to
that one,' he said."

I smiled across the table. "I'll remember that, especially because you told it to me," I said. "Thanks, honey."

My most difficult case was a student named Tarell—a bully—who was teetering on the edge of failing seventh grade, even though his intelligence scores showed him to be above average. He'd be okay for a while, getting passing grades and not causing trouble, and then he would do something especially cruel or humiliating to one of the sixth graders—yank his jeans down in the hallway, perhaps, or heckle him in the cafeteria about the shoes he was wearing. He would often latch on to one particular boy and taunt him for several weeks, then drop him and pick on someone else. He seemed especially determined to show that nobody could beat him up.

He'd had detention and been threatened with expulsion, but he remained silent when spoken to, passively aggressive. In my office he would invariably arrive late, throw himself into a chair reluctantly, and stare out the window, just putting in his time, answering my questions in monosyllables but rarely offering me anything substantial to work with.

One day after he'd been in detention for breaking a boy's glasses, we sat across from each other while Tarell, as usual, stared sullenly out the window, occasionally glancing at his watch and shifting in his chair.

Finally I broke the silence and asked, "Tarell, who did this to you?"

He still didn't look at me, but I saw his body tense. "Did *what* to me?"

"Turned you into a hostile, unhappy bully."

This time he jerked about and faced me. "Nobody does *nothing* to me! I can take care of myself!" he said.

"Who are you trying to get back at here?" I continued. "You can't possibly be mad at some ninety-pound sixth grader who never did anything to you. Who are you really angry at?"

The breakthrough didn't come all at once, but once the floodgates were opened, I heard about his sadistic father, a man who never laid a hand on him, in either affection or anger, but who also never had a kind word for his son. Who was as abusive with his put-downs and insults as some parents were with their fists. And as the anger eked out in my office, it wasn't as necessary for Tarell to take it out on other boys. At the end of the year he still had problems, a lot of them, but he also smiled more and had actually made a few friends.

"So how are you liking your job, Al?" Dad asked me one evening when we had him and Sylvia over for dinner.

"Love it!" I told him. "I can't think of anything I'd rather do."

"Same with me," he said. "I can't imagine retiring, though I suppose I'll have to one of these days. It's just too much fun at the store."

But I was having problems I didn't tell him about. Just as Tarell seemed unable to get to our sessions on time, I seemed to continually turn in reports late to Marsha Sims, and I couldn't understand why. All through high school and college, I managed to get assignments in on time, yet now I invariably discovered that the day I was to hand in a report on a student, I'd left the papers at home. Or I had done all but the last part. Or I had misplaced test scores that were to accompany it.

"Just get on the ball, Al!" Patrick said to me when I confessed. "Put it on your calendar. Write yourself a note." I did, and it helped some, but not a lot. It almost seemed as though I were asking to be called into Marsha Sims's office, and one day it happened.

She sat behind her desk in her navy-blue suit with the navy and turquoise pin on the lapel. With her fingertips together, lightly tapping her chin, she studied me.

"You know, Alice," she said, "I can't quite figure you out. You get along well with the staff, the students like you. You never seem to miss appointments, you rarely take sick days. And yet . . ." She pointed to some papers on her desk, and I knew what was coming. "At least a third of your reports are late. I'm supposed to schedule conferences with parents, and I have to nudge you to get a report to me when it should be in my box without any prompting. Do you have any idea what's going on?"

I began apologizing all over the place, but Marsha waved me off. "That's not needed here," she said. "You don't have to like me, Alice. Not everyone does. But you do have to work for me and respect my rules. And one of my rules is that I have to have reports on time. I've got enough problems on my plate without the added annoyance of having to nip at your heels to get something done."

I nodded.

"If there's anything I can do to make this easier for you . . . ," she said.

"I think it's my problem, and I'm going to have to solve it," I told her.

"Good," said Marsha. "I hoped you'd see it that way."

As soon as I got home that day, instead of sitting down with a cup of tea and a cookie and scanning the newspaper, I went out for a walk. I walked several miles hardly aware of where I was going.

I was behaving just like Tarell, passively aggressive. I'd felt I couldn't really tell Marsha Sims that she gave orders like a martinet. That she treated me, in particular, like an adolescent. So I'd been displaying my resentment in childish ways, and the one way I could annoy her, without actually realizing what I was doing, was to get my reports in a day or two late. They were well-written reports, meticulously done, and in every other way I did my job well. Yet I was like a fly buzzing around her head.

And strangely, once I knew why I did it, I stopped. The missing test scores were found, the test papers attached, and the reports were in on time. I learned to speak up at faculty meetings and found that if I made a humorous comment without being hostile, she would listen. I was growing up along with my students.

18
THE BIG EVENT

I'd been off birth control for the past six months, and we weren't "working" at getting pregnant, just ready for a child if it happened. I was now three weeks late, and that had never happened before. Were my breasts more tender than usual? I wasn't sure. I bought a pregnancy test one day after work and nervously took it home.

It was as though I were carrying something alive in my bag, and I realized I was driving ten miles under the speed limit. I went straight up to our bedroom and sat staring at the kit, reading the instructions again and again, too nervous to absorb them at first. Finally, my heart beating double time, I got a cup, peed in it, and inserted the test strip. Then I sat on the toilet seat, hands folded in my lap, and watched the clock.

One minute . . . two minutes . . . I'd heard that, years ago, a woman had to go to the doctor for a pregnancy test, and then her urine went to a lab where a rabbit was sacrificed or something after it was injected. It sounded almost superstitious. I don't know if it was good news or bad when the rabbit died, but all the while the woman was wondering whether or not her life would change, and here I was, simply watching the minute hand on the clock.

Three minutes. *Stay calm,* I told myself. I picked up the instructions and read them again. *One line, no baby; two lines, pregnant.* Like Paul Revere and his lanterns or something.

I took a deep breath and lifted out the test strip. *Two lines.*

I screamed with excitement. Then I walked around the bedroom, whispering, "I'm pregnant! I'm pregnant!" When I looked at myself in the mirror, I looked different somehow. My cheeks were flushed. I sat down on the bed, my hands on my abdomen, and couldn't stop smiling.

I was twenty-six, my third year as a counselor. Liz hadn't conceived again—she and Moe were planning another trip, this time to South America. Neither Gwen nor Pamela was married, so it appeared that I'd be the first one of us to have a baby.

Everything swirled around in my head at once. We needed to start saving every cent for the baby! What would we name it? Where would we put the crib? What about maternity clothes? Oh, God, *clothes*!

It was late May, and I was probably three weeks pregnant, so the baby was due around February 1. I could probably get through the summer without showing too much, but by fall and especially winter . . .

I leaped up and grabbed my pillow. Unzipping my black pants, I opened the top as wide as possible and stuffed the pillow in. Then I pulled my jersey top down over the pillow and stood sideways, looking in the full-length mirror. I looked like a woman with a pillow in her pants, and I was stretching my jersey top.

Coats! What about a winter coat or jacket? These were expensive, and I wondered if my old one would do. I ran to the coat closet, holding my false abdomen, grabbed my down jacket, and ran back again. Standing in front of the mirror, I lifted the hood, with the white fake fur forming a wreath around my face.

Omigod! I'm pregnant! I'm really, really pregnant! I kept thinking. There were two of us now snuggled all cozy inside my down jacket. But I had to struggle with the zipper and knew I'd never get it up even halfway.

Suddenly I saw movement in the mirror and looked behind me to see Patrick standing in the doorway, staring at me, shirt-sleeves rolled up, suit jacket over one arm.

"Snow in the forecast?" he asked quizzically.

I whirled about so fast that the pillow came halfway out and my pants began to slide. With Patrick staring at me bug-eyed, I yanked them up and waddled across the bedroom, then threw my arms around his neck.

"Patrick, I'm pregnant!" I cried. "We're parents!"

He made some kind of noise, a little gasp or gurgle, and then, holding me out away from him so he could see my face, he cried, "Really? *Really?*"

"Really," I told him, and he let out a whoop of delight, lifting me off my feet and whooped again.

"When?"

"February, I think. I'm trying on coats," I said, and we fell on the bed laughing, tossing our pillow baby around and reveling in our May delirium.

It was one of the happiest evenings of my life—second only to getting engaged, I think. Suddenly there's a whole new subject to talk about, plans to make. There would be another person in this house. We wouldn't just be a couple, we'd be a family.

We decided not to call anyone, though. Most miscarriages happen in the first three months, we knew, so it was better to keep the secret for twelve weeks or so, as Liz had tried to do until I'd heard her in the restroom on my wedding day. It was hard to keep the secret, but we did. And when the time was up, Patrick called his folks and I called Dad and Sylvia, and I think Dad yelled louder than I had, he was so happy.

When I called Gwen, I said, "Maybe I shouldn't tell Elizabeth. It will just make her sad."

"Alice, that's life," Gwen said. "She'd feel a lot worse if she knew she was out of the loop, being treated differently than everyone else."

So I called Liz, and Gwen was right. In characteristic

Elizabeth fashion, she said, "Oh, Alice, I'm so happy for you!" and I'm sure she meant it.

Dad was the one, though, who couldn't stop smiling. Every time I saw him, there was a smile on his face. There were also lines on either side of his mouth that seemed to be getting deeper, reminding me that he, like everyone else, was getting older. But it didn't seem to bother Sylvia. They were always holding hands, every chance they got.

"Well, what are we going to name that baby?" he said one night when Les and Stacy were in town and we were all there at the house for dinner.

"How about Myrtle?" said Lester. "Myrtle Louise or Henrietta? Clementine? There are dozens of good names out there."

"You're just assuming it will be a girl?" said Patrick, laughing.

"Oh, I've got boys' names too," said Lester. "What about Alonzo Homer? Horatio? Sylvester? No, wait. I've got it! The perfect name if it's a boy."

I grinned. "What?"

"Are you all with me now?" said Lester. "Are you listening? This is it: Lester."

Stacy laughed loudest of all.

What I'd always worried about most when I thought of being pregnant—other than the birth itself—was morning sickness. I hate feeling nauseated and disliked the thought of Patrick hearing me barf in the bathroom. Hated the thought of being afraid to go anywhere for fear I'd throw up. Just thinking about Liz gagging in her bridesmaid dress made me scared. Miraculously, though, I only felt queasy a couple of times during the whole nine months. Sometimes we worry about all the wrong things.

For the most part, I liked being pregnant. I enjoyed just sitting quietly, one hand on my abdomen, feeling the baby move. I liked taking baths with Patrick, leaning back against him in the tub, his legs on either side of me.

"There! Feel right there!" I would say, placing Patrick's hand over a particular spot. "What's that, do you think? A knee? An elbow?"

Patrick would press and poke, and sometimes the bump would move or disappear. "Probably his rump," he said once. "Going to be one of those pointy hind-end kids with big ears and a snotty nose." And we laughed.

What I didn't like as the baby grew bigger was the pressure on my breastbone from inside. And especially the pressure on my bladder.

One day in my eighth month, Valerie was in town and Liz had arranged a "lunch with the girls" at a favorite little restaurant in Chevy Chase. I had started carrying a small pillow with me for my back, and while the others sat at a booth, I was seated on a chair at the end of the table, where I could give my belly plenty of space.

We all laughed about it, and it was no big deal. Val was still employed by the museum in Oklahoma City—was co-director now, in fact—and Claire had photos of her husband in the Coast Guard. We shared appetizers and tried a new dessert, and finally, when we collected our credit cards as the server returned, I started to scoot away from the table and felt myself pee right there in my clothes.

I froze, not daring to stand up, embarrassed to pieces. I wondered if the others could smell it. How could I explain this? I just plain-out peed!

There was only one thing to do. I leaned forward to put my napkin back on the table and knocked my water glass over, gasping as a deluge of ice water poured over the edge of the table and right into my lap.

"Oh! I'm so clumsy!" I cried, inching my thighs apart to make sure the water soaked all the way through, breaking out in goose bumps as it passed between my legs.

Val shrieked in merriment, and everyone began grabbing napkins to soak up the water as a waiter hurried over with some extras.

"No problem," he said.

Claire was on her cell phone taking pictures to send to Abby.

"At least you waited till the end of the meal, Alice," Liz joked. "We'll go to the restroom and get some paper towels for you to sit on in the car. It's okay."

"Happens all the time," said the waiter reassuringly.

"That's good to know," I said. Yeah, right.

In her car Liz said, "Want to go to our place and watch a movie? You can use a hair dryer on your clothes. Luckily, it was only water."

"Pee," I said.

"*What?*"

"I peed all over myself, and the water was a cover-up."

Liz burst into laughter. "Alice, do you realize that someone could do a comedy series on your life? *The Situation Room with Alice* or something."

"How about *Saturday Night Schnook*?"

"Whatever. The ratings would be off the charts."

"Great. But right now I'm getting rancid," I told her. "Dry pants never sounded so good."

I worked up until the ninth month, then took a four-month maternity leave, which would expire at the start of summer vacation. That meant seven months off at home with my baby. And the first day I spent at home, I got a call from Elizabeth.

"I'm pregnant!" she cried. "I've made the first trimester, and the doctor says I'm doing fine!"

"Oh, Liz! That's *wonderful!*"

"They'll grow up together!" she said. "They'll only be five months apart. Maybe you'll have a boy and I'll have a girl, and they'll marry and we'll be parents-in-law!"

That's Elizabeth! But I just let her burble on, basking in her happiness. Every woman is entitled to go a little crazy when she's pregnant.

Patrick had asked his office that no trips be scheduled for him during the last month of my pregnancy, and everyone seemed in agreement with that. As it turned out, the baby came only a week and a half earlier than expected, but Patrick was out of town anyway. He had been asked to fly to Chicago when another man couldn't make it and was told he could fly out and back on the same day.

"Are you *sure* you're all right with this?" Patrick had asked before he left.

"I feel exactly the same as I felt yesterday," I told him, not wanting him to worry. "I'll be fine, Patrick. Les and Stacy are in town, so I've got the whole family here if I need them."

Lester and Stacy had driven in the day before to celebrate her mom's birthday. Now they were spending their second day with Dad and Sylvia before they headed back to West Virginia. I'd be going over to Dad's for dinner.

But only an hour after Patrick left, I had my first pain—like a menstrual cramp. *What's a single cramp,* I thought, *and a mild one at that?* Even if I was in labor, first-time mothers sometimes take thirty-six hours to deliver. Besides, I had spent the previous day cleaning out the refrigerator and felt sure the cramps had something to do with all that exertion. About twenty minutes later I felt another one, even milder, so I lay down and took a nap.

I woke about one that afternoon feeling very different. This time there was no mistaking it. The pains were coming about twelve minutes apart, and my back ached. I phoned the doctor.

"Well, well," he said. "Looks as though one of us miscalculated, doesn't it? Or else that baby has a mind of its own. It's your first child, Mrs. Long, and they usually take their own

sweet time, but when the contractions get to be about six minutes apart, I think you'd better get to the hospital. And please
don't eat or drink anything."

Patrick's plane was due in at seven, and I wanted to wait for
him. If I called him, he'd still be in the meeting, and for a while
it seemed the contractions had slowed. Another false alarm. But
around five, when the pains were seven minutes apart, I called
Dad's number. Les answered.

"So how's the mom-to-be?" he asked. He sounded a bit
drowsy, and I imagined I'd interrupted a nap.

"About to become a mother sooner than I thought," I told
him. "Patrick's flying back from Chicago, Les, and I'm in labor.
The doctor thinks I'd better get to the hospital. Could someone
drive me over?"

I heard him choke. I had purposely tried to stay calm, because
I know how Lester reacts to anything remotely resembling childbirth.

"It's okay, Lester. We've got a while," I told him, then paused
and held my breath because I had a really strong contraction.
"Uuuaah," I groaned.

"Oh, my God!" Lester yelped. "Dad's at that new Wegmans
store with Sylvia and Stacy, picking up dinner. Al, why do you
do this to me?"

"Just call him on his cell phone," I said.

"Our father doesn't *have* a cell phone!" Lester said. "He is
still in the Neanderthal Age. I'll try Stacy, but they're at least a
half hour away."

"Want me to call a cab?" I asked, trying not to laugh. I don't know what was keeping *me* so calm. The fact, I guess, that none of the pains were new to me—just like really strong menstrual cramps.

"No, no, no, I'll be right there. I'd better not take the beltway in case traffic gets tied up somehow. I'm coming by East-West Highway, Al," he said. "Are you bringing the towels?"

"Towels?" I asked.

"In case it *comes,* Al! A sponge? A mop? What do *I* know?"

"Les, just relax and get over here, will you?" I said. I threw a few things in a bag and figured Patrick could bring the rest. I left a voice mail for him for when he landed and was waiting outside our building when Les pulled up. He squealed to a stop, jumped from the car, and helped me down the steps.

A neighboring couple saw us leave. "Good luck, Alice!" the woman called.

"Make it twins!" yelled her husband.

I started to get in the front seat, but Les said, "Not there, for Pete's sake! Get in back so you can lie down."

"Lester, I'm not planning to deliver in your car," I said. "It's going to be hours yet!"

That seemed to calm him down, and when he saw how easily I was breathing, he relaxed a little.

"Have you called Patrick?" he asked.

"I left a voice message. There's really nothing he can do."

Les practically braked right there. "He could come *home,* Al! He could catch the first plane home!"

"He's *already* on a plane, Les. It gets in around seven."

"Did you tell him to go directly to the hospital? To take my place in the delivery room?"

"I did, Lester. But I doubt very much I'll be in—" I paused as another pain roiled my insides.

"So this is it, huh?" Les asked, looking over at me when we came to a stoplight. "My little sis is going to be a parent before I am. What's it like, kiddo? Not that I could ever understand."

"A cross between a menstrual cramp and a really bad belly-ache."

"I don't think I could ever be a woman."

"Well, that's one thing you'll never have to worry about," I told him.

At Sibley Hospital, Les pulled up to the entrance. He went inside and returned pushing a wheelchair. An aide was holding the emergency room door open, smiling at me. She reminded me of Gwen.

"So today's your lucky day," she said cheerfully as Les helped me into the wheelchair. "And here's the proud papa."

Les opened his mouth to correct her, but I said quickly, "Yes, he's just wonderful. He's going to stay right by my side during the delivery, aren't you, darling?"

Les looked at me in terror.

"You can bring your wife's bag after you park," the aide instructed. "We'll meet you up in maternity."

"Good-bye, sweetheart!" I called over my shoulder as I was wheeled away.

The truth is, I was more frightened than I looked. I'd always tried not to listen when I heard other women talk about their childbirth experiences, because they always managed to scare me. I remember Dad telling me that everything stretches down there, but what did *he* know? Not even Sylvia knew what it was like. If ever I needed my mother, it was now.

I glanced at my watch. Patrick's plane was due in a half hour, if it was on time. It would be another hour before he got here.

After I registered, I was taken to a room and given a gown to put on, one of those white numbers with tiny blue squares on them. A nurse gave me a pelvic exam.

"Your cervix is dilated four centimeters," she said. "That baby's on its way, all right."

I tried to remember all the things I'd learned in my childbirth class that Patrick and I had taken together. The relaxing, the breathing. It was easy to do between contractions, of course, but not so easy when a big one hit.

Lester came warily into the room with my bag, and his face was pale. "I checked with the airline—at least his plane took off on time," he said.

I closed my eyes and gripped the bed as another contraction came. They were stronger now than any menstrual pain I'd ever had and were more typical of bellyaches. *Big* ones. My back ached and I felt I might throw up, but I didn't.

When it was over, I said, "If you were a proper husband, you'd offer to rub my back."

"Will you *stop*?" Les said, looking around. "I already set them straight about that."

"Well, I told them that you're my *first* husband masquerading as my brother and that my second is due any minute," I said.

"Stifle it," said Les, but he was instantly sorry when I clenched my teeth against another contraction. "Okay," he said. "I'll rub your back." I'm not so sure it did anything for me. There's a lot of difference, I decided, between a brother awkwardly rubbing your back and a husband doing it just the way you like it.

"Well, Al," he said, "I thought I'd be going through this with Stacy one of these days, but so far it hasn't worked out."

I glanced at him over my shoulder. "Really, Les?"

"We haven't given up—there are a few more procedures to try—but we're just not having any luck so far."

"Oh, Les, I'm sorry," I said.

"Yeah. Figured a big beautiful stud like me would be procreating all over the place. Maybe you'll have to have all the grandkids for both of us."

I wished I could think of the right thing to say, but just then another contraction came, and I didn't want to talk at all.

Between contractions I tried to think how I could describe them to Elizabeth and Pamela if they asked. Like a rolling gut ache, I guess—the kind you get just before you're going to be sick. I found myself counting by fives each time a contraction came, timing it. Five . . . ten . . . fifteen . . . twenty. . . . The pain grew stronger, swelling and reaching its peak about the time I got to eighty-five, and then it tapered off. By a hundred ten, it was gone and I could rest a little. Lester looked relieved.

"Well, Mrs. Long, how are you feeling?" came the doctor's voice as she appeared beside me, and from then on, it seemed I was concentrating mostly on my pains. I wasn't conscious anymore of time—whether it was minutes or hours.

At some point I heard Les say, "Hey, Al, Patrick's here. I'm going to go home and let Dad and the others know how you're doing, okay?" I just opened and closed my eyes, and he added, "Hang in there."

And then Patrick was bending over me, kissing my forehead, and for a while I wasn't sure who was in the room and who wasn't. The doctor examined my cervix, and then I was back to the contractions again. I knew that once I counted to eighty-five by fives, they would start to go away, and knowing that helped me deal with them.

I felt Patrick rubbing my back, wiping my forehead with a cold cloth. I squeezed his fingers when the contractions came and heard myself grunt. I closed my eyes when the pain was the worst, but there wasn't any feeling of ripping or tearing. It was more like everything in my abdomen was playing musical chairs, changing places. If I could just have a five-minute break between pains, I thought, I could handle this pretty well, but that didn't happen.

The anesthesiologist arrived and asked if I wanted an epidural—an injection in my back.

"Yes!" I said, wanting to rise up and kiss the man. After that, the contractions were a breeze. I felt no pain.

Patrick stayed with me the whole time. I could see it was dark outside the window and I was hungry, but they wouldn't let me eat anything. Patrick slipped little slivers of cracked ice in my mouth when I was thirsty.

"Okay, Mrs. Long," came the doctor's voice finally. "Let's go have that baby."

They arranged a mirror so that I could watch my baby being born, and I suddenly began to laugh. All I could think about was that summer Elizabeth, Pamela, and I had taken a class called "For Girls Only" at the Y, and a nurse suggested we go home and look at our genital area with a mirror so we could see how we were made. And here I was again with a mirror, and this time there was a live audience.

"Well, *she's* in a good mood," said the anesthesiologist.

"It'll be one cheerful baby, I'll bet," said the nurse.

They put my legs in stirrups, the doctor down at the end of the table, and I heard her say to Patrick, "Now would you like to help that baby along? Press your hands gently on your wife's abdomen, just about here, and let's push that little monkey out."

I never knew if what Patrick did actually helped or not. I was busy with my own pushing. But now and then I raised my head a little, and I do remember seeing a pinkish-orange ball emerging between my legs.

"Push now," said the doctor. "Big push," and I strained. I took a breath and pushed again.

And a few minutes later I heard a faint cry, then a louder

one—a tremulous *"Waaaah,"* like a doll makes—and Patrick said, "Honey, we have a little girl!"

Then Patrick was kissing me, tears in his eyes, and the doctor laid this small, warm, moving bundle on my abdomen. The baby was coated with some sort of white stuff, but I could feel her little chest heave as she squalled again. She had bright orange hair like her daddy. Her head looked like a wet fuzzy peach.

Patrick and I were laughing and crying at the same time, and the doctor and nurse were smiling. "How about naming her 'Cantaloupe'?" the doctor said.

I shook my head. "Patricia Marie," I announced, the name Patrick and I had already chosen. And I could not believe, as I held my baby, that Patrick and I together had produced this wondrous little bundle of life, with her orange hair and fair skin and toes so tiny, they looked like peas.

When Dad and Sylvia came to the hospital later, Patricia Marie had been cleaned up, swathed in blankets, and was asleep in my arms. Dad could barely speak. I handed the baby to him, and he held her as though she were made of glass, looking down at her with such wonder.

"Marie! You named her after your mother," he said, slowly leaning down and kissing the baby's forehead. "Oh, Patricia Marie, you've got to be *some* girl to live up to the likes of your grandmother."

19
BALANCING ACT

I've heard that some women are uncomfortable around newborns and prefer their children after they learn to walk and talk. But I loved all the different stages of infancy and could hold my baby endlessly and talk to her, watching her little mouth try to copy the movements of my own. I think I was in a state of euphoria all during those early months, and I especially enjoyed nursing her at night. We had turned our study into a nursery, and when I heard her cry, I'd bring her into bed with Patrick and me. Lying in the fetal position with my knees bent, Patricia Marie at my breast, I could feel her little feet digging into my thigh as she drank. It was easy to feel that nothing else mattered in the whole wide world—just Patrick and me and Patricia Marie.

Sometimes, just to amuse her and us, we'd bring her into

bed with us on a weekend morning and playfully put her between us as we hugged—our "Patricia sandwich," we'd call it.

Dad and Sylvia couldn't seem to get enough of her.

"So what do you want to be called, Sylvia? Mom says you get first pick," said Patrick. "Will it be 'Grandma' or 'Grandmom' or 'Nana' or . . . ?"

"We'll see what's easiest for her to say—I don't care," Sylvia said.

Did everyone take as many pictures of their babies as we did? We sent slide shows by computer to Les and Stacy, Dad and Sylvia, and any relatives or friends who showed even remote interest in them. First smile, first tooth, first car ride, first word . . . And then, one night, after finishing a small bag of cashews, Patrick blew the little bag full of air and popped it. First Patricia startled, her eyes huge, and then she broke into a loud belly laugh that took even her by surprise.

"Listen to her!" Patrick cried. "She loves it!"

We popped another bag, then another, and each time, as though it were the first, Patricia startled, then laughed, an infectious belly laugh that doubled us both over.

Les teased us about all the photos we took when he and Stacy came to celebrate Sylvia's birthday at my folks' house. Sylvia had said that all she wanted was to hold the baby, and she did, until Patricia finally fell asleep, and we put her in her portable crib in my old bedroom upstairs.

"Babies, yabies, they give me the willies," Les said, and when we all turned on him, he said, "It's the way they *stare* at you. No self-consciousness whatsoever. You can stare right back, and it doesn't faze them. It's like *Twilight Zone* for little monsters."

"Oh, Les!" we all cried, and even Stacy beat him on the back.

It was later, when Stacy was showing Sylvia how to play the dulcimer she had brought her as a present, that we heard a soft "Ba-by" coming from the kitchen. We all stopped and stared. "Ba-by," came the voice again. Surely not Patricia's.

"Baby girl, are you Uncle Lester's bitty baby girl?"

Our mouths opened in surprise, and we suppressed our laughter as we crept toward the kitchen and over to the baby monitor on the counter.

"Are those your little toesies?" came the voice, and when Les came down at last, holding Patricia, awake from her nap, we all chorused, "Ba-by. Baby girl." His face reddened as he stared first at us, then at the baby monitor in Stacy's hand.

"Busted," he said. "But it was worth it. She gave me a great big smile."

Six months later, when Gwen was in her first year of residency at Johns Hopkins in Baltimore, she called to say that she had a weekend off and was coming home to see her grandmother, now in her late nineties. Could we possibly get together? She had news. . . .

I immediately called Pamela in New York and virtually ordered her to come down. Patrick was in London, and it was a rare—very rare—chance for the four of us to be together. "We'll make it a sleepover," I said. "There's room." Patrick and I were talking about buying a house, but it hadn't happened yet.

Elizabeth had a baby of her own now—also a girl, Janine—whom she brought with her because she was still nursing. When Pamela came, we played with both babies, but when Gwen arrived, all eyes were on her left hand. There it was—a small, sparkly diamond—and for a moment Gwen almost lost her balance as we hugged her.

"Charlie came up a month ago and made his 'It's now or never' speech, and I fell for it," she laughed, the dimples in her cheeks deeper than ever. When I looked at her skeptically, she said, "No, Alice, I wasn't pressured into saying yes—it was only a matter of when. The wedding's still a long way off, but at least now we're committed to each other and can make plans for when my residency's over."

Janine and Patricia Marie were distracted by all the laughter and chatter in the room. They were still too young to object to being passed from lap to lap, hugged and bounced and kissed, Gwen cooing over their sweet baby-skin scent. When Liz nursed Janine, I was intrigued to find that her little girl also wriggled her small toes in pleasure as she drank, kneading her bare feet into Elizabeth's lap.

"Amazing how one end can smell so sweet and the other end smell so awful," Pamela commented, handing Patricia back to me after holding her for a few minutes, and we laughed.

Finally, when both babies were asleep in the study, we ordered a white pizza like we used to, opened some beers, and settled down for some serious gossip. For tonight, Gwen and

Pamela would be sleeping in our bedroom, Liz and I would share the pullout couch (when or if we ever went to bed).

"Has anyone heard from Jill or Karen? Penny?" I asked.

"I get an e-mail from Karen every so often," Pamela said. She had changed from her designer jeans into blue silk pajamas. She was wearing her blond hair shoulder length and gently curled. It was a dark blond, probably because she wasn't out in the sun so much. She'd taken off all her makeup and looked a lot like the Pamela we once knew. It was as though we were all fourteen again.

"Where *is* Karen now?" Gwen asked.

"Pittsburgh. And guess what Lori and Leslie are doing?"

I took a guess. "Tour guides in Yellowstone Park?" That was what they'd talked about doing back in high school.

"Wrong. They've started a website devoted entirely to travel sites and suggestions for gays and lesbians—discounts on airfare schedules, hotels, the works. I hear it's doing well."

"Good for them! And Jill and Justin?"

"Still in Baltimore, I think. Karen says they separated for a while, then got back together."

We sighed in unison.

"Penny?"

"Married. Tucson," said Pamela, who seemed to be social secretary for our group. She stared at the three of us in astonishment. "Don't you guys keep up with Facebook?"

"Are you kidding?" said Liz. "If I have two free minutes in the day, there are a dozen things calling to me more important than Facebook."

"I haven't even cut my toenails in two months. *Look* at them!" Gwen said, holding out her bare feet. "That's *one* thing I'm going to accomplish tonight." She was sprawled out in Patrick's favorite chair in flannel pj's with penguins on them, legs draped over the arms, a plate with two slices of pizza on it, resting on her chest.

"At least the four of us are still in touch," I said. "We all have careers, two of us are married and mamas. . . . Did we turn out at all the way we'd thought?"

"You did," said Pamela. "You always talked about being a counselor or a psychologist—picking people's brains."

"I don't *pick*," I said, and took another swallow of beer.

"And for a while we thought Liz would be a nun," Pamela joked.

"We never did." I looked over at Elizabeth, who was still wearing a maternity top with her jeans. "Some nun," I said. "What about you, Pam?"

"Well, I thought I'd go into theater but ended up in advertising, and I like it."

"Is marriage in your plans somewhere?" asked Elizabeth.

"Far, far down the road, if ever," Pamela said.

"Don't you ever get lonely?" Liz persisted.

"I've got friends. I've been dating one guy for six months now, so I guess you could say we're semi-serious. But we're not talking marriage yet. Just having a good time being together."

"Well, so are we. Wow, it's so nice to see you guys. Just to have time to talk like we used to," I said. I padded out to the kitchen in my floppy slippers to get a can of nuts and returned. "What about you, Gwen? For a while you were talking about going into pediatrics. What happened?"

"It was a hard decision, but I finally settled on gynecology because women make easier patients. You don't have to coax or trick them into letting you have a look. And I especially like working with young women. I get lots of students, especially those asking specifically for a woman doctor."

"It just makes sense, you know?" I said, reaching for the scrunchie that was dangling over one shoulder. I gave my pony tail a twist and secured the blue band again around my hair. "No matter how good a male doctor might be, he simply doesn't have the female parts that we do. He can't possibly experience the same thing."

Gwen sat up and reached for a paper napkin. "Many of my patients still have a hard time asking their questions, though. Usually I'm doing a follow-up after prescribing birth control pills or treating a vaginal infection. And what they usually say, once they're on the exam table, is, 'Dr. Wheeler, could you just check to see if everything looks normal?' And then I have to guess what's really on their minds."

"Which is what?" I asked.

"Could be anything, but often they're afraid that some part of their body isn't attractive or isn't working right. We females can be one insecure bunch!"

"Gwen, the Reassurer of Worried Women," I said. "I'll bet you're good at it."

"But that's for starters. The big worry, but the one most unspoken, is that they don't climax during intercourse. It's like the six-hundred-pound gorilla in the room that everyone knows is there but they never talk about. They'll wait till the very end of their visit and then say, 'By the way, Doctor . . .'"

We'd all stopped chewing then, and I wondered if that six-hundred-pound gorilla was sitting right there with us.

"And . . . ?" Pamela said, bobbing one foot up and down.

"And they assume that because I'm close to their age and probably have a boyfriend that I've worked it all out."

"Well, darn!" said Pamela. "We hoped you had!"

We laughed a little self-consciously.

"We had a good lecturer on female sexuality in my last year of med school," Gwen told us. "She was a psychologist and researcher from somewhere in New York, and all the ob-gyn students were supposed to attend. She said that although some women do occasionally climax during intercourse, expecting them to is like expecting a man to ejaculate simply by stroking his thigh."

"Hear, hear!" said Pamela.

"Really?" said Liz. She looked thoughtful. "Hmm. I wonder if Moe could . . ."

We laughed, but Gwen continued:

"None of the women students looked surprised. Relieved, maybe, but you should have seen the men's faces. Disbelief? I'm not sure. She suggested that when a female patient brings this up, we should reassure her that her anatomy is just fine and suggest that she discover how she most likes to pleasure herself when she's alone, then see how she and her partner can incorporate that in their lovemaking."

"Wow!" I said. "When do you suppose movies and novels will catch up?"

"It'll be a while," Pamela said. "That came up in a rehearsal at theater arts school. The scene was supposed to portray two people making love in silhouette, and the actress was complaining that both of them climaxing at the same time was a male fantasy. There's too much faking going on, she said."

"Man oh man, I'm going back to school," said Liz. "Where were these discussions when *I* was in college?"

"The thing is, though, men usually can't tell the difference," Pamela went on, looking around to see if anyone agreed with her. "And it's more convenient for them if we climax together— less work. So we fake a lot."

"Well . . . that depends," said Liz. "But don't we worry sometimes that our guy will meet up with a woman who climaxes easily, no matter what? And he doesn't have to work so hard to satisfy her?"

"Exactly!" said Gwen. "And we just assume she'd automatically be gorgeous, sexy, and slim, a temptation any husband couldn't resist."

We sighed, signaling it's something we'd all thought about at least once.

"Maybe people should take turns," I ventured, trying not to get too personal. "Like one time they do everything the man likes, and the next time it's *her* turn to choose."

"That is so . . . so *Alice!*" Pamela exclaimed, laughing. "Gosh, you're so democratic!"

"Every couple has to work out their own unique way of making love—that's what I tell my patients," said Gwen. "And that can be half the fun. You know how the psychologist concluded her lecture? She said that she knows for sure that God is a man, because if God was a woman and wanted her female creations to climax during intercourse, she would have put that little button of pleasure *inside* the vagina where it would do the most good."

"Oh, I don't know. I find it handy right where it is," said Pamela.

When school started again, I felt I could not bring myself to leave Patricia Marie. We needed a second income to buy a house, however, but Patrick and I talked it over and decided that was off for now. We missed having a study, but somehow we made do.

It would have been great if Patrick's grandfather had written his trust so that Patrick got twenty thousand a year until he was twenty-five or even thirty, and then got the whole thing. But obviously his grandfather, like Patrick's parents, wanted him to make his own way in the world, with just enough money from the trust to keep him from being destitute. And there's something to be said for that.

Every day with the baby was different; every day a new discovery—the day she discovered her navel, the day she started to sing. I told Marsha Sims that I could not come back to counseling until Patricia was in school. She was more understanding about it than I had imagined, and she worked out an arrangement where I could do counseling one day a week on a consulting basis, keeping up with a few of the students I'd worked with before, and I was willing to entrust my daughter with a sitter for that long.

The first Halloween with Patricia, she wore a little clown costume, and I drove her over to Dad and Sylvia's so they could make a fuss over her and put candy in her plastic jack-o'-lantern.

When she was two, I found a darling goblin suit and walked her to a few of the neighbors, where she determinedly climbed the steps to each house, pressed the doorbell, then stood dumbfounded when the door opened, forgetting the magic words but usually remembering to say a loud "Tank you" when the candy was dropped in her pumpkin.

When she was three, I pondered the little princess costumes, the cowgirl skirts and boots, and the pink tutu of a ballerina, and asked what she would like to be for Halloween.

"A box," said Patricia.

I stared at her. "A box?" Could she mean a bat? A boy, even? A fox? "Wouldn't you like to be a little princess or a ballerina?"

"No," she said emphatically, and pointed to a cardboard box in a corner.

I couldn't understand it, and neither could Patrick, but if Patricia Marie wanted to be a box, a box she would be. At the supermart I found one that had held a dozen packages of toilet paper. I cut holes in the bottom, one for each leg, holes in the sides, one for each arm, and a large hole in the top flaps for her head.

On Halloween night she stepped into the leg holes, thrust her arms out through the sides, and then we closed the top flaps where the half holes created a large circle around her neck. While the sidewalk filled with little witches and pirates and Supermen, Patricia Marie awkwardly made her way up the steps and across the porches.

"My goodness, what do we have here?" neighbors remarked thoughtfully as they opened their doors. "And what are you?"

"A box," Patricia replied, and she took the Milky Way bars or the packages of M&M's, dropped them through the neck opening of her costume, and listened for the thud as they hit the cardboard bottom. If they fell out the leg holes, I collected them as I followed along.

When the other children's plastic jack-o'-lanterns were full, their parents told them it was time to go home. For Patricia Marie, however, she was just getting started.

"*I* want to be a box," one child complained as Patricia added another Mars bar to her collection. The trick impressed even the older children.

"I bet she gets to stay out all night," another kid said.

I smiled at my daughter, whose gait was even more awkward with the addition of still more lollipops between her legs. Neither princess nor pirate, she was her own little self, just the kind of daughter I'd hoped to have.

* * *

Two and a half years after Patricia was born, we had Tyler, and if we had felt cramped with Patricia occupying the study, it was really difficult now. Tyler's crib and changing table took over half the so-called master bedroom. If either of us was foolish enough to get up in the middle of the night to use the bathroom, we ran the risk of stepping on Kermit the Frog, and one loud rubbery croak at three in the morning would send the other partner bolting upright, heart pounding.

We decided that it was time to buy a house and settled on an old Victorian on a tree-lined street in Chevy Chase. It was the cheapest in the neighborhood because it needed a lot of work, though basically it was sound. An elderly man had kept it long after his wife had died, and he sold the house "as is." Patrick and I figured we could do the inside painting and small repairs ourselves and would hire someone to install central air-conditioning when we could afford it.

But the wraparound porch made the peeling paint and missing shutters bearable—a wonderful place for Patricia to play in rainy weather while Tyler, in his playpen, would crow at her antics, and I kept a watchful eye folding laundry at a window. In winter we had our own backyard to cover with snow angels and a door to decorate at Christmas.

One Friday evening it had started to snow just after we put the children to bed, and around eleven, when I looked out, I saw that it had snowed three inches, then stopped. The moon was big and yellow, and the branches on the maple in the front yard were still. I stepped out on the porch to find that it was a perfectly lovely night, mild for winter, just cold enough to snow. I went back inside.

"Patrick!" I said. "Let's take the kids for a sled ride."

He paused with the apple he was eating. "They're in bed."

"Let's get them up and take Tyler on his first sled ride."

Patrick started to protest, then his eyelids crinkled into a smile. He woke Tyler and zipped him up in his snowsuit, and I woke Patricia.

"Sweetheart," I said, "this is a secret. We're going on a midnight sled ride." Patricia rubbed her eyes and stared up at me, her hair dangling in front of her face. She simply watched sleepy-eyed as I pulled on her heavy pants over her pajamas, then her boots and cap, and tied a scarf around her neck.

Patrick and I hastily dressed, and then we were all out in the front yard in the big silent night with the cold moon looking down on us. Patrick got the sled from the garage, and Patricia Marie climbed on. We put nine-month-old Tyler between her legs, and she folded her arms around him as we started off down the street.

"Is it still a secret?" she whispered hoarsely, her eyes wide.

"Yes," I whispered back, "because no one knows we're out here. We're the first ones to make tracks in the snow. The very first. Everyone else is asleep."

"Everyone else is sane and sensible," Patrick put in, laughing.

"And it's just us and the snow?" said Patricia.

"Yes," I said. "Just us and the snow."

When we took them back a half hour later, their cheeks

were a bright pink, but no one complained, no one whimpered. I made hot cocoa for Patricia Marie, and we gave the baby a few sips.

"That was the best night I ever had," Patricia told us.

"One of the best," I agreed, and gave Patrick a kiss.

Tyler turned out to be as different from Patricia as salt from pepper. He was quiet, thoughtful, and dreamy, while Patricia was stubborn, outgoing, and vivacious.

"How can they be so different, when we're raising them exactly the same?" Patrick said to me one morning.

But they each had their own set of genes, their own rank within our family. I wrote little stories for each of them, and each was the main character in his own drama. Patricia liked stories where she was the heroine venturing out in danger-ous territory, while Tyler preferred gentle stories of animals befriended.

Patrick reveled in both of our kids. His favorite activity was to stretch out on the floor on his stomach after dinner and let them maul him, roll him over on his back, pull at his hair, try to lift his legs, and shriek when he'd grab them.

The most wonderful thing about children is that, with you, they are experiencing something for the very first time. The waves at the ocean that chase them screaming up the beach and send them padding back down to be chased again. The little holes in the sand where the sand crabs hide. The holes to be dug that mysteriously fill up with water.

I loved taking the children to an apple orchard, where Patrick picked the apples too high for us to reach, and the children ran from tree to tree, astounded at all the apples at their feet, showing each one to me to exclaim over and declare, "Perfect!"

"October has got to be my favorite month," I said to Patrick as we watched the kids examine a wormhole in a Stayman. "I'm going to remember this day forever."

Elizabeth had become pregnant again almost immediately with her second child, another girl. But she chose to keep teaching, and her mother took care of the children while she worked. Moe and Patrick hit it off, so we often got together on weekends and took the kids to a park or the zoo. If life ever seemed idyllic and serene, those were the years.

The main problem in our lives was the balancing of time— work and play, spouses and children, parents, friends, house, yard. . . .

"I can't even find time to get a haircut!" I complained to Elizabeth after I'd picked up Patricia and Janine from their soccer game, and our four children were playing in her backyard. "The bathrooms need painting, Dad's birthday is coming up and I don't have his present yet; Sylvia's having a knee operation and I want to take them some meals next week. Life is crazy!"

"Tell me about it," Elizabeth said dryly. "I haven't even had a chance to shave my legs!" She was wearing her dark hair in a French braid that looked glorious on her, but I was surprised—*startled*, in fact—when I noticed a couple of silver hairs in back. Gray hair! In our thirties! One of us was actually starting to go gray!

"Your life is just as hectic, huh?" I said, still obsessed with her hair.

She gave me a little smile. "And I'm pregnant again."

"Really?"

"I just found out. This is absolutely, positively the last child. Moe wants to have six, so I told him if he wants to carry the babies and do the deliveries, that's fine with me." I'll say this for Elizabeth: Marriage made her feisty.

When Tyler was two and a half, I took him to our pediatrician for a three-week check following a urinary tract infection and some pain in one ear. But now, as far as I could tell, both had cleared up.

"How you doin' there, soldier?" Dr. Freeman said when he came in the room. "Got any more pain, buddy?"

Tyler solemnly shook his head.

"Can I peek in your ear?"

"I guess so," Tyler said, and continued to sit stoop-shouldered on the examining table.

Dr. Freeman always stood to one side, I noticed, away from Tyler's feet whenever he shone the light in his ears, having dis-covered long ago that a child in pain is capable of delivering a deadly blow to a doctor's groin.

"Ear looks fine to me," the doctor said. "Let's get another

urine specimen to make sure that's okay, and then you can go home."

I was angry at myself for not plying Tyler with juice or something before we came. I might have known they'd need another specimen, and getting Tyler to urinate on command was like asking the sky to rain.

"Want a drink from the water cooler?" I asked him as we left the room. He liked to press the little blue handle and watch bubbles rise in the jug. I gave him a small paper cup, which I'd filled. He drank two sips of it and poured the rest out.

"That's all you want? Oh, it's so good! Nice and cold!" I said.

He shook his head, so I guided him into the restroom.

"We need you to pee in this little cup so the doctor can check it out," I said.

"I don't have to go," said Tyler.

"I know, but he only needs a bit. Just a teeny . . . tiny . . . bit." I lowered Tyler's little jeans and underpants and held the cup below his penis.

Tyler looked idly around the restroom and ran one finger through a drop of water on the edge of the sink.

"Try to pee, Tyler."

"I can't."

I turned on one of the faucets so he might emulate the sound of running water. The minutes ticked by. I tried to think if I knew any songs about water. "Swanee River" was the only thing that came to mind, besides "Old Man River." I didn't think either would help.

"One little, two little, three little raindrops; four little, five little, six little raindrops . . . ," I chanted in a singsong voice, totally off-key, of course.

Tyler frowned at me. "That's not right. They're supposed to be Indians."

"Oh," I said. "Well, this little Indian better be careful, because they're paddling a canoe that's coming to this big waterfall—water coming down everywhere—sloshity, sloopity . . ."

Tyler continued frowning. Someone tapped on the door.

"We're just leaving," I called, and pulled up Tyler's pants.

We went back out in the waiting room and watched the other children building something out of Tinkertoys in one corner. I gave Tyler another cup of water to drink. He drank about half. I looked at my watch.

"Tyler, I need to get home. Patricia's at a neighbor's, and I have to pick her up." I took him into the restroom again when it was vacant and once again lowered his pants.

"Don't look," Tyler said.

"I won't." I turned away. But after waiting thirty seconds, I turned back and Tyler was impishly running a bar of soap along the edge of the sink.

"Tyler," I pleaded, "please try to pee. Just a little bit. Patricia's waiting for us, and there's an ice-cream bar in the freezer waiting for you."

Tyler tucked his head to the left and continued rubbing the soap.

"Please?"

"Go away and I will," he said.

"Really? If I leave the room, will you pee in the cup?"

He nodded.

"All right. And then be very, very careful. Don't spill any of it, okay?" I handed him the cup and left the room, then stood just outside the door. Minutes went by.

"Tyler?" I called softly. "Are you ready? Did you do it?"

"Almost," came the reply.

Finally, "Ready!"

I went inside, and miraculously, there was a small amount of urine in the cup, a few tablespoons, perhaps. I helped him pull up his pants, then carried the sacred specimen to the lab technician.

"Please tell me this is enough," I begged. "We'll be here till midnight."

She smiled and looked at it skeptically. Then, "I think it will do," she said. "Have a nice afternoon, Mrs. Long."

"Can I have my ice cream?" Tyler asked as we walked to the car.

"Indeed you may, the minute we get home. Thank you, Tyler. That was a big help."

I had barely pried Patricia away from her play with a neighbor and walked back in our house when the phone rang and I answered. It was the pediatric office.

"Mrs. Long, the doctor wants to know if you could bring Tyler right back? His urine specimen was a little unusual, and he'd like to talk with you."

I felt the blood draining from my face, my chest tightening. "W-What does he suspect?" I asked, barely audible.

"I think he just has some questions, but he wants to see both you and Tyler. Could you come?"

"All right," I said. "We'll be right there."

I let Tyler eat his ice-cream bar on the way, Patricia assigned the job of wiping his hands and face when he had finished. I tried to drive extra carefully because I knew my mind wasn't completely engaged in what I was doing. What could a urine specimen show? I thought of my mother. Leukemia? Sepsis? Kidney failure?

"Why do we have to go back?" Tyler complained when we parked.

"Honey, the doctor forgot something and he wants to see you again," I said. "I'm sorry. Patricia, do you want to bring your book with you?" Reluctantly, the children followed me inside.

In the doctor's office Tyler sensed my worry.

"Why does the doctor have to see me? Do I have to pee again?" he asked.

"You might."

"Is he mad?"

"Mad at you? Of course not. Why would he be mad?" I asked, putting one arm around my little boy, who might have only a few more years to live.

"Mommy . . ." Tyler looked up at me. "I ax-i-dentally got some spit in it," he said.

I stared down at him. As gently as possible, I said, "You spit in the cup?" I could imagine it now. A little boy impatient to get home, figuring that one body fluid was as good as another.

The doctor stepped into the waiting room, and I realized we were the last patients of the day.

"Dr. Freeman, he spit in it," I said. "He just told me."

The doctor stared at Tyler, who had his head buried against my arm, and suddenly he began to laugh. "That explains every-thing," he said. "There were things in that urine that never should be, but I'll give Tyler an A plus for creativity."

Dinner was late and no one cared, Patrick as relieved as I was. It seemed like such a small thing to happen now that we knew Tyler had been spared the unimaginable, whatever that might have been, but that I had imagined anyway.

A week later we took the children to Cumberland Falls, first to hike in the woods, then wade and splash and climb over the rocks at the base of the falls.

On the long drive home again in clean clothes, their bodies dry, their tummies full of the picnic lunch we'd had afterward, Patricia softly began a song she'd learned in summer camp. I stole a glimpse of her over my shoulder, reclining there in her corner of the backseat, eyes half closed, her voice hitting every high note. And Tyler, occasionally recognizing a tune, would sometimes sleepily join in.

Patrick and I exchanged smiles. *What I would give to bottle this moment forever,* I thought, if only to celebrate the fact that my children-of-a-tone-deaf-mother could, miraculously, sing. And how that pleased their grandfather, who was already giving Patricia piano lessons.

Maybe this day would be even more precious than the day at the orchard, I thought. But then, what about Tyler's performance at the day-care center he occasionally attended—the boys dressed up as bees, the girls as flowers? As they'd lined up to recite the bee poem for their parents, Tyler had seen us in the audience and stood there smiling his shy, delighted little smile, waving one small hand slowly in front of him, oblivious of his classmates reciting in chorus.

There were so many of these moments that could never be captured accurately, even on the camcorder, only in the heart.

As much as I loved my children and enjoyed being with them, I also felt torn when I saw other people getting on with their careers, and then I doubted both my ability to advance in my profession and my sincerity as a mother. How could there be any question which was more important?

Sometimes I thought of Pamela and wondered if she had any problems balancing the various facets of her life. She was advancing in her job and seemed to have plenty of time for her friends. Her dad had remarried, and that was going well. Still, with a mom like Pamela's, even with the help of Alcoholics Anonymous, there were worries I probably knew nothing about.

As for Gwen, Charlie had moved to Baltimore and found a place for them to live. And Gwen got married without any of her friends present. She told us about it later. Her grandmother, now a centenarian, was in kidney failure, and the one thing she had wanted was to see her granddaughter married.

So on a Sunday that Gwen had off, close relatives had gathered in the Wheeler home. Granny had been wheeled into the living room and carried to a recliner. And Gwen, in a white, filmy, floor-length dress and a bridal veil that her grandmother had worn, said her vows in front of the fireplace with Charlie, who, Gwen said, recited his with tears in his eyes, never letting go of her hands.

"We took pictures," Gwen said, and then they had a good old Southern dinner that Granny would have loved if she could have eaten it. But she sat there enjoying the people and the music until she fell asleep. "I'm so glad she lived to see me married, because she died the following week."

That's Gwen. She has no trouble figuring out *her* priorities. A month later her parents gave a reception for her and Charlie so they could celebrate with friends. About a hundred invitations went out to come celebrate with the Wheelers at the Cosmos Club in DC, where Mrs. Wheeler was a member.

We all came bearing gifts to make up for the shower Gwen never had, the bachelorette party that never was, the church wedding that wasn't there. And for a woman who had been in medical school practically all her life, it seemed, Gwen sure remembered how to dance.

She had the most shapely legs of the four of us, and in the white filmy dress with the swishy skirt she'd worn for her vows, she whirled and swiveled like a college freshman as we applauded and cheered from the sidelines.

Charlie, only an inch or two taller than Gwen, was almost a one-man show in himself. He had taught ballroom dancing at an Arthur Murray studio part-time to put himself through college and grad school, and he outdid Gwen in the rumba. But it was when they did the tango that we knew Gwen hadn't spent *all* her nights in medical school studying.

They flew off to Hawaii for a five-day honeymoon, and Liz, Pam, and I helped the Wheelers take all the gifts back to their house and do whatever else her would-be bridesmaids might have done to be helpful.

"Three down, one to go," we told Pamela.

"It'll never happen," she said.

Patrick, too, was advancing. He'd been offered a position in a nonprofit branch of IBM. He would be based in Bethesda, only a short distance away, but there would be more travel involved. No matter where he worked, it seemed as though he was bound for a promotion every year. That was Patrick.

We talked about the job offer before he decided. I loved living in my old area—only twenty minutes from Dad and Sylvia, a couple hours away from Les and Stacy. We weren't far from Liz and Moe or Gwen and Charlie, and I could see Val and Abby when they came back to visit in Maryland. I was grateful that Patrick had taken a job here to begin with and had known in my heart of hearts that it might not last forever.

But if Patrick accepted this new job offer, there was the possibility that he would be transferred later on, and how could I give up this house I loved? In any case, there would be more travel, and he might be gone one week out of every four. How would I feel about that? How would he? And how would it affect the children?

I played it over and over in my mind. I knew that Patrick could have had at least two other jobs when he joined the Washington think tank before we married. A man with his scholarship and linguistic abilities could almost write his own ticket, but he had taken a job near my hometown because he knew it meant a lot to me, especially once we had children. To be away so much, though?

"How much do you really want this job, Patrick?" I asked. "On a scale of one to ten?"

"Eleven," he said. "But I would do everything in my power to be home for the big occasions and to make my time home count."

"Then take it," I said. And he did.

I'd lie in bed sometimes in the mornings when Patrick had an early meeting, watching him loop his tie in front of the mirror. The same slim body I'd always known, the orange hair. I knew his profile as well as I knew every little mole on his body.

I'd smile to myself, thinking how this was the same Patrick who used to hold my hand as we walked around the block on a summer evening back in sixth and seventh grades. Who

French-kissed me once in a school broom closet. And here he was in our bedroom, the father of my children. He didn't play the drums anymore—he'd sold them after college—but he still liked to run, and that's how he stayed slim.

After having two children, I wasn't as slim. On my thirtieth birthday I weighed twelve pounds more than I had when we married, but I think I still looked pretty good. I had a great haircut, kept my makeup fresh, my clothes in good shape.

In the years I was home with the children, there was no end to all the things I wanted to do with them before they started school, and one of the things was a visit to the fantastic new elephant enclosure at the National Zoo, with woods and ponds and acres to roam.

Liz had come along with her three girls, and we'd managed to visit the animal each child specifically wanted to see—the giraffes, the tigers, the monkeys—while Liz and I felt closer to the maternal elephants, patiently herding their young.

We had come to the end of the spectators' walkway, and were getting ready to leave for home when I caught sight of a woman staring at me. After turning away self-consciously, I glanced back again and saw her mouth, which had turned down slightly at the corners, stretching into a smile. She looked to be a sturdy thirtysomething in a National Zoo uniform.

I stopped fussing with Tyler's backpack and straightened, returning her smile. Something familiar . . .

"Rosalind!" I cried as she came toward me, and we hugged.

When I backed away from her and noticed the "Elephant Trails" pin on her shirt, I grasped her arms.

"You did it!" I cried.

"Yep. Not only do I get to work in an elephant house, but I'm part of the planning for raising herds of Asian elephants here in DC."

"It's beautiful," put in Liz, and I introduced them.

"Rosalind Rodriquez is an old friend from long ago," I said. "I'm surprised we even recognized each other. I knew her back in grade school."

"And these are your kids?" Rosalind asked, grinning at Patricia and Tyler.

"Yes."

"Well, I'm married to my elephants, I guess. Right now I'm starting my shift, but e-mail me here at the zoo. We'll catch up."

"Of course I will. It was *so good* to see you, Roz."

"You too. Take care," she said, and disappeared behind an Employees Only door.

All the way home I entertained the children with tales of Rosalind—all the trouble she got into when she came over.

"She really buried you in a snow cave once?" Tyler asked.

"I guess we could call it 'accidentally on purpose,'" I told him, "but it didn't keep me from missing her after we'd moved. Wow! The Elephant House! Good for Rosalind!"

I wasn't the first mother to discover that everything I'd ever planned ended up taking twice the time I'd expected, of course. But I also had a "bucket list" of things I hoped to accomplish when the kids were down for their naps: a scrapbook for each child's primary years; a quilt I had started some time ago; all twenty of the novels on my list, beginning with Dostoyevsky and including D. H. Lawrence and Philip Roth. I wanted to keep up with my professional journals and possibly take a yoga class. . . .

Just remember that the children come first, I'd tell myself every so often, and not always successfully. *D. H. Lawrence will always be waiting, but you might get only one chance to look at the spider-web Tyler found.*

With Patrick's new job, however, there were more trips overseas, and though he kept his promise and tried to be home for major events, there were so many times—just ordinary times—that I wanted him to be there to hold me, stroke me, talk to me, make love to me. But he wasn't.

"Sweetheart, you know I want to be here with you as much as you want me to," he said once as he packed for a trip to Montreal.

"Do you?" I asked. "You fly all around the world, Patrick, and meet fascinating people, and then you come home to meat loaf and car repairs and fixing Tyler's bike."

"Sometimes that's the best kind of life to come back to," he said, and leaned over the bed to kiss me before he left.

I knew what he meant—a refuge, a place to be himself—but I didn't want him to see us as dull. Me, in particular. And if I dug even deeper than that, I worried he might find one of his business associates more interesting and attractive. *"It's forever, Alice,"* he had whispered on our wedding day. But don't most couples believe that when they marry? Don't they all think that the way they feel about each other then is the way they'll feel forever?

It was a combination, I guess, of facing my early thirties and seeing a photo of the nonprofit group Patrick was working with—seven men and two women. Attractive women, beautifully dressed.

"Patrick," I asked him once, "How would you rate me on a scale of one to ten?" We were in bed together and had made love.

I could tell by his voice that he was smiling. "In what department?" he asked, lazily stroking my breasts.

"Uh . . . desirability," I said.

"Hmmm. Eleven?"

"Be serious."

"Because?"

"Because I really want to know. You meet exciting, worldly women in gorgeous clothes, and then you come home to me in jeans and a sweatshirt. You're away a lot, you know."

"But you always look great in your jeans and sweatshirts," he said. "Besides, with Tyler in day care, you're a pretty girl alone all day, and the men *you* meet must find that awfully appealing." He gave me a playful shake.

I traced one finger down his cheek and around his ear. "I'm not a girl anymore, Patrick."

"I like you just the way you are," he said, and we went to sleep after that, but it didn't really answer my question.

20
CRISIS

Once Patricia was in first grade, we discussed enrolling Tyler in preschool and my going back to work. While our daughter was a full-steam-ahead kind of child—build it, play it, ride it, float it—Tyler's head was in the clouds, and his imagination was most active when he was quiet.

He was shy around other children, and while we were ready to accept him as the little introvert of the family, we also felt that being with other children more might make kindergarten a bit easier for him.

At the same time, I longed for adult conversation—about students, not sandwiches—and didn't want to lose the edge in my professional life. So we decided I would return to work full-time, and each morning either Patrick or I would first drop

Patricia Marie off at her elementary school, where there was a before- and an after-school program for children of parents who worked. Then we would drive Tyler to his preschool class at the Y.

One morning Patricia, true to form, decided she didn't want to go to the before-school program. Never mind that only two days before, she had loved it.

"It's borrr-ing!" she said, folding her arms across her chest, refusing to get out of the car.

Seeing his sister object, Tyler became weepy and clingy. "I don't like it either," he said of his own preschool.

I tried the objective approach. "That may be true some-times, but the other day you told me about all the fun you were having. There are games and snacks and stories and—"

"The crackers are awful!" Patricia said, her lower lip jutting out. "They taste like paste."

"Well, whether you're bored or not, I'm afraid you two will have to do the best you can," I said. "Both your dad and I work, and I have to get to my job early."

Patricia got out of the car then, scowling, and Tyler was sniffling when we got to the Y.

"It's not fair!" he said. "You don't *have* to work, Mommy! You didn't used to. You used to stay home with me."

That night after the children were in bed, I said to Patrick, "Why is it that everything I do for myself makes me feel guilty? You go off each morning to work you love, but when *I* try it, I get a ton of guilt."

"Because you're their mom, that's why," Patrick said affectionately.

"Well, I want somebody else to be Mom for a change. *I* want to go to exotic places and meet fascinating people. *I* want to fly around the world without feeling guilty."

"I could probably ask to be demoted to maintenance supervisor, and you could apply for an exchange counselor position for a year," he said, not at all helpful.

"You know what I mean, Patrick," I said sulkily. "I'm tired of feeling guilty."

"Then don't," he said. "Listen, Alice, you stayed home with the kids for six years when they were small, and you were a good mom then. You'll be an even better mom if you do something for yourself now. If you don't, you can be sure Patricia will call you on it when she's a teenager and ask why you sacrificed your own dreams."

I smiled at him. "Exactly what I wanted to hear," I said. "What made you think of that?"

"I just didn't want to have to apply for maintenance supervisor," he told me.

Aunt Sally died that winter. Carol had called to say that her mother had had a massive stroke and was in intensive care. Dad and I were making arrangements to fly to Chicago when Carol called again to say that Aunt Sally was dead.

Next to Sylvia, I guess Aunt Sally was as close to a mother to me as anyone, because I have only a few memories of my own mom. And even the few I have get mixed up now and then with memories of Sally.

Patrick was in San Francisco, so Sylvia said she would come over and take care of the children, and Dad and I flew out together. Les and Stacy would meet us there.

"It's too bad it takes a funeral for you and me to find some time just to be alone together," Dad said as the seat belt light came on and we prepared for takeoff. "How are things going, honey?"

"Busy," I told him, and related all the things we were doing. "Patrick's promised us a trip to Quebec this summer. He says he's always looking for places the family might enjoy when he travels on business."

"Now, that sounds wonderful! Sylvia and I are talking about Florence and Venice. She's always wanted to see Florence again, and we might even get to Rome while we're at it."

"Oh, Dad, I'm so happy for you!" I said. "She's made such a difference in your life, hasn't she?" Dad beamed, and remembering Sylvia's old flame, I got up the nerve to ask, "Does anyone know what became of Jim Sorringer?"

"He married," Dad told me.

"The P.E. teacher he was dating after you married Sylvia?"

"No. He went back to California, took a position there, and married the woman he'd met while he was working on his Ph.D."

"A woman he'd been seeing all the while he was supposed to be serious about Sylvia, I'll bet," I said.

"Now, honey, we don't know that," said Dad, and laughed.

* * *

Uncle Milt just wandered around like a lost soul. I guess Aunt Sally was so good at directing other people's lives that she had also directed his all these years. Carol stayed right by his side through the funeral and made arrangements with neighbors to look in on him every day with an occasional roast chicken or some home-made bread, but we could see it was going to be hard for him.

We all went out to dinner the following evening, and Dad and Les and Stacy took Milt on a shopping trip the day after that to buy him some clothes he needed and restock his refrigera-tor. Carol and I sorted through Aunt Sally's things—the personal stuff that Uncle Milt didn't feel he could handle—her clothes and jewelry, all the things in her closets and drawers.

She had already, we discovered, put Carol's name on a few things she wanted her daughter to have. But I was surprised to find a small flat box in a bottom drawer with my name on it as well as Carol's. We opened it up.

"What *are* they?" Carol wondered, looking at the strange assortment of plastic Baggies filled with bits and pieces. Each Baggie in turn had a label with either the name MARIE or SALLY on it.

"Baby teeth!" I exclaimed, looking at them more closely. "These must be my mother's baby teeth. And the others are Sally's."

"And infant bracelets . . . the kind they put on newborns," Carol said.

There were Baggies with locks of hair in them, dime-store photos of both sisters together when they were little, teething rings, hair ribbons . . . all the things my grandmother hadn't been able to part with as her daughters got older.

Carol cried softly, fingering her mother's baby teeth, and we hugged. Carol had told me she'd decided not to have children, and I wasn't sure just what she was feeling at that moment: grief over losing her mother; the fact that she would have no baby teeth of her own children to treasure; or the thought that some-day relatives would be looking through her own things, sorting them out, discarding some of her keepsakes.

I carefully wrapped up the relics of my mother and put them in my suitcase.

"Thanks for coming, Alice," Carol said when it was time for Dad and me to leave. "You were part of the one bright spot in this whole weekend. I'm glad I could share it with you."

In the next few years, as our own lives became even busier, I tried hard to pay more attention to my dad. Most of the time he was his usual sweet self, but as he aged, he became grumpier, easily irritated over small things that wouldn't have bothered him before. He often complained he didn't see enough of his grandchildren, and sometimes I would just pack overnight bags for the kids and let them stay at the old house for the whole weekend. Dad and Sylvia were glad to have them, and it made a nice holiday for Patrick and me. Tyler was still very much a "grandpa's boy" and loved to cuddle up to my father, but

Patricia was already beginning to pronounce even these events "borrr-ing."

Does every mother, I wonder, reach a point with her children when she wishes they would grow backward? When Patricia Marie was a baby, we eagerly awaited her first steps. We encouraged her to drink from a straw and brush her own teeth and go down the slide alone.

And then . . . You miss that chortle of delight when the juice comes up the straw the first time. You miss that baby voice singing the alphabet song in the dark.

I didn't think Tyler would ever be potty trained and wished him to grow up faster. Now I missed the way his small hand used to rest on mine as we read his evening storybook. I missed the feel of his head resting against my shoulder there on the couch.

You blink your eyes, and suddenly your children have teeth too big for their faces. The baby shoes are replaced by smelly sneakers left just inside the front door. *Come back!* you want to call to the little boy of yesterday, at the same time you're thinking, *Grow up!* of the girl who just angrily slammed the door of her room.

"Enjoy every minute," Patrick and I always reminded each other. And we really tried.

Now, however, in addition to Patrick's travels and my counseling, Tyler's playdates and Patricia's soccer, there were piano lessons, nature club meetings, and karate classes; there were PTA and parent conferences; there were faculty meetings and dental appointments, birthday parties and sleepovers. It seemed sometimes that even when Patrick was home, one of us was always off chauffeuring the kids somewhere.

"Hello. Have we met?" Patrick joked one evening as we passed in the front hall. I had eaten early and was preparing to drive Patricia to a play rehearsal, and he was just getting back from a soccer game with Tyler.

I smiled ruefully. "How about a date Friday night?"

"I'll probably be too tired," he said. "Saturday?"

"I'll put it on the calendar," I laughed.

I got in the car with Patricia Marie. She zipped up her white Windbreaker and fastened her seat belt. Then she turned in my direction and studied me with her green, green eyes.

"Does that mean you're going to have sex?" she asked.

"W-What?" I said, swallowing quickly.

"Sex. You know." She rolled her eyes. "Sexual *intercourse*, Mom! Is that what you and Dad do on a date?"

I suddenly saw myself at that age, badgering Dad about his love life. "Sometimes," I answered. "And sometimes we just watch a video and make popcorn, or listen to music and talk." I couldn't help smiling. "Is there anything else you want to know?"

Patricia wrinkled her nose. "It sounds pretty gross," she said. "When I'm married, can I just watch the video and eat popcorn *without* having sexual intercourse?"

This time I couldn't help laughing. "Of course," I said. "But don't be surprised if you change your mind."

* * *

Phil Kirby was the reading teacher for our school, and his office was next to mine. We shared the same copier and supply cupboard and, in general, kept tabs on each other's lives.

When I was having a bad day and work piled up, Phil would say, "Here. Let me copy those off for you," if he saw me heading for the copying machine. And when I knew he had back-to-back sessions that ran into his lunch hour, I'd sometimes bring him a sandwich from the cafeteria.

He was a tall man, like Patrick, but more muscular—he'd played football in college—and he also had a gentle take-charge manner that made you feel like whatever problem you might have, he could solve it. He used the most marvelous aftershave, and he was a spelunker—he liked to explore West Virginia caves with a local club, rappelling into dark holes, not knowing what was down there, and this sounded enormously scary and exciting to me.

More than that, however, I could tell that he was attracted to me. I knew by the way his hand would linger casually on my shoulder or by the quick neck rub he would give me when he knew I was tense—that if I gave him the slightest encouragement, we could have an affair.

And I have to admit his flirtations were flattering. I didn't encourage him, but I didn't discourage him, either. He made me feel interesting and alive. Not that my husband didn't, but Patrick was away so often, and more and more of our spare time was spent hauling the kids from one activity to the next. I wasn't thinking of giving in to temptation, but . . . it was another fine line to walk—another balancing act—between enjoying Phil's attentions as a coworker and leading him on. It was a heady time, actually. I felt loved at home, desired at work, appreciated by the other counselors, and liked by the students. Patrick and I were thirty-five, Patricia was nine, Tyler six and a half, and life was good.

Patricia, in fact, reminded me of myself when I was her age—Patricia and all her questions.

"Mom," she asked me once, sitting at the table eating a biscuit and jelly and swinging her legs, "what's a vibrator?"

I was at the counter making a barbecue sauce for spareribs, and I paused, blinking. *Stay calm,* I told myself. *She may have something entirely different in mind.*

"Well," I said, "there are different kinds. Rocking chairs sometimes have them. Mattresses . . ."

"Mrs. Ryder's comes in a little box," Patricia said.

"Oh," I said. "That kind. Were you and Mindy going through her mother's things?"

"No. Her mom circled it in a catalog and it came in the mail. What's it for?"

I rummaged through my spice drawer, stalling for time. "Some women use it because it feels good and relaxes them," I said.

"Oh," said Patricia, and continued chewing. Then, "Are spareribs the ones we can eat with our fingers?"

Yes, my darling daughter, I wanted to reply. *You may eat them with your fingers, with your feet, in your chair, or on the floor.*

"Those are the ones," I said. *Thank you, thank you for not asking any more questions.*

Oh, God, I remembered some of the questions I used to ask Dad and Lester at the dinner table, because I felt safe asking. And how patient they were—Dad, anyway—though I embarrassed Les to death. Payback time? I hoped I'd handle things as well as they did.

We were often invited to receptions and dinners at IBM functions, and when I possibly could, I went with Patrick. I enjoyed dressing up and accompanying him—Patrick splendid-looking in his three-piece suits and occasional black tie. Sometimes I wondered why every woman in the corporate office wasn't mad about him. And then I discovered that one of them was.

She was an ash blonde, a little bustier than I am, had great legs, and though you wouldn't call her a beauty, she was certainly attractive. She spoke with a slight accent—Austrian, maybe. There was something about her eyes when she talked with Patrick, something about his voice when he spoke to her, that made me take notice. I knew they had gone on trips where three or four executives traveled together. But then I had long ago realized that Patrick would always be surrounded by admiring women, and when I worried, I'd remember his words: *It's forever, Alice.*

After his next trip, however, when Helene was along, he

seemed different when he got home. More quiet. Why is it that when you desperately want to talk with your husband in private, the kids seem ever present, as though they can tell? Several times that evening, I thought perhaps now was the time to ask what had happened, and always Patricia or Tyler interfered. I thought Tyler was asleep when he came downstairs upset because he'd forgotten to do his arithmetic homework, and the book had to be found and he had to be helped.

Then Patricia, who had gone upstairs to bed, decided she was hungry and came down to make cinnamon toast. And instead of taking it up to her room as she usually did, she brought it into the living room where Patrick and I were sitting together on the couch and plunked herself down across from us.

"What's wrong?" she asked, her mouth full.

"Nothing. Why?" I answered.

"Why are you watching me? All I'm doing is eating toast," she said.

"I guess I was wondering why you didn't take it up to your room," I said.

"Oh, I get it. You want to have sex," she said.

"What?" said Patrick.

But she laughingly picked up her saucer and went upstairs.

"Kids!" Patrick said, smiling a little. But after a few general comments before we could really discuss anything, Patricia was back down again to put her plate in the sink and ask if someone could drive her to school early the next day. It was all I could do not to yell at her to leave us alone.

Finally, when we were sure they were settled for the night, Patrick didn't wait for me to ask. He reached over and took my hand, and I felt dread welling up inside me.

"I'm feeling pretty unsettled about something," he said.

"I know," I told him as lovingly and calmly as I could. "I can tell."

He smiled again. "I can't keep anything from you, can I?"

"Why would you want to?"

"I guess I don't." He tipped his head back and gave a long sigh till it seemed all his breath was gone. "In Seattle," he said finally, "the others went out for the evening, and I found myself having dinner alone with Helene."

"You *found* yourself?" I questioned, and instantly regretted the sarcasm in my voice.

"Okay. Correction. I invited her to have dinner with me. The others were going to a steak house, and I'd had steak two nights in a row and wanted seafood. Helene said seafood sounded great to her too, so I invited her to go along."

I waited, my chest feeling heavy and tight.

"Nothing happened, Alice. Nothing overt, anyway. But it was a long dinner . . . I liked the smell of her perfume and . . . at one point I did reach over and touch her hand. I told her I found her very attractive, and she said she's attracted to me too."

Anger stirred inside me, and I had to struggle to keep it down. Looking at Patrick's hand—imagining his fingers on hers, possibly caressing her thumb—almost made me sick.

"But I reminded her that I'm married," Patrick continued. "And she said, 'Yes, I know. A pity.'"

I closed my eyes for a moment, hating the woman, but knowing that the worst thing I could do right now was lose my temper. How many other husbands would even tell their wives about this? Didn't Patrick get points for being honest? When he didn't say any more, I said, "And . . . ?"

"And that's about it. She's married too, but they're separated. Her husband's evidently been talking divorce for a long time, but neither of them has acted on it. She did say that . . . that sometimes affairs can actually help a marriage, put some spice back into it."

That really got to me. "That's about the worst excuse I can think of, Patrick. So every time she makes love to her husband, she thinks of you and gets off on that? And when you make love to me, you're mentally caressing her instead, and that will strengthen our marriage?"

"I didn't say I agreed with her," he said, and his voice had a note of defensiveness in it, so I kept quiet and let him talk. "I just said, 'Well, I'll sleep on that,' and she said, 'With or without me?' 'Without, I guess,' I told her. So . . . we said good night. I kissed her forehead, and we went to our separate rooms and stayed there. But I just . . . I don't like to keep things from you. You and I agreed that we wouldn't."

We were still holding hands but they felt wooden. I desperately hoped I would say the right thing: "So that's the end of it?"

"Yes. But I . . . I was really tempted, Alice. I don't quite know what to make of it, and I know there will be future trips where she's included."

There was silence between us, but my brain was reeling. Was he asking my *permission*? What I *did* know was that if Patrick was going to be faithful to me, it had to be because he *wanted* it that way, despite his temptations, not because I made him promise.

"I can't make up your mind for you, Patrick. The decision has to be yours," I told him finally.

"I know."

"Have you asked yourself how you would feel, or how it would affect our marriage, if *I* had an affair with a coworker?"

Patrick glanced over at me. "I'd probably feel horrible. I know I'd be jealous. And I don't *intend* to have an affair, with her or anyone else. But I'm not one hundred percent sure that if the opportunity came again and circumstances were right . . ."

"The opportunity will always be there. You know that. And what are the 'right' circumstances for breaking our vows?"

"I know, I know." Patrick tipped back his head again let out his breath, then straightened up. "I'm talking like an idiot. Looking for justification, I guess. I'd hate myself if I did it. I want to be the kind of husband you can trust."

I closed my eyes momentarily, almost too frightened to speak. "But you really *want* to sleep with Helene?"

"Listen. Probably every man wants every attractive woman who comes along, and maybe vice versa, I don't know. That doesn't mean I'm going to do it. But this particular night was different somehow, and it surprised me. To tell the truth, it scared me."

I rubbed my thumb over the top of his hand. "I guess I'll have to say it scares me, too. Because if you go down one road, Patrick, you can't go down another. You can't undo it."

He didn't answer.

"And while I can understand that you'd be tempted—Helene *is* attractive and she obviously likes you—and while I might even be able to forgive you in time, I'm not at all sure I could forget. I'm just afraid that . . . that things would never be the same between us again, no matter how hard we tried. My resentment would keep cropping up, and I'd take it out on you in other ways. That's what really scares me."

He didn't answer. Just drew me to him and we kissed. There were tears in my eyes. "Patrick, I love you so much," I said.

"I know," he said again. "And I don't ever want to do anything that would hurt you."

In a way, I guess, things are never quite the same again after a confession like that. For a while, even though Patrick and I were loving and gentle with each other, the fact that he was that attracted to Helene was a weight on my heart. My mind kept drifting to him all day at work. Was he talking to her right now? Having lunch with her? Would she actually proposition him sometime and would he accept?

At work, Phil noticed immediately that I was upset about

something. One day after school we were both working late, and I was in a panic because Patrick and Helene and six others from IBM were flying to Tulsa for a conference and would be there all week. I couldn't keep my mind on my job and realized I was copying the wrong things on the copier. Suddenly I felt tears running down my cheeks. I'd thought no one had seen, but Phil had.

The next thing I knew, he was walking toward me. "Alice," he said, "what's wrong?" and he put one arm around my shoulder. "Tell me."

I thought how satisfying it would be if Patrick knew I was desirable to other men, if he realized that *he* had better worry about *me*. Then I asked myself, *Which do I want more? To get even and really hurt him? Or do I want my marriage to work?* And I knew without a doubt: make it work.

"I'm okay, Phil," I said, backing gently away from him. "Don't you ever have one of those days where it takes only one small thing to set you off? I'll feel better tomorrow."

"Sure?" he asked.

"Trust me," I said, and went back to the copier.

21
TIME-OUT

A wonderful thing happened just before school started the following September. I was offered the job of supervising the counseling staff of all the county's middle schools. It meant I'd be going from school to school consulting on various problems, writing up reports, working out schedules, and attending meetings.

The problem with being promoted is that you're often taken away from what you love to do most and put in charge of other people who get to do the best stuff.

"What should I *do*?" I asked Patrick. "It's a great step up, and the pay is good, but . . ."

"But you'll miss working with students," he said. "Tell them the truth."

So I did. The miracle was that they wanted me anyway and said I could still do part-time counseling at my old school. So I accepted, and the family decided I should have a party. It was weeks before we could all get together, but when it was time, Patrick's parents even flew in from Wisconsin for the occasion. It seemed strange to be celebrating me for a change, not Patrick.

"Hey, Al," said Les. "Nice going!"

"I'm so proud of you," said Dad, hugging me. Sylvia hugged me next.

Tyler had made place mats for the table, with pictures he had drawn of me on each of them—as a mother holding a baby, another with a crown on my head—and Patricia made a pineapple upside-down cake, my mother's recipe. Patrick, meanwhile, had grilled steaks for all of us, and it was a festive meal. Mine was a small accomplishment compared to Patrick's many promotions, but I had so few that perhaps this is why everyone made such a fuss.

"I can't tell you how many times I talked to a counselor about a student when I was teaching," Sylvia said to me. "I always got such good insight and suggestions."

"I probably learn as much from the students as they learn from me," I told her.

When I'd found out that Les and Stacy had come in two days earlier and were staying at Dad and Sylvia's, and then when Patrick spent most of Saturday over there, I suspected something was up.

And now, as we cleaned up the dishes, I noticed whispers

being exchanged, and Patrick invited us all to the family room for a special presentation. I immediately looked around to see who was missing—if the kids were about to perform—but the children looked as surprised as I was. The chairs and couches had been turned toward the TV, so I sat down with Patrick on one side of me, Dad on the other, Patricia and Tyler at my feet, and suddenly the strains of Vivaldi's *Four Seasons* filled the room. The screen lit up and we read:

ALICE KATHLEEN MCKINLEY LONG: THIS IS YOUR LIFE
As told by your brother, who is not entirely well

The roar of laughter served as prelude to what was to come. As the homemade video continued, I realized now what Lester and Patrick had been up to at my parents' home—that someone had gone through all the old photographs on Dad's shelf, the girlhood scrapbooks still in the attic, the boxes of photos waiting to be sorted here in my office—and I surrendered myself to the fun, as Lester's recorded voice provided the commentary.

While one of Dad's much-loved pictures of me as a baby asleep in a laundry basket, in nothing but a little shirt and diaper, appeared on the screen, Les intoned in his most dramatic voice, "Born on May fourteenth to a poor but honest musician and his wife, little Alice Kathleen McKinley had only the clothes on her back and a laundry basket to serve as her crib. But she was loved." The children shrieked with laughter.

Lester's voice continued: "Though the hardworking parents

tried their best to keep the family clean, water had to be hauled in from the well, and there was no money for soap. Many times, unfortunately, it was difficult to keep little Alice clean." And there I was in my high chair, trying to feed myself, with strained spinach and beets all over my face, my tongue sticking out one side of my mouth.

Tyler doubled over.

Next there was a picture of the four of us lined up to have our picture taken. I don't know where or when this was—I must have been about three—but I was holding a limp doll over one arm, squinting at the sun, and my underpants were in danger of falling, dipping low beneath the hem of my dress. Lester intoned: "The family consisted of Ben, the father; Marie, the mother; Lester, the brother; and little Alice . . . the littlest."

Immediately following was a photo the photographer must have shot the minute after the first one was taken, because my underpants had obviously given way and were down to my ankles. I was crying and trying to pull them up, and part of my bare bottom was visible to the camera.

"When at last the family acquired county water, they could not, alas, afford a bathroom, and so little Alice had to bathe outdoors the best she could." And there I was, squatting over the water sprinkler in the front yard, hair bedraggled, looking very satisfied with myself.

We were all enjoying ourselves immensely. An almost continuous chuckle came from Dad's throat as he recognized old-time photos and we listened to Lester's droll, but theatrical comments: "As a widower, Ben McKinley did his best to show his children the world. There was North Chicago . . ." (a photo of us by the Wrigley Building with Aunt Sally and Uncle Milt), "South Chicago . . ." (a photo of us by Lake Michigan), "and West Chicago . . ." On and on the photos went.

"Little Alice had to endure the taunts and teasing of her older brother, but finally, in a brave show of retaliation . . . she broke his leg." And there was a picture of Lester looking forlorn with his leg in a cast, propped up on a chair.

Tyler turned around and stared up at me. "*Did* you?"

"No, but there were plenty of times I would have liked to," I laughed. "And it was only his ankle. Don't you kids believe anything in this movie."

"At last a fairy godmother came into the family to bring peace and joy," said Lester's voice, and we saw a photo of Sylvia, to which someone had added a pair of fairy wings, and the kids cried, "Nana!" turning toward Sylvia, who was sitting with the Longs on our second couch.

The video continued with a picture of me at sixteen with obvious pimples sprouting up here and there: "To supplement the family income, little Alice, now a teen, was poster girl for Noxzema," the commentator's voice went on.

"Euuu, Mom, you looked awful!" Patricia gasped.

"But we all did. We were all going through the same thing," I assured her.

And when a photo of a pickup truck came on the screen, loaded down with all the stuff going to my dorm room the first day of college, someone had taped a chorus singing, *"She's off to see the wizard, the Wonderful Wizard of Oz."* And then Lester's voice dramatically shouting, "She's off to college, folks, and we're free of Alice! Free at last! Thank God, we're free at last!"

A wedding picture, a honeymoon photo, a picture of a squalling Patricia at three days old, with the announcement that she was elected Loudest of the Newborns; a close-up of Tyler in an enormous yawn and Lester commenting that there was an admissions fee to enter the cave, which sent both Tyler and Patricia leaning and howling against each other. A photo of me at my desk at school, to which someone had added a star above my head as my promotion was noted. And finally the concluding announcement, "Alice Kathleen McKinley Long, this is your life."

We all clapped and laughed and clapped and laughed some more. The kids, of course, wanted to watch it again.

I looked lovingly over at Les. "This must have taken a *lot* of work."

"All I did was put it together and add some sound," he said with uncharacteristic modesty. "Dad and Patrick supplied the photos."

I squeezed Dad's hand and leaned over to kiss Patrick. "Thank you, all of you," I said. "That was one of the funniest things I ever saw. And yes, it's been a wonderful life."

"Mom! You're not dying or anything!" Patricia scolded.

"I'm still allowed to say how much I've enjoyed my life," I told her, laughing.

✳ ✳ ✳

Later, when I was sitting out on the porch with the Longs while my family did the dishes, Mrs. Long said, "I think you and Patrick were meant for each other, Alice."

I smiled. "So do I."

And Mr. Long squeezed my arm. "You're the daughter we never had, and now we have grandchildren, too. You've made us both very happy." I noticed his hand was shaking, and then I remembered the slightly forward gait he used when he walked and realized with a pang that he probably had early Parkinson's disease. I wondered if Patrick knew.

Mrs. Long set a little box on my lap. "Perhaps I should have given this to you sooner, dear, but it's been in the family a long time, and I thought you might pass it along to Patricia someday."

I opened the box. There was a bracelet—obviously valuable— but I knew I'd seen it before.

"It's lovely," I said. "It's very old, isn't it? I feel I've seen it before. Maybe you were wearing it once."

"Perhaps," she said, and smiled. "I don't know if you remember, but a long time ago when Patrick first became your boyfriend, he gave that to you for your birthday. Or maybe it was Christmas, I can't remember."

I stared at it, then at her.

"He didn't steal it, exactly. He just thought that since I didn't wear it often—the stone seems too big for my wrist—he figured I wouldn't mind if he gave it to you."

I burst out laughing. "I do remember now!" I said.

"When he told me later," she went on, "I had to call and explain and ask for it back. It was so embarrassing."

We laughed together on the porch, and I told the story again when the others came out to enjoy the air.

Now that her girls were fairly self-sufficient as far as getting themselves off to school each day, Liz and I had this mad desire to *go* somewhere, *do* something—if only for a few days.

"You could always fly to London for the weekend," I joked as we shared a cup of coffee one Saturday afternoon after I'd dropped off a book on bed-wetting for her youngest child.

"I'd settle for the International Reading Association Conference in New Orleans," she said. "I've never been to an IRA conference. In fact, I've never been to New Orleans, and it would be fun to just take off and *do* it." She put down her cup. "Why don't you come with me?"

I blinked. "When?"

"The week before Thanksgiving. *You* suggest books to teachers. *You* keep up with what kids are reading. And now that you supervise other counselors, it's even more important!"

I was allowed to choose two professional conferences a year, and I hadn't attended any yet. I put down *my* cup. "I'll do it!" I said, and we gave each other a high five.

"What about Pamela?" said Elizabeth. "Would she go?"

We immediately called her, but she didn't think she could get off work. But the big, huge surprise was that Gwen wanted to go!

"You can take off work?" I asked incredulously.

"One of the doctors in our practice asked if I could cover for him between Christmas and New Year's, in exchange for Thanksgiving, and I said I'd let him know. So I say, let's DO it! I missed that trip out west that you guys took, and—except for my honeymoon—I haven't had a real vacation in years."

Liz made the hotel reservations, I made the plane reservations, and two weeks before we were to leave, Pamela phoned: "I can't stand the thought of you three down in New Orleans without me. I'm coming too," she said. We whooped.

The Sunday before Thanksgiving found the four of us eating beignets and drinking lattes in the French Quarter. Elizabeth and I had each marked off the seminars and lectures we wanted to attend while Pamela and Gwen went on an airboat tour of the swamps and had a Cajun culinary lesson, but we set aside a few of the evenings and all day Sunday to hang out with each other.

We'd been sitting at a table in Jackson Square for about a half hour when a man of fifty or so in a pale yellow suit got up from a neighboring table, introduced himself as Marcel, and said that he was French-American, though his accent seemed a little off. He asked if he could join us.

I was on the verge of telling him politely that we were old friends, cherishing our time to catch up on each other's lives, but Pamela, of course, scooted over to make room and invited him to sit down. Gwen and I looked at each other with concealed amusement. It was so *Pamela*! Men seemed to gravitate to her like paper clips to a magnet.

"I've been watching you enjoying one another's company, and I'm curious as to how long you've all known each other," Marcel said. He had thick graying hair, elegantly trimmed, and piercing gray eyes to match. "I'd almost guess you were sisters, except for"—what a line; we were sure he was referring to Gwen, but he turned, smiling, to Elizabeth—"the dark-haired one."

"Almost sisters, but not quite," said Pamela. "We *feel* like sisters, though."

Marcel said he was a writer and that he needed a scene between a group of adult women. Having grown up with only brothers, he didn't quite have a feel for intimate female conversation, and he would love to observe and listen.

"To eavesdrop, in other words," I said, amused at his boldness and curious as to why a middle-aged man would not have picked up the cadences and rhythm of women's voices by now, sisters or no sisters.

He talked a little of his life, of a few articles and short stories he had published, but it became quite clear that the focus of his attention was Elizabeth, who did look ravishing in a teal knit top and linen pants.

I needed a restroom, and when I got up to find one, Elizabeth came too, leaving Pamela and Gwen to entertain our gentleman friend, which they seemed quite happy to do. As soon as we were out of earshot, we started to giggle and bent over double after we'd rounded the corner.

"Hey! We're still babes!" I laughed. "*You* are, anyway."

"Pamela will probably have a date with him by the time we

get back," Elizabeth joked. "I'm going to have to tell Moe about this."

"Is this guy for real?" I asked. "He actually thinks we're going to have intimate conversations with him around?"

We found a restroom, and when we returned to the table, Marcel was still there. In fact, he sprang to his feet when he saw us and gallantly pulled out two chairs at once, waiting to push them in after we sat down.

Pamela caught Elizabeth's eye and had that mischievous set of the mouth that meant she was up to something: "I told Marcel about your husband dying so young," Pamela said, an expression of concern on her face, "and how we're here trying to get your mind off things, Liz. I hope you don't mind."

Before Elizabeth could protest, Marcel reached across the table and put one hand over hers. "I'm so sorry," he said, and kept his hand there.

I expected Elizabeth to say, *What are you* talking *about?* but she fell right into the role. "Thank you," she murmured. "It's been very difficult."

Pamela, who was sitting between us, bumped my knee with hers and probably bumped Elizabeth's, too. I decided to go along with the joke.

"This is the first time Elizabeth has been without a man in her life," I said sympathetically.

"I understand," said Marcel, and it looked to me as though he gave Elizabeth's hand a squeeze. "Perhaps if you would allow me to show you the sights of the city . . ." He paused, wondering,

I suppose, if he was going too far, too fast, and added quickly, "The *four* of you, of course!"

Gwen took over this time. "We just don't know yet how we want to spend our time here," she said. "I think we'll take Elizabeth back to the hotel to rest, then make plans for the afternoon."

"I am at your service," Marcel said, and pulled out a small notebook from his breast pocket. He jotted down his phone number, then tore out the sheet and thrust it in Elizabeth's hand. "Rest," he said. "And then I will show you the city. Not enough to tire you, only delight you."

Pamela got up. "You've been so kind."

"I am at your service," Marcel said again, bowing ever so slightly in his pale yellow suit.

Back in our room we howled like hyenas. But Elizabeth stopped suddenly and gasped, "He knows where we're staying!" We remembered that Pamela had mentioned it. This sent Gwen and me into spasms again.

"Naturally," said Pamela. "That's part of the fun."

We sprawled out across the two beds. "Gosh, it's good to be with you guys," Gwen said. "It's like old times."

Elizabeth looked at Pamela. "How did you explain my wedding ring?"

"I told Marcel you couldn't bear to remove it—that you vowed it would stay on your finger until you went to bed with another man."

"*What?*" cried Elizabeth, and that set us off again.

We got out a map of New Orleans and decided we really wanted to see one of the "cities of the dead," the aboveground cemeteries where bodies are buried in small crumbling mausoleums, one of them containing the body of a voodoo queen. The concierge told us what bus to take, and we rode through the city until we came to the walls of the cemetery.

Gwen was especially fascinated, because she liked to guess what the children in a family might have died of when the gravestones indicated that several died at the same time. We were walking among the tombs, reading inscriptions, looking for the voodoo queen, when suddenly Elizabeth said, "Oh . . . my . . . gosh!"

We looked where she was looking, and there was the man in the pale yellow suit at the far end of the cemetery, looking around. I grabbed both Pamela and Elizabeth and yanked them back behind a tall mausoleum with a lamb sculpted on its door, and we clapped our hands over our mouths, eyes wide with laughter.

"How did he know we were *here*?" I asked Pamela.

"I told him we wanted to see one of the cemeteries, and he recommended this one," she said.

"You *didn't*!" I peeked around the wall. "He's coming this way!" I said, and we darted over to the next tomb, and then the next.

"Oh, my gosh, I think he saw me," Elizabeth said as we zigzagged our way along the back row of grave sites.

"Elizabeth!" came Marcel's voice. "*Ma chère*! Let me show you New Orleans!"

Pamela slipped on a piece of masonry and fell, letting out a little shriek. We yanked her up just as Marcel came around the corner a few tombs down.

"Elizabeth!" he called again.

But we were running back out to the street where, miraculously, two cabs were cruising by. We managed to flag the second one and pulled away from the curb just as Marcel came out of the cemetery, his arms spread dramatically in a gesture of despair.

We figured the guy was either clueless or a grade-B actor who was having as much fun as we were. But we put our minds to other things that night, eating at a Cajun restaurant that Moe had recommended before we left, then strolling along the streets in the French Quarter, listening to the sounds of jazz coming from various clubs, ever alert for a man in a pale yellow suit. We managed to squeeze onto the floor where the Preservation Hall musicians were playing Dixieland, and we fell into bed about eleven, declaring that this was the most fun we'd ever had.

Pamela had just come out of the bathroom when there was a light tap on the door and a man's voice called, "Room service!"

We looked at each other.

"I didn't order anything," said Elizabeth.

"Neither did we," I said.

The three of us tiptoed to the door and took turns peering out the peephole. We could see a man's shoulder, garbed in a white shirt, but he had turned away from the door and we couldn't see his face.

We didn't move. The hand knocked again.

"Room service," came the call, a little louder.

"Marcel!" we whispered to each other as we recognized the voice. We still didn't answer, and finally, at long last, he went away.

"How did he know what room we were in?" I wondered.

"He probably has an in with the night clerk," said Pamela. "Gave him some story about researching a novel . . ."

"If he bribed someone to tell him the room we were in, he could bribe someone to give him a key," said Elizabeth.

Laughing hysterically, we chained and double locked the door, then pushed a chair, two suitcases, and a lamp in front of it.

Marcel didn't press his luck. He never returned or called, and after talking well into the night about Gwen's practice, her family, and her marriage, we slept contentedly, deliciously, until late the next morning.

When we got back home, Patrick asked if I'd had a good time. He and the kids had made a welcome-home dinner of chicken, macaroni and cheese, and applesauce, but, hey! I only had to eat it. I didn't even have to clean up afterward.

"A *wonderful* time!" I said.

"What all happened, Mom?" asked Patricia Marie.

"Well," I said, "a strange man in a pale yellow suit sat down with us one day at breakfast, chased us around a cemetery, and tried to get in our room at night."

Patrick lifted one eyebrow and surveyed me across the table. Tyler looked at me with wide eyes. But Patricia balanced a bite of macaroni on her fork, gave me a sidelong glance, and said, "Yeah, Mom. Right!"

22

DECISION

For the next few years, my job kept me busier professionally than I'd ever been before, but I loved it. Patricia was in sixth grade now, Tyler in third, both at very manageable ages.

It would be nice to say that I had been successful with each of the students I counseled, but I wasn't. Sometimes I was asked to take over some of the more difficult cases, and one of them, in one of the schools, was an eighth grader, Nicole Butler. She had been referred to a counselor for her suggestive behavior with her boyfriend, and had been admonished by the vice principal. It hadn't affected her at all, however, and she'd told the overworked counselor that she would not even talk with her unless she could guarantee 100 percent that their talks were confidential and that her parents would never know what they talked about.

Sensing that this was going to take far more time than she could give, the counselor asked if I would see Nicole. I had time that week for only a short preliminary session, and when I arrived for it, I found myself looking at an attractive brunette in a too-tight jersey top who sat with her arms crossed, staring at me defiantly. What made it interesting was that she obviously wanted to talk, but only under her conditions.

"I know why the teachers want you here," I said, "but I don't know why you wanted to come."

"Because there are some things I want to talk about, but not to my parents, especially my mom."

"Then I'll tell you up front that if you're involved in anything illegal, I have to tell them. If you are drinking and getting drunk or taking drugs, or if you are being sexually molested, I have to report it."

"Define 'molested,'" Nicole said.

"When an adult is taking advantage of you sexually, whether you agree to do it or not."

"And if it's not an adult and you're not doing anything you don't want to do?"

"Then, technically, I suppose, it's not molestation."

"And you don't have to report it? To my parents, I mean?"

"Not unless you want me to."

"God, no," she said, and for the first time in our session, she relaxed a little, letting her hands drop in her lap.

"From what your teachers tell me, you and your boyfriend

are behaving pretty inappropriately in the halls and the class-rooms. Any thoughts on that?"

"Define 'inappropriate,'" said Nicole.

I smiled. "Your turn," I said. "What would your definition be?"

She didn't hesitate, and stared straight into my eyes as she answered: "The teachers would say it was touching a guy in any way, shape, or form. It freaks them out." She almost smiled, sure, it seemed, she had shocked me.

I didn't hesitate: "They report long tongue kisses, groping each other in the genital area, rubbing bodies together . . ."

"If it's so offensive, they don't have to look. It doesn't involve them," she said quickly.

"You've heard the expression 'Get a room'?"

"Yeah, we would if we had the money. Where are we sup-posed to get a room if both our moms are home all day? I'm highly sexed, what can I tell you?"

It was an interesting case, because her grades were above average, she hadn't been in any other trouble with her teachers, and she was active in a few extracurricular activities, but she was determined at thirteen to have sex, as much of it as she could get.

"Are you prepared for sexual relations, Nicole?" I asked. "I assume you've started your periods, so you know that preg-nancy is a possibility."

"Ha. My mom would call it a catastrophe! But we're going to do it! Yes, we'll use condoms. Ethan's got them already."

"So . . . what is it you want from me?"

Here she took a deep breath and slid down a little farther in her chair. "I don't know, just . . . Well . . . We sort of tried it once, before his mom came home, and I don't think we were doing it right. I just . . . And he's got this pimple down there, and we don't know if that means anything or not."

She was still testing me to see how I'd react. I could tell by her eyes and the hidden smile, but at the same time, she was fishing for information. I decided to play it straight.

"I certainly can't take the place of a doctor," I told her, "so Ethan should at least have the nurse look at it. But we cover a lot of things in the sex education course we give to eighth graders in the spring."

Nicole gave a sardonic laugh. "Mom won't sign the paper. She's already said."

What the girl wanted, I realized, was a short version of the sex education course here in my office. What she wanted, in fact, was a far more graphic explanation than what she'd get in the spring. And I had no authority to give it to her.

I remembered my twenty-year-old self (was I really that old?) walking into a Planned Parenthood clinic, the embarrassment I felt then, and here was a mere child of thirteen, fumbling her way into sex. . . . A girl who obviously thought that if I outlined the moves like a football play, she and her boyfriend would know how to do it.

"The best sex," I told her, "is between two people who are in a private, comfortable place, with all the time in the world, and who really care about each other."

"Tell me something I don't know," she said, and then, immediately apologized. She also glanced once or twice at the door, as the halls were filled with the chatter of students changing classes. I wondered if her boyfriend was waiting for her. "It just . . . really hurts," she said, a bit more humbly.

"Most girls need plenty of lubrication the first time," I said, knowing that this alone had crossed the line, but if I gave her nothing of value, I was certain she would not come back and I'd have no chance of influencing her decisions.

"What kind?" she asked nervously.

"You can buy it in any drugstore, next to tampons," I said.

She suddenly picked up her books. "I have to go."

"Well, I'm going to get together some materials for you, and I think you'll find them helpful," I said. "We'll go over them together in our next session when we have more time. Okay?"

She nodded and stood up, then opened the door. The minute she stepped out into the hall, I heard her say, "Kirsten, what are you doing here?"

And a younger girl's voice sang out, "I have just as much right . . ."

"Quit spying on me . . ."

Their voices faded off as they moved away, and I'll never know what happened, because Nicole didn't keep the next appointment. Nor did she attend the sex education course when it was offered in the spring. I had to chalk it up as one of my failures.

Summer came and the semester ended. *What could I have done differently?* I kept asking myself.

Two weeks into the fall semester, however, I read in the *Post* that a parents' group had gathered the necessary number of signatures for a proposal to be sent to the school board advocating abstinence-only sex education. I hadn't read the article yet, but several faculty members asked if I'd seen it, and the health teacher running the program begged me to come out strongly for continuing the present program.

"Of all people, counselors know how desperately students need this information," she said.

"Of course I'll support you," I told her. "Let me read the article, then I'll know better how to respond."

I had to visit two other schools that morning, but I finally got a copy of the *Post* on my lunch break and sat down in a Panera Bread café to read it over an egg salad sandwich.

The reporter quoted one of the founders of the TTT movement—"Tell the Truth" (about abstinence)—and the facts were questionable from the get-go: that students who attend abstinence-only courses instead of the usual sex ed courses have fewer out-of-wedlock pregnancies than students who are introduced to contraceptives; that teens who have access to contraceptives misuse them; that the rate of sexually transmitted diseases is higher; and so on. All the statistics quoted were highly debatable, and I was particularly interested in a few lines near the end of the article: *"Everyone knows that once our young people have experienced sex, they are far more reluctant to give it up. And it can become as addictive as drugs or alcohol,"* said Emma Butler, co-chair. *"Put simply, we believe that we have a mission to save our middle school students from themselves and to let the school board know that we are a force to be reckoned with."*

I closed my eyes, but I think I'd already made the connection. When I got back to the office later, I checked Nicole's records, and yes, of course, her mother's name was Emma, and already there was a message from a *Post* reporter wanting to talk with me about the guidance department's slant on abstinence-only education.

"I think I'm in this deeper than I ever intended to be," I told Patrick that evening. It had been fairly easy to challenge the statistics that the TTT was distributing, but that didn't get at the heart of what was worrying the parents. For them, life was moving too fast. Their children were more sophisticated than they'd been at their age, and while parents couldn't stop what came on TV screens or what their kids heard on the bus, perhaps they could have some influence on what their kids learned in the classroom. Teachers should not be making it easier for young teens to have sex, they should be teaching that no sex until marriage equals problem solved. Except, as Nicole and her boyfriend demonstrated, it didn't.

"You've got to choose your battles, and if this is one you want to fight, go for it," Patrick said.

"It's going to mean endless meetings, conferences, press quotes, rebuttals . . . ," I said. "But yes, I really want to fight."

Patricia Marie came through the living room just then in her Snoopy shirt with a box of crackers she was returning to the kitchen. "Are you guys talking about that sex ed course at school?" she asked, stopping long enough to pop one more cracker in her mouth.

"That was the topic of discussion," I said wryly, one eyebrow raised. "Have you been listening from the stairs?"

"No, I just heard you talking when I came through the room. We took a poll on the bus, and everyone we know can take that course, except I don't think kids would admit it if their parents said no."

And that was another problem, I realized. No kid should be ostracized because of a parental decision.

"Well, if you hear any more talk, remember that every parent wants what's best for her child. We just don't always agree on what that is," I told her.

Patricia lingered a bit longer.

"Since I'm here, I might as well ask another question of both of you," she said, and waited.

"Yeah? Shoot," said Patrick.

She leaned against the door frame, feet crossed, and gave an embarrassed little giggle. "I know that when a man and a woman get engaged, either one can pop the question, but it's usually the man, right?"

"Right," said Patrick.

"So when a guy and a girl—well, a man and a woman—want to have sex, who asks?"

That was a new one. I deferred to Patrick, trying not to smile.

"Well . . . uh . . . I'm not sure asking is actually necessary. I mean . . . if their sexual activity is that far along, then it's the next logical step and . . ." He looked at me helplessly. "Of course, I would expect they'd known each other for a long time. . . ."

"Actually, either one could suggest it, Patricia, and the next logical step would be to make sure the boy was using a condom," I said.

"Okay, thanks," Patricia said quickly, and disappeared.

Patrick sat staring after her. "Did that just happen?" he asked. "Is *that* the kind of question you get from students?"

"You've no idea. A few months ago she wanted to know if you can tell by a girl's fingernails whether or not she's a virgin."

"*What?* Did you have all those questions when you were in seventh grade?"

"And then some," I told him. "And I'll bet you did too. You just don't remember."

It was only October, and the critical decision coming up for spring semester was whether the sex ed course should be canceled until a committee had a chance to study the issue further. Never mind that the committee had studied it to death before it was ever decided to teach the course in the first place. The TTT group wanted even more, however. Not only did they want it canceled, but they wanted an abstinence-only course to be taught in its place, and they already had the materials they felt we should use.

I already knew of half a dozen middle schoolers who had engaged in intercourse and countless others who, according to their peers anyway, "fooled around." Did we abandon these pseudosophisticated kids to a no-sex rule even after they had experienced the thrill of it and then trust that our admonitions and persuasions would be sufficient? Or did we equip them for their soon-to-be-even-riskier sexual life so that they would have a basic knowledge of what "a pimple down there" means and other matters? At the very least, we felt—and experience bore this out—the fact that we were talking in the classroom about sex meant that it was okay for kids to discuss it with us.

As the battle became more heated, Emma Butler became more strident. Every other day, it seemed, the *Post* reported a new allegation or statistic from TTT, and because there was such emotion on both sides, a reporter was always around to pick up the next newsworthy pronouncement, and these would land on my desk seeking a rebuttal.

And then one night the phone rang still again. As soon as I said hello, this steely-sounding woman said, "Am I speaking to Alice Long?"

"Yes," I said, trying to be pleasant. "And you are . . . ?"

"Emma Butler," she replied. "And I think you should know what you are doing to young minds in the schools."

"Oh, Mrs. Butler," I said, "I'm glad to have the chance to talk with you personally. Would you like to come to the office and we could have a discussion?"

"No, I would not want to waste my time. Everything I have to say to you I can say over the phone," she replied.

I've learned when to let silence bring out feeling, and when I didn't reply, her words came out in a rush: "Little children enter middle school just after fifth grade. They come as innocent youngsters off the playground, used to skipping rope and playing kickball. Most of them don't even know what a condom is, and *we don't want* them to know! Call us old-fashioned, but we think of ourselves as sensible; with all the sex going on on television, magazine covers that make you blush, stories about priests seducing children and homosexuals hugging right out in public, someone has got to say, 'Enough.' We can't stop the movies and TV and the perverts, but with God's help, we can stop the schools from the early sexualization of our children."

She stopped for breath, and her voice was trembling. I think she had just coined a new word, but I really felt for her then. In my mind she was one woman struggling to hold back a crumbling dam, water already pouring over the top.

"Do you have children, Mrs. Butler?" I asked.

"Yes, I do—a ninth-grade daughter and another in seventh. Sex is the last thing on their minds. I know, and our daughters know, that the only way they'll get a car when they graduate from college is if they remain virgins till then."

"Well . . . back when we were in middle school, and certainly when our mothers were," I said, "many of us didn't menstruate until we were twelve or older. Now puberty begins earlier. For some girls, it's ten or eleven. And with it comes sexual maturation and all the normal feelings."

"Maybe so, but they don't have to act on them. If schools start giving out condoms, you'll see them all over the playground for children six and seven to pick up. Girls will start having babies before they graduate eighth grade. This is only the start of the degradation of America, and I and my committee intend to stop you and your agenda for our county. I have nothing more to say to you."

And Mrs. Butler hung up.

I sat down with tears in my eyes for her daughters. What a shame we couldn't have a responsible dialogue, I was thinking. She had brought up a number of points that many parents worry about—risque-looking clothes designed for nine-year-olds and younger; child molestation by the clergy; movies depicting sexual violence toward women. But we can't deal with problems if we pretend they're not there, as well as normal sexual feelings that arise naturally in adolescent youngsters. I wished Nicole could have gone through the sex education course I'd had in my church as a teenager, where I learned that sex and love and respect and responsibility go together, and I wondered how we could incorporate more of that in the course we give in the spring. Was I in this battle now, heart and soul? Absolutely.

Both Emma Butler and I appeared on the local news from time to time, and I was shocked one evening to see a brief ad for TTT, showing Emma Butler with her husband and both daughters by her side. "The abstinence-only philosophy works for us and our family, and I've never had to worry about my daughters," she announced. The younger daughter looked beatifically up at her mother, but Nicole stared stonily at the camera as the letters TTT took over the screen.

* * *

The middle of November, with both Christmas and the abstinence-only decision hanging over me, Patrick excitedly announced at dinner that IBM was entering a partnership with Spain to provide more grants to Latin American countries to start business courses in schools. He would be actively involved in helping set up the program, and IBM wanted to send him to *Barcelona*.

"Patrick," I said, my body frozen. "You'd be there for . . . ?"

"Two years! All of us! We'd all go!"

"*What?*"

"Think what a fantastic opportunity this would be for you and the kids. I've always wanted to take you there!"

"Dad! Wow!" Tyler cried excitedly, not waiting for my reaction. Even Patricia Marie, who I thought would never want to leave her friends, looked interested.

I couldn't believe it! "Barcelona! Oh, Patrick! They'd take care of the move and everything?"

"Down to the last dresser drawer. All we'd have to do is give them the key and walk out. The kids would be in English-speaking classes, of course."

"It's . . . it's wonderful!" I gasped.

"We're going to Spain, we're going to Spain!" Tyler said, his voice riding up and down.

"I can even speak a little Spanish," Patricia said, repeating something she'd learned in Scouts: "*¿Cómo está usted?*"

"*No comprendo,*" Patrick said, and we laughed. He was still looking at me.

"My head's spinning," I said, and I had to admit that almost every day since the sex ed debate began this fall, I felt I would take the first plane leaving for almost anywhere, as long as I never had to put up with Emma Butler and TTT again. "Of course I want to do it! I'd love to live in Spain, Patrick! Especially Barcelona. How did you manage that?"

"They're simply expanding their program and offering more grants. Of course, they think that partnering with Spain on this one would also increase their business. Actually, I'd be based in Barcelona, but also working in Madrid. I'd be with the family a lot more, though."

"Let's do it, Mom!" Patricia Marie said. "I could e-mail all my friends in Spanish."

I looked at Patricia Marie and Tyler, then at Patrick. "When do they want us to go?"

Now Patrick looked a little sheepish. "As soon as we can get there. They thought maybe . . . over Christmas vacation."

"Over Christmas! Patrick? That's less than six weeks away—are they out of their minds?"

"No, but I think it's time we did something fantastic and out of our minds, don't you? They said they'd even provide a housekeeper."

I thought of the job I'd be leaving behind—how lucky I'd been to get it. The big vote on the sex education course scheduled for the end of January. How could I walk out now? It would be like I couldn't face it.

"Patrick, I—I can't! I need to be here! I've worked so hard, given so much time to this."

I could see the disappointment in his eyes, the children's fallen faces.

"Aw, Mom!" said Patricia Marie.

"We never do anything fun," Tyler said, and strangely, that made us all laugh because he says that five minutes after riding a roller coaster.

"I'll tell you what," I said, my brain on overdrive. "Let's fly there right after Christmas and find a place to live, and you kids can stay there with your dad while I come back and finish out the school year."

Patrick looked stunned. "Would that work?"

"If we get a good housekeeper who can run things when you aren't there, Patrick. I think you guys can manage till I come in June."

"Are you serious, Alice? Would you do that?"

"Why not? Let me be the one who travels back and forth. I can come in mid-February, I can come again over spring break, and I'll ask for a leave of absence come summer because . . . we're going to *Barcelona*!" I shouted out the last word, and the kids took up the chant.

Patrick was like a little boy himself. I was in the other room when he called work and told his boss we were going. All evening he seemed dazed—we all were—and kept grinning at me as we prepared for bed that night.

"That's a solution I'd never thought of, and I'm not sure what I'm in for, taking on the kids by myself," he said.

"They're potty trained," I joked. "They can dress themselves and comb their own hair. I'll drop in now and then to see how you're doing."

"Come here," said Patrick, pulling me over to his side of the bed. "I was worried you wouldn't do this for me."

"I'm doing it for us, Patrick," I said. "I think it's going to be great. I *expect* it to be great. I'm going to be a Spanish woman with a basket on my arm, doing the baking, and eating flan, and looking out over the sea."

"And I'm going to be a very proud Spanish papa when I show you off to the locals," he said, reaching over to turn out the light.

23

BARCELONA AND BACK

The years we spent in Barcelona were some of the best of our lives. I was truly away from home and family—my childhood home and family, I mean. Even when I was away at college, I was only a half hour from Dad. Now I was a world away.

The first six months, of course, I was still working, traveling back and forth at IBM's expense. I was the one taking cabs to the airport—and even flying first-class. I was there over Christmas vacation to help choose the rental flat where we'd live and to approve the full-time housekeeper. I was there to meet Patrick's associates, and best of all, I was there to announce the school board's decision to reaffirm our sex ed course for the county. As a result, Emma Butler had appeared on local TV, declaring that she was enrolling her youngest daughter in a private school. She did not mention Nicole.

And the children will never forget the months alone with their dad in Spain.

"I was walking right where Columbus was when he got back from discovering America!" Tyler said over the phone.

"And Dad lets me walk to the *panadería* each morning to buy rolls for breakfast!" Patricia boasted.

Patrick bought a motor scooter and had taken each child on a sightseeing trip around the city. On the phone at night, they argued over who got to tell me about the spiral staircase and the building that looked all wavy and the huge Ferris wheel and roller coasters at Tibidabo.

I couldn't wait till the semester was over, and the very next day I was on the plane to Barcelona, this time to stay out the remainder of the two years. The housekeeper greeted me with exclamations of either welcome or relief, but she was joyful, and so were Patrick and the children.

What happened was that we all grew closer—Patrick and Patricia and Tyler and I. Patrick loved his work, Patricia had a couple of Catalonian boys flirting with her, and Tyler blossomed into a lanky, self-confident kid who drew his own map of our new neighborhood, adding streets as he discovered them. Each day I could see his little world expanding there on paper. For my part, I recorded our adventures as a personal travelogue and enjoyed the family's response when I read them aloud at night.

Patricia and I bought a traditional Spanish outfit for her—

the embroidered skirt, fringed shawl, and lace mantilla to wear over her hair. I took her picture to enclose with our cards at Christmas, and we bought a toreador costume for Tyler. He consented to put it on but, in typical Tyler fashion, insisted on posing cross-legged, sitting in the grass beneath an actual cork tree, with a flower in his mouth, like Ferdinand, the peaceful bull—and what better message to send at Christmas time, anyway?

Because none of our close friends were here, Patrick and I relied more on each other, asking each other questions in Catalan, exploring together on weekends, eating paella, shopping for sangria pitchers or chocolates or fans for gifts. Our time there seemed more like an extended vacation. Patricia wanted to attend a Catalan school her second year, and she was so warmly received that it seemed the perfect thing to do—she could catch up if she fell behind once we got home. And it was wonderful when Les and Stacy came for Christmas.

The kids were at a birthday party one evening for one of their new friends, after which they were going to spend the night with one of Patrick's coworkers who said he'd pick them up with his own kids. So Patrick and I walked La Rambla hand in hand, stopping to watch the mime artists, the musicians, and the street vendors who thronged the place. We talked about his work, and Patrick mentioned that one of the men told him that Helene had received an offer from AMOCO and was working for that company now in Dallas.

"That's nice," I said blandly. Then we looked at each other and laughed.

"I'm glad things turned out the way they did," he said finally.

"So am I."

His hand tightened on mine. "Were *you* ever tempted, Alice? Truthfully?"

I told him about Phil.

"You never mentioned him before," he said.

"I thought you'd feel I was digging him up to throw in your face."

Patrick thought that over. "You had every right . . ."

"I know."

Patrick pulled me toward him sideways. "I would have been jealous as anything," he said as we staggered along, lockstep.

"Good!" I told him.

"Beaten his brains out. Smashed him to a pulp."

"Even better," I said, and laughed.

"Did he ever . . . ever kiss you?" Patrick asked tentatively.

"On the forehead," I said.

"That's far enough," he said, and we stopped right there on La Rambla and kissed under a Catalonian sky.

There was also romance in the air for Pamela, we heard, because she e-mailed that she was seeing a lot of a suave New Yorker named Nick who owned a men's clothing store. She sent us photos of him, and Liz e-mailed that she had met him, and Pamela and Nick seemed to have a lot in common. *This might be the one!* she'd written.

The real surprise was that Gwen and Charlie were expecting.

Who does an ob-gyn ask to deliver her own babies? I wondered in an e-mail to Liz.

Someone she sees every day at the office? Liz e-mailed back. *You think?*

But there was sad news too. We received word that Uncle Milt had died. It wasn't entirely unexpected, because he had a number of health problems. And not wanting to interrupt our trip to Madrid that Patrick and I had planned, Dad didn't tell us until after the funeral.

I called Carol as soon as I could.

"I'm so terribly sorry," I said. "I just found out."

"I know. It was my decision that we shouldn't call you, because I was afraid you'd zip right back. I had a lot of support from your dad and Sylvia and Larry and all my friends, Alice, and I think I was prepared for it, anyway."

But I wasn't. I must have felt that Uncle Milt, being older than Dad, was sort of insulation between my own father and death. That Dad couldn't possibly die before Uncle Milt. And now Dad was next in line.

Carol and I talked as long as we dared, bringing each other up-to-date. While her husband was managing hotels, she had an executive position in a nursing association and loved it.

"Take care," I told her as we signed off. "Be good to yourself now."

"And you take care of your dad when you get back," she

told me. "We don't realize how much we'll miss them till they're gone, Alice."

Dad, however, seemed to be doing all right, and we settled back into our Spanish routines in the months we had left. What we did not expect at all was the death of Patrick's mother, from an embolism in her lung following a hip replacement. We'd arranged to come back to the States two weeks earlier than we'd planned when we first found out she needed surgery, claiming our house once again in Chevy Chase. But her death took us all by surprise, and we didn't know what would happen to Patrick's father, whose Parkinson's disease was getting worse.

This was so difficult for Patrick. *It must be especially agonizing for an only child,* I thought. I knew how hard it had been for Pamela dealing with her mom's problems.

I don't remember much about my own mother's funeral, but helping plan Mrs. Long's service with Patrick, watching him struggle with his grief, I had a vague sense of *déjà vu.*

It was the first funeral that Patricia and Tyler ever attended, and they were solemn throughout, their attention primarily on their dad. When the casket was lowered and Patrick wept, I saw Tyler swallowing and swallowing, and I squeezed his hand.

Just coming back to the States was, in itself, a shock I hadn't expected, and the funeral came only a few days before Christmas. There were many more decisions to be made, more choices to be had. I just wanted time to stand still for a while and let me get my bearings. And driving to Baltimore to see Gwen and Charlie's new baby boy was just what I needed.

Gwen had e-mailed me a few pictures of him at six weeks old, and he had his mom's dimples. His huge brown eyes took over his whole face.

"He's simply adorable, Gwen. I'd want to hold him twenty-four/seven," I told her, cuddling the chubby little cherub in my arms.

"That's my problem. I want to play with him forever. Liz and Moe came to visit last week, and their little girls could hardly keep their hands off him. How are *you* doing, other than the funeral?"

"We're all going a little bit nuts," I told her. "Patricia's starting high school next fall, and she didn't do nearly as well as she thought in Spain, so she'll have to go to summer school to catch up. She's pretty upset about that."

"Wow. I should think so," Gwen said. "She'll catch up in a hurry, but try telling that to a teenager."

"Meanwhile, Tyler will be starting middle school next year, and that's a trial for every kid, no matter what. And everything's changed in my department. I'm going to be supervising counselors who are used to doing things their own way now. I won't even know some of the new ones at all."

"Alice," Gwen said, "trust me. It could be so much worse for both of us. I had a patient just last week who had her third miscarriage. . . ."

I was instantly humbled. "You're right, you're right," I said.

"I'm not trying to belittle your problems, but . . . well, I can think of a dozen women who would kill to have spent two years in Barcelona."

I needed that, and I was determined to be more positive about things. Patrick was worried enough about his dad. He had asked for less travel in case he was needed at home, which meant that many of his coworkers got the work he loved to do while he was stuck with paperwork. And finally one night he said the words I'd been dreading to hear: "Al, do you think it would upset the family too much if Dad moved in with us?"

When I didn't answer right away—because the truthful reply would have been, *Yes, of course it would!*—Patrick answered for me: "I was hoping it wouldn't come to this. But he doesn't want to live on an assisted-living floor of some retirement complex, and who knows how much time he has left?"

I sat down across from Patrick, and we just looked at each other for some time.

"If it were my dad, I know I'd bring him here," I said, "but I won't pretend it's going to be easy."

"I know."

"And everyone's going to have to cooperate and share the work."

"I know that, too. You can count on my help most of all," Patrick said.

So we converted our family room into a bedroom, installed a hospital bed for Dad Long, and had a nursing attendant come in during the day to take care of him until Patrick or I got home at night. But it was the simple fact of having his dad in our house that unnerved us all. Patrick relieved his own stress by jogging, and it seemed to suit Tyler's tall frame as well. He began going along with his dad, and finally it was a weekly occurrence, sometimes even more often, and it was great to see them have their own thing together.

Patricia and I were having a harder time of it, and somehow having Dad Long living with us led to our worst battles. Most of the time, unlike many teenagers, Patricia wore her heart on her sleeve. We didn't have to ask what she was thinking or feeling. She would stand behind me at the sink and give me a hug as readily as she would drop her schoolbooks on the floor and bellow, "I hate life!" She could be sunny one minute, grabbing her father and dancing around the living room to her favorite song, and five minutes later be fighting heatedly with Tyler over whose turn it was to empty the dishwasher. But it was Dad Long who upset her the most.

"He's always *staring* at me! Just *staring*!" Patricia complained one day, coming in the kitchen.

"Shhh, Patty. He's not deaf!" I scolded. "That's the way people with Parkinson's often look. He doesn't mean to stare."

"Well, if he doesn't mean to, then make him stop!" she said, and I felt like grabbing her by the shoulders and shaking her.

"Could we have a little more empathy here, please?" I asked, knowing her grandfather might not last out the year. "Can't you even imagine what it must be like for him to be so dependent on us?"

"No, I can't, because I'm *not* him! I'm *me*! And I only know what it feels like to be *me*!" she said.

I was furious with her. "Then I pity you!" I said. I'd had a difficult day already. I'd forgotten to pick up the ingredients I needed to make dinner, I was facing a root canal in a couple of days and the tooth was hurting again, and now this. I turned on her. "I'm embarrassed for you, that you have so little feeling for other people."

"I do too have feeling for other people!" she shrieked. "I just can't get along with *old* people! They're weird and they're creepy and they *smell* and—"

My patience gave out and I slapped her. I had never slapped either of my children before, other than a quick swat on the seat, and I was as shocked as she was.

"Mo-ther!" she gasped, her face flushed, one hand on her cheek.

I started to say, *Oh, Patricia, I didn't mean that!* when she rushed upstairs and shut herself in her room.

I leaned against the stove, stunned. What was I thinking? Was *I* never young and self-centered and thoughtless?

Upstairs, I tried to open her door, but it was locked.

"Patricia," I said, "please let me in. I'm sorry."

"Go away. I *hate* you!" she cried. I could hear the sob in her voice.

Sadness welled up in my throat, almost choking me. "Patricia . . . ," I began again.

"Go *away*!" she wept.

I sat down on the floor outside her room, my head on my knees, hugging my legs. I didn't want things to be like this between us. I wanted us to be close. The phone rang, but I didn't answer. I heard Tyler come in for a drink of water and run back out to his buddies on the basketball court. I didn't move.

I don't know how long I was there. I leaned back against the wall and closed my eyes, trying to remember *any*thing about my own mother, any fights we might have had, but I had simply been too young. I did remember several big ones I'd had with Sylvia. What would Patricia remember of me?

Finally I heard the door open. Patricia started to come out, then stopped. I said nothing. She said nothing. She went on to the bathroom and closed the door. I heard the toilet flush.

When she came out again, hesitantly, I turned in her direction, and for a long moment we studied each other. I held out my arms.

Wordlessly, she came over and collapsed on the floor beside me, both of us crying. I hugged and rocked her.

"I'm so, so sorry, Patricia," I said. "I'll never do that again."

"I'm sorry too," she sniffled. "And I . . . I hope he didn't hear me."

"So do I," I said. I waited until we were both more composed, and then I told her, "Parents have bad days too sometimes. I have problems and worries you don't know anything about, and sometimes, if you catch me at a bad moment, I thoughtlessly take it out on you. You'll probably do the same to your own children now and then. Not often, I hope, but it won't mean you don't love them."

We continued to hug, her arms tentatively creeping around my waist, her wet face against my neck.

"Are . . . are there any big problems?" she asked.

"None that we can't handle," I said, and kissed the top of her head.

24
CATCHING UP

I knew that Les and Stacy had been trying without success to have children, and over the years I had hoped they might adopt, but they didn't. It was a topic we didn't discuss any longer, and never, of course, unless one of them brought it up. Les was forty-six, Stacy forty-one, and they seemed more or less settled as a childless couple.

They had moved to Virginia, where Lester became head of personnel at George Mason University, and Stacy taught physical education at a nearby high school. They often drove back to Silver Spring so that we could celebrate holidays together, and we all planned to gather at Dad and Sylvia's for Father's Day. We brought Patrick's dad with us, helping him out of the car and moving slowly up to the house as he shuffled along the sidewalk.

My own dad was semi-retired now from the Melody Inn—he only went in three days a week. He and Sylvia were talking about a trip to Scandinavia, and that was beginning to appeal to him a lot.

"It's probably time to turn the store completely over to another manager," he said.

"I don't want you to give up the work you love," Sylvia told him, carrying a stack of plates to the table. Her hair was thinning prematurely, so that pink scalp showed through in places, and she was self-conscious about this. But she still dressed in those delicate filmy clothes of gorgeous colors. I think Sylvia was born beautiful.

"Well, I love *you* even more," Dad told her. "I can't very well take the store to Norway, can I?"

We heard a car door slam outside, and then Les's and Stacy's voices as they came up the walk. They descended on Dad with a bottle of wine and a bouquet of flowers from their garden.

"Happy Daddy's Day," Stacy said playfully, kissing Dad on the cheek.

"Thank you, honey," he said.

Lester, I noticed, gave Dad a hug, not the usual man-to-man handshake, and he seemed different to me somehow. Dazed, maybe. Distracted. I was instantly overcome by the thought that he might be sick.

They were late in arriving, and Sylvia had the roast ready, so we sat down almost at once to eat. Dad poured the wine Stacy had given him, and we all raised our glasses for a toast. He had filled Mr. Long's glass only half full, and still Patrick's father, holding it shakily, had a difficult time with it.

"To Dad," Stacy said. "The best father-in-law a girl could have." Then she looked at Lester and said, "And next year there will be *another* daddy at this table."

It took a couple of seconds for the announcement to sink in, and then we all went wild.

"You're expecting?" Sylvia asked.

"Yes! I'm pregnant!" Stacy said delightedly, and we cheered and screamed some more. "We've known for three months, but I was afraid to tell anyone for fear it . . . the pregnancy . . . wouldn't take." She smiled at Lester. "And . . . Les, tell them what we found out yesterday."

I turned to my brother. He still looked like a deer caught in the beam of headlights. He opened his mouth and said only one word: "Triplets."

This time it was pandemonium. There were shrieks and laughter and clapping, and both Les and Stacy were swallowed up in hugs.

"When are they due?" I cried.

"The week before Christmas," said Les, suddenly a man of very few words.

"Yuk!" said Tyler, wanting to be in on the fun. "Three diapers to change all at the same time." We whooped some more.

"Three hungry mouths," I said. "Three noses to wipe."

"Three *bottoms* to wipe!" said Patricia.

Lester was slowly coming out of his fog. "We're going to raise them on a rotation basis," he said. "Got it all figured out."

"How's that?" asked Sylvia, chuckling already.

"Switch 'em off weekly. First week you and Dad will take Kid

Number One, Alice and Patrick can have Kid Number Two, and we'll take the third one. The next week we'll switch so each of you will have a different baby." We laughed.

"Oh, Les," I said, getting up and hugging him again. "I can't believe you're going to be a dad!"

"What I am is scared half out of my wits," he said.

It could only happen to Lester. Triplets!

"Cheer up," I told him. "You could be the one *carrying* them, for heaven's sake."

We all offered to help when the time came, of course. Stacy and Lester became totally baby-centric. They began picking up books on breast-feeding and infant care, pediatric medicine, and *How to Finance Your Baby's Education*. We knew that fertility drugs sometimes meant preemies, and didn't want to worry them, so we worried each other.

"I wonder if I should take off work a few days to be there for them when the triplets come," I said to Patrick.

"I think if they want you there, they'll ask," he said.

We already knew the date the babies would be born because Stacy was to deliver by Cesarean section. As fate would have it, the day before the delivery was scheduled, the forecast was horrible. Heavy snow was expected, and already the announcement came that schools would be closed. I'd made Belgian waffles— one of Dad Long's favorites—for a festive breakfast, as much to occupy my mind as to please the family, because we were all thinking the same thing: worrying about Stacy.

The phone rang at twenty past ten, just as I had placed the last waffle on the table and Patricia and Tyler were dividing it meticulously. It was Lester.

"Al?" he said.

"Les! What are you going to do about tomorrow?" I asked. "We've all been wondering."

"The five of us are doing fine," he told me.

"What?" I yelled as the family gathered around and Mr. Long looked confused there at the table by himself.

We heard Les laugh. Two days before the snow began, he told us, they had heard the forecast and simply called the hospital to see if they could move the C-section up. The doctor had been thinking the same thing, so that's what they did.

"And now we're parents!" he said joyfully. "And you have two nieces and a nephew!"

We all went bonkers."Oh, Les! I'm so happy!" I cried, and one by one, I had to put the family on the line, speaker setting so we could all hear.

"What are their names, Uncle Les?" Patricia asked.

"Wynken, Blynken, and Nod," Lester told her.

"Uncle Les-ter!"

"Dopey, Sneezy, and Grumpy," said Les.

"*Les-ter!*"

"Their names are Sara, Hannah, and Benjamin," said Les.

"Another Ben in the family!" said Patrick.

"Dad must be totally thrilled," I said, and could imagine his smile, as wide as his face.

* * *

Parenthood, for better or worse, shows us parts of ourselves we didn't know were there. I was more impatient at times with my children than I ever thought I would be, while Lester, who usually gagged at even the words *dirty diaper,* threw himself into parenthood with abandon.

He took a month's leave and organized his life with the "Tumultuous T," as he called the triplets, so that he would be around when Stacy needed him most. I would often visit to find one baby slung over his shoulder for burping, one in his arms getting his supplemental feeding, and the third sprawled facedown over Lester's knees for a "burp in progress," as Les described it, each of them expertly pinned in place by a finger, a hand, or an elbow.

"Look at you!" I said to him once. "Les, you're fantastic. Who would have thought!"

"The older, the wiser," said Les. "When I'm eighty, I'll be so smart, they won't be able to stand me."

We'd had to put Mr. Long in a nursing home at last because he'd fallen and broken a hip and needed more care than we could give him. I think even Patrick finally realized it was the best place for him. I noticed Patrick was developing deep creases on either side of his mouth, and I found myself staring in the mirror, pushing the skin up a little on my cheekbones to see how nicely it tightened the jawline, wishing I looked that way again. I hadn't minded my thirtieth birthday at all, because I'd felt trim and healthy and pretty, but my fortieth . . . !

"Patrick, do you think I need a face-lift?" I asked.

He was shaving at our double sink, and he eyed me skeptically.

"No, I'd be afraid that when I kissed you, something would fall," he said.

"Be serious," I told him. "Look." I pulled skin on my cheeks back again to tighten the chin line. I opened my eyes as wide as possible to demonstrate an eyelid lift and pouted my lips to show what a collagen injection might do.

Patrick stopped shaving and stared at me.

"Alice," he said, "that looks like a dead fish. Please don't tinker with the woman I love. I like her just the way she is."

Still . . . a new wrinkle here, another gray hair there. They kept coming, all the same. And parenthood was like that too. Just when I thought we had a handle on Patricia's assorted problems, we found that Tyler needed our attention. And once we'd worked through his difficulty, Patricia would confront us with a new crisis.

Our children seemed to be changing from week to week. Patricia's body was curvaceous, lean as a gazelle, while Tyler was a gaggle of arms and legs and ethereal as fog. One day they were perfectly normal children on the verge of adolescence, and the next I hardly recognized them.

One morning, Patricia came down to breakfast wearing raccoon eyes; she had bought some mascara and applied it along with eyeliner so thick that when Patrick glanced up from his newspaper, he actually jumped.

"My God!" he said, without thinking. "What *is* it?"

Patricia fled the table crying, and I had to get the cold cream and help her wipe it off.

A few evenings later Tyler put down the magazine he was reading and yawned, slowly unkinking his arms and legs, and then, elongating his body in a giant stretch, he slid off the couch, under the coffee table, and, completely oblivious to us, it seemed, used his forearms to inch his way across the room on his stomach, into the hallway, and, step by step, up the stairs.

Patrick looked at me. "What was *that*?"

"Our son, I think," I answered, and knew I could never love my crazy kid more than I did right then, the very epitome of adolescence. "You'd better quit asking and just accept that they live here," I told Patrick.

But Patricia was fifteen now and not nearly as communicative as she used to be. If acne wasn't ruining her life, it was her super-strict parents. Like a puppy straining at the leash, she longed for more independence. We tried to give her all we felt she was ready for, but to Patricia Marie, it was never enough. The rules were absolute: no smoking, no drinking, no drugs, no sex, no riding with anyone who hadn't been driving for at least six months without an accident, and no parties where adults weren't present.

Patrick, however, surprised me by how strict he was with her. It was not the rules so much as the authoritarian way he presented them. Maybe all dads were so protective of their daughters, I thought.

"What do you mean, 'sex,'?" Patricia demanded, standing

belligerently in the doorway with her arms folded, glaring at us. *It could so easily have been me at fifteen,* I thought.

"Anything that leads to intercourse," Patrick said, heedless of the quicksand he'd just stepped into.

"Daaaaad!" she wailed. "That could be *any*thing! Sex always starts with *some*thing! A look, a touch, a word, a smile!"

"So don't look, touch, speak, or smile," Patrick told her. He was trying to be funny, but this was lost on our daughter.

"I won't have intercourse, but you can't dictate *every*thing I do!" she insisted. "*You* kissed when you were fifteen, I'll bet! I'll bet you even *French*-kissed, and did a lot more than that!"

I was making tomorrow's lunch at the counter and cast a side-long glance at Patrick. What *did* we do at fifteen? Everything we could get away with, I knew. I wasn't about to tell Patricia, but I remember how Patrick first tried to French-kiss me when I was twelve. When I was babysitting, yet! Good gosh, should I be worried about what Patricia might be doing when she was out babysitting?

"Blow jobs," said Tyler, who was eating a bowl of ice cream at the table.

"*What?*" I said, turning around.

"Where did you hear about that?" demanded Patrick. We were both surprised. Tyler was only twelve!

"Oh, everybody knows about oral sex," he said nonchalantly, digging out the chocolate chips to savor when he was through. "We watched them do it on cable over at Bernie's house."

"And when was that?" I asked in the calmest voice I could muster.

"A sleepover. After his parents went to bed."

Patrick gave me a look that said, *Don't react now. We'll talk to Bernie's parents later.*

"You kids grow up too fast," I told my children. "There won't be anything left to discover or appreciate when you're older. You'll be jaded."

"Mom, just because we *talk* about something doesn't mean we do it," said Patricia after Patrick left the kitchen.

"I know," I told her. "And I understand that. But it's important that you know how we feel about things, and dads are pretty protective of their lovely daughters. I not only thought about all kinds of things, but I fantasized about doing them, even though in real life, I never would. Although I *do* remember riding around a few blocks on a motorcycle with the kind of guy I would never seriously consider going out with."

"Really?" Patricia stared at me, grinning a little. "Did your dad ever find out?"

"No. But Sylvia did. Because she was having lunch with someone and saw us go by on the street. And, bless her, she never told him. She talked to me about it instead."

"Well, I think about a lot of things I'd never do either," said Patricia.

That was encouraging, if true. Liz and Pamela and I certainly knew about a lot more than we had actually tried, but we wanted to know about things just the same. It helped us feel sophisticated without taking any risks. Patricia, however, was still testing the limits, it seemed, because it was only a few weeks later that we were faced with a serious infraction of our rules.

She had asked to go to a party at a friend's house—the parents were divorced—and to our question, would the mother be home? Patricia had answered that she thought so.

"Think so or know so?" Patrick asked.

"It's Melissa's mother, and she's always there," was the reply.

"Well, you have to make sure," Patrick told her.

The party was coming up Friday night, and still Patricia was evasive. Finally she said yes, Melissa's mother would be there, but she didn't convince us.

"Give me Melissa's number and I'll check myself," I told her.

"Mo-ther! Nobody does that. You can't go around calling *parents!*" she wailed.

"*We* can, if you want to go to this party!" said Patrick.

She burst into tears. "It's like I'm seven years old!" she cried.

"Exactly," said Patrick. "No. Make it five. At seven you would be able to say definitely whether someone would be home or not and recite a phone number."

Sarcasm didn't help. Patricia alternately cried and screamed for the next two days, refusing to give a phone number or Melissa's last name, and so she was grounded on Friday night.

She spoke only when spoken to. She went about with a determined look on her face, but at the same time, she did all her appointed chores, didn't quarrel with her brother, didn't make waves. It seemed she was making sure we could not find fault with anything else she did, and this, for some reason, set off an alarm in me.

On Friday night she went to her room with a stack of magazines and a box of chocolate-covered grahams. She had also, I noticed, carefully polished her fingernails and toenails. Tyler was on a sleepover at a neighbor's. Patrick and I looked at each other across the living room, where we were enjoying the quiet.

"What's this? A new era of cooperation from Patricia?" he asked.

"Don't count on it," I told him.

About eleven I tapped on her door and looked in. She was still dressed, surrounded by magazines.

"Everything okay?" I asked.

"Everything's fine," she said, biting off her words.

"Well, we're turning in. Thank you for cooperating tonight, Patricia." I paused. "We do love you, you know."

She didn't answer.

"Good night," I said finally.

"Good night."

I lay in bed beside Patrick, who dropped right off to sleep, wishing I could see inside Patricia's head. Was she angry? Or did she realize we were right to keep her home? Was she plotting some future revenge? If only she'd *talk*! If only I could ask the right questions. I was a school counselor, for heaven's sake, good with other people's children, so why was it so hard to get my own to open up and talk to me?

When an hour had gone by—then two—and I was still awake, I was debating whether to get up and read awhile or stay put when I thought I heard a noise. It was so indistinct, I couldn't tell if it was inside or out. I opened my eyes and listened. Nothing. I waited a minute longer, then sat up. Nothing. I could have imagined it.

I slid out of bed, into my robe, and went out in the hall. Patricia's door was closed. I didn't want to go in her room and wake her if she was sleeping, so I went downstairs to check. The front door was still bolted and chained. I was relieved.

Then I heard another sound, possibly someone talking. I checked the back door. Locked. I tiptoed back upstairs again and softly opened Patricia's door. I could see her form in bed. The window was slightly ajar, but most of us slept with our windows open on mild nights.

I went over and looked out. No figures in the yard. No ladder. Still suspicious, however, I turned around and gently lifted the covers. There were Patricia's pillow and stuffed animals arranged beneath, like a sleeping person. I raced back into our bedroom and woke Patrick from a sound sleep. I was almost hysterical.

"Right under our noses!" I kept saying. "She went out, deliberately disobeying us!"

Patrick threw on his robe and came downstairs, checking the door as I had done.

"Both doors are locked from the inside, so she must have climbed out her window and onto the garage roof," I said. "It's all I can figure."

He sat down with the phone book. "What's Melissa's last name?"

"I don't know," I said. "I never got that far with her."

"Well, I'm going to find Patricia if I have to wake the parents of every friend she has," he said angrily.

I guess there are bound to be highs and lows in a mother's life that she will remember forever, and this was one of the lowest. I sat on the couch trying not to imagine what would happen at Melissa's. Imagining Patrick going after Patricia, walking up to the door and knocking. The kids peering out. Patricia's humiliation as he dragged her home. Would things ever be the same for us again? Were we about to lose our daughter?

Stay calm, I told myself. *Keep a united front. Be firm, but let her know she's loved.* All the things I told other parents with troubled teenagers over and over again seemed to help so little here.

"Hello," Patrick said into the phone. "Mr. Gordon, this is Patrick Long, and I'm so sorry to call you at this hour, but Patricia has gone out without our permission, and I wonder if anyone can tell me the last name and address and phone number of the girlfriend named Melissa. . . . Yes, of course I'll wait. . . ."

I sat on the couch, hand over my eyes, embarrassed for Patrick, for us both. I could picture Tom Gordon waking his wife and possibly having to wake Christin, too. Unless Patricia's friend Christin herself was at the party.

I could wring Patricia's neck, I thought at the same time I desperately feared for her safety. It seemed like yesterday that Patrick and I were pacing the floor with a crying baby, taking turns in the middle of the night, and how I longed then for her to be older. Now I felt I would give anything to have her in my arms, bawling or not.

"Yes . . . all right. I'm so sorry to have wakened you," Patrick said, and hung up. "Christin isn't sure. She thinks it's Phillips, but that's the dad's name, and he and Mrs. Phillips are divorced. Melissa's living with her mom and the phone's under the mother's maiden name. She said Emma would know and gave me her number."

"Oh, my God," I said.

The noise again.

"Patrick!" I said, sitting up straight.

There was the soft thud of footsteps coming up the stairs from the family room, and then Patricia came into the living room, rubbing her eyes.

We stared at her.

"What's the matter?" she asked.

"Why aren't you in bed?" I demanded.

"What are you so mad about? I couldn't sleep and went downstairs to watch TV. I guess I fell asleep."

Patrick gave me an exasperated look, but I wasn't fooled. "No, Patricia, you arranged your bed to make us think you were in it. What's going on?"

She shrugged helplessly and looked at Patrick, as though I was making a mountain out of a molehill. "*Nothing!* I just didn't want you to worry if you were checking up on me, which, of course, you were."

"There's a TV set right there in the kitchen," Patrick observed.

"I didn't want to *wake* you if you heard it! Jeez! Try to be considerate and you get the third degree!" she said.

Patrick stood up and started toward the stairs to the family room.

"What are you *doing*?" Patricia demanded. "I turned out the lights."

"I'm checking anyway," he said.

"Dad!" Patricia sank down on the couch and covered her face.

And a minute later I heard Patrick's voice below. "Get out!"

Muffled voices, noises, footsteps on the stairs, and then two boys I'd never seen before and a girl I'd seen only once or twice came parading past me, eyes averted, and stood at the front door staring at the double locks.

"Wait here," Patrick said. "I'm driving you home."

The girl, a somewhat large brunette, stood with her back to me and was wearing her shirt inside out. Patricia was crying and I noticed that her jeans were partially unzipped. Before Patrick could come back down from upstairs with his keys, however, one of the boys fumbled with the dead bolts himself, opened the door, and in seconds, all three had disappeared.

That seemed to make Patrick even angrier, and he stormed down to the family room to make sure no one else was hiding there.

I let Patricia cry for a while. And finally I said, "*What* were you thinking?"

"As though *you* never did anything your dad didn't like."

"I didn't say I hadn't. But this is about you. I was punished and you will be too."

"Like how?" she asked tentatively.

"We'll discuss it when your dad comes up here."

We both sat silently for another few minutes, and finally I heard Patrick's footsteps on the stairs.

He was carrying a wastebasket half filled with beer cans. I wished we could discuss the evening calmly, but Patrick wasn't at his best in the middle of the night.

"Care to explain yourself?" he asked Patricia, sitting down on the couch beside me. "Now that you've awakened us, the Gordons . . . ?"

Patricia's head jerked up. "You didn't call *Christin's* parents?" she cried.

"Yes, we did. I woke up her father, he woke up her mother, the mother woke up Christin. . . ."

"She wasn't supposed to know about the party!" Patricia wailed. "Melissa told her there wasn't any . . ." Her voice trailed off and she stared down at her lap again.

"How did your friends get in here?" Patrick demanded.

Patricia's voice was almost inaudible. "I let them in through a basement window."

"Who were the boys?" I asked. "They looked older than you and Melissa."

"Just some guys she knows."

"And what were you doing?"

"What do you mean?" She gave us a quick glance, then down again.

"What was going on in the family room?" Patrick said in a measured tone.

"Nothing bad. We were just playing cards."

"Patricia," I said. "Melissa had her shirt on inside out when she came up. And in case you hadn't noticed, your jeans are unzipped."

She immediately gave her zipper a quick jerk, then gave us an exasperated look. "We were playing strip poker, okay? But I still had on my underwear. Nobody was totally naked." And then she asked defiantly, "Are you proud of yourselves, humiliating me in front of my friends?"

I studied my disheveled daughter. "Are you proud of yourself, Patricia?"

When she didn't answer, Patrick said, "Whatever, she's grounded for a month. No friends, no parties."

Patricia broke into tears again. "A *month*! You're so unreasonable! You don't trust me at all!" she wailed.

It was almost laughable, but I managed not to smile. "You lie to us, you help friends crawl in a window and play strip poker when you make us think you're asleep upstairs, and *we're* unreasonable not to trust you?"

"I only did it because you don't trust me to take care of myself at a party. I don't smoke and I've only ever taken one single sip of beer, and I wouldn't ever let a guy go all the way with me, so why are you so *worried*?"

Patrick had calmed down now, and he was good with her. "Patricia, we trust your good intentions, but what we *don't* trust is your judgment. By your own admission, you've been to parties where alcohol was provided for minors, strictly against the law.

And what about the kids you're with? Kids who may have had more than 'a sip of beer'? Who might want to have sex enough to put drugs in your drink? If I could, honey, I would protect you physically for the rest of my life, but I can't. And so we worry."

Patricia continued to cry, but I knew she was listening to him. She went up to her room, and Patrick went back down to the family room again to check the basement window. Then we all went to bed.

For the first week of her detention, Patricia was furious. Patrick was out of town for a few days, and when he came back, he said that someone at the office suggested he check Facebook—that Patricia had posted a photo of him he may not appreciate.

"Did he say what it was?" I asked.

"No. We were both leaving work and he had a train to catch. He said someone had sent it to his daughter, and she made the connection."

Patrick and I went into the den and signed on. We looked up Patricia's account, to which, strangely, she had never "unfriended" us. As we'd suspected, there was no mention of the party Melissa had been planning to give while her mom was away. Instead, as we scrolled down, we were suddenly confronted with a full-page photo of Patrick's face, asleep on the couch. I remembered that photo. She had taken it for fun a year ago when he'd dozed off on a Sunday morning reading the *Times*. His cheeks and chin covered with stubble, glasses askew over his nose, his mouth hanging open at one side, saliva eking out one corner, unwashed hair hanging over his forehead. Underneath, the caption: *Meanest man in the world.*

We stared at it a moment or two in silence.

"Well, at least she didn't say she hated you," I said, and suddenly we burst out laughing.

It was really such a perfect cartoon of an unshaven man at his worst, and it could have been any man on a weekend morning.

"I suppose it could have been me in my underwear," Patrick said. Then he added thoughtfully, thinking perhaps of the few times one of us had been naked in the bedroom when a kid walked in, "Or no underwear at all."

"Maybe that's coming next," I said.

"What do you think we ought to do?"

"I don't know. Let me handle it, though. I might get more out of her," I suggested.

We could tell by the number of calls Patricia was receiving on her cell phone, and the constant *ding* of her computer when a new message arrived, that friends were reacting to the posting, and she ate dinner hurriedly, eyes on her plate to discourage conversation.

Later that evening as she came through the dining room she found me at the table with her and Tyler's medical folders there in front of me, cleaning out old papers and bringing their charts up-to-date. And there before me was a large photo of Patricia's face when her acne was at its worst. Her dermatologist had been on vacation, and she wanted to prove to him when he got back that the medicine he had prescribed was not working. A more miserable girl you never saw. I was holding it out in front of me when she passed my chair.

Patricia stopped, as I was sure she would.

For a few seconds she remained absolutely silent. Then, in a small voice, she asked. "What are you going to do with that?"

I looked up at her innocently. "Well, what do you think we should do with it?"

"Mom," she said, and swallowed. "Don't. Please."

"Don't . . . ?"

"*You* know. Post it. On Facebook." She crumpled into the chair beside me. *"Please."*

"How could we ever do such a disrespectful thing to you, Patricia? We love you, no matter how angry we might get at you. Nothing would justify embarrassing you like that."

She struggled to say, "I'm sorry! I . . . really . . . am!"

"Once it's out there," I told her, "you can't take it back."

"I *know*! And . . . and . . . now I feel terrible!" she wept.

"Your dad needs to know you're sorry. He needs to hear it from you."

Slowly, Patricia got up and walked into the living room. Patrick was doing a crossword puzzle, and she sat down next to him, newspaper in his lap. I saw her head tipping in his direction until it rested against his shoulder, and I folded up the medical folders and put them away.

* * *

Of her own volition, Patricia made an apology of sorts to her dad on her Facebook page. She insisted the photo was a joke and posted another of her and him together. Oddly, it was that pathetic picture of her face plus her boredom at being grounded that prompted her to ask what she could use on her skin in the future to hide small blemishes. She pointed to a little red spot on her chin.

Every so often in a mother's life, the Fates come together and agree to give her a break. Did I see an opportunity here? Do cars have wheels?

"I could let you use some of my concealer," I offered. "Want me to show you how to apply it?"

She shrugged. "Okay."

We went upstairs to the master bathroom, and I pulled out all the stops. Actually, I pulled out the drawer with my cosmetics in it.

"Wow," she said, looking at the array of little jars and bottles and brushes and tubes. "What *is* all this stuff?"

"Things that women of a certain age use to beautify themselves," I said, and jokingly added, "Want a makeover?"

She laughed. "What do I have to do?"

"Just hop up here on the counter where there's good light," I said.

I envied the deft way she hoisted herself up.

"Just a quick wipe to get everything off that's on there," I said, and she allowed me to take a washcloth and wipe her face clean. I looked into the green eyes of my fifteen-year-old daughter. Same freckles I'd had, right there over the checks and forehead. Same heart-shaped face . . .

"Okay," I said, giving her a hand mirror so she could watch the process. "Free service today. You're in luck."

First the moisturizer, then the makeup base, then the concealer over the blemish . . . Creme rouge on the cheeks to emphasize the cheek bones, then the powder . . .

I worked in slow motion, and along the way, we talked.

"When did your mom let you wear makeup for the first time?" she asked.

"Well, remember that from kindergarten on, I didn't have a mom."

Patricia sucked in her breath. "Ooh, I forgot. What did you do?"

"Just experimented with stuff that other girls were using. Some days I'm sure we looked hideous."

Patricia giggled.

"How did you learn about everything else? You know . . . periods and cramps and stuff."

"Well, there was always Aunt Sally."

"Not Aunt Sally!" We both laughed then.

"She did the best she could," I told Patricia. "And Lester's girlfriends helped a lot. So did my cousin Carol. Then Sylvia came into my life . . ."

"But all the rest!" Patricia said. "I mean, buying a bra and everything."

"I remember Lester taking me to buy my first pair of jeans," I said. "In the *boys'* department. It was a disaster!"

"Tell me!" Patricia begged.

"I was in a dressing room, and he kept bringing me the wrong size. Finally I came out to look at myself in a three-way mirror, and when I went back to the dressing rooms, I opened the wrong door."

Patricia gasped.

"A guy, I'll bet!"

"Yep."

More giggling.

"Was he naked?"

"No. He had on his Jockeys. Know who he was?"

She shook her head.

"Your dad."

I had started to do her eyebrows, but she exploded with laughter and I backed off.

"And I was *so* embarrassed," I told her. "To make matters worse, when school started, I discovered he was a patrol boy, and I had to walk past him every morning. Of course we recognized each other."

I had to wait for her to stop laughing and then I did her eyebrows. As I filled them in with feathery strokes, she told me about a girl at school who chose to live with her dad after her parents divorced, and about Melissa, who never got to see her father.

When I lined her eyelids with a soft eye pencil and added bronze shadow, I told her how I started out using green eye shadow on myself and how my dad used to hate it.

And about the day I dyed a huge hunk of my hair green and went to school that way after he told me not to.

"Did he punish you?"

I didn't answer until I'd finished the left lid. "He told me that he was very, very disappointed in me, and I think that hurt worse than anything."

Patricia didn't respond to that, and we were both quiet while I applied the mascara to her eyelashes, then pale melon-colored gloss on her lips.

"Whew!" she said, when I'd finished. "I don't ever want to be a model. This takes forever."

"That does it," I said.

"Tell me when I can look," she said.

I gave her hair a few swipes with the comb. "How about now?"

This time Patricia turned toward the big mirror behind her, and her eyes lit up in surprise. "Wow, Mom! Deceptive advertising." We laughed. She leaned a little closer, then backed away again. "Is this really me?"

"Only at prom time," I said. "But I'll make you a gift of my concealer."

As we were clearing off the counter, she said, "About the other night . . . I've never played strip poker before."

"Oh? Why do you think you did it this time?"

"I don't know." She stood holding the little jar in her hands, absently turning it around and around. "They were just . . . older guys. I didn't want them to think I was a kid."

"So that's not the kind of thing you do with friends you generally hang with?"

"God, no! It's like . . . you know that story you told me? About you and the motorcycle guy?"

"Yes."

"It was like that. But don't think I do that all the time. I want you to trust me."

"That's the problem with trust, sweetheart," I said. "Once you've broken it, you have to win it all over again. But this is a start."

When she was allowed to go out again, Patrick bought a large windup alarm clock and explained the rule. There was a nine o'clock curfew on weeknights, eleven on Fridays and Saturdays. After she went out for the evening, we would set the alarm for nine or eleven, depending on the night, and place it in the hall outside our bedroom. If she was home by curfew, she would turn the alarm off. If she came home late, the alarm would wake us and we would start calling her friends. It was her responsibility to get home before it went off.

A perfectly brilliant idea, the same one that Dad had used for Lester and me. And it worked.

We had barely recovered from worry over Patricia when I discovered a lump in my breast. I'd had a mammogram a year before, and everything had looked fine. Yet, as I was showering and my fingers soaped my breasts, I felt it—firm and hard beneath my skin.

My fingers pulled away momentarily, my heart beginning to race. And then, tentatively, I reexamined my breast, hoping to discover that the hardness I felt was only a rib. But there it was, a lump—definite and distinct. I quickly dried off, wrapped a towel around me, and went back in the bedroom, where Patrick was pulling on his socks.

He began filling me in on his schedule for the week. "I'm supposed to fly to San Salvador on Wednesday and—" He saw my face and stopped.

"Patrick, there's a lump in my breast," I said.

He slowly pulled up his sock, his expression changing from nonchalance to concern. "You've had these before, haven't you? Is this different?"

"I think so. I'm not sure."

"Can you see the doctor today?"

"I'll call as soon as I get to work," I said. "The office isn't open yet."

Patrick got up off the bed and hugged me, encircling me with his strong arms. "Let's don't borrow trouble," he said. "If necessary, I'll get someone else to go to El Salvador for me. I'd just as soon stay, anyway."

I nodded, needing the safety of his arms.

At work I phoned and got an appointment for three that afternoon. The doctor could see I was scared. But when he examined me, he frowned as he explored the lump, examining it with one finger, then another, mentally measuring.

"It doesn't feel quite like a cyst," he said. "But we can't be sure of anything until we biopsy."

"And then what?" I asked.

"Well, if it does prove to be cancer, then we need to know what kind it is, how aggressive it is, and how best to treat it. But that's putting the cart before the horse. Here's the name of the surgeon I'd like you to see about the biopsy." He wrote something down on a card and handed it to me. "You'll be in good hands, I promise."

What's hardest is trying to keep things normal for the rest of the family when you're feeling so fragile yourself. When Patrick got home that evening, he immediately took over, and when the kids had finished eating, he helped Tyler with his homework and searched for Patricia's jacket when she complained she'd lost it.

"What's the matter with Mom?" I heard Tyler ask. "Is she sick or something?"

"She's just had a really hard day," Patrick answered. "So we're letting her take it easy. What do you want in your lunch tomorrow?"

But it was Patricia who came in our bedroom that night as I was taking off my robe.

"Mom," she said, cautiously putting one hand on my shoulder. "Dad says you had a doctor's appointment today. It's . . . it's not anything serious, is it?"

I tried to be as matter-of-fact as possible. "We don't know yet, Patty, but it's probably not. Just one of those things doctors like to check up on." I gave her hand a playful squeeze.

But waiting was the next most difficult thing to do. A wait to see the surgeon, a wait for the biopsy itself, a wait for the report. All I wanted was to get it over with.

Patrick didn't go to San Salvador. The biopsy showed it was cancer. I felt as though my chest had become a cement block, icy cold, and I could feel my pulse pounding in my temples, so loud I wondered if Patrick could hear it.

"Mrs. Long?" the doctor said, leaning forward.

Even before he could tell me that the cancer was in an early stage, I had planned my memorial service and written notes to my children!

But it was Patrick's strong hand on mine, his take-charge attitude that calmed me enough to discuss the next step.

I was scheduled for a lumpectomy. Sylvia and Dad came over to stay with the kids the day I went in the hospital, and Patrick drove me to Sibley. My thoughts raced on ahead of me as I watched an ordinary day roll past me out the window, men and women on their way to work. *I* wanted to be out there having an ordinary day. I didn't want to leave my son and daughter and husband behind, as my mother had done when she died, and I felt I was experiencing all the agony she must have felt when she got leukemia. I wanted to see Patricia and Tyler grow up to be whatever they wanted. I longed to see Patricia wearing Mom's wedding dress. To see Patrick hold his first grandchild. I wanted to hear about Tyler's career, to grow old with my husband. . . .

Tears streamed down my cheeks and I choked off a sob. Patrick reached over and clasped my hand. "Just remember, sweetheart, we're in this together," he said.

* * *

Except that we weren't, really. Only one person was lying there on the operating table. Only one person was given an anesthetic. But as I felt myself drift off, I knew that Patrick had said all he *could* say.

Motion around me, voices. I felt as though I were at the bottom of a deep well, unable to speak or respond. Someone was gently slapping the back of my hand.

"Alice," a woman's voice was saying. "We need you to wake up now. Your husband's here beside you. Alice?"

I felt my eyelids flutter.

"She's coming out of it," the female voice continued.

And then Patrick's hand was on my forehead. I could detect his scent. He stroked the side of my face. "Honey? Can you hear me?" he kept saying.

I struggled to open my eyes, but the brightness of the room overwhelmed me and I closed them again.

"The operation's over." The hand continued stroking.

"What . . . did they . . . ?" I asked.

"A lumpectomy, like they said. There's no evidence of spread, and your lymph nodes are fine."

I started to cry. Relief, mostly. But I knew that there might be radiation ahead for me, possibly chemotherapy.

"You still have your breast," the nurse was saying.

But Patrick said, "Al, I'd love you with no breasts at all. You know that."

And I did know that. I let myself drift off again, squeezing his fingers.

25
TOURING PARTNERS

Cancer treatment was far more advanced for me than it was for my mom, even though she had had leukemia, not breast cancer. The radiation treatments were fewer than I'd expected, and the chemo not nearly as bad as I'd believed. I didn't even lose much hair, and what I did lose came back again.

It was Gwen who helped the most. She was raising two children—she and Charlie had had another boy two years after their first—and working part-time, but she was my unofficial patient advocate, driving down from Baltimore once a week. She explained the procedures in detail, held my hand when I went back for my six-month checkup, read the statistics for my type of cancer (which cheered me), and always had a hug when I needed one most, if not in person, then by phone.

"I hope Charlie appreciates you," I said. "I hope he knows how wonderful you are."

"Oh, he does," she assured me. "I rubbed his back and held his hand when he passed a kidney stone, and now I'm the best thing that ever happened to him."

"Well, you are!" I said. "How are the boys, Gwen? I feel I've kept you away from them too much."

"Inseparable one minute and impossible the next," she said. "But I love them to pieces. I've thought of trying for a girl, but if we got another boy, I'm not sure either of us could take it." I laughed. If anyone could take it, Gwen and Charlie could.

On March 1 of Patricia's junior year, Patrick came home and said, "Does anyone have something special planned for spring vacation?"

He looked around the kitchen, where the three of us were making lasagna—Patricia layering the noodles, Tyler the mozzarella, and I was spooning the sauce.

"I was going to shop for a rug," I said. "You're invited to go along."

"Emma and Katie and I are going to hear the new band at the Night Owl," Patricia told us.

"I don't know. Sleep late, eat lots," said Tyler, sneaking a bite of cheese. "Why?"

Patrick was grinning, so I knew something was up. "Wouldn't you all rather see the Tower of London and Buckingham Palace?"

"We're going to *London*?" Patricia asked.

Tyler pumped one hand in the air and yelled, "Yes!"

"I just up and decided that this family needs to go somewhere," Patrick said. "You'll have to be all packed and ready, because we leave a day before spring vacation starts and get back a day after school begins." He looked at me. "I figure we can write excuses for those two days. Would it be okay with your job?"

"I'll make it work!" I said. "This is wonderful, Patrick!"

"Well, I thought so too," he said, obviously proud of himself. "No downtime afterward, but it'll be worth it."

And it was.

I was surprised, actually, that Patricia agreed to go with us, but I guess London trumped even her friends. When Tyler's best friend, a collector of foreign beer cans, heard where we were going, he begged Tyler to collect all he could find and bring them back, for a percentage of the profits when he sold them.

"Now, Tyler, how are you going to manage that?" I asked.

"That craze was over years ago," Patrick pleaded with him.

"Not for Matthew. He inherited his uncle's collection, and he's going to sell them all on eBay," Tyler explained.

We gave in, and Tyler crammed a box of plastic bags into his backpack.

We talked of nothing but the trip in the week before we left, and each of us decided what we most wanted to see or do. There were a few things we all agreed on—the Tower of London, as Patrick had said, Buckingham Palace. But Tyler, for some reason, really wanted to say he had been to Wales, so we bought BritRail passes to do that. I most wanted to see the old medieval towns of York and Chester, and that would take up another two days. Both Patricia's and Patrick's desires were in London itself. Patrick wanted to look up the buildings of Christopher Wren and explore some art galleries; Patricia wanted to see Chelsea and visit shops and bookstores and buy something for her English literature teacher, who had impressed her most this year.

I don't know that any of us slept much on the plane going over. We decided to spend our first night in York to escape the London crowds when we were so tired, so as soon as we got our money exchanged, we took the train to Victoria Station, where we had to catch a cab to get to the second train station for York. We stood in a famous British queue to take our turn, and when we finally got in the cab and told the driver we had twenty minutes to catch our train, he gave us the ride of a lifetime. As this was my first taste of driving on the left instead of the right, I was sure we would be killed on our first day there. If we were half asleep before, we were wide awake now as the driver careened by Buckingham Palace, tore around monuments, and zigzagged through lines of pedestrians.

Patricia made gasping noises, her face against my shoulder as huge double-decker buses seemed to be coming right at us, and just when disaster was all but certain, the taxi would swerve the opposite way. We made it onto the train with fifty-five seconds to spare.

Tired as we were, the city and suburbs were just too different from ours for us to sleep.

"Look, Mom, how small the yards are!" Tyler exclaimed. "And every one has a wall or hedge or something around it."

"And flowers!" Patricia added. "Did you ever see so many flowers?"

In York we were fascinated by the pull chain toilet and a bathtub high up on a pedestal. We spent our second day there too and found we could walk around the entire city in an hour or two, much of our sightseeing taking place on the old Roman wall that still surrounded portions of the city. I had read up on York before we came and pointed out the huge Micklegate Bar, one of the four gates leading into the city. "It was up there on the crest of this gate that the heads of traitors were once exhibited on iron spikes until they rotted away, their eyes pecked out by marauding crows," I told the kids.

"Cool!" said Tyler, gazing upward.

I also pointed out the Treasurer's House, where the ghosts of Roman soldiers were said to appear. Clearly, I was caught up in the history of the place. We hired a guide to drive us out in the country to see a church dating back to 654, the tombstones in the graveyard so close together that mowing was impossible, and so sheep grazed on the tall grass.

I could have stayed in York the whole time we were in England, but it was on to Chester next. The trains there, which seated passengers at tables much like a diner, were conducive to eating and conversation. They were also a magnificent opportunity for Tyler.

"I can't watch," said Patricia as Tyler went up and down the aisles, keeping his eye out for empty beer cans on the tables and asking politely if he might have them.

"Collectin' the rubbish, are ya?" asked a cheerful woman, tossing in a paper bag and a half-eaten sandwich, and Patrick laughed at the look on Tyler's face as he accepted the trash and thanked the woman.

He had collected some cans in York as well, so by the time we reached Chester, he had half a plastic bag full. He had gone eight cars away from where we were sitting, looking for beer cans, and thought he'd allowed enough time to get back to us before our stop. And he had, except that people ready to get off at Chester began gathering at the exits, their suitcases blocking the aisles and making it impossible for him to get by.

Each of us had been assigned two bags to carry each time we went from one place to another. Tyler's bags were still on the rack above us. We hoped he would assess the problem, figure out we had his bags, and just get off at our stop and wait for us on the platform. But when we realized he wasn't getting off and the train would move on, Patricia ran to find the conductor, Patrick went along the outside of the train calling Tyler's name, and I stayed with the bags. Finally they found him, shaken and pale, seconds before the train pulled out, and we stood on the platform, a little foursome with our arms around each other, breathing deeply and trying to laugh at our adventure.

As we signed in at our second hotel, the helpful porter, hearing the sound of clinking beer cans, reached out his hands and said to Tyler, "Shall I chuck those for you?" at which Tyler yelped, "No!" Patrick had to explain—not for the first time—that these were quite precious to someone back in the States, and he endured the stares of the hotel personnel.

In Chester we gaped at the ancient two-story buildings, some of which leaned slightly inward over a narrow lane, and shops so old, we read, that knights had patronized them to buy their armor. Another walled city, and Patrick pointed out the sharp spikes along the top in places to keep the enemy out.

To do all we wanted to do in London, we could spend only a few hours in Wales. But we loved riding the train to Holyhead, water on one side, mountains on the other, and trees bent double by the force of the wind that blows off the Irish sea.

We did our best to pronounce the names of streets and towns along the way, and Patrick tried to photograph some of the signs as the train sped along. One was so long that the sign itself seemed to go on forever. The amused conductor, who must have seen tourists struggle over this many times, came by later with a piece of paper imprinted with the name: LLANFAIRPWLLGWYNGLLGOGERYCHWYRNDROBWLLLLAN-DOSILIOGOGOGOCH.

"What does it mean?" I asked.

"Turn the paper over," the conductor said. The translation read: *Church of St. Mary in a hollow of white hazel near to a rapid whirlpool and St. Tysilio's Church of the red cave.*

We had a few hours to wander around Holyhead—it, too, once occupied by Romans—before we caught our train to London. But the journey to the end of Wales and back was worth it if only to see the Church of St. Mary sign, which we tried again and again to pronounce.

We spent the rest of our time in London. At breakfast the next morning in a hotel on the outskirts, we were marveling at the breakfasts served in some of the hotels, especially the one in York. "We'll remember that as 'Hotel Near Wall with Bacon and Tomatoes and Ham and Eggs and Kippers and Fruit on a Big Platter with Cream on the Side,'" said Patrick.

For the rest of the trip that was the trigger that could get us all laughing, and the kids tried to top each other with outlandish names. We visited the British Museum and the Tower of London. The changing of the guard at Buckingham Palace became, for Patricia, Place-of-Young-Hot-Guy-in-Beehive-Hat-and-Red-Jacket-Holding-Rifle-and-Not-Even-Looking-at-Me-When-I-Said-Hi.

We set aside one afternoon for each of us to go our separate ways and meet again for dinner. Tyler had a map of the London Underground, and just as he'd enjoyed mapping out the streets of our neighborhood in Barcelona, he enjoyed taking the different routes of the subway. Patricia haunted the shops and bookstores of Chelsea and came back with a paperbound copy of *New Voices in Poetry* by young British authors to give her teacher and some earrings for her friends. Patrick went to the observatory at Greenwich.

I simply explored the neighborhood outside our hotel, watching the preacher who stood on a trunk denouncing a demonstration a few feet away of a man lying on a bed of nails; the trio of young men playing a guitar, a flute, and a hurdy-gurdy; the proper-looking lady in hat and suit pedaling sedately down the street. I drank in the dialect, the wonderful cockney—a woman complaining to another about a friend who had invited her to tea, with nothing to eat, "Just a cup w'out anythin' to hold in your han'." Like Tyler, I loved the signs at important buildings or driveways that read DEAD STOP or DEAD SLOW.

But there were places that made me sure that, were I to die in London, it would not be in a cab but by the simple act of crossing the street—places where, even though I checked for traffic on my right instead of my left, there was no walk light, and it was just a contest between cars and pedestrians.

I stood timidly by as swarm after swarm of cars and cabs and buses trapped me there on the curb. And then, on some unseen signal, the crowd waiting beside me would suddenly defy all odds and surge into the street with traffic coming right at them. Miraculously, the oncoming herd would stop, then inch forward again until, on that same unseen signal, all engines revved up and they were off again.

I couldn't do it. When it was a wager between me and the grille of a double-decker bus, my bets were on the bus. I was trapped at Piccadilly Circus until a proper English gentleman suddenly took me by the arm, hustled me across, tipped his hat (yes, he wore a hat), and walked on.

* * *

Our most expensive outing in London was a medieval feast we had signed up for in advance. We'd read about it when planning our trip. Tyler was up for anything having to do with food, and Patricia had a special dress she thought would be just right for Elizabethan times.

The morning of the banquet, I woke feeling slightly feverish, with an unsettled stomach. Something I'd eaten, I thought, and I was careful of what I ate the rest of the day. By evening I didn't feel better, but arguably, not any worse. *I am not sick,* I told myself as we climbed into a cab. *Not at the price we paid for these tickets!*

We were deposited in front of a hotel and led to the Elizabethan rooms by a minstrel strumming his lute. The banquet hall was lit by candles and, probably because of his height, Patrick was chosen as lord of the manor, and instructed to greet each arriving guest with a hearty "Drink! Hail!" to which the guests replied, "Wassail!"

Patrick took his role with gusto, and the four of us were seated at the head table. As all the other guests were "seated below the salt," they had to come to him to ask for a pinch from the salt box. Specifically, the men sent their wives, and Patrick took great pleasure in the custom of requiring a kiss of each fair maiden before he obliged, to much laughter from his children.

The menu consisted of dishes served in medieval times, and everything was done to make the meal as authentic as possible, down to the chipped platters, the wooden bowls, and the straw on the floor. We were to drink our soup right from the bowl, then wipe our bowls clean with huge hunks of bread. I stared down at the grease left in my bowl and realized that dinner, for me, was over. I was going to have to fake the rest of the evening. *I am not sick,* I reminded myself.

Patricia leaned around Patrick to say, "Isn't this fun, Mom?" and I gave her a wan smile.

I watched as my glass was filled with fermented apple juice. Each course had to be presented first to the lord of the manor, and when a costumed wench appeared with a huge platter of shellfish, I held my breath while she heaped a pile of mussels onto each of our plates.

"Are you all right?" Patrick asked me as I tried unobtrusively to stuff each gray creature back into its shell.

"Don't ask," I said. "Carry on for old England."

The fish was followed with an assortment of chopped vegetables that looked like cold chop suey, and then the minstrel came in with an authentic boar's head, high on a platter, singing all the while, and when he presented it to us, its foggy eye staring up at me, the apple askew in its hairy mouth, I changed my mantra to, *I am not going to throw up.* I had not vomited even once when I was pregnant, I told myself, so I wouldn't now. This medieval feast was my idea, and I was jolly well going to sit here and watch my family enjoy themselves.

Chicken pâté was served along with the boar's head—its cheeks, I imagine—with admonitions that we would be fined if we did not leave some on our plates to give to the poor, and I was the most charitable one in the room.

Then the main course—huge slabs of roast beef that the wenches forked off slovenly onto our plates in a splatter of fat and grease. Where were those medieval dogs under the table when we needed them? I silently moaned.

Tyler, who had finished his beef, noticed me sliding my portion back and forth across my plate, and asked, "You going to eat that, Mom?" I told him to wait until the guests were pounding the table again to applaud the minstrel at the other end of the room and then I would slide my serving onto his plate.

When the main course was finished, the wenches came around with a large bowl, into which each guest unceremoniously dumped all leftovers. I stared down into the gray shellfish, the chop suey, the fatty slabs of leftover beef, and—I couldn't help myself—the desecrated boar's head, with one eye still intact.

Then I turned suddenly and asked permission of the lord of the manor to use the restroom. Out in the hall, I remember one of the wenches saying, "You don't want to miss the raspberries with clotted cream," and the next thing I knew I was lying on a sofa outside the hotel kitchen, with three wenches, two chefs, and one minstrel looking down at me.

I had not thrown up. I had evidently thrown myself onto the floor, or started to, until a wench caught me when I passed out and, once revived, I begged to be allowed to remain there until the feast was over. The lord of the manor and his children, I instructed, were not to be disturbed.

Later, back in our hotel room, as the kids were enthusiastically recounting the evening, Tyler summed it up in one sentence: "Feast-of-Boar's-Head-and-Mussels-and-Eating-with-Hands-While-Mom-on-Couch-Turns-Green."

I recovered soon after, and for our final night in London, we splurged and stayed in a hotel in the heart of the city. Up until now we had been sleeping in two bedrooms, females in one, males in the other, so there wouldn't be a pileup in the bathroom. But to save money in this expensive hotel, we got a room with two double beds; I slept with Patricia in one, Patrick with Tyler in the other.

After we'd turned out the lights, we were talking about all the trips we'd taken as a family—what we remembered most.

"I remember our trip out west, when we got out of the car at the Grand Canyon and you held on to our shirts because you were afraid we'd fall in," Patricia said, and they guffawed.

"And you and Dad never told us that our last stop was going to be Disneyland! And every time you talked about it, you called it Frisbee Water. What was that all about?" Tyler demanded.

I laughed. "Because if you guys knew that the last stop on our trip was Disneyland, you would have wanted to rush through everything else, and we didn't want to spoil the trip listening to, 'How long before we get there?'"

"Oh," said Patricia. And a minute later, "Remember when we stopped at the Dinosaur National Monument just before dark? And we were about the only ones there? And Dad locked the keys in the car, and we were afraid we'd have to be there all night, and we didn't have any water, and—"

"I know, I know, and we didn't have food, and we were all going to starve to death before they found our bodies in the morning," Patrick finished.

"And that ranch outside Yellowstone, remember?" Patricia went on, and we started laughing even before she told the story. "You were afraid Tyler might be too little, Mom, so you asked for their most gentle horse, and every time we turned around, Tyler's horse was just standing there!"

"Dead stop," said Patrick, and we roared.

I lay there beside Patricia, smiling up into the dark. *Maybe this will be the favorite part of this trip for me,* I thought. *Lying here with my family, laughing and sharing memories, knowing that someday this night might be one of the ones they remember and laugh about too.*

The next morning Patrick and Tyler packed all the collected beer cans in boxes the concierge had found for us and took them to customs to mail home. Patricia and I used the opportunity for one last stroll around the neighborhood, and as we were admiring a jacket in a shop window, we were assailed by a confused English tourist from some small town wanting directions to Victoria Station. She had her coach tickets and knew her son would be frantic, and somebody had told her to go down to the bridge and turn left, but she was all confused. We finally found a local to explain the directions to her, but the station was still a long way off. She started out, and we followed her for a bit and saw that she was doing exactly the opposite of everything she'd been told to do. So we chased her down, called a taxi for her, and paid the driver to take her to the station. By then she was in tears of frustration, and I kept thinking that little old woman could well be me in twenty years, every bit as overwhelmed and baffled by London as she was.

"That was a nice thing to do, Mom," Patricia said.

"Just paying it forward," I said, and told her about the man who had changed a tire for us when Pamela and Liz and I were on that trip to California years ago.

When Patrick and Tyler came back, Patrick said, "Alice, you should have seen the face of that man at customs. We got out of the cab, carrying all these boxes that weighed hardly anything at all, and he asked what we wanted to declare. When we told him they were empty beer cans, he actually stepped back a little, like we were lunatics."

We were still laughing as we loaded our bags into a cab for our final journey to the airport. Every day since we'd left, my thoughts had been centered on what we were going to do the next morning in the next city and the next and the next. And then, seated beside Tyler on the plane, clouds appearing and disappearing outside our window, all I could think of was home. There's a comforting familiarity in the usual buzz of activity and urgency of tasks—the old routines. Two weeks after we returned from London, Patrick was deep in a new project at work; I was sitting in on a support group for eighth graders, anxious about attending high school in the fall; Patricia was shopping for pants to go with a pair of shoes she'd bought in Soho, and within minutes of Tyler's boxes arriving from London, his cell phone was ringing like the New York Stock Exchange, and he was trading cans right and left with friends willing to sell not only their souls but their baby brothers for a British beer can.

This is my life, and I like it, I thought one evening as I checked a lasagna in the oven. The bustle, the humor, the spontaneity, the teasing . . . I smiled as I thought of the name we would give our home, were we to have a sign above our door frame as they had in Wales: "House of Four People in Town of Chevy Chase with Big Hearts and Usual Frailties Living Joyfully the Best They Know How."

About three months later, Mr. Long died. It wasn't unexpected, as he'd grown increasingly frail. He died in his sleep, and Patrick took some time off work to arrange the memorial service, the burial. . . .

Patricia and Tyler went about the house soberly and helped out where they could. The obituary in the *Post* gave an extended account of Mr. Long's years in the State Department—the many overseas assignments and the countries where he had served. The mail brought numerous notes from people who had known Mr. Long in government, but few came to his memorial service, because most of his friends and coworkers had scattered to other parts of the country.

As he had at his mother's memorial service, Patrick stood up and gave a moving tribute to his dad. He choked up once or twice and had to stop momentarily, but I was glad that Patricia and Tyler could see this depth of feeling in their father, who obviously seemed so strong and capable to them over the years.

Later, when the service was over and friends had come and gone, Patrick and I sat out on the glider on our back porch holding hands. We were watching two sparrows building a nest under the eaves of our toolshed—one flying in and out with a piece of string or straw, then the other taking its place. Soon, just as the sparrows had done last year, there would be nests on both sides of the toolshed, parents teaching their young to fly, until one day they'd be gone and the nest empty.

"I guess it's just beginning to hit me that I'm an orphan," Patrick said.

I caressed his hand with my thumb.

"Never really thought of it that way before, but now the realization has struck that if I ever need advice—help, consolation— my parents are gone. Not that I ever really asked their advice once I was grown, but it's the knowledge that I couldn't now if I wanted. That if there were ever any questions I wanted to ask them—about their lives, about myself as a child or places we had lived before I was old enough to remember—I've lost the chance. Strange . . ."

"I imagine so," I said.

"I'm glad we had two children," he said after a bit. "They can lean on each other after we're gone. Share memories."

"True."

"And someday we'll be the old wise ones," he said. "Our children will be coming to us for advice."

"Or not," I said, and finally saw him smile.

IBM was starting another charitable grant program, this time in some African east coast countries, and once again, Patrick was offered the job as coordinator. But this time he turned it down. With Patricia applying to colleges and Tyler now a freshman in high school, he didn't want to uproot the family; and, as he admitted to me, all that travel didn't appeal to him as much as it used to.

Tyler had joined the track team, and he and his dad were still enjoying those five- and ten-mile runs on Sundays. Patricia had enrolled in a number of advanced courses and was showing a remarkable aptitude for science, surprising us both.

So Patrick took a different job within the company and also signed on to head a committee to reelect one of the best congressmen we'd had in our district.

I smiled as I rubbed his feet for him after a long Saturday campaigning door-to-door.

"What's so funny?" he asked, raising his head off the pillow and looking at me. "My feet stink? I just washed them."

"No, I'm just thinking that trying to harness your energy is like trying to harness the sea. Just when I think I've got you home for a spell, you're out campaigning."

"I'm home!" he protested.

"Yes, but your mind is always on the next job or project and the next and the next. I'm not complaining, really. Just observing."

He wiggled his toes in my hands. "I like to make a difference."

"I know. That's what attracted me to you. Last year you headed the food drive at the church and the—"

"You were part of that too."

"As I said, I'm just observing. And I also observe that someone's toenails need trimming. Stay put. I'll get the clippers."

Patricia was accepted at William & Mary—a college that had turned me down—and we joked a lot about that. She and I were closer now—no doubt because of the cancer scare, but I'd take whatever I could get! It had made us both more aware of our mortality—mine, anyway—and we didn't want to waste time quarreling with each other.

Once she left for college, she frequently called home, and I loved being there for her—mostly listening, sympathizing, once in a while telling her about an especially hard time for me, like my experience with my first roommate, Amber, and her boyfriend. She thought that story was hilarious and told all her friends.

When she came home to visit, I tried to respect her privacy. I let her sleep in and I didn't nag her about picking up her things, but I would still invite her to help me out sometimes—make a special supper or bake a cake—something that helped us both feel she was still a responsible member of our family. Every so often, she'd ask about my health, and lucky for me, the answer was always positive. I was doing well.

Just when I was confident that every member of my family was feeling settled and secure, we discovered that Tyler was in love.

26
MOVING ON

I'd never known how much a boy could suffer. Tyler had always gone out with a group of friends before, never paired off with anyone in particular, and suddenly, in his sophomore year of high school, he had a girlfriend.

It first caught my attention when I noticed him sniffing his armpits one morning before he went to school. Funny, I thought, how Elizabeth and Pamela and I used to do that back in junior high. About the worst thing you could say to a girl, even worse than *What happened to your hair?* was to insinuate she smelled.

The generic deodorant stick in the bathroom was replaced by one with a designer label. Shirts that had been worn only once were tumbling into the clothes hamper at an alarming rate.

"Mom, I have to know," Tyler said hesitantly one morning before he caught the bus. I braced myself, then had to choke back a laugh when he asked, "Tell me honestly if my breath stinks."

I looked at the boy with the dark blond hair and brown eyes, who was now several inches taller than I was. It was hard to imagine that I had given birth to those extra-long arms and legs. He approached me—embarrassed but sincere—and blew his breath in my face.

"Crest, with a little bacon on the side," I told him.

He put his book bag down in disgust and headed for the stairs once more. "I'll brush again," he said.

"Tyler! You're perfectly fine!" I called after him. "She won't mind a bit."

But he retorted, "It'll be like she's kissing a pig!"

So he's at the kissing stage now, I thought, smiling to myself. The year before Patricia had left for college, she'd become very solicitous of her younger brother, giving him advice and buying him shirts she thought he should wear. But she wasn't here now, and the current heart-stopping event for Tyler was a party being given in the home of a *junior,* to which Tyler and his girl-friend had been invited, because both girls were friends. Tyler's girlfriend's brother had offered to drive them over.

For a week Tyler had battled a nervous stomach.

"I just know I'll do something stupid," he murmured the night before the party. "I'll probably get something stuck in my windpipe and have to have someone do the Heimrick maneuver on me."

"I believe that's Heimlich," I said. "Hey! I thought this date was supposed to be *fun*! You're not going to your execution, you know." And then I added, "I'm more worried about the brother's driving."

"He's okay," Tyler said, and we could usually trust his judgment. "Jon's on the basketball team, and they can't smoke or drink or anything."

"Yeah, but how's his driving?" asked Patrick.

"Got his license ten months ago, and if he even dents their dad's car, he has to take it to a body shop himself for estimates and pay for repairs," Tyler told us.

Chalk one up for those parents, I thought.

"How far away is the party? We'll need a phone number," I said.

"Somewhere off Norbeck Road. I'll give you the name and everything," Tyler said, and he did.

Patrick and I decided not to set a curfew. We knew how embarrassing it would be if Tyler were the only one of the four, and probably the youngest, who had to be home at a certain time. Frankly, he was more trustworthy than Patricia had been at that age. He was generally open about what he intended to do, and if we ruled against him, he'd argue it out, not sneak around behind our backs. And yes, the parents would be home. The mom was going to make tostados for the crowd, and they'd be playing blackjack and stuff, he told us.

"If you see that you're going to be really late, though, could you call us?" I said.

"Of course," Tyler said, but we failed to pin down "really late."

The day of the party it didn't just rain, it heaved rain. Water cascaded down the roof and gushed in torrents out of the rain spouts. There were flood warnings for Maryland, Virginia, and the District. I could have sworn Tyler almost looked relieved when he came home from school, speculating on whether or not they would still hold the party.

But the rain finally stopped around five. The trees and bushes dripped, the back of the yard was flooded, but the sun peeped out from behind rolling gray clouds, and a phone call from Tyler's girlfriend assured him that the party was still on. The creek across from her friend's house had flooded, she said, but the water hadn't reached the road, so all the streets in that neighborhood were passable.

Tyler couldn't eat anything, even though I suggested a sandwich to keep his stomach from growling. Five minutes before he was to be picked up, he decided he had perspired so much that he should change his shirt, and when the brother pulled up and honked, I was relieved to have Tyler out of the house.

"Enjoy!" I said as he went out the door, but he didn't answer, only swallowed.

Patrick and I watched discreetly from a window.

"This reminds me of the night you invited me to dinner at your parents' country club," I told him. "It was one of the most exciting, terrifying evenings of my life."

Patrick looked at me in surprise. "It *was*?"

"I was only twelve, Patrick."

"Well, so was I! I thought you had a good time."

"I did, but I was so nervous! Besides . . . there's something I never told you."

Patrick grinned. "What? You wet your pants?"

"No, but when I got home and opened my purse, I discovered I'd stuffed the linen napkin inside!"

Patrick burst out laughing, and so did I.

"I was embarrassed out of my mind! You were so smart and sophisticated and—"

"At *twelve*?"

"Well, you seemed that way to me," I said, sinking down on the couch.

"And now?"

"Now you're smart and sophisticated and sexy," I told him.

He came over, sat on the hassock, and began stroking my leg. "Let's go to bed," he said.

"Now?"

"Sure. Tyler's out for the evening."

I started to smile. "Well then . . . !"

We woke about eleven feeling as though we'd had a night's sleep.

"Is it raining again?" I said. "I wonder how long that's been going on. I didn't think the sky could hold any more." I rolled over and put my arms around Patrick.

"Hmmm," he said. "I like rainy nights. Let's see. We could

get up and make waffles, or we could stay in bed and do this all over again."

"I'm hungry," I told him.

Patrick laughed. "So am I."

We got out of bed, put on our robes, and were eating Belgian waffles at a quarter of midnight.

"Do you suppose he's having a good time?" I said, running the last bite of waffle around the edge of my plate to soak up the raspberry syrup.

"Must be. Probably having a blast. He should be calling pretty soon, though. Have you checked your cell phone?"

"Several times, actually. But we didn't set a curfew, remember?"

"Then he's probably on his way. I don't think he'd stay out past midnight without calling."

But midnight came, twelve fifteen, twelve twenty . . . and the excitement I'd felt for Tyler earlier turned to cold, hard fear.

"I'm texting him," I said, and thumbed in, *Tyler, where are you?*

Twelve twenty-five, no answer. Twelve thirty-five . . .

"Hand me your cell," Patrick said. "I'm simply going to call him."

My insides ached as I sat watching Patrick's expression. He shook his head finally. "Voice mail," he said. And then, into the phone, "Tyler, call home. *Now!*"

We called the house where the party was being held and got no answer.

"What about this Jon fellow? The girlfriend's brother? Do we have his family's number? They've got to be worried too." Patrick got up and went into the bathroom while I searched for the notepad. I thought I might throw up.

But just as I was about to pick up my cell phone again, it rang. I grabbed it.

"Tyler?"

Instead, a man's voice said, "Mrs. Long? This is Officer Harding and—"

"No! No!" I cried, my strength giving way.

"Hey, hey, hey!" the voice said. "I'm just calling to tell you that your son and his friends were trying to push a neighbor's car out of a creek. They weren't successful, but everyone's fine. I'm calling from my patrol car while we wait for a tow. But you should have some towels and newspapers handy when he comes in, because these kids are mud from their shoulders to their shoes."

There is no fear as intense as the fear you feel when a police officer calls you about your child at one in the morning, and no relief quite as profound as when he says your boy is safe.

"Evidently, a neighbor was in such a hurry to get inside that she parked uphill in her driveway with the car in neutral, and it rolled backward, crossed the road, and went into a creek," the officer continued.

"I'm . . . so relieved!" I said, my voice trembling.

I heard him chuckle. "I'm a dad myself, which is why I'm doing the calling. The boys left their wallets and cell phones in the house so they wouldn't get wet, and got themselves filthy.

Two of them asked if I'd call their parents and explain. One of the girls' parents is driving them home."

"Thank you," I kept saying. "Thank you, thank you . . ."

When Tyler came in, we had the newspapers and towels ready.

"You should have *seen* it, Dad! Both of her back tires were in this creek, and we were in mud up to our ankles, and we all pushed, but the car still kept rolling backward. Mr. Eddy came out with a flashlight, and the girls were standing up on the porch, and everybody was yelling and giving directions and cheering. And then another neighbor called the police because he thought we were drunk, and—man!—what a great night!"

Patrick was not amused. "Tyler, that was dangerous! Cars have been washed away in flash floods!" he lectured. "You guys should never have been in a creek after all this rain."

Tyler was standing on the newspapers I'd strewn in the hallway and had begun stripping off his clothes. He looked chagrined. "Well, that's about what Mr. Eddy said, but the water had gone down, and the neighbor was crying, and she wanted us to get the car out before her husband woke up and saw what happened."

"Have you any idea how worried we were?" I put in. "I texted you, your Dad called . . ."

"I didn't have my cell phone on me, Mom! It would have been ruined."

"We tried the number you gave us—the girl who was giving the party . . ."

"Everyone was out on the porch watching."

How can you love your kid and want to throttle him, both at the same time? I was speechless.

Tyler took off one shoe and water poured out. He took off the other, then looked up at us, beaming. "That was one of the best nights of my entire life," he said.

Patricia enjoyed the story enormously when I called her the next day. Somehow the brother whose very existence she ignored back in middle school she now seemed to cherish, if not adore. She sent him sweatshirts with WILLIAM & MARY on it, introduced him to the best bands and comedy teams.

"What's with her?" I asked Liz once as we were gift shopping at a Greek bazaar during the holidays. "She's even taking him to a concert over winter break. *Patricia! Tyler!*"

"I think he's become her mascot," Liz guessed. "She focuses all her homesickness on him. Easier than saying she misses Mom and Dad." But Patricia admitted to that, too. Once she was away from home, she didn't seem to have the same need to oppose us. I tried to keep our phone conversations nag-free, and it paid off. She called frequently and let us in on her life. She had started out in journalism but switched her major to biology.

And no sooner had she settled on her major for good than she also fell in love, and she called home about that, too. Life was so good, so varied, so exciting that she just had to share it, and I felt incredibly lucky that she wanted to share it with me.

* * *

Patrick and I celebrated our twenty-fifth wedding anniversary snorkeling in the Caribbean. It was something I'd always wanted to do, so we flew to St. John's, where we rented a condo overlooking the sea, and took an expedition out the very next morning. We swam together, grabbing each other by the arm when we saw another spectacular fish or a bank of coral we didn't want the other to miss.

I had more fun than I could remember, just losing myself in the sea, the sound of my breathing replacing the voices of the other snorkelers; I swam with the swarms of exotic-looking fish that noiselessly glided by, free as the fish, happy in my aloneness.

But back at the hotel, we lay happily together on a chaise lounge for two, my bare legs entwined around Patrick's, remembering the way we had lain together at Ocean City the weekend he proposed. Now he was stroking my hair at the temples and I was on the verge of sleep when he said, "So, Alice, would you do it all over again?"

I opened my eyes, then let them close. "Marry you?"

"Yes."

"In a heartbeat," I told him.

He smiled. "Good. We still have that second trip to Ireland to take, remember. It's nice to reach your twenty-fifth anniversary and want to do it all over again, isn't it?"

I smiled. "Mm-hmm. Did you ever think we wouldn't make it?" I rolled over on my side and put an arm around his waist.

"Not really. And you know how I decided that?"

"What? My brains? My beauty? My sexual allure?" I teased.

"Nope. Your dad."

I pushed away from him. "My *dad*?"

Patrick pulled me back down beside him. "No. Just watching him—I mean, him and Sylvia together. And I thought, 'That's what I want. That's the way I want Alice and me to be when we're in our sixties'—warm and affectionate and honest with each other. I didn't want us to end up like my folks."

"What do you mean? They always seemed to get along to me."

"Oh, they did. But there was a sort of . . . sadness in the marriage, I think. I didn't realize it till I was in my late teens and asked Mom about it once. I'm not sure how we got on the subject. But I guess Dad had a couple of affairs when he was traveling—always in a different country, you know. Mom said she forgave him, but she could never respect him as much as she once did." Patrick touched my forehead with his lips. "I didn't want something like that to come between us. And that was the best decision I ever made, next to marrying you."

A brochure arrived in the mail one day showing a cozy bed-and-breakfast with a wide porch and rustic-looking rocking chairs. There were tall trees in the background and, beyond them, snow-covered mountains beneath a spectacularly blue sky. *Haynes Hideaway, in glorious Hailey, Idaho,* it read.

What was this? I wondered. Someone who loved alliteration,

obviously. I glanced again at the envelope. My address was handwritten. I opened the tri-fold brochure.

> *Co-owners Lori and Leslie Haynes invite you to enjoy their newly remodeled bed-and-breakfast and the splendor of the Wood River Valley. Only minutes away from skiing in Sun Valley, gay-friendly Haynes Hideaway offers guided hiking and biking tours in the Sawtooth National Forest as well as all the comforts of home. . . .*

Lori! Leslie! They were still together! They owned a business! A bed-and-breakfast.

I grabbed my cell and called their number, trying to picture them both—Lori, tall and a bit stoop-shouldered, a shy brunette with bangs, and Leslie, short and blond—the blondest girl I'd ever seen.

"Hello? This is Lori at Haynes Hideaway," came a cheerful voice.

"Oh, Lori! It's wonderful! Your bed-and-breakfast!" I cried.

There was a pause. Then, "Is this . . . *Alice?*"

"Yes!"

"I found you!" Lori said excitedly. "Leslie and I have been tracking down all the people we ever knew, and I wanted to hear from you most of all. I found out that you and Patrick were married. So are Leslie and I."

"Congratulations, Lori! That's terrific!" I said.

She laughed. "You know the old joke: 'What do lesbians

take on their second date? Answer: a moving van.' We were both a little scared that maybe it was true—that maybe Leslie and I were so glad we'd found someone like ourselves that we wanted to move right in. So we decided to separate for six months and date other women, and we did. Actually, it lasted only five months. We missed each other so much that we not only got back together, we went right to the courthouse there in Seattle and applied for a marriage license. And Leslie decided to take my name. . . ." I'd never known Lori to be so talkative, and it made me smile just listening to her.

"I'm so happy for you," I said. "The last I'd heard, you'd started a travel website that was doing really well."

"So well, in fact, that—along with our other jobs—we were able to save enough to afford a down payment on this place. We thought about what part of the country we loved the most, with all the activities we liked to do, and here we are! If you're ever in Idaho for skiing . . ."

"If we're ever in Idaho for *any*thing, we'll visit the Haynes Hideaway," I promised.

Shortly after we celebrated our anniversary, Pamela and Nick broke up. They'd been living together so long that it was hard to think of them as not married, and they had seemed so handsomely matched. They both were style-conscious, both loved New York, both liked to visit the trendy clubs and restaurants, and neither wanted children.

"What happened?" I asked when Pamela was in town one

weekend and I invited her and Elizabeth and Moe over for dinner with Patrick and me.

"I don't know," Pamela said. "I just looked at him one morning and decided he was running on empty."

"Come again?" said Moe.

"He just seemed like a shell of a man. Nothing inside! I suppose he could have said the same about me. We shared a lot of external things, but . . . I realized I didn't know how he felt about all kinds of issues, things we'd never talked about. And every time I brought up a topic, he said he hadn't thought much about it and he didn't want to start now. We just lost interest in each other, I guess."

I felt cold all over, because that's exactly the way it had been between Dave and me. And I could almost see us now, in Pamela and Nick. It was the feeling you'd get after you'd escaped a car crash by a sudden swerve.

"Sure there's no one else?" Liz asked.

"No. And you know what? I'm happy being single. Not that I wouldn't consider having a man in my life if I found someone just right, but I'm not lonely. And besides, I've got some growing to do."

"Don't we all," Patrick said.

Patricia Marie and her boyfriend wanted to get married. She was twenty-three, exactly the age I was when Patrick and I married, yet why did it seem so young? I knew if I tried to talk her out of it, she'd be all the more determined. Both she and her

husband-to-be were a year out of grad school and were looking for work there in Massachusetts in molecular biology, so it
wasn't as though they were clueless about life.

I wonder if any parent ever feels that her son or daughter
marries the person she had in mind. I never thought a lot about
it, but I suppose if I had, I would have imagined that Patricia's
fiancé would greet me for the first time with a firm handshake
and a gracious, *Hello, Mrs. Long. It's a pleasure to meet Patricia's
mother.* A young man in a suit and tie, maybe. A young man in a
suit and tie holding a bouquet of flowers. A young man in a suit
and tie holding a bouquet of flowers and looking at my daughter with such love and devotion that I knew he would care for
her the rest of her life.

Instead Patricia had come home for spring break in her
senior year with a short, curly-headed young man, in torn jeans
and a T-shirt, whose sneakers seemed impossibly huge to me.

"Mom, this is Zack Sheldon," Patricia had said on her way to
the kitchen to get a soft drink for him.

"Hi. How you doin'?" he said, not even bothering to shake
my hand.

At first, Patrick and I figured he was one of many boyfriends
she'd have. Zack made himself comfortable on our hide-a-bed
in the family room, stayed up late at night playing cards with
Tyler when he was here, helped himself to whatever food he
found in the fridge, and generally made himself at home.

But when he came back for a week over the summer and
we began to suspect that Patricia was not staying in her own

room the latter half of the night, and when we heard them talking about the various companies and labs they might apply to after grad school, we realized they were serious about each other.

It wasn't that Zack was objectionable, exactly. It was just that he was so different from what we had imagined.

"Does he have to *slouch* that way?" Patrick said, observing Zack out on the deck with a beer can in one hand, the newspaper in the other. "Can you see this guy going on a job interview with curvature of the spine?"

"Can you see him waiting for Patricia at the altar with his shirt tail hanging out?" I asked, a bit more to the point.

But Patricia loved him, so we decided to be as accepting and supportive as possible. After all, they shared the same interests, the same kind of work, they both liked to ski—something Zack had taught Patricia—they both wanted children, and when they argued, they seemed to do it intelligently, always coming up with reasonable solutions.

"Well, Zack," Patrick said, shaking his hand, "welcome to the family."

"Yeah, thanks," Zack said.

Couldn't he show just a little more enthusiasm? I wondered.

His family lived in Rhode Island, and when we went up to visit, at their invitation, we found them warm and down-to-earth, and liked them immediately.

But almost everything I had imagined about having a daughter—a daughter preparing for marriage—turned out to be wrong. Patricia did not want a big wedding, a church wedding. And most disappointing of all, she did not want to wear my mother's wedding gown.

"But . . . but I had it preserved! I've saved it all these years for you!" I said.

She stared at me incredulously. "I wasn't even here! I wasn't born yet! How could you be saving it for someone you didn't even know!"

I tried to calm myself. "You're right. But . . . well, you're named after the woman who chose it. I'd sort of hoped that dress could become a tradition, passed down from mother to daughter to—"

"Or not!" Patricia wore that amused look she gives me sometimes when we disagree. "Mom, it looked great on you in your wedding photos, but I want a simple sheath dress, cocktail-length. I don't want a veil or any of that jazz. It's just not me. Okay?"

I looked at my grown daughter and decided she was right. She *would* look better in a simple sheath dress. She *didn't* need any of that "jazz," as memorable as it was to me. Hadn't I changed the dress to suit me? Patricia deserved the kind of dress, the kind of wedding, the kind of husband that suited her best, and she would have it.

"What do you think, Dad?" I'd asked one weekend, helping him plant more tulip bulbs in his side yard. His back had been bothering him a lot, and Sylvia had arthritis in her hands, yet they both loved working in their garden. We wanted them to be able to enjoy it as long as possible. I'd been telling him the latest incident of "Patricia Gets Married" as we worked.

"I think Patricia is going to do whatever she wants, and you'd better let her make her own decisions," he said, smiling a little. "I know. I had visions of her in Marie's dress too, but when you come right down to it, what's a dress? Choose your battles carefully, Al. If you're going to disagree with your only daughter about something, let it be more importan than a dress."

I looked at him fondly. "How did you ever get to be so wise?" I asked.

He laughed. "By raising you," he said. And then he asked, almost bashfully, "Did I do a good job, do you think?"

It occurred to me that up until then in my relationship with my father, I'd wanted him to be proud of me. I'd wanted to prove that I was a wise mother, a supportive wife. I wanted, spoken or unspoken, his approval. I had never thought that he might need mine. There were times I still longed for reassurance from Patricia that she had really forgiven me for that slap, understood our disagreements, knew how much I loved her and cared. How pleased I was whenever Tyler thanked me for something or told me I'd made a great dinner! How eagerly I wanted my own children's approval!

"Dad, you didn't just do a good job of raising Les and me, you did a spectacular job," I said. "You were father and mother for both of us, and I used to tell you more personal stuff at the dinner table than my friends told their parents in a lifetime. I don't know how you managed it so well."

He beamed. His laughter came in short, jerky little chuckles, the kind he couldn't hold back when he was happy, and I reached out over the bag of potting soil and gave his shoulder a squeeze. The older we got, the more alike we were, father and daughter, man and woman. The more human.

No matter how "simple" someone wants a wedding to be, it's not. In fact, Pamela, a bridesmaid multiple times, once remarked that the simple weddings are sometimes the hardest.

"You won't have to reserve a church because we're holding the wedding outdoors," Patricia told us. "We want the reception outside too."

"Outside," Patrick and I repeated numbly.

"No roof?" asked Patrick.

"We'll tell the guests that if it's raining, they should bring umbrellas," said Zack.

I believe he was serious.

I imagined blue sky when the guests left home for the wedding, clouds rolling in when we started up the hill to the little circle of pines where the ceremony would be held, and a cloudburst right after the "I dos." I imagined the bride's four-inch heels sinking down into the mud and the bride's mother sliding unceremoniously down the bank on her backside.

I phoned Gwen as soon as I could.

"The wedding's going to be outside?" she repeated. "What are you going to do for chairs?"

Chairs? *Chairs!* If we had the wedding in a town hall, there would be benches. If we held it in a church, there would be pews. If we held it outside, it meant we'd have to rent chairs and pay to have them hauled up the hill, set up, and hauled back down again. Either that or all the guests would stand.

I phoned Elizabeth.

"Outside?" she exclaimed. "What will you do for air-conditioning?"

Was this a generational thing? I wondered. Something that people Patricia's age just take in stride? Were we showing our age with all this fretting?

"You know," said Sylvia, "these things tend to work out. If everything goes smoothly, it will be a day they always remember. And if there's some major mix-up and we can keep our sense of humor, they'll always have an interesting story to tell about their wedding. That's the stuff memories are made of."

It was indeed a lovely wedding. The evening before, showers were predicted, but Patricia was nervous enough without me reciting the weather forecast. She'd given the impression of being so relaxed, so cool, but obviously, she wasn't that way at all. I sat with her in her room, giving her a pedicure and trying to be funny while she did her nails. She had scoffed at the idea of having anything done professionally except for her hair.

"Well, Patricia, it's the night before your wedding. I've never been the mother of the bride before. What do we do now? Are we supposed to have a mother-daughter talk?" I was massaging lotion between her toes, her green cotton robe pulled up above the knee.

"You mean about sex and stuff?" She grinned.

"If you want."

"Sure, Mom. What do you need to know?" The old joke. We laughed.

"Did I tell you that the night before I was married, Aunt Sally and Uncle Milt were staying with us to attend the wedding. I was upstairs packing my suitcase, and Aunt Sally came in my room, looking very uncomfortable. 'I haven't done a very good job by you, Alice,' she said. 'But this is something a mother should do, and I have to take the place of Marie.' She slipped a little tube of something in my suitcase and whispered, 'Lubrication.' I stood there trying to think what needed lubricating. My suitcase? Our car? And then it hit: *me*."

Patricia and I howled.

"She was right, of course. Except that Patrick and I were beyond that point by then."

Patricia wriggled her big toe affectionately against my hand. "You've done a good job, Mom," she said. "You always answered the questions I asked, and then some."

"Then some?"

"Everything you told me, I told the girls at school, and then I started bringing their questions to you, pretending they were mine. 'Ask her about this,' they'd say, or 'Ask her about that.' You were educating a whole class and didn't know it."

"Are you serious?"

"Cross my heart." She had no makeup on at all, and looked like the impish girl she was back in seventh grade. She cocked her head, then, and studied me: "You must have missed a lot, Mom—growing up without a mother."

"I suppose I did," I told her. "But you know what? I've come to know her better than I ever thought I would from the things she left behind: her books, her pictures, her recipes, her letters. . . ."

I massaged Patricia's foot there in my lap. "I would have liked my mom, and I think she would have liked me. And she absolutely would have *loved* you."

"I hope Zack and I are as happy as you and Dad," Patricia said thoughtfully. "You've had a really happy marriage, haven't you?"

"Yes, I think you could say we have," I told her. "But no one is *always* happy . . . or *always* angry. In a good marriage you feel content most of the time, satisfied with the way your life is going and with the person you married. Most important, satisfied with yourself."

The showers tapered off by morning, and by the time the catering service arrived to put up tents, the grass was drying. The tables and chairs were set up in the big tent, the food brought in, and at four o'clock the justice of the peace arrived, a jolly, good-natured man who seemed in no hurry to rush through the ceremony.

All of us looked splendid in our finery—the Sheldons with their three other grown children; Lester and Stacy wearing the adoring expressions of a fond uncle and aunt, the triplets in the row beside them; and Dad and Sylvia, holding hands.

As the bridesmaids started up the hill in their buttercup yellow gowns and slippers, I noticed proudly that Tyler, who stood beside the best man, seemed mature beyond his years. He was in his third year at Oberlin, considering a career in social work. He had girlfriends, but no one special yet, and made a handsome addition to the wedding party. As for the groom, I'll have to admit that I looked more favorably on his best man than I did on Zack. Why couldn't she be marrying *him*? I wondered guiltily.

But as I watched Zack's face as he waited for Patricia to be escorted up the hill on Patrick's arm, the way his own arm encircled her when she reached him, the rapport they had with their friends at the reception, I realized that if Patricia married a man *I* liked best, she would not be Patricia, but merely a clone of me. And as our eyes met when the ceremony was over and she started back down the hill as Mrs. Zack Sheldon, I told myself once again that often our children know far better than we do what's best for them.

To recuperate, Patrick and I returned to Ireland, something we'd promised each other a long time ago. We went over the summer and allowed ourselves to do all the things we hadn't had time to do on our honeymoon. Yet there were favorite places we remembered and wanted to see again, and if we decided we'd seen enough of Ireland, we'd hop over to Scotland for a while. After living so regimented a life between his job and mine, it was delicious just to wake up in the mornings and say, "What shall it be today? City or country?" And then take all the time our hearts desired.

When the trip was over and Patricia found out we'd been away, she said, "What's this about a second honeymoon?"

"Not even the second. We're still celebrating the first," Patrick told her.

27

VIVA LA ALICE

Patrick and I, Dad and Sylvia, were going to Virginia for Christmas. It was weird to see Lester the father of ten-year-old triplets. Definitely weird to see him at the age of fifty-seven. Patricia and Zack were with the Sheldons up in Rhode Island this Christmas, and Tyler was at his girlfriend's, so it was no problem for us to get up early and head for Fairfax.

Sara, Hannah, and Benjamin had curly brown hair like their mother, but they looked more like Lester around the face—the mischievous eyes, the straight-lined smile. They enjoyed each other's company and had secret words, secret phrases, secret gestures to amuse themselves.

It had always been the rule in Stacy's family that no one could open presents on Christmas morning until everyone had eaten a proper breakfast. It was the policy now in Lester's, too. Stacy didn't want people filling empty stomachs with chocolate and candy canes, so we arrived around nine thirty, and as soon as we sat down at the table, Lester's children appeared with a "Christmas Manifesto," printed out on their computer. Each of us had to sign that we would not "dawdle over breakfast" past ten o'clock and that anyone who wasn't finished eating by then would have to open his gifts last.

"Honestly, now!" Stacy said, embarrassed, but both we and her parents thought it funny, and we all managed to take our coffee cups with us into the living room by ten and gather around the tree. When the big red box in the corner was opened, however, revealing Rollerblades not only for the "Tumultuous T" but for their father as well, we reached for our coats and gloves and headed outside to watch the maiden voyage, the triplets filling the house with deafening shrieks and Lester protesting all the while.

"I haven't been on skates since I was seven!" he kept saying.

"You've been on ice skates, and that's good enough," Stacy told him.

"I think we'll watch from inside," Stacy's mom said, opening the curtains a little wider, but Dad and Sylvia went outdoors with us.

Les and Stacy lived at the bottom of a gentle hill, and in winter the street was sometimes closed off for sledding. It was the first Christmas Stacy could remember that the children hadn't prayed for snow. Now they wanted bare streets and side-walks, and bare is what they got.

They practiced clunking around on the sidewalk for a while, perfecting their balance, but within twenty minutes, the triplets were taking long, jerky strides, arms out at their sides. At last, when they were all adept at staying upright, Les included, they turned their feet sideways and climbed to the top of the hill.

Being Christmas morning, and a Sunday at that, there was almost no traffic, and the sun shone warmly down on our little audience of five as we sat on Lester's front steps and waited for the show to begin.

"This is more fun than a circus," Dad chuckled.

"And there's not even a safety net," said Patrick. "The world's most daring—" He stopped mid-sentence when we saw the first performer coming down the hill—Benjamin, his knees bent, face aglow. We clapped and cheered as he aimed his feet toward the lawn at the bottom and managed to stop just short of the maple tree.

But there was no time to comment because Sara was next, shrieking all the way down, followed by Hannah, the smallest, who didn't make a sound till she got to the bottom and then split the air with a victory yell.

There seemed to be a rather lengthy intermission before the last performer appeared on the scene.

"Maybe he went out for coffee," said Sylvia.

"Maybe he took the first bus out of town," joked Dad.

"No, here he comes!" I said, leaning forward to get a better view as the triplets gathered at the bottom of the hill.

"Yay, Dad!" yelled Sara.

"Come on, Pop!" cried Benjamin.

"You can do it!" Hannah encouraged.

The hill seemed gentle enough to look at it, but Lester was picking up speed as he came down. The kids had been practicing for weeks on their friends' skates, hoping they would get Rollerblades for Christmas, and had mastered a few of the finer points, but no one had taught Lester to stop.

Faster and faster he rolled, his arms flailing like windmills, eyes huge, legs unsteady, a terrified wail coming from his lips. Patrick leaped off the steps to run out and stop him, but he missed. Lester zoomed right past us toward the house at the curve of the road and, seconds later, had gone headfirst over a row of azalea bushes flanking the street.

It was all we wanted to talk about for the rest of the day.

"You should have seen your face!" I told him.

"If only I'd brought the camera!" said Stacy.

"I would have paid admission to see *that* show!" said Dad, laughing.

Later, as Lester was collecting the utensils for carving, I offered to hold the turkey steady while he worked.

"It's really been a marvelous day, Les. I'm so glad you invited us here," I said.

"Humph," he mumbled, and gingerly laid some more slices on the platter.

I was trying not to laugh. "The triplets were over the moon with their skates, and I have to tell you, that was some performance from you."

Les frowned at me, but I could tell he was holding back a smile. "I have only two words to say to you, Alice," he said. "'Bah' and 'humbug.'"

Two years later, three months before Dad's eighty-eighth birthday, I got a call from Sylvia saying that he was in the intensive care unit at the hospital.

"Sylvia!" I cried. "What is it?"

"He's been having some chest pain, Alice, and didn't want to worry anyone. I didn't even find out about it until last week. He was to see the doctor on Thursday, but obviously, he was sicker than we thought. They're going to do a quadruple bypass in the morning."

I didn't even bother to lock up my office. I asked my secretary to cancel my last meeting of the day and drove ten miles over the speed limit to Holy Cross, yanked the ticket from the machine, and parked my car at an impossible angle.

He was lying amid a tangle of tubes and monitors, and I stood just inside the curtain, afraid I'd burst into tears if I went any farther. His body seemed so small under the blanket. Had his legs always been so short? I wondered. I sucked in my breath and heard him say, "Come on over, honey."

Tears came in spite of myself. He put out one hand, and I went to his bedside, clasping his fingers.

"Dad . . . ," I said.

"Just like an old car." His lips were dry and stuck together.

"What?"

"One part wears out before the rest."

A nurse came into the cubicle to check his IV and stopped to survey us. "You must be Alice," she said.

"Yes."

"Well, I know your dad would rather be anyplace but here, but I want to tell you, he's my best patient."

"He's always the best," I said, and squeezed his hand.

Dad didn't take his eyes off me for a second. "I'll be going in for surgery first thing tomorrow morning," he said. "But you don't have to be here, sweetheart."

"Of *course* I'll be here, Dad!"

"Dr. Rankin is one of the top doctors in his field," the nurse told me. "Your dad will be in good hands."

Dad and I chatted a bit more, and I left with the promise to return after dinner. We called Tyler in Ohio, and he said he'd take the first plane he could get. We couldn't reach Patricia and Zack, who were skiing somewhere in Colorado, but I left a message on Patricia's cell phone. Les and Stacy were fighting rush-hour traffic to get to the hospital, and Patrick met Tyler's plane at the airport. By eight that evening, the six of us, including Sylvia, stood awkwardly around Dad's bed, curtained off from the other beds in the ICU—no room for cards or flowers or balloons in here.

Dad repeated his joke about being like an old car. Lester put one hand on his shoulder and said, "Don't knock it, Dad. I once had a car that made it to two hundred thousand miles. You've still got a lot of mileage in you."

Dad maneuvered his hand around the tangle of tubes and put it over Lester's, but he didn't respond.

The nurse came in then and said they needed to do some prepping to get Dad ready for surgery the next day, so we began saying our good nights. I lingered in the room a minute after the others had said their good-byes, though, and tried to hold back tears.

"Dad, I wish I could go through this with you. I mean, really," I said.

"Don't say that, honey," he told me. "We all have our own battles to fight, and sometimes we have to go it alone. I'm stronger than you think, you'd be surprised."

"I hope so," I whispered, memorizing every line of his face, every tiny mole, the deep-set eyes and the brows that grew more unruly with each passing year.

The nurse was waiting, so I leaned down and kissed him. Dad smiled up at me and whispered, "Like me?" Our corny old joke.

I smiled back. "Rivers," I said. "And I love you oceans and oceans."

Out in the waiting area we sat with Sylvia awhile before we drove her home. She looked tired, and I was conscious of the fact that her clothes did not fit her well anymore—her frame was no longer big enough to fill them out.

"How are you holding up?" Patrick asked her.

She leaned into a corner of the couch. "All right, I guess. I just wish . . . I wish I'd known sooner that he was having symptoms. Why didn't he tell me?"

Les smiled. "It's called 'love,' Sylvia. He didn't want to worry you, and it's possible he was also keeping it from himself. In any case, we'll all be here tomorrow. Try to sleep. It's the best thing you can do for both of you."

Patricia called that evening to say that she had just got off the slopes and found my message. They'd be taking a red-eye flight to Washington that would get here early the next morning. Tyler said he'd meet them at the airport, and I knew how important it was for him to be helpful somehow.

"Mom," Patricia said before we signed off, "it's . . . it's really serious, isn't it?"

"Yes, but it's not a rare operation anymore, sweetheart," I said. "A lot of people have it. And your grandpa has all the family rooting for him. I'll tell him you're on your way."

As Patrick and I drove to the hospital the next morning, I thought of all the things I wanted to say to my father, just in case. I felt I ought to apologize for everything I'd ever done that upset him, any grief I'd caused—the time I'd dyed my hair green, the time Pamela ran away from home and I hid her in my room, the unkind things I'd said to Sylvia once after they were married. . . . There were so many things left unsaid.

Patrick seemed to know what I was feeling because he reached over and patted my hand.

But when we got up to Dad's floor, we were not allowed in the ICU. A nurse got up from behind a desk and ushered us down the hall to the solarium at the end, where Sylvia was sitting white-faced between Les and Stacy.

"What is it?" I asked the nurse.

"Dr. Rankin will be with you shortly," was all she said.

I hurried over to Sylvia.

"I don't know," she said. "We got here just a few minutes ago, and there's all this commotion. . . ."

I sat down before my legs gave way. I remembered the day my wonderful teacher, Mrs. Plotkin, had died, the code blue, and the way the medical staff had congregated at the door of her room.

"Just tell us . . . has Mr. McKinley gone up for surgery already?" Sylvia asked the nurse. The nurse shook her head and held the door open for Dr. Rankin, who was coming out of the ICU.

I knew even before he told us. I seemed to hear the words before they were spoken: "I'm so terribly sorry."

"No!" I cried, and felt Patrick's arm tighten around me.

Sylvia, her eyes wild, reached out wordlessly toward the doctor, and he pulled up a chair. "About fifteen minutes ago Ben had a massive coronary. He had signed a Do Not Resuscitate order, so we honored that. And even if we'd tried to revive him, he wouldn't have lived long or been the same." He clasped Sylvia's hands in his. "I wish for all the world I didn't have to tell you this."

It was as though I were going numb all over. Even my lungs felt paralyzed, and I didn't think I could breathe. I turned toward Patrick, wanting him to breathe for me. *Bring him back!* I wanted to scream. *Please, please try!* I looked over at Lester. He sat with his elbows on his knees, face in his hands, his shoulders shaking. Sylvia leaned against Stacy and cried. I had honestly thought that as long as my dad was in a hospital, they wouldn't let this happen. And when we went to see his body at last, I thought I knew what it would feel like if I were to die of a broken heart.

Outside in the parking lot I couldn't stop crying. I vaguely remembered visiting Mom in the hospital not long before she died. I'd sat on her lap and she had sung to me, softly in my ear. I wanted to sit on Dad's lap just one more time. I needed to feel his arms around me and his prickly cheek against mine. I wanted this. I *needed* this. As if thinking or saying this over and over would make it happen. Patrick didn't tell me I was embarrassing him. He didn't seem to care that people glanced at us warily as they hurried on by. He just held me in his arms beside our car, his face nuzzled against my neck, infusing his own strength into me.

"There were still things I wanted to tell him!" I wept. "There was so much more I had to say. *Why* didn't I tell him before? Why did he have to die *now*?"

"Maybe there's never a 'good' time to die, hon. There are always things we wish we'd said or done." He guided me over to the passenger side of the car, then went around to the other door and got in. "Alice, when I watched you and your dad together," he said, "you showed you loved each other in a hundred different ways. Whatever you might have said or done would only have been icing on the cake. He already knew whatever it was you had to say."

I swallowed and tried to speak through my sobs. "Patrick, if . . . if I die before you . . . or if you die suddenly and I don't have a chance to tell you . . ."

"I'll know you loved me in a hundred ways you never said. Even if we've just had an argument and I get run over by a bread truck, I'll always know I had your love. Okay?" He jostled my hand and coaxed a smile out of me.

"You'll know that the argument was just on the surface? And that there was a river of . . . an ocean of love underneath?" I asked.

"Absolutely."

We drove home slowly through the late-morning traffic. Patrick had phoned Tyler at the airport and left a message. Patricia's plane would be arriving soon, and I knew that I was going to have to help her make peace with the knowledge that she had not been able to say good-bye to her grandfather. The fact that I had not said all the things I'd wanted to say would let her know that life goes on in spite of regrets, and that it's not the things left unsaid that are so important but rather the feelings underneath, too deep for words.

✳ ✳ ✳

Dad had asked that his body be cremated. "I don't want it taking up precious space on a shrinking planet, and I especially don't want something that you kids and Sylvia have to look after," he had told me once.

So we held a memorial service at the church on Cedar Lane—the church where they'd been married. I sat staring at the ebony container holding his ashes, the remains of my father. How could that possibly contain all that he was—his kindness, his laughter, his music, his love?

I tried to comfort Patricia and Tyler before they went back to their own lives. They were emotional during the service, unable to hold back tears, and just watching them kept my eyes red and brimming.

"It will get easier, I promise," I told them as Patricia sobbed first on my shoulder, then Zack's.

"I know, but if I feel this bad for Gramps, how am I going to feel when it's Dad?" Tyler told me.

"You'll feel even worse, of course, but you'll carry on, because happiness has a way of creeping in again. It really does," I said.

A few days later, when Tyler and Patrick embraced at the airport, it was a long and tender hug.

The following afternoon I went over to Sylvia's to keep her company. She was out in the yard in her jacket, looking over the remains of their garden to see if any mums could be rescued for inside the house. I simply fell in beside her as she traversed the yard, and we walked with our arms around each other's waists.

"I didn't get to tell Dad all my thank-yous, but I won't make the same mistake with you," I said. "Thank you for loving him, Sylvia. And thank you for coming into our lives and filling in for the mom I never had."

"They were some of the happiest years for me, you know," she said, and gave me a little hug. We walked in step around the garden, surveying the dry, crumpled stalks of flowers.

"I still wish I'd had a chance to tell Dad all the things I wanted to," I said. "Apologize for some of the things I said to you. But really, you're the one who should be hearing it. I really am ashamed and sorry."

"Oh, I knew that, Alice. That was forgiven ages ago," she said.

"Do you ever have regrets about your life, Sylvia? I'm asking in a general way. Is there anything you'd do differently, or something left undone?"

"Of course. That's the human condition." And then, reminiscing, she said, "I was in community theater for a while when I first began teaching, and I loved it. I always thought I'd like to combine the two. But teaching takes up all your spare time, it seems. It was just a choice I had to make, and no great sacrifice. And I was probably a better teacher than I was an actress. But still . . . that's one of the things I left undone."

"You were a wonderful teacher," I told her. "The boys were all mad about you, and I think we girls were a little jealous."

She laughed, but after a while she grew quiet again, and we stopped to sit on a wrought-iron bench at the back of the garden.

"And I wish I had made up my mind sooner about marrying Ben," she said. "I regret I had to go to England for a year to even think about it. I miss him so much already." Her lips trembled slightly.

"So do I," I told her.

"And now . . . that's a whole year we could have had together." She shook her head. "Sometimes . . . when I used to think of how it would be if Ben died first, I figured if I could just remind myself of the things I *didn't* like about him, I wouldn't be so sad. But I'm not so sure. Right now I'd give anything to have him sitting across the room from me, reading aloud parts of the newspaper and interrupting whatever I was reading." She smiled at me through her tears.

I smiled back. "That used to drive Les nuts too, I remember."

"And his moods . . ." Sylvia thought about it a minute. "The thing that nobody tells you about husbands, Alice, is that they don't always react the way you think they will. Before we married, I used to imagine that when Ben was sad or worried, he'd tell me. Just come to me and say, 'Sylvia, my stomach hurts' or 'I'm afraid I made a big mistake on the income tax.' And I'd comfort or reassure him."

I nodded.

"Instead, an ache somewhere just made him withdrawn and silent. A mistake might make him irritable and short-tempered. I might spend half the day trying to figure out what was wrong. Women are more likely to talk it out."

"That's why we live longer," I told her, and squeezed her

hand. After a while I asked, "Any thoughts on what you want to do now?"

"I've been thinking of inviting my sister to visit. She's out west, and we've seen so little of each other. I'd really like to ask her to live here with me, but I thought if I just invited her for an extended stay, we could see how well we get on with each other before we take such a big step."

"That sounds wise," I told her.

She looked into my eyes. "Thank you for coming by today, Alice. I think I needed to talk even more than I knew."

The year of our sixtieth birthdays, Patrick saw a notice in the county paper announcing the opening of a time capsule. It had been buried, the paper said, forty-eight years ago by a seventh-grade class at Colesville Junior High School, taught by Elmer Hensley, and former students were invited to attend the ceremony. According to instructions, the capsule was to be opened when the class reached their sixtieth year. Then it listed all the students who had taken seventh-grade history with Mr. Hensley that year: Pamela Jones, Mark Stedmeister, Alice McKinley, Elizabeth Price, Brian Brewster, Patrick Long. . . . I wondered why Gwen wasn't mentioned, then realized that she had had a different teacher for history.

I mentioned the capsule to Patricia and Tyler, who were both home for the weekend. Tyler and his longtime girlfriend had announced their engagement, and Patricia's little boy was having his third birthday. Little Lyle had been born up in

New Hampshire with only Zack and a midwife in attendance. (Patricia, at thirty-four, still wanted to do everything herself. "But I remembered what you said about counting to eighty-five by fives, Mom, each time a labor pain began, and that really helped!" she confessed later. "Just knowing the pain would subside by the time I got to a hundred and ten got me through it.")

"*Go,* you guys!" said Tyler, when he heard about the time capsule. Now a thirty-one-year-old social worker, he put the emphasis on *social* where his parents were concerned. "It should be fun!"

"Of course we'll go," Patrick said. "Wouldn't miss it!"

I called Pamela, who was now Mrs. William Harris, having been married on a cruise ship to a husky, kind man with shaggy gray eyebrows who treated her like a queen—when she deserved it—and whom Pamela adored.

"Pamela, do you remember burying a time capsule back in seventh grade?" I asked.

"What?" she said.

"The time capsule we buried in Mr. Hensley's class. We all put something in it and wrote letters to our sixty-year-old selves. Don't you remember?"

"Vaguely."

"And the guys had just named you Wyoming, while I got North Carolina."

"*What?*" she said again.

"The seventh-grade boys gave each seventh-grade girl the name of a state, based on the size and shape of her breasts. And you were so proud of getting Wyoming that you said you were going to put your measurements in the time capsule. Did you?"

"Alice, how do you *remember* all this stuff? I scarcely even remember seventh grade!" she said.

I guess I do have a good memory for the past. Sometimes I wish I didn't. I think I remember every embarrassing, agonizing, humiliating thing that ever happened to me. "Hensley was the history teacher nobody liked much—until he retired, that is, and then we gave him a party," I told her.

"I guess I do remember the party," Pamela said.

"Why don't you come down for the opening, just to see who shows up. It might be fun," I said. "I guess the idea is that those of us who are still local will contact the ones who left. That's why I called you."

"I'll see," she said.

The thirteen or so men and women who got out of their cars and crossed the playground came tentatively, as though we were kids again and it was our first day at a new school. I imagine each of us thought we hadn't changed much since seventh grade and were shocked at how old some people looked and surprised that others hadn't changed much at all.

I was wearing a white tee, khaki skirt, and thong sandals, my blondish-gray hair swept back away from my face, little gold hoop earrings in my ears, and the gold heart on a chain that Patrick had given me around my neck. Patrick and I hardly knew a few of the people, but we recognized the others—Pamela and

Elizabeth, of course. Pamela was as svelte as ever, even though her shoulders were somewhat stooped. She kept her hair a lovely shade of blond, while Elizabeth's hair was totally white—beautiful and wavy—and she was heavier now, thicker about the waist. But her skin was as gorgeous as ever, and Liz still looked about the same to me somehow because we got together so often. Her children were grown and married, and she seemed at peace with the world. Gwen came because she wanted to see all her friends.

"Brian?" I said, looking at a pudgy man who was bald on top. None of us had seen Brian for decades.

"Alice! Oh, wow! You've still got some red in your hair!" Brian Brewster said, giving me a bear hug. He was living in Nevada now, he told us, and a relative had seen the piece in the paper about the time capsule and sent the clipping to him.

"Jill!" I cried, recognizing the still-attractive woman—trim and tanned—despite her unusual number of wrinkles. "How *are* you?"

"Doing good," she said. "And you look great, Alice. Isn't this a hoot? My mom read about it in the *Gazette*."

It was Karen I hardly recognized because she had gained so much weight. There we were on this warm May Saturday—Jill and Karen, Pamela and Elizabeth, Brian and Patrick and me, and five other members of our class. We stood at the center of the small crowd that had gathered to watch—friends, relatives, young women with strollers, and a few businessmen who seemed to have stopped on their way to lunch.

Two photographers were there with reporters from both the

Gazette and the *Post,* and someone from the board of education was waiting for us with a ceremonial shovel.

Patrick couldn't believe we got press coverage. "News must be slow today," he joked to a reporter.

"We're always interested in a good human interest story," she said. "People like to read about time capsules."

Our old school had been converted to a county recreation and day care center. A cluster of boys stood to one side with their basketball to watch, while small children peered at us from a fenced-in playground beyond, then continued chasing each other about, disinterested.

"What do you remember of seventh grade?" one of the reporters went around asking. What do you remember of Mr. Hensley, the school, the city, the world—as though we were the last members of a lost civilization.

"Ask Alice," people kept saying. "She remembers everything."

When we'd all given our names, we took turns digging in the spot Hensley had marked on a map of the school property, measuring exactly from the corner of the lot. He'd had the foresight to file the map with the board of education and leave the spot unmarked so vandals wouldn't dig it up and destroy our project. He'd even left a copy of the map, we found out, in his will. Now, that's planning ahead!

With each thrust of the shovel, we seemed to remember more and more and couldn't stop talking. Seventh-Grade Sing Day, which had frightened us so; Denise "Mack Truck" Whitlock, an eighth grader who ended her life by standing in the path of an Amtrak train; the talent show; the "Our Changing Bodies" seminar at the Y ("Omigod! *That!*" one of the women cried); gourmet cooking; Patrick's drum solos; gym. . . .

Patrick was using the shovel when it struck the canister, and he hauled it out. It was a large metal milk can, actually, so rusty that we had to borrow a hammer and screwdriver from the building custodian to pry off the lid. But as we gathered around and the cameras clicked, we greeted each of our treasures with cries of, "Oh, look!" and "Who put that in there?" and "Brian, that must have been *your* idea."

It was a strange assortment there on the picnic table, where we spread everything out. A copy of the *Washington Post,* dark and yellowed, with headlines about the old Soviet Union; a Michael Jordan poster; a SAY NO TO DRUGS bumper sticker . . .

We gingerly examined our treasures, passing them around. One was a bracelet made in Hawaii.

"What in the world is *that*?" asked Pamela. "Whose was it?"

No one seemed to know, but everyone was looking at me for the answer. It did seem familiar somehow. And then I remembered. Denise Whitlock's bracelet—one of the personal items she had given me before she committed suicide. I had put it in the capsule so that we would remember a girl we hardly knew.

"A bracelet from a friend," I said, slipping it on my wrist. "Denise Whitlock's."

"The girl who . . . the train?" asked someone. I nodded.

"She left it for you?" asked Jill.

"Among the things she gave me that last day, before I knew. Before anyone knew what she was thinking about."

The keepsakes continued to come—a wrapper off a McDonald's Big Mac, a photo of our seventh-grade class, a girl's halter top, a report card . . . and finally a clutch of lined note-book pages.

At Hensley's insistence, each of us had written a letter to our sixty-year-old self, and as they were distributed among us, we moved over to the swings and merry-go-round, where we could sit and read them. The rubber-strap seats of the swings weren't nearly as comfortable as those old wooden seats I remembered—the kind a guy could stand on, with a girl in the middle, pumping it high into the air.

It was a strange feeling holding a piece of notebook paper I had held as a twelve-year-old girl writing a letter to the woman she would become:

Dear Alice:

I can't believe that when you read this, you'll be sixty years old. Right now that seems ancient to me—older than Dad, even. I wonder if you feel ancient inside or if you still feel like you always did.

I smiled and continued reading.

Dad will be gone, of course, by the time you get this letter. Maybe Lester too, and it's hard for me to even write

*about that. But maybe you'll be married and have children
and grandchildren, and when you do, I guess that makes up
for the people you lose. Does it? A little, even?*

Among the soft chuckles here and there, I detected more
than one sniffle. As several women dug in their bags for a tissue,
the boys who had grown restless and were passing their basketball back and forth stood still again and watched respectfully
from a distance.

*What I want to know is how your life has been so far,
and what you decided to be. Did you ever get breasts as big
as tennis balls, and was it still important to you when you
did? Do you still have any red in your hair, or is it all gray?
Are you fat? Do you wear orthopedic shoes? Can you still
wear shorts in the summertime?*

I had to laugh out loud. Patrick looked up from his own
letter, and we just exchanged smiles. I didn't want to share my
letter right then, so I kept reading:

*Is your favorite food still fried onion rings? Is your
favorite color still green? Does the name "North Carolina"
ring any bells? Do you ever hear from Elizabeth or Pamela?
Whatever happened to Patrick?*
*Maybe what I really want to know is, did you ever reach
an age where you could forget all the stupid, ridiculous things*

you've done and said, or do you still wake up in the middle
of the night and remember each one exactly, embarrassing
you all over again?

Maybe you're a famous chef by now. Or maybe you stay
home and feed your cats. But whatever you are, I hope you
never forget me, the girl I am now.

Love,
Alice

I wasn't the only one who was crying. I guess I thought
we'd laugh and hoot and pass our letters around, but except
for a passage read here and there, most of us folded them up
and tucked them away in a purse or pocket to read again and
again.

Suddenly I felt the swing I was sitting on lurch, and my
arms tightened around the chains as I found myself being pulled
backward, higher and higher. I gave a little shriek as Patrick let
go and I went sailing forward, my legs straight out in front of me
to keep them from dragging the ground. When the swing came
back again, Patrick gave another push.

"Hey! Nice legs!" Brian called as my skirt billowed out over
my thighs, and I laughed.

Then the swing to my left was moving with Liz in it, and Jill
was on the other side of me as Brian gave it a push.

"Way to go!" laughed a reporter, as one by one, each swing
in the row got in motion. The squeak and creak of the moving

swings had a rhythm all their own, and no one cared that the photographer snapped a picture. The spring breeze fanned our faces, the sunshine warmed our legs, the guys doing the pushing were obviously in competition with each other, and it seemed perfectly natural that one of the men watching from the sidelines should bound forward and climb deftly to the top of the jungle gym while we cheered him on.

Standing on the next-to-the-top rung, the familiar-looking man suddenly beat his chest and let loose with the most magnificent Tarzan yell.

"Donald Sheavers!" Liz and Pamela and I all shouted together, and as we screamed his name, the former boyfriend of all three of us did a couple of flips, then dropped to the ground and came over to say hello.

"Just read a piece in the paper about the time capsule and thought I'd stop by to see who showed up," he said, grinning.

He was still in the area, he told us, and worked for a Ford dealership in Wheaton. And because he knew all the new establishments in Silver Spring, he suggested a good place where our little crowd could have lunch.

Seated around three tables pushed together there in the restaurant, it was like old times. We talked nonstop, just as we used to in class. We overlooked the gray hair and the trifocals, the pants with elastic at the waists, because those weren't important anymore. *We* were. We had survived illnesses, divorces, disappointments, and worse. All of us had lost people we loved, and some had lost jobs. But we were here, we had good things to share as well, and best of all, we were still *making* memories, not just reliving them.

Just for fun, we each took out photos of our children and mixed them up there on the table to see if the others could guess whose they were. I added a photo of Patricia's little boy just to confuse things, and we all laughed when Pamela, who was raising border collies with her husband on a farm in Connecticut, slipped in a picture of their dogs.

A few of us were retired, but all of us had plans.

"I'm going to do some part-time consulting for IBM," Patrick told the others. "They need someone to go to Japan a couple times a year, and Alice will be going with me."

"I'm enrolled in a language course, and Patrick and I are allowed to speak only Japanese at the dinner table," I explained, and everyone laughed.

Elizabeth and Moe had started a foundation to help finance foreign adoptions for childless couples; Pamela and Bill were going to Scotland to look at a special breed of collie; Jill, divorced from Justin, was a talent scout in L.A.; Brian owned a sports franchise; and Karen worked in a bank. Gwen was invited to join in, of course, and told us that she and Charlie have been hosting some foreign medical students in their home.

Each of us talked about the milestone of reaching our sixtieth birthday and how we planned to celebrate it. When they got to me, I started to say that we hadn't really done anything special, but Patrick rested his arm on the back of my chair and smiled.

"Alice doesn't know it yet," he said, "but I'm taking her back to the Caribbean for snorkeling, something she's been wanting to do again."

"Patrick! Really?" I cried, and hugged him as the others cheered.

We stayed another hour, reluctant to leave, exchanging cell phone numbers and e-mail addresses, vowing to keep in touch. But as I rode home contentedly beside Patrick, I knew I hadn't shared quite everything with my friends. I hadn't even told Patrick yet about the project that excited me most: I wanted to write some books about what it had been like growing up with three best friends and marrying my childhood sweetheart. About what it was like to grow up without a mother and about all the things Dad and Lester had to teach me. I wanted my children and grandchildren to know that no matter when you are born or where you live, happiness and disappointments have the same flavors the world over. I think that Mom, and the girl I was back in seventh grade, would have been pleased.

And so, when we reached home and Patrick had gone into his study to check his e-mail, I took my laptop out on our screened porch and sat down on the glider. I looked out over the backyard, at the forsythia Dad had helped us plant at the edge of the garden, and thought of all the things I would put in my first book—all the embarrassing, weird, wacky, wonderful things that happen as a girl goes from child to woman.

I smiled as I wrote down the title of the first book: *Starting with Alice*.

* * * * * *

AFTERWORD

To my readers:

I started writing my first Alice book thirty years ago, and *The Agony of Alice* was published in 1985. I didn't know at the time that the book would become a series—I'd only planned to write about a motherless girl looking for a role model, and who finds her not in the most beautiful sixth-grade teacher, but the homeliest. Then the fan letters started coming; reviewers said things like, "Alice's many fans await her further adventures," and I said, *"What?"*

My wonderful editor at the time, Jean Karl, and I talked it over, and I agreed to do a series, provided I would not have to write more than one book a year and that Alice could grow a little older in each one; I didn't want to find myself stuck in a sitcom year after year.

As the series progressed, it seemed most natural that each book cover about four months of Alice's life—fall semester, spring semester, and summer. For a time, Jon Lanman edited the books, then they were passed along to Caitlyn Dlouhy, who was raising two daughters in real life, and continued as editor to the end of the series.

When we discovered that very young girls were reading their older sisters' collections, I wrote three prequels, beginning with *Starting with Alice*. And, somewhere along the way, I recklessly promised my readers twenty-eight books. I would end the series with Alice and the members of her seventh-grade world studies class meeting again to open the time capsule they'd once buried. Since my mother, her sisters, and my grandmother all lived to a grand old age, I figured I would too. What's to worry?

Still, at some point, even though I had six or seven books yet to go, I wrote a quick draft of the final book and stuck it in a fireproof box in my office. I didn't want to leave readers hanging, never knowing how things turn out for this little community of people I had created, should anything happen to me. Of course, when all the books had been written and it was time to submit the final manuscript, it took many more drafts and ended up twice the length it had been originally.

Several of my readers suggested the title of the book, *Always Alice*, and we started out with that—then decided we needed a title with a bit more *oomph*. And because I'd been promising to tell readers everything they wanted to know in the final book, *Now I'll Tell You Everything* seemed perfect. Zillions of you asked—no, *demanded*—that Alice and Patrick get married, and on that, I was way ahead of you. I even knew about their engagement before they did.

What made me write the Alice books in the first place and why did a series appeal to me? It's probably true that Alice represents the daughter I never had, though I didn't start out thinking that way, for I've written lots of books about girls. It's immeasurably easier to raise a child on paper than it is in real life, but it was Alice who determined what would happen next. Once she became a full-fledged person in my head, she directed the way she wanted to go. She never played on a sports team, and I never had either, nor did she sing in a school choir or a madrigal group—and this was something I had loved. Alice never even sang in the shower. Yet this seemed true to the person I had created, and I was determined to let her lead her own life. More than that, I wanted to share the journey with her.

I received many suggestions over the years from my readers. Give her a dog, a sister, a car, diabetes . . . Make her play soccer, smoke pot, go to Paris, sleep with Patrick . . . Making Alice do something that didn't fit was like trying to cram on a shoe that was the wrong size. It just didn't work. But your letters and e-mails describing your own problems and your own lives helped more than you'll ever know.

If you see yourselves in Alice and her friends, rest easy. The things that happen in these books are partly me, partly you, partly things friends have told me or newspaper stories and articles, all mixed up with imaginings.

Some of you were intrigued almost as much by the book jackets as by the stories, and were often confused by the different covers for each new edition. A few of you asked for the names and addresses of some of the models (sorry!) and a lot of you pleaded to see Patrick or Lester on a book jacket. Quite a number of you asked if there was a movie about Alice (Yes! *Alice Upside Down*) and offered to play the role of Alice or one of her friends in future films.

When my husband was alive, he read each Alice manuscript before I turned it in. Both he and my agent, Bill Reiss, were especially fond of Lester, and chuckled over the conversations between him and Alice. But keeping track of what went on in each book when it came time to write the next one was my biggest headache, not only for me but for the editor and copy editor. In the early books, I believe, Alice's birthday falls on three different dates; Elizabeth has her ears pierced in one book but not in the next.

Finally the copy editor, Cindy Nixon, took on the tedious job of creating an Alice "bible," rereading each of the Alice books and recording every friend's temperament, hair color, likes and dislikes; every holiday, every gift, every vacation, every kiss . . . Each of the twenty-eight books is summarized, and the copy editor even included all the discrepancies from book to book. These hundred or so pages were collected and revised every few years, and now, as a special gift to my readers, the publisher has made this collection of facts available for free, online. Just go to the Alice website, www.alicemckinley.com, and click on "Just the Facts" in the heading at the top of the screen. You can find every possible thing you ever wanted to know about Alice from each of the twenty-eight books.

But some of you have asked if I would ever tell you how long Alice lives and, if she dies, how it happens. The rest of her story is up to you. She and Patrick are taking lessons in Japanese, preparing for Patrick's short-term consultant job in the Far East. You can be sure she won't want to stay away from her grandchildren long, and will need to check in on Lester's triplets too. And, of course, she is writing some books about her life. . . .

I want to thank the many girls and guys and the moms and dads who wrote to me about the series. I'm grateful to the librarians and teachers who stood up for me when the Alice books were challenged in their schools, sometimes even risking their jobs. My sons, Jeff and Mike, unknowingly helped, because their experiences in growing up are often there in the background. And I've e-mailed my granddaughters, Sophia and Tressa, numerous times with questions about high school and college. But special thanks goes to Caitlyn Dlouhy and her staff, who not only kept me focused, but up-to-date. Caitlyn offered some terrific suggestions along the way that made this a fuller, richer series.

I'm also grateful for the troop of noisy, chattering characters who travel with me inside my head. As long as they are poking, prodding, demanding a place in a book, I have new things to do, new stories to tell.

A READING GROUP GUIDE FOR
THE ALICE SERIES

ABOUT THE SERIES

To hear grown-ups talk, the years before you turn twenty-one
are a joyous, carefree time that you will eventually think of as a
high point. But how could this possibly be true when there are
so many things that can go wrong every single day? You could
fall down the stairs at school . . . and wet your pants while you
are falling. Your boyfriend could tell you that you're chubby.
You could make a fool of yourself in a talent show. You could
wear really bad eyeshadow. You could even get accidentally
locked out of your house while wearing your underpants. The
list is endless!

Luckily, there's Alice McKinley, in a whole series of books

by Phyllis Reynolds Naylor. Alice faces the same problems and emotions that you do, and deals with them in a manner that everyone can relate to. She may not have a mother to guide her, a plan for the future—or even, sometimes, a clue—but she does her best and muddles through. She is the friend that every girl needs . . . to laugh with, to cry with, and to face the mysteries of growing up with.

When Alice McKinley first burst onto the scene more than twenty-five years ago, readers and critics immediately welcomed her into their hearts. "A wonderfully funny and touching story that will make readers smile with wry recognition," *Booklist* wrote in its starred review of the very first Alice book, *The Agony of Alice*. Since then, the number of titles in the series has grown and so has Alice, from a third-grader anxious about finding her place in a new town . . . to a teenager eager to discover her own individuality. It's clear in book after book, each a witty and often moving portrayal of everyday disasters and occasional triumphs, that effervescent Alice is maturing into someone pretty fabulous.

DISCUSSION QUESTIONS

1. Alice deeply misses her late mother and imagines that a mom would be able to handle every awkward situation or answer all of Alice's questions. Discuss the relationships that Alice's friends have with their own mothers. What is the difference between living with a real mother and living with a faint memory of one?

2. "I kept wondering who makes the rules," Alice muses in *Alice in Rapture, Sort Of.* "I just don't understand how one day you aren't ready for something and then, after a birthday party, you are." Do you think arbitrary age limits make sense? Why or why not?

3. Bullied by Denise in *Reluctantly Alice*, Alice ends up reaching out to her tormentor. Why does Alice do that? How does Denise respond? Do you think anyone could have spared Denise from the tragedy she suffers in *Alice in April*? Why or why not?

4. As many of the titles in the series suggest, Alice has her fair share of embarrassments and disappointments. Yet somehow she is able to rise above her troubles. What are some of Alice's character traits that help her weather the bad times?

5. At the beginning of *Reluctantly Alice*, Alice decides she wants to be liked by everyone, but her father insists: "People who try to please everybody all the time turn out like oatmeal." Do you agree with Mr. McKinley? Why or why not?

6. Although Alice insists there are no racial divisions in her junior high, a school-wide experiment in *Alice on the Outside* shows her how easy it is to slip into ugly prejudices. Discuss race relations in your own school or community. Is your neighborhood racially mixed? Is your school? Do you see any evidence that individuals are treated better or worse based on their race or physical appearance?

7. Why does Alice keep turning to her Aunt Sally for advice? Does she ever take any of it?

8. Despite her many complaints about living with only men, Alice is deeply attached to her father and older brother. How do they look out for each other? Does the absence of a mother in the house make them closer somehow?

9. *Alice In-Between* is the title of one of Alice's adventures, but is it also a theme that runs through the whole series? In what ways is Alice in-between girlhood and womanhood? Are there other ways that Alice is in-between?

10. The Alice books, especially *Alice on the Outside*, are forthright about Alice's curiosity about sex and her growing understanding of her own sexuality. To whom does Alice turn when she has questions about sex? How reliable are each of these sources? What do you think are the important values she's learning?

11. Alice feels like she spends a lot of time making mistakes and embarrassing herself. What are some of the embarrassing things she's done? Do you think she makes more mistakes than other people? Does the embarrassment she feels match the things she does? Is it the most important thing about her?

12. In *The Grooming of Alice*, Pamela and Elizabeth want to get in shape in part because they have too much stress in their lives and

they want to have control over some aspect of themselves. What are some other ways that characters in the books—or people that you know—deal with stress? Are these healthy ways to relieve tension? What are some things that you can do to reduce the stress in your life, before it becomes such a major issue?

13. Pamela, Elizabeth, and Alice are blown away by parts of their "For Girls Only" day at the Y. What is it about the day that they find so effective? Why do you think that it moves them so? Do you think that the things they learn during the day are true? Are they helpful?

14. When Patrick and Alice break up, Alice feels like she can't go on without being part of a couple. Why, then, doesn't she take her friends' advice and look for another boy to date? What does Alice think is the most important part of being in a relationship? What do you think is the most important? How does Lester feel about dating?

15. Alice often feels nervous and awkward about kissing Patrick and being intimate with him, and at one point breaks up with him because she doesn't feel ready to have a boyfriend. In your opinion, is this normal for a girl her age? How does her nervousness—and how she deals with it—compare to Pamela, Elizabeth, and their other friends? Which members of their group are most ready for mature relationships, and how does this compare to the way they each act?

16. Who does Alice turn to for mothering, since her own mother died when she was so young? What does each of these people provide for Alice? Does Alice give anything in return for this nurturing? What does Alice have from her real mother?

17. Alice has been waiting a long time for her father and Sylvia to get married. Why is it so important to her that this happen? Why did she choose Sylvia Summers? Do you think that having Sylvia in the family will turn out the way that Alice thinks it will?

18. Alice is so certain that something is going to ruin her dad's wedding, but it ends up being one of the most beautiful days of her life. But was the day perfect? Is there such a thing as a perfect day, where nothing goes wrong? Can you think of other times in her life when Alice was expecting things to be perfect and they didn't turn out as she had planned? What was important about each of these days? Does Alice—or anyone else—have the right to expect certain days to be perfect?

19. In what ways does Alice's relationship with her father and Lester affect how she thinks about other boys? Are these influences good or bad? Does the fact that she's the only girl in their house put her at as much of a disadvantage as she thinks?

20. How does Alice's relationship with Pamela and Elizabeth change over the years? What is it that keeps the three girls together? What separates them?

21. Alice struggles because she wants to fit in and be part of the group, but also wants to be a distinctive and special person. How does she go about achieving each of these things? Why does she sometimes choose to do things that she knows will keep her from being accepted? Do you agree with her choices?

22. In *Alice on Her Way*, Alice really hits it off with Sam—but when she starts to get to know him better, she is surprised by his opinions on certain topics. Have you ever dated someone who had very different opinions from you? Did this affect *your* opinion of *them*?

23. Faith believes that her boyfriend only hurts her because he cares so much about her. Discuss whether this is true. How can thoughts like this be dangerous? If you had a friend in Faith's position, what would you do?

24. When one of Alice's friends gets sick in *Alice in the Know*, it prompts her to ask her father questions about her mother, and together the two of them discover that sharing their memories of her mother helps them. Why do you think this is? Have you ever had the experience of remembering someone you love who is no longer with you?

25. Discuss a time when a friend has gone through something sad and scary. How did you help them through it?

26. Race is a huge issue in *Alice in the Know*. Do you agree with Tracy's rejection of Lester's proposal? Why or why not?

27. Responsible, dependable Alice is fired from her department store job! Do you think her dismissal should have come as a surprise, or should she have been expecting it? What did she learn from the experience?

28. Do you agree or disagree that a person who worries all the time about something awful happening is already ruining the good times?

29. In *Dangerously Alice*, Alice has a hard time dealing with the Miss Goody-Two-Shoes label she has been given. Have you ever been called a name? How did it make you feel?

30. Alice seems smitten with Tony Osler from the first time he asks her to dance. Analyze Alice's attraction to him.

31. Alice's speech teacher, Mrs. Cary, has each student choose a controversial subject and defend his or her own view on it, without knowing that later they will all be asked to research and defend the opposite view. Do you think it was a fair assignment?

32. Alice hides in her dad's closet because she suspects Sylvia is going to tell him about the fight they had. Instead, her parents have sex, all while Alice can hear. Lester advises her to never,

ever tell her dad what happened. Discuss the wisdom of this advice.

33. Alice and Liz spend the night out in the city so that Alice can write an article for the newspaper. Do you think the article made the risk worthwhile? Why or why not?

34. Alice finds out from Sylvia that her father had been terribly anxious when she missed her curfew. Role-play her dad's anxiety.

35. Sometimes Alice feels that she is just treading water, waiting for her real self to emerge. Is this a feeling you can relate to? Explain.

36. In *Almost Alice*, Patrick reveals to Alice that he won't be able to attend the school dance in February, and suggests that Alice take someone else. What do you think of this suggestion?

37. David points out that different people handle doubt in different ways. Do you think this is true? How do you handle doubt?

38. In *Intensely Alice*, Alice lies to her father about where she is going to sleep while she's in Chicago. Provide examples of things you still feel obligated to tell your parents as you get older—and some that you might keep to yourself.

39. A man named Doug Carpenter puts his hand on Alice's knee on the plane and makes her uncomfortable. Discuss her handling of the situation. Would you have reacted like Alice did or differently?

40. How did Alice and her friends deal with Shelly and her evangelizing? Do you think they handled the situation correctly?

41. What helped Alice and Sylvia finally be honest with each other? In your experience, what types of settings make it easier to talk about difficult things?

42. Without planning or foresight, Mark's friends gather at the Stedmeisters' house. Discuss this silent tribute. Who do you think this might have helped? How effective do you think this was in expressing their feelings?

43. In *Alice in Charge*, Alice is shocked to discover that there is a neo-Nazi group in her school. Why do people join hate groups? What need do you think this could fill?

44. Alice's family is fascinated by the traditions of Daniel's family—and vice versa. Does your family have any old traditions related to their country of origin?

45. Alice is horrified when she realizes that Mr. Granger has taken advantage of Amy. Discuss molestation. Who do you think is most vulnerable?

46. In *Incredibly Alice*, Alice manages to overcome her fears and tries out for the school play. Have you ever had to find the courage to try something new? How did you do this?

47. Sometimes, trusting your own judgment can mean disappointing a parent or a teacher. Have you ever had to decide between your own heart and that of someone who is looking out for you?

48. Discuss Alice's decision about how she would like things to be when she has sexual intercourse for the first time.

49. It's not just *Alice on Board*—Pamela's parents are on board too! That's bad enough, but then her mom starts acting out to get attention. Discuss some instances in which a family member or relative has embarrassed you in public. How have you handled it? How would you like to handle it in the future?

50. As a member of the crew, Alice learns all sorts of things, from how to clean a bathroom in record time to how to help a passenger into a life jacket. What are some things that Alice learned that would be helpful in future jobs but are not part of her job description on the ship?

51. Even with all the work that needs to be done, Alice manages to find time to have fun—and ends up particularly close with fellow shipmate Mitch. How are Mitch and Alice alike? How are they different?

PROJECTS AND RESEARCH

1. Each of the Alice books is distinguished by sparkling dialogue. Choose a favorite scene and act it out. If the scene features both young people and adults, try switching age roles. The adults in your group could read the younger parts and the younger members can tackle the adult parts.

2. Imagine Alice is part of your reading group. Write her a letter that describes yourselves to her. Who is in the group? What are your goals? What else have you read together?

3. In *Alice in Lace*, each student in Alice's health class has been assigned a hypothetical real-life problem to figure out. Most of the older members of your group already have plenty of experience with practical problems. How prepared were they for the decisions they had to make? Do they have any regrets?

4. At the close of *Alice in April*, Alice writes a letter to herself at age sixty. Your group can do the same thing, but with a slight twist. The younger members compose letters to their older selves. Their older members write a note to their younger selves, back when they were adolescents.

5. In *All but Alice*, Miss Summers asks her language arts class to find a song or musical or book title that best reflects the personality of each member of their family. Alice picks *Funny Girl* for

her mother and *Annie*, as in the musical version of Little Orphan Annie, for herself. Ask all your members to think of popularly known titles that describe themselves and everyone else in the group.

6. Alice has a number of people whom she can turn to with questions about sex and her body, but sometimes it can be hard to bring up the topic. Find someone in your community—a doctor, teacher, or social worker—who is knowledgeable and willing to speak to you and a group of your friends. Including your parents in this group can spark some interesting discussions, in addition to ensuring their support. If you are all still feeling too embarrassed to ask questions, perhaps you can create an anonymous question box, which you could use to get the discussion started.

7. Several times throughout the books, Alice makes a pineapple upside-down cake using her mother's recipe. Ask around for some of your family's recipes and try them out.

8. Working on her school newspaper is something that brings Alice both pleasure and recognition. Volunteer to work on your school newspaper. If this is not an option for you, then perhaps you could create a newsletter for some group that you are part of—your family, reading group, or workplace are all possibilities. Get others to help you with the creation of this newsletter.

9. When Alice first starts babysitting Jimmy Benton, she has a frightening experience when he chokes on a grape. Research opportunities in your community to learn CPR, the Heimlich maneuver, or first aid, so that you will be prepared for such emergencies.

10. Alice often tries to help out others who are in need, inviting them to Thanksgiving dinner, befriending them if she senses they are lonely, or buying holiday gifts that they might not otherwise get. Find a local organization that fits your interests and beliefs, and volunteer there.

11. Patrick and Alice help out their teacher and have a good time when they create a timeline of the Russian Revolution. Create your own timeline—choose a historical event or something that happened in your own life—and have fun finding creative ways to illustrate it. Use it to decorate your classroom or your bedroom.

12. Although she resisted at first, Alice joined a few school clubs, where she met new people and discovered new interests. Join a club that interests you, or sign up for classes about something you've always wanted to learn.

13. For Alice's three-minute speech in *Dangerously Alice*, she talked about the cruelty of animal experimentation. Investigate the truth of her talk.

14. Role-play the thoughts and feelings that a guy might have when he finds out his girlfriend is pregnant. If he says he'll "be there for her," what might he mean by that? What might she think he means?

15. In *Alice in Charge*, we meet Daniel Bul Dau, a foreign exchange student from the Sudan. Brainstorm ways to help a new student feel welcome.

This reading group guide has been provided by Simon & Schuster Children's Publishing for classroom, library, and reading group use.

It may be reproduced in its entirety or excerpted for these purposes.